CLAIMED BY THE ALPHA

THE ALPHA KING'S BREEDER

BOOK ELEVEN

BELLA MOONDRAGON

For Charlie

CONTENTS

1

ARCANA UMBRA

Misty

I FLIP A PAGE IN MY JOURNAL, SQUINTING AT THE TERRIBLE handwriting I'd scribbled down last night when I'd woken from my latest dream. I can't comprehend what I'd been trying to say. Dark? Hurt? Silver? Those words look somewhat clear. I can't even remember writing them down.

I close the journal with a sigh and slip it back in my purse, hanging the bag over the back of my chair in the common room of my dormitory. It's a massive building with a pitched roof, several towers, and spooky, darkened alcoves, but it's home, and right now, I'm sure I'd be able to hear Georgia singing her heart out in the shower if the nagging, incessant voice in my head would shut up for a single, blissful second.

I've come to the conclusion after two years of hearing what I can only describe as white noise and the occasional static screech, like I have a radio fixed inside my skull, that the voice isn't my internal dialogue. No, that's a separate entity in itself, and I'm constantly at odds with the unfamiliar, genderless, and distorted whisper I hear from time to time. It's like someone's trying to talk to me underwater or by using a crappy walkie-talkie that only works well if you're within a few feet of the other unit, which totally defeats the purpose. I think this might be some new power developing. It would make perfect sense, given that I'll be coming into my wolf soon.

Still, I can't stop the voice from breaking through my daydreams and moments of strict focus. Right now, I can hear someone talking, maybe to a group, but static blurs their words. Earlier today, I heard the voice loud and clear for the first time. *Do not go to the party.*

Other times, usually in the dead of night when I'm unable to sleep, I'll hear whispers. Like prayers, they're soft and personal. I can't tell what the voice is trying to say, but I feel like... it's asking for something. Begging for something just out of reach, and in those quiet moments, I empathize with it.

Mostly because I've been begging for it to shut the hell up for two years.

I rub my temples, which causes one of my curlers to come undone. I curse under my breath as I roll the curl back in place and check my watch again. I came down here to pass some time before I needed to finish getting ready for the party, but I need to get dressed soon. I start packing up my things when familiar footsteps come up behind me, and then more foam curlers are coming undone, and Nathan is pressing a sloppy kiss to my cheek, smudging my carefully crafted makeup.

"What's on your head?" he asks, hovering beside me and preventing me from rising from my chair. He flicks one of the curlers, which immediately comes loose and bounces several feet away, rolling to a stop under a sofa.

I glare at him. "Do you mind? It takes forever to set my curls after a blowout."

He arches a brow, his mind probably settling on the word blow, like I'm about to get on my knees in public. "I went upstairs, but your door was locked."

"It normally is," I reply, a little peeved by the teasing glint in his brown eyes. I look him up and down. He obviously just came from practice. He's a bit sweaty and wearing joggers and a gray shirt that hugs his muscled frame. "What brings you here?"

"I came to see my girlfriend for a minute."

"Just a minute?"

"I have plans tonight–with the guys. It's Rodney's birthday tomorrow, but we have a track meet, so we're going out for drinks tonight instead."

I purse my lips, looking at him. "Drinks the night before a track meet?"

He waves me off, not bothering to sit down in the chair beside me, obviously not planning to stay long. "I just wanted to pop by and tell you that, in case you were planning to come over tonight, seeing as you got all dressed up for something."

"I have plans tonight, actually. Georgia and I–"

He presses another kiss to my face. "That's great, babe. I'll see you tomorrow night–probably, okay?"

"Oh–"

He turns on his heel and walks away, just like that. I frown at the place where his body faded into the shadowed hallway outside the common room entrance and lean back in my chair, crossing my arms under my breasts. I've come to the conclusion that, while Nathan is handsome and… has a nice body, and is comfortable to sleep on… he's not that smart. He just… doesn't have much going on upstairs, which are words directly from my grandpa Maddox's mouth after I brought him all the way to Maatua to meet some of my family for the first time over spring break.

I'd scoffed at Grandpa when he said that to me, but now I'm wondering if he might have been onto something. It could be worse. Nathan could be a meathead like Ryan. He could be strict and bossy like Sydney. He could be all-powerful and scary as fuck like my uncle Ryatt.

I don't mind having a dumb boyfriend. I'm smart enough for the two of us, I guess.

But now I'm heavily suspicious, and this is one of those times I wish phones worked out here in Eastonia. I'd be looking up not only him on social media, but his friends, confirming it is, in fact, Rodney's birthday tomorrow and they are, in fact, going to get drinks later. Then, I'd look up the sports schedule and confirm there was, in fact, a track meet tomorrow.

If the dots didn't line up, I'd guess Nathan would be going to the Arcane Umbra party tonight just like I think he is.

I roll my lip between my teeth and let it go with a pop before rolling my eyes, shrugging my shoulders, and walking through the narrow, darkened hallways toward my dorm room. Four flights of stairs later, my thighs burning, I test the door and find it unlocked, and Georgia isn't in our room. She's still singing in the communal shower down the hall, which means Nathan lied.

"What do you need me to do?"

I whirl back into the hallway. "Hello?"

The hallway is totally empty, only Georgia's beautiful singing echoing off the walls. A chill runs up my spine as I glance around and step into the room, shutting the door and my eyes as the voice echoes through my head again, loud and clear.

"It's too late." Static. Static and the beating of a heart.

"Too late for what?" I say as if I'm using the mind-link, and I swear I *feel* a pause like the voice heard me, too.

The voice doesn't answer. Instead, my mind goes blissfully quiet.

Georgia bursts through the door, which nearly hits me in the back, carrying the scent of sweet pea and violet body wash and coconut lotion with her. "Oh, shit! What are you doing standing against the door?"

"I thought I heard…. Nothing."

She tightens her towel around her chest and reaches up to pull off her shower cap, her perfectly dry, bouncy ringlets falling free over her shoulders. "You're not freaked out already, are you? We can't chicken out now."

"I'm not chickening out." I sniff indignantly and cross the room to my desk, switching on my lamp, and pulling my makeup bag out of a drawer to fix the damage Nathan's mouth caused to my perfectly executed bronzer.

Georgia continues to sing as she gets ready. I zip up the black bodycon dress she picked out for the party which hugs her curves and makes her look like we had to sew it on. She looks like she just walked out of a magazine as she checks herself out in the mirror while the sounds of campus nightlife starts to sizzle through the air outside our single, open window.

"Are you really wearing… that?" she asks, looking me up and down as I step into a pair of heels that make me six inches taller than I am.

She's not talking about the shoes, however.

I run my hands down the length of black satin that rests mid-calf. The dress is simple, borderline elegant, nothing like what I imagine people are wearing to this party. I pull a black cloak over the strapless dress, which is tight around my breasts and shows off just enough cleavage to make it seem like I'm dressing to impress and have a good time.

But I'm planning to do a lot more than that. I'm going to find out everything I can about the Arcane Umbra. I will leave no stone unturned.

Georgia wiggles her fingers at me. "You look like a sexy witch. Are you going to put a hex on me, Misty?"

"Don't tempt me," I giggle, following her out of our dorm. We keep our masks tucked under our arms as we cross the campus square. The bell tower rises above us as we close in on the entrance, which I expected to be teeming with party goers, but it's empty.

Georgia clutches the invitation and looks around, confused. "Is this right?"

"It said the bell tower, nine P.M." I try the main door, which is little more than a service entrance. "It's locked."

"Maybe someone pulled a prank on us." She pouts, her mouth sagging with disappointment.

"I bet each invitation has a different location," I mumble, trying the handle again, frowning in frustration. "Different locations so the invitees don't meet or see each other coming into the party."

"That doesn't make any sense."

"It does if my catacomb theory is correct," I whisper, yanking on the handle with all of my strength.

"Catacomb–oh!" Georgia shrieks as the door flies open, and a cloaked figure darkens the already shadowed doorway. A sleek black mask covers the upper half of his face, and his head is shielded by a hood made of the same pitch-black fabric.

His mask doesn't even have eye holes, but I can feel him looking at us–at me–as he turns his head from side to side.

Georgia hands him the crumbled invitation with a trembling hand. He plucks it from her fingers and turns back into the shadows without so much as beckoning us to follow.

I'm absolutely buzzing with excitement as I firmly take Georgia's hand and drag her inside. The door shuts with a snap behind us, and a lock clicks into place. I feel a second presence in the darkness–another man, judging by the strong scent of aftershave–but I don't turn to look. I don my mask and pull my hood over my head, covering my perfect blowout, hiding my perfect makeup.

A door opens somewhere nearby, and faint light spills over our feet. Georgia gasps as we're led into a tight corridor of ancient gray stone.

"You were right–"

I clap my hand over her mouth as my vision clears enough to see the narrow stone staircase leading down into the darkness, into the tunnels I knew–I just knew–lay deep underneath the university, possibly stretching all over Tarsian, connecting ancient temple to ancient temple, castle to castle, fortress to fortress.

I shush Georgia, but she's already forgotten she was about to give away my secret–that I've spent two years trying to research this secret society in an attempt to gain entrance to their world and unearth their secrets. The *why* of it is what's keeping me going as the air starts to cool the further we travel underground and the stairwell becomes increasingly narrower until my shoulders brush each wall.

But my eyes are wide when we finally reach the bottom level of the hallway, and the first thrums of music reach us.

"Oh. My. Goddess," Georgia gasps, and I *smile*.

2

STOLEN KISSES

Misty

MUSIC BLARES FROM HIDDEN SPEAKERS. PURPLE-HUED LIGHT COVERS the wide, open ballroom of sorts in dim colors as bodies move to sensual, thrumming songs that I don't find even remotely familiar. Men and women alike are all dressed in black—black masks, black dresses, black suits. Some wear hoods to cover their hair, but I can't tell who's who... I can't tell who belongs to the order and who's just an invitee.

A screech of excitement barrels toward us as we edge down a short row of stone steps. Two women in black masks launch themselves at us—Fia and Darby—and I catch Darby at the very moment she wobbles in her impossibly high heels.

"No freakin' way!" Fia shouts over the music. "We were wondering if you guys got invited!"

"Why didn't you say anything?!" Georgia gasps, clutching Fia's face. "We could've all gotten ready together!"

Darby bounces up and down beside me, clutching a plastic cup in her hand full of what smells like cheap beer. "Isn't this great?"

Georgia, Darby, and Fia shout back and forth about our good luck in getting invited, but I'm instantly suspicious. I turn to look over my shoulder at the heavy, wooden double doors we'd been led through to the ballroom of some ancient underground… castle? Temple, more likely, but still.

The men who'd escorted me and Georgia here are gone. I would have noticed them stepping past us into the depths of the party.

If they're not here, where did they go?

"They have like… anything you want to drink. Wine, beer, the hard stuff." Darby ropes her arm through mine and begins dragging me into the fray while Fia drops into conversation with Georgia, our little group splitting the crowd.

But I don't make it to the tables of food and drink resting along the far wall. Distracted by the music and dancing, my friend's don't notice me slipping my arm from Darby's grasp. They don't notice me wading back through the crowd, my chin tilted toward the massive domed ceiling, to the ancient, candle-lit chandelier made of hundreds of silver shards. No one notices me slipping through a darkened archway leading off the ballroom and into a dimly lit corridor.

I try to keep my footsteps as light as possible as I pick over broken cobblestone, resting my hand along the wall. I test every door I pass. Some are unlocked, but the rooms within are empty and dark. Some doors open to nothing but stone rubble and the smell of mildew and dust. Other doors are locked tight, but their handles are… warm. Warmth and a metallic taste coats my tongue each time I try to yank open the locked doors.

I'm not dumb enough to ignore the taste of magic in my mouth. I've grown up around magic.

"Spells," I murmur to myself, smirking with excitement. This is going to be great, I can already tell. This place must be where the order regularly meets, tucked deep below the teeming campus sprawled above it. Maybe the locked doors house staircases that lead to specific entrances in the old buildings scattered across campus? The library, the dormitories, the halls and meeting spaces… I've been living here for almost three years and researching the strange, magical history of Eastonia, and my kind, all while a secret society has been lurking below me.

I turn a corner to another long, dimly lit hallway. It's uneven, the hallway curving slightly as I follow it on silent feet. It takes me a while to reach the end because of my new heels. I don't want anyone to know I'm here. I don't want them to hear me coming.

What I'm hoping to find is a meeting room or a library of some kind. Somewhere the order would keep their secrets about membership and their history.

But instead, at the very end of the hallway, I find an open door.

And then I find Nathan, my boyfriend of two years, bending a young woman dressed in black over a desk.

I stand numbly just a few feet away from the open door as the woman's fingers travel up the back of his neck to where his mask is tied behind his head. He grunts, mumbling praise under his breath while she writhes beneath him.

My lips part in surprise, but I stifle any noise about to fall from my tongue as he throws his cloak back, revealing his favorite TU crewneck sweatshirt, his joggers, and boxers pulled down to his knees. Sloppy. He's always been sloppy. I watch him thrust into this total stranger without even using protection, and now I'm... sick to my stomach.

I whirl, not bothering to hide the *click clack* of my heels on the cobblestone, and sniffle with absolute, unfiltered rage. Not heartbreak. Not rejection. *Fury.*

I have no idea where I'm going, but I end up in a web of crisscrossed corridors that I don't recognize. Frustrated, I choke out the first breath I've remembered to take since catching my boyfriend red handed with his pants down in a grimy alcove and bend at the waist to try to fill my lungs with much needed air.

"Misty," I whisper to myself. "You idiot. Grandpa was right about him all along."

"You shouldn't be here."

I freeze. At first, I think it's the voice in my head, but as I straighten, a shadow comes into view, followed by its owner.

He's tall. The tallest man I think I've ever seen. Taller than Ryan and my Uncle Ryatt, I think, which is wholly uncommon, and honestly, startling. He's wearing a black cloak and a mask that covers half of his face, only his chiseled, clean shaven jaw visible through the shadows dancing over his profile.

The buttons on his all black suit glint in the dim light coming from torches along the walls around us.

I take him in, my gaze doing a thorough sweep of his outfit, and spot a serpent cast in silver, or white gold, hopefully the latter, eating its own tail. He wears it as a cufflink.

He tucks his arm behind his back when he notices me looking at it.

"You shouldn't be here," he repeats, his voice deep and full of smoke.

"I don't know where I am," I admit, not bothering to hide the pained bite in my voice as I straighten up fully and rest my hands on my hips. I have to crane my neck to look up at him as he steps closer. "You're part of the order, aren't you? Why aren't you at the party?"

"Why aren't *you* at the party?" he echoes.

"I needed some fresh air," I lie, and he smirks, glancing back and forth. There's no fresh air down here. None at all. It smells like damp stone and dust, but his scent breaks through it all. I can smell his aftershave–clean and brisk. A hint of woodsy, spiced cologne on his clothing, and beneath that, his skin. A scent that's his–and his alone.

He smells good, and for a moment, my inhibitions slip. "Do you want to have sex with me?"

He stares at me. At least, I think he's looking at me. I can't tell beyond the mask, but his lips part in surprise before pressing into an amused smile. "No."

"Well," I huff, sniffling. "No worries. I'll find someone else."

I pull back my hood and untie my mask, letting it fall into my hand before wiping away smudged mascara from my undereyes.

He continues to stand there, silent and still like a statue.

I glance up at him, wiping my smudged fingers on my cloak. "What?" I growl, sniffling again, feeling utterly pathetic.

"Why are you crying?"

I sigh, then laugh bitterly. "Because I just found my boyfriend, one of your *brethren*, fucking someone in your creepy, underground lair." More tears spill over my lashes, further smudging my makeup. It was a waterproof mascara night, for sure. "And now–" I laugh, tears spilling down my cheeks. "Now I'm asking a total stranger to fuck me just to feel something other than how I feel right now."

He tilts his head to the side in a curious stance. "How do you feel right now?"

"Like killing him," I admit, and it's the truth. "Like breaking his fucking neck."

"Why don't you?"

I narrow my eyes at him. "Because that would be *murder*."

He purses his lips. "So?"

"So? Murder is bad." I stare at him for a moment, feeling uneasy in his presence for the first time, but here I am, in the underground, standing in front of an order of Arcane Umbra member. This has been a dream of mine since I first heard whispers about them when I was a freshman. I might not get this chance again. I blink the tears away and dry my cheeks. "Is that what this is? A sex and murder party?"

"No," he says, amused. "Not tonight, at least."

"Then what's the reason? The order is so secretive. Why invite students to a party, go about the whole secret invitation and mask process? Why have everyone use a different entrance?"

"You've put a lot of thought into this."

"These catacombs stretch all over campus, don't they?" I edge a step toward him, unable to shut my mouth. "They stretch every-where–to the Firestone temples lost in the sand outside Serpentia and Oasia, right?"

"They do," he says, his wide mouth and full lips twitching into a smile that he quickly lets fade. "But these aren't even the catacombs."

"Then what is this place?"

He lifts a shoulder in a shrug. "Old facets of the campus, back when it was a castle housing whatever Alpha reigned here. It's easy enough to access."

I stare blankly at him.

"Are you disappointed?" he edges, smiling again. It's a cocky, smooth smile that makes me think he's probably drop-dead gorgeous behind his mask. "Did you think you'd come here and find out all of our dirty little secrets?"

"What are your dirty little secrets?" For some reason, that question causes that smile to fade, his mouth pressing into a tight line.

"You're not going to find what you're looking for here. You should stop looking, actually. It's pointless."

"How do you know what I'm looking for?"

"You're a protohistory student."

"How do you know that?"

"Because you stupidly took off your mask," he replies, stepping forward, coming to a rest a mere foot away from me. "Princess Mystica of Crescent Falls, is it? That's your name?"

"Misty," I correct, thankful for this distraction but also feeling rather small in his shadow. I can't look into his face–his mask–without my neck feeling like it's about to snap. "And who are you?"

"That doesn't matter," he rasps, but then footsteps sound in the hallway nearby, followed by hushed male voices.

He stiffens and turns ever so slightly toward the noise.

"Put your mask on," he commands in a low, serious voice. "Now. Do not take it off again."

"Why?" I mumble as I raise my mask to my face. I'm moving too slow for his liking, apparently. He lets out a sigh of frustration and snatches the mask from me, tying it to the back of my head tighter than necessary.

"Pull up your hood to cover your hair."

Two masked figures come into view. They stop to stare at us at the very moment I pull my hood up. The masked man stares them down. He's standing close enough to me for it to feel intimate, and my heart rate spikes as he leans down, caging me against the wall.

"What are you doing?" I hiss, pressing my back against the wall, but the words are stolen from my tongue as his lips crash into mine–hard.

My head bounces against the wall. I hiss a breath in pain, but his hand cups the back of my head and then he's… deepening the kiss, chasing my tongue with his and I'm… kissing him back. His mouth is warm and perfectly fitted to mine as he holds us there, his free hand sliding into my cloak to clutch my hip.

"Who is that?" one of the men asks.

"Fuck if I know," his companion laughs then says loudly, as if to get our attention, "Someone's who's about to miss the meeting with the Umbra Mortis if he doesn't get his ass to the rectory in five fucking minutes!"

Their footsteps begin to retreat, but the kiss isn't stopping. I clutch his cloak as he leans his body against mine, sighing breathlessly against his mouth. He groans as his mouth leaves mine to trail kisses along my jaw as my arms rope around his waist.

But the second I lay a hand on his back, he hisses in pain and pulls away.

We stand there for several seconds staring at each other, panting.

"Are you hurt?" I ask as reality crashes down around me. I just kissed a total stranger. I kissed a stranger after finding out Nathan cheated on me. I kissed a stranger at an Arcane Umbra party.

His lips, slightly swollen from kissing me, part, something silent passing between them, like a prayer.

Then, he says, "Go back to the party, then go home, Misty."

He turns on his heel and stalks away.

3

A WHISPERED WARNING

Misty

BURNING SUNLIGHT STUNS ME INTO ALERTNESS. I OPEN MY EYES TO slits and promptly close them again. A dull pain spreads through my head, reminiscent of the type of hangover I wouldn't wish on my worst enemy, but that doesn't make any sense.

I'm standing in the damp, dusty corridor in the web-like underground beneath campus... right?

I open my eyes against the light and stare blankly at the ceiling of my dorm room. Soft snoring echoes all around me. Ignoring the sickening pain in my head, I turn ever so slightly to look at the person whose arm and leg are draped over my body, finding Georgia sleeping peacefully, still wearing her black dress. We're in her bed on top of the bedspread, and one quick glance across the room shows me a tangle of cloaks and shoes separating Georgia's section of the tight room from mine where Fia and Darby are fast asleep in my bed.

I sit up. Georgia's arm slips from my waist as I slide out of bed and walk on unsteady feet to the door, grabbing my shower kit, a robe, and a towel. Trembling with confusion, I fumble with the door with numb fingers that just won't do what I need them to do.

The hallway outside our door sways as I stagger down to the communal bathroom. Normally, the bathroom is a wash of hairspray, steam, and girlish banter, but right now, it's silent. Empty. I didn't bother to check the time, but it must be the early hours of the morning.

I set the water as hot as I can possibly handle and let it wash away the numbness coasting through my veins, trying to put together the pieces of my night. I don't remember anything past meeting that order member in the corridor. Touching my fingers to my still swollen lips, his kiss comes hurtling back to me with startling clarity. I remember the other men walking away and the knowledge that this could stop but it… didn't. We kept kissing. We kissed like we knew each other, like our souls were intertwined.

But I remember him pulling away the second I touched his back, and he hissed in pain, then he told me to go back to the party and to go home.

Well, I made it home. But I have no idea if I made it back to the party and what happened afterward.

I shake out my tight muscles and sink to the floor of the shower, leaning my head against the tile as steam rises all around me. I close my eyes as the pain in my head starts to recede. I'm not hungover. I'm a terrible lightweight. A single glass of wine has my cheeks burning red and a migraine creeping into existence. I know better than to even touch hard liquor. Even the smell of it makes my stomach turn.

I wouldn't have been drinking at all. Not with plans to unravel the mysteries of the order.

Was I drugged?

If so, how?

Voices drift into the bathroom. Women who live on our floor are shuffling in, talking in soft tones about their nights. Another shower starts, then another, but I continue to sit, battered by hot water, for several more minutes. Eventually, I step out of the shower dressed in a robe with my hair twisted in a towel and smile in greeting to the four women crowding a long, narrow counter, all of them chatting over the sound of hairdryers and the clink of makeup compacts opening, but I hurry back to my room without so much as drying my hair.

My friends are still fast asleep.

I pour three glasses of water, force myself to cry, which isn't that hard when I let my memories flood back to catching Nathan cheating on me, and let the tears drop into the water. I still feel like shit, but my friends don't have to.

I let my hair air dry, curling softly at the edges while gathering up the scattered shoes and cloaks covering the floor. I tuck everyone in, change into my usual shorts and tank top, and make a snap decision to grab my bathing suit and gym bag along with my backpack. I plan my day out in my head to stop from thinking back on what I remember from last night, which is becoming hazier by the second. I'll go to the athletic center first. I'll use the pool, swim laps until I feel satiated, and then I'll go to the library and spend the rest of the day studying.

My heart rate is already spiking as I cut through the campus square, lugging two bags with me, my freshly washed hair curling into soft waves around my face. It's going to hate being stuffed into a swim cap, but my options right now are severely limited. I can spend the day wondering what the hell happened to me or go about my day like I normally would.

I simply chose the latter.

"Misty, hey!"

I slow my pace with a sigh. Jogging footsteps rush in my direction, and then I'm being cast in shadow by a young man I know through Nathan.

Declan steps in front of me, looking me up and down before saying, "Going to the gym?"

"Yes," I reply sweetly, biting down on my tongue before I can say something like, *What does it look like? Get out of my way.*

"Did you, uh, do anything fun last night?" He runs his fingers through his shaggy brown hair, looking down at me with an odd expression. Admittedly, I don't know Declan very well. He's a jock, like Nathan, and they run in the same crowd. He has bright, sandy-brown eyes and a pleasant, quiet personality that makes him an outlier in their group of friends. I've never seen him as a threat.

Until I remember that my now ex-boyfriend is part of the Order of Arcane Umbra.

How many of the track team guys are part of it, too?

I narrow my eyes at him. "Not really. Why?"

"I was—was just wondering," he stammers, shoving his hands in his pockets. "I didn't see you at Leroy's last night."

Leroy's, the campus tavern. I roll my eyes, deciding to drop the act. "I wasn't invited to Rodney's early birthday party."

"Oh," he says as I turn toward the door of the athletic center. "I mean, it wasn't really a birthday party, just a few drinks—"

"Declan, I need you to listen to every word I'm about to say to you, okay?" I turn to him with my hand on the doorknob of the very old building housing a state-of-the-art pool, gym, and indoor track. "Tell Nathan he's pathetic, and I never want to see him again. If he asks why, tell him it doesn't matter, and if he gets all sad, confused, and pouty, tell him to go seek comfort in the girl he was fucking last night." I pull open the door, walk in, and let it slam shut behind me.

Declan gapes through the glass in the door but doesn't follow, thank the Goddess, because now I'm about to start crying again.

I hurry to the locker room, change into my one-piece suit, stuff my hair into a swim cap, and beeline for the pool, ignoring the other students milling about. I didn't even check the pool schedule, but it doesn't matter. The tangled voices and images in my head are growing so overwhelming that I find it hard to catch my breath as I burst into the pool area and rush to the edge, diving in gracefully.

I slip into the deep end, and the second my body fully submerges, my head goes blissfully quiet once again.

I swim over a dozen laps and finally come to rest on the edge of the pool, panting, resting my head on my arm as I catch my breath. The pool is empty. A few people are walking laps on the track over-looking the pool, but that's it. I'm alone here.

I suck in a breath and slip underwater in preparation to pull myself out of the pool and go about my day when the voice echoes through my head so loud my ears ring.

In the still emptiness of the water all around me, the voice is loud and crystal clear.

'*Get off campus. Now.*'

I've rarely ever talked back to it, not until yesterday when I heard the distorted whispers and finally decided to ask what the hell it was going on about.

'*Why?*' I ask into the nothingness, opening my eyes underwater.

A hushed sigh echoes through my head–very male, honestly. '*Just listen–for once. Don't bother packing. Just leave.*'

'*Who are you?*'

'*The fucking devil on your shoulder, Mystica. You have to LEAVE.*'

I close my eyes again, trying to pull the voice closer, to see the person, or being, behind it. It's not nearly as distorted as it usually is. I can hear the infliction in each word, the sheer frustration and concern, and it's definitely a man talking to me.

'*What god are you?*'

He laughs. '*I'm not a god.*'

This doesn't feel like the mind-link. I don't have the ability to shut it off, tune it out, or seek it like I can do with my family. It doesn't tickle the same parts of my brain, either. This is... deep. Overwhelmingly so. It blurs my other senses. I open my eyes, focusing on the glimmering far wall of the pool.

'*Tell me why I need to leave and maybe I'll listen to your warning, demon,*' I reply hotly.

'*Just listen to me–*'

My lungs burn and warning bells skitter through my brain. I'm still underwater. I'm sitting at the bottom of the pool with my eyes open. Suddenly frantic, I tuck my legs beneath me and leap up on my toes, grasping for the surface as the voice's words coast through my mind, but the end of his sentence is cut off when I breach the surface and suck in much needed oxygen.

'*What did you say?*' I fire down the... line? Whatever this is, it's nothing but static now, then echoing, deafening silence as the sounds of the athletic center fade back into view.

Uneasy, I pull myself out of the pool, standing at the edge to glance around. I'm still alone. There isn't a single, other soul in the pool area. There's no music blasting over the speakers or anyone sitting in the stands, watching me. No one that could have been talking to me somehow, mind-linking with me.

I can't even mind-link with my friends here. I'm too far away from my family to use it with them.

I hurry back to the locker room, wash the sharp, chemical laden pool water from my skin, and redress. I pull the swim cap off in a huff and grip the porcelain rim of the bathroom sink as I stare at my reflection, my eyes rimmed red from holding them open underwater for what could have been seconds–or several minutes.

Does water somehow... hold whatever link I have to this voice... open?

I've never heard of this before. This... power? Maybe. It could be a power. A new power emerging in time for my upcoming birthday.

Within minutes, I'm in the library, shuffling down the wide, amazing, seven story spiral staircase that leads three stories down to the recesses of the library and four stories up to the domed ceiling leagues above my head.

My usual study spot is shockingly busy today, but Saturdays are always busy in the library. I chew the end of my pen as I scan racks of ancient tomes and books in the "magic" section, aptly named. I have special access to this section because the librarians were sick of me asking them for new books every five seconds. I'm the only student in the entire university who's allowed to just take these books off the shelf, and the strange library knows that.

The library has the same kind of magic as my cousin Kenna's castle in Veiled Valley. It's *alive*.

I turn with a tome about magic communication in my hand and watch hundreds of books zooming in a spiral against the turns of the staircase at the center of the library, sorted by magic.

But as I pick through the racks back to my usual table, I spot someone else there.

"Oh, thank the Goddess," I rush out, slamming my book down in front of Georgia, who jostles at the noise, choking on her iced coffee.

"Did you just see a ghost… again?" She laughs, shaking her coffee to better mix her hazelnut and vanilla flavor. She gets the same coffee every morning. She's a creature of habit and has a wicked memory. She knows the name of every member of my family and remembers their birthdays, anniversaries, and any upcoming due dates when I honestly grapple to hang on to that information, and I'm related to them.

"How did we get home last night?" I hiss as I sit down, glancing up and down the table. There's a group studying nearby but hopefully out of earshot.

"What do you mean? We walked." She narrows her eyes at me. "Don't you remember? After we left Leroy's–"

"Leroys?" Something like unease curls in my belly. "But we didn't go to Leroys."

She searches my face for understanding. "Have you had any coffee yet today?"

"No, but–" I suck in a breath as tingles whisper over my skin. "We didn't go to Leroy's last night. We went to the bell tower."

She arches a brow. "The *bell tower?*"

Does she seriously not remember? "We went to an Arcane Umbra party! How did we get home from it?" My tone takes on a desperate edge as Georgia shakes her head, her eyes filling with concern.

"Misty, what the hell are you talking about? We got dressed up and went to Leroy's, remember? Darby was there celebrating Rodney's birthday and asked us to come."

My heart races as I lean back and look at her. I rack my brain. I'd cleaned up this morning in our room and didn't see the masks anywhere.

Something's wrong.

"You look exhausted, Misty," she whispers, but she still looks concerned as she rises and gathers her purse. "I'm going to go get you a coffee, okay? They messed up my order, anyway. I'll be right back. Maybe instead of hitting the books, you chill today. You danced until like, three in the morning."

No, I didn't. I wasn't dancing at all. I was kissing an order member in a shadowed corridor deep underground.

I watch her walk away and turn to my book… just as the magically sorted books still in midair, then plummet to the ground.

4

THE WORLD CRASHES DOWN

Misty

GEORGIA TURNS TO THE RAILING IN AWE. THE STUDENTS SHARING OUR little alcove rise from their chairs in confusion as the books crash to the ground.

My already thundering heart nearly stops, skipping several beats, and in that time, the first screams echo all the way down to us on the second to last floor, splitting the normally silent air into pieces. I stand, my chair falling over backward, as green-hued light blasts through the upper section of the library.

"GEORGIA!" I scream, lunging for her as debris–a tangle of stone, books, and paper–cascade down the open space housing the staircase. A shockwave slams into us, knocking Georgia away from the railing and sending me backward into one of the racks, my spine singing in pain. More screams follow, growing in intensity, as I open my eyes to thick dust and the haze of magic I can taste on my tongue.

Shadowed figures move down the staircase. Wolves follow, their eyes glowing red and green in the haze. I choke on the pain coasting through my body as my healing powers ignite, quickly fading bruises

23

and knitting together broken ribs, but Georgia is lying face down covered in books.

"Ge-Georgia," I croak, falling to my knees and crawling to her, finding the puddle of what's left of her iced coffee soaking the carpet. I pull her toward me as the students behind me hush each other's sobs of fear. One of the figures senses my movement and stops on the staircase, looking through the fog of dust, right at us.

"Georgia, wake up," I hiss, rising and dragging her across the coffee-stained floor. I reach the other students, who part to allow us space in their not-so-well-hidden shadowed alcove, but it's too late. The cloaked figures are running now, reaching our landing of the staircase, and moving in our direction.

I shove a barely conscious Georgia behind me, thrusting her into the arms of a terrified looking young man whose glasses are cracked, his face covered in dust.

"What's happening?" one of the women behind me asks as I turn back toward the staircase.

I glance around, noticing a break in the toppled racks, and motion toward it. "Go, get out of here and hide!"

The group nervously looks at where I'm pointing, tears in their eyes.

"Go!" I hiss, giving one of the women a shove, but it's too late. Two wolves dart out of the gloom, snarling and clacking jaws lined with massive, sharp teeth. Shadowed figures appear behind them in black cloaks and black masks. Arcane Umbra members.

They're attacking the university.

I spin on my heel as the wolves lunge at us and splay my hands out wide, screaming as I send a blast of bright blue light sizzling through the air between them and us. The light explodes, creating a force field I can barely contain. "GO NOW!" I shout at the group of terrified students, who are whimpering and gaping at me in shock. Tears of frustration well in my eyes as a few of the girls skitter away, tripping over fallen books and toppled shelving, but the young man holding Georgia struggles to carry her over the racks.

My powers are barely holding. I take several steps forward,

blasting my light, pushing the wolves back even further until they're forced to retreat in the direction from which they came.

"Get out of here!" I scream at the student holding Georgia.

He drops her and runs.

"No! Fuck!" I scream in frustration and sheer, unfiltered rage.

Georgia sputters, blood streaming from a gash on her forehead as she tries to lift her head.

"GG!" I yell at her, and she blinks at me, confused. "Georgia!" I take another step, pushing the wolves back again, but my magic is starting to fizzle. "Georgia, look at me. You need to get up! You need to run!"

"M-Misty?" she murmurs, blinking into the bright light cast by my magic.

"GEORGIA, PLEASE!" I scream. "RUN!"

I take another step, reaching the railing, turning and sending my magic in a straight, bright line that fans out over the balcony over-looking the staircase. Above me, other balconies come into view, and several students are running for their lives while others are screaming in the arms of order members carrying them away.

The worst of it are the bodies with their arms draped through the breaks in the railings, blood dripping from still fingers onto the books covering the floor.

Tears burn my eyes, blurring my vision. I scream again, so loud my voice cracks and breaks, as I send my magic hurtling in a deadly wave.

"The net! Drop the fucking net!" Someone above me shouts through the chaos.

"GEORGIA!" I bellow, craning my neck to watch her struggle to her feet. She wobbles but manages to grip a toppled shelf and pull herself upright just as something heavy is thrown from three stories above my head, metal singing through the air as it falls.

I make a snap decision to not look up. I watch my friend instead, silently pleading with her to hurry.

The wind is knocked out of me, then searing pain erupts all over my body as a metal net made of silver drops over me, extinguishing my powers completely. I crumble, screaming in pain, for help, for anything. My healing powers aren't quick enough to fix the burns left by the silver as it touches my bare legs, my bare arms. My hair gets tangled in the net, exposing my neck, and the net settles against it, forcing me to curl my chin into my chest to try to get away.

"Ge-Georgia!" I sob, watching in horror as she slips, falling backward off the shelf she was trying to climb over. Two shadow figures reach her within seconds and roughly tackle her to the ground. "NO!!! NO! STOP!" I scream her name over and over, trying to find my powers, but the silver is eating me alive.

The wolves are nowhere to be seen, but several figures surround me, blocking my view of Georgia and her assailants.

"Get her up and cuffed, quickly," someone sneers, and the net is lifted. I immediately try to wrench away, but I'm tackled to the ground, a boot flat against the back of my neck.

I scream, kicking and writhing as multiple hands touch my body, flattening my arms to my back. My healing powers work overtime, soothing the silver burns, but pain ignites again on my wrists as silver cuffs are tightened in place.

I kick wildly, the heel of my sneaker meeting someone's jaw with a satisfying crunch.

"AH! Fuckin' bitch!" I'm kicked hard in the ribs. It knocks the wind out of me. I choke on a scream as another kick snaps at least two ribs.

"Stop! He wants her in one piece!"

Someone kneels on my legs, preventing me from moving, and another set of silver cuffs are fastened around my ankles.

The burning sensation blinds me. My vision blurs around the edges, going dark. I open my mouth to scream Georgia's name again, but someone stuffs wadded up fabric between my teeth. I bite down the best I can on his fingers but he pulls away and slaps me so hard my ears ring.

"Pick her up."

I'm lifted and thrown over someone's shoulder like a sack of potatoes. I spit out the gag, still screaming, and wriggle, trying to throw myself off his shoulder.

"Fuck, I'm going to drop her!"

I bite down on his back, and he screams.

I'm dropped flat on my back, my body crunching against books and shelving.

My world blurs as my head bounces against the hard, stone ground. All around me, books are falling from the shelves. Paper dances through the air, drifting like feathers. I can't tell if the metallic taste in my mouth is magic–or blood. I go still for the first time, the pain too overwhelming to move, let alone think past.

Masked faces funnel around me, staring down at me. I can't tell who's speaking, who's telling me to *fucking chill*, that if I don't stop trying to fight them, they'll kill–they'll kill Georgia. Tears fall freely down my cheeks. I can't move. I'm losing feeling in my arms and legs. My back. My back has to be broken.

I slip away, mentally trying to grasp anything to hang onto. I find… something. Something deep in my mind, and tug tight.

"*Help,*" I manage to whisper, sending the word down whatever line this is to the voice in my head. "*The–the university is being attacked–I'm–I'm hurt–They're taking me away–*"

"*I warned you,*" the voice echoes back, and it's the last thing I hear before my vision goes black, and everything goes completely, utterly silent.

* * *

I'm thrown to the ground, which wakes me up. I'm not sure how long I've been out, but I know the second new air fills my lungs that I'm not in the library anymore. I don't recognize the scent filling my nose at first. I blink away the darkness in my vision, lifting my head to murmured voices. Dark stone fills my eyes, followed by green-hued light. Dim light, thank the Goddess, because my head is killing me.

Someone releases the cuffs around my ankles. I don't waste any time. I pull myself up to a kneeling position and it... takes all of my strength. My healing powers are trying to knit me back together, but it's slow, especially while they focus wholly on the silver cuffs burning my wrists, trying to heal the skin there again, and again, to no avail.

I sway, swallowing back the urge to throw up all over the damp stone floor, but eventually lift my head to the two-dozen or so men standing in a semicircle on the far end of the room, arranged on shallow stairs that lead to a platform.

Most are wearing masks. Some aren't, and as I sweep my gaze over the group, I come to a stop on Nathan. He stares at me, inhaling deeply as his dark eyes fill with dampness.

I bare my bloody teeth at him and rasp, *"You."*

He closes his eyes and looks down at his feet.

A shuffling echoes through the... ballroom. That's where I am. I'm in the ballroom from the party last night, the party that *definitely* happened. I wasn't imagining it. I scan the men again, looking for the man with the silver snake on his cuff, but they're all wearing them. The silver glints in the dim light as an elderly man parts the crowd and comes to a stop a few feet away from me.

He smiles with malice, chuckling to himself. "What a lovely little treasure you are, Princess Mystica. Quite the fighter. A pretty little warrior."

I slowly turn my gaze up to him. "Who the fuck are you?" I growl, shaking from pain and the utter shock of what just happened to me. "Where is Georgia?"

"Do not speak." His slap echoes through the ballroom.

I sneer up at him. "Fuck you."

He lifts his hand again, but a deep voice nearby says darkly, "That's enough."

His voice is smooth like a fine, expensive scotch. His footsteps are heavy and trained as he moves down from the other men. "Umbra," he says as he reaches the man's side, wearing a mask. He leans in to whisper something to the man, who keeps his eyes on mine.

Impatient, I writhe against the cuffs holding my wrists behind my back. "Let me go, you fucking monsters!"

"You're not going anywhere," the elderly man replies sharply.

"Her hands are glowing!" one of the other men shouts in warning, and the elderly man's hand comes down so hard on the side of my face that I topple over and see stars for several seconds. My vision clears enough to see the way the masked man has a death grip on the elderly man's arm.

"Do I need to remind you of the deal we made?" the masked man sneers. He shoves the elder.

"I am the Umbra Mortis," the old man growls, straightening his cloak. He turns to his assailant, giving him a deathly glare.

"And I am the *king*," the man says, reaching up to take off... to take off his mask.

Dark gray eyes meet mine as the fabric falls away. Prince Cole looks down at me with disgust.

He just called himself the king, though. I don't understand....

His gaze holds mine for several seconds before he turns to glare at the Umbra Mortis, who I assume is the leader of this group of criminals, and then faces the crowd of men standing in silence behind him. "If anyone so much as touches a hair on her head, they die. Am I understood?"

A murmur of acknowledgement passes through the crowd. But the Umbra Mortis is glaring down at me, his upper lip curled over his teeth. I'm not watching him, however. I watch as Prince–*King*–Cole stares into the crowd, right at Nathan, who still has his head bowed.

King Cole turns on his heel, and two masked men come down the steps, following him as he walks toward the same shadowed archway I'd explored last night. He pauses at the archway, turning toward the men again. "I want her sedated for the journey. Fully sedated."

"Wait–" I rush out, and his eyes fall on mine. "My-My friend–Georgia–"

To my shock, one of the men at his side removes his mask, revealing... Declan. Declan's eyes are pleading as he gives what I believe is a wobbly attempt at a reassuring smile. "She's okay. She's all right, I promise."

Utter confusion blurs my senses. King Cole is still looking at me as I'm dragged to my feet by masked men. He holds my gaze for several more seconds before saying to no one in particular, "Alert her father that we have her, and he'll heed my demands if he ever wants to see her again." He turns and stalks into the darkness.

5
THE B WORD

Aviva

I've never been to Crescent Falls before. I imagined something different than quiet, somber hallways and hushed murmurs. I guess, in any other circumstance, we would have been able to drive here in a real car from the border with Eastonia, taking several days to travel through the sweeping plains of Moorn before reaching the mountainous, sprawling mecca of the capitol while Ryan told me stories about growing up in this fascinating place but that's... not how this is happening.

We arrived an hour ago to chaos. Now, I pace behind a couch, watching my mate lean into conversation with his twin brother Sydney and their father, Alpha King Isaac. Ryatt, the Alpha King of Eastonia, isn't here. Neither is his wife and mate, Ella, Ryan's aunt.

Evander's here, however, and he keeps stealing glances in my direction while I do my best to fade into Maddy's floral wallpaper.

One second, I'd been tucked into bed with my mate, reveling in the absolute bliss of our impending parenthood, and now I'm here, after hours' worth of jumping from place to place, learning the horrific details about an attack that will go down in Eastonia's sordid history as one of the worst offenses to our people we've ever experienced.

Over a hundred young university students are dead or badly injured. Dozens more are missing.

Princess Misty, Ryan and Sydney's little sister, is one of those currently unaccounted for.

Maddy sits in silence on the couch with her hands knitted so tightly together her knuckles are white. I pace behind her again, laying a hand on her shoulder. She briefly leans her cheek against my hand ,and it shatters my heart.

"When did this come?" Isaac asks like someone took a rake to his vocal cords as he lifts his eyes to Evander. An envelope so black it sucks the light from the room rests in the center of a table where the men stand in a semicircle, looking down with bated breath at the note that came in it.

"Last night," Evander says with a short nod. "Ryatt killed the messenger."

"Of course, he did." Isaac closes his eyes and stands with the letter in his hands, crumbling it in his fist.

We brought the letter. Ryatt showed up in the middle of the night last night, covered in blood, and whisked us away to the Roguelands where we joined Evander and jumped all the way to Crescent Falls. Ryatt promptly left us behind to deliver the letter to Isaac ourselves, and now we're… trying to grapple with what comes next.

Ryatt opened the letter first. He read the neat handwriting. He learned Misty's fate and used his powers to turn the mysterious man who'd delivered it to a bloody pulp. At least, that's what Evander told us. I have a feeling it wasn't a swift death.

Maddy wouldn't read it. Even now, as she watches her mate squeeze the paper in his fist, her eyes remain dry and emotionless. I know that inside she's falling to pieces.

I can't imagine how they feel.

Isaac takes a deep breath and looks up from his hand just as Sarah walks into the sitting room.

She looks around, her cheeks flushed and eyes heavy with worry. "The boys are playing in the library with Cosette and Hanna."

Sydney gives her a quick, tight smile that she returns as she moves toward the center of the room. A man I haven't been introduced to yet, who goes by the name Cassian, leans against the wall by the window, tapping the fingers of his mechanical right arm on his thigh.

Silence settles as we all look at Isaac for some semblance of a plan.

He looks at his mate, though, with glassy blue eyes full of grief and vengeance. "I'm leaving for Eastonia—immediately."

Maddy nods, sucking in a breath as she looks down at her hands. Isaac looks at Sydney, then at… Sarah.

"You and I will go within the hour. We'll travel with Ryan and Aviva."

Sydney's head whips to his mate, then back to his father. "What are you talking about?"

Sarah's lips part in surprise. "Me?"

To the group, Isaac says, "Sarah is going to scry to give us a better idea of where Misty's being held."

"Isaac," Sarah pleads, shaking her head. "I can't—Tarsian is too far away for me to see anything clearly—"

"That's why we'll be staying in the Deadlands, in Silverhide." Isaac's gaze sweeps over my face before resting on Ryan. "You're going to meet with each patriarch in the Deadlands and have them prepare their warriors." He turns his gaze to Evander. "You're going to gather your Ghost army and be prepared to meet us in the event Misty is closer to the border with the Deadlands."

Sarah looks at Sydney, confusion blurring her features. Sydney shakes his head, straightening as he turns to his father to argue, but Isaac beats him to it, continuing, "Sydney, you will be staying here and preparing our army for war."

War. The word echoes around the room, burrowing into each of us and burning into our minds.

"You're not separating me from my wife," Sydney growls, but Isaac holds up a hand.

"Every capable warrior in Crescent Falls will be dispatched to the border within the next day."

Maddy stands abruptly. "Isaac, you're getting ahead of yourself."

He licks his lips. "Ella has already declared war on Tarsian. It's done. Their forces are already being gathered in the Roguelands in preparation for an… invasion." Even Isaac chokes on the word.

My own mind spins. We've just gone to war. My hands shake as I clutch the back of the couch, imagining the blood of rogues oozing between my fingers. Ryan holds my gaze with hooded eyes. He's thinking what I'm thinking. We're tired.

"Our troops can't invade until we know where our daughter is," Maddy argues through gritted teeth, tears spilling down her cheeks. "Misty will get caught up in the violence. You read the letter–you know what he'll do to her if they–if they cross the border into Tarsian!" Maddy starts to shatter, trembling as she wraps her arms around her stomach. "That's our baby, Isaac. You can't let them do this yet. We need time to find her first!"

Isaac swallows hard, closing his eyes as he says, "Everyone out."

None of us move right away. I make a single step toward the doors when he shouts, "Out, *now!*"

I scurry out of the room, Sarah mere inches behind me. Sydney continues to argue with Isaac as Cassian, Isaac's Beta I've gathered, grabs Sydney by the rough of his neck and drags him out into the grand foyer of their beautiful castle. The doors slam shut behind my mate, who's the last to leave the room, but Maddy's soft cries echo through my veins, slicing me into pieces.

I resist the sudden urge to wrap my arms protectively around the tiny flicker of life resting in my belly. We haven't told his family yet.

Sarah grabs my arm and walks me down the hallway in silence. The heavy tread of Ryan, Sydney, and Evander follow, but a glance over my shoulder shows me that Cassian is heading upstairs.

Closeted in a kitchen in the very back of the house, I turn toward the windows overlooking the back garden while Sydney and Ryan lock the doors, closing us in.

"What," Sarah says harshly, turning to the men, "did the letter say?"

Ryan runs his hands through his hair, shaking his head. His lips part, but he can't bring himself to say it. Even Sydney looks green as he drops his gaze to his feet, rolling his lower lip between his teeth and squeezing his eyes shut.

Their little sister is caught at the center of this madness.

I turn to Sarah instead. I'd rather this news come from me instead of either of them having to find the strength to say the words out loud.

"Misty was taken by Cole, the new Alpha King of Tarsian." I lick my lips, finding them dry and cracked from anxiously gnawing them raw over the last day. "He's said that as long as the Allied Kings stay out of Tarsian, she'll live. If the Allied Kings invade, he will kill her." I swallow past the lump forming in my throat.

Sarah scoffs, looking wildly around the room. "Then why the hell are Ryatt and Ella planning a full invasion–backed by Isaac's army?" She settles wild eyes on her mate who can't bring himself to look up from the black and white tiled floor.

Ryan speaks, his voice low and calm despite the words I know are about to fall from his lips. "In the meantime, he's using her as a... breeder. She'll be returned to the family once their child is born but only as long as our armies don't cross the border. That's why it's imperative we find her and stop that from happening."

The word breeder bounces through the room, echoing like a death knell.

"No," Sarah whispers, shaking her head. "No, Misty's so young. She's not–she hasn't even come into her wolf yet. This isn't... that can't be what the letter said." Her mouth continues to move, but words don't come out. "No, Sydney."

"The deaths from the attack on the university spanned three king-doms," Ryan says painfully. "There were students from Crescent Falls, the Roguelands, and even Celestoria studying there and they…. Ryatt and Ella don't have much of a choice. Alpha King Cole knew exactly what he was doing. He wants this war, for whatever reason."

"Then why try to make deals?" Sarah argues through tears. "Using Misty?"

"I don't know," Sydney whispers, shaking his head.

"Will he kill her?" Sarah looks murderous as she sweeps her gaze around the room.

"This man killed his own father," Ryan says, "to take over as Alpha King. None of us should doubt what he's capable of."

"So Misty is going to die because our kingdoms are going to war?" Sarah looks horrified and broken as she gestures to the door of the kitchen, like Misty is standing just beyond it, out of reach.

"No," I say softly, shaking my head. Something clicks in my head. Ryatt was adamant that I came here, with Ryan, to see Isaac. "No, because you're going to find her, and I'm… I'm the one that's going to go get her, aren't I?" I look from face to face.

"No–" Ryan rushes out, but Evander sighs and cuts him off.

"Yeah," he breathes. "You and I are going to Tarsian, Aviva."

"She can't," Ryan cuts in, shaking his head. "I won't allow it."

"None of us have a choice about the roles we're about to play," Evander says sharply.

Ryan looks at me with fury flashing through his deep, blue eyes. He's about to say it… to say I'm pregnant.

What would we do if this was our daughter trapped behind enemy lines, forced to be a monster's breeder?

We'd be going after her, hell or high water. We wouldn't question a single decision we had to make. We'd find her.

Into his head, I whisper, *'Don't.'*

Ryan holds my gaze for several seconds. Mingled anger and resignation flare behind his eyes before he finally sighs and looks down at his hands, which curl into fists.

Resigned to the reality of our situation, Sarah looks at Sydney with a heartbreaking expression. "But what about the boys?"

Sydney looks like he's about to break at any given second. Their family is about to be split up for Goddess knows how long–with him dealing with the royal army, and Sarah in Eastonia with us, trying to find where Misty's being kept.

I don't realize Ryan's suddenly right by my side until he knits his fingers in mine and tugs me toward the door. We follow Evander out, leaving Sarah and Sydney to discuss what happens next for their children.

"Where do you think she is, right now?" I ask Evander as we walk down the hallway.

Evander sighs, "Your guess is as good as mine. Tarsian is huge. It's bigger than the Deadlands and Roguelands combined. She could be anywhere."

6

LOOSE TONGUE

Misty

I open my eyes to darkness, blinking it away. My body aches like nothing I've ever experienced before, but I'm alive. I'm alive, and in a dungeon.

I rise to my knees, crawling to the bars that separate me from a dingy, damp hallway lit by flickering torches.

I hesitate before gripping the bars, but it's iron, not silver, thank the Goddess. I'm not sure how much more I can take... *wait a minute.*

I lift my wrists to the torchlight. Twin silver bands–wide, and seamless–hug each wrist. They're no chains between them. Nothing keeping me bound to the wall. Manacles. I immediately try to pull them off, but I can't. It doesn't hurt, though. I wedge a pinky between my skin and the manacle on my left wrist and feel... leather? Some type of barrier between the silver and my skin.

Still, even without the silver resting directly against me, it's close enough to keep my powers at bay. My fingertips sizzle and send puffs of mist through the bars instead of strips of bright light. My healing powers gnaw at the deep bruises covering my body but don't make much of a difference.

I grit my teeth and inhale deeply through my nose, then let the air out in a rush, my eyes going wide. "Georgia?"

Her sweet pea and violet scent is faint, but she's here. She's been using the same body wash since I met her. I'd recognize the smell anywhere. "GG? Where are you?"

"Misty?" Movement catches my attention in the cell across from mine. She reaches for the bars, but then thinks better of it, her hand retreating back into the shadows.

"It's iron, Georgia, it won't hurt you!"

She clutches the bars and painfully pulls herself into view. She's horribly battered but alive.

Thank the Goddess. I'll never skip temple services again once we're out of this.

"Misty, what happened? Where are we?" Her voice breaks. "Where is everyone else?"

"I don't know," I rush out, shaking my head as I press my face against the bars. She's wearing manacles too. Probably so she can't shift, but she's my age. Neither of us have come into our wolves yet. "I got knocked out. I saw you get tackled and then... I don't remember. Georgia, why don't you remember going to the Arcane Umbra party?"

"The party?" she whimpers, shaking her head. "I don't remember, Misty. My head–everything in my head is a mess. I remember... I remember getting ready with you and taking a shower and then it goes hazy."

"Don't worry about it now, okay? I'm going to get us out of this, I promise."

She nods, tears sliding down her face. A low groan echoes nearby, and we both go still.

"Hello?" Georgia croaks.

"Ah–fuck–what the fuck–" A male voice, obviously in pain, echoes toward us. "H-Hello?"

"Who are you?" I shout, unease prickling over my skin.

Another set of silver manacles catch the faint light in a cell next to Georgia's. A young man grips the bars and grunts with effort as he pulls himself into view before slumping, resting his cheek against the iron. He looks familiar. I've seen him around campus, and... on the expedition this summer, during my internship. He's a... cryptology student, I think. One of those weirdos that specializes in breaking ancient code, unlocking secrets from the past in languages we've lost to time.

"Are you Luke?" I ask on a whim. He's one of only three people in that specialized program, so my odds are good.

"Yeah. Misty? Where the fuck are we?"

"I don't know," I reply, swallowing hard. "I have no idea."

"How did you get here?" Georgia asks, scooching toward him and reaching through the bars to grip his shoulder in solidarity.

He's too tired to even flinch away from her. I can see his arm from here. His left shoulder is hanging at an odd angle. It's likely dislocated. He has to be in an immense amount of pain.

"We were dosed with wolfsbane, weren't we? I can taste it," he murmurs, wincing as Georgia runs her fingers through his hair to try to comfort him. I can hear dried blood cracking beneath her fingers, which turns my stomach.

I lick my lips and taste the same slightly sweet flavor. Wolfsbane, for sure. "Where were you when the attack happened? In the library?" I'm hoping the attack was contained to the library only, not the whole campus.

"No," he croaks. "I was in the–the dormitory. I was just leaving to meet some friends for study group, and I–something exploded in the campus square. It's hazy, the memory, but I remember running outside with a group to find out what happened, and it was just... madness. I tried to pull a girl out from underneath some rubble, but she was obviously dead and then... then the glass dome of the library shattered and...." His head slumps forward. I can smell blood in the air. He's hurt badly, I can sense it. My healing powers–dim as they may be right now–prickle with the need to assist.

"Try to stay awake," Georgia coaxes, her voice heavy with grief.

"I got tackled. Someone hit me over the head with a brick, I think, or a really fucking heavy book. I don't remember anything past that."

A door opens nearby, spilling bright light into the hallway. Luke doesn't have the strength to shy away from the bars like Georgia and I do. We watch a hooded figure open Luke's cell door, and another figure wearing a mask and hood helps his companion lift the injured man to his feet.

Luke cries out sharply in pain. Goddess, he can't even use his legs.

"Let–" I cry out, clutching the bars again. "Let me help him. I can heal him! Please!"

They ignore me and drag him away. Georgia chokes on sobs. "What are they going to do to him? Misty? What's happening? What's going to happen to us?"

"I don't know, I don't know," I tell her, trying to remain calm, but I'm crumbling to pieces.

Two more people enter, this time opening Georgia's cell. I shout at them, and she's screaming in fear as they roughly drag her away.

I'm next. I have to be next. When my cell door opens several minutes later, I swing my fist, meeting the groin of the man that's come to try to drag me away.

"Gods damnit, Ashton," his companion curses as the man kneels in pain, taking several rapid breaths. I'm grabbed and lifted by my grimy, tangled hair and hauled upright.

I try to spin out of his grasp, but he's twice my size. He leaves his friend behind to tend to his busted balls and unceremoniously marches me, kicking and screaming, out into… daylight.

A sun-soaked staircase leads up high to a wide balcony over-looking miles and miles of desert. Nothing but bright blue sky and endless, golden sand.

Sand races in a soft breeze from the roofs of several golden towers, glass windows glinting in the unforgiving sunlight. This is a huge fortress. A castle. An ancient one. It reminds me of the castle in Moonrise. And as I'm led down a long, open air corridor overlooking a patchwork of courtyards six stories below, I realize with shock that this has to be a Firestone castle, one that rose out of the sand over twenty-five years ago when my aunt put on her crown.

I close my eyes for a moment, feeling faint and weak. This is impossible. No one, and I mean no one, knew there was a Firestone fortress like this in Tarsian. We are likely very far from Serpentia... and even further from any help.

I think of my parents. My heart lurches as fresh tears spill from my eyes, which I squeeze shut. The hot breeze blasts my raw skin with sand. I cry out in fear, grief, and frustration.

I tell myself to turn those feelings into anger. It's the only way I'll survive this hellscape.

When I open my eyes again, I'm being bustled through an archway into a wide, brightly lit throne room. There's a crowd here–men in black cloaks watch as I'm led to the center of the room and thrown on the ground at the feet of the Umbra Mortis.

In the light, I can see his features clearly. He's old and gnarled. He looks older than my grandpa by decades, but they're likely the same age, based on how spry he is when he moves in my direction. Hatred can do that to a person, I guess.

"Princess Mystica," he grins. "Pleasure to see you again."

I scream, trying to get my powers to respond, but nothing happens. I'm too weak to even rise to my feet, so I stay kneeling. I'm not in cuffs. No chains bind my hands and feet together. Just the manacles on my wrists, and they're light as air but powerful enough to make me useless.

"I am going to gut you like a fucking pig," I sneer, raising my eyes to meet his.

"You have a foul mouth for someone of your rank."

I laugh at him. "If you were expecting a fucking damsel in distress, you're going to be sorely disappointed by me."

"Ah, we've heard about you," he says, pacing back and forth in front of me. I crane my neck to try to catch a glimpse of the twin thrones at the far end of the room, expecting to see Cole resting in one, but I can't see him through the haze of black fabric blocking my full view.

"I'm sure you have. You can think about me when I slit your throat," I croak, giving him a deranged smile. "I'll make it slow, so we can savor the moment together."

"You must think your family is going to show up any moment now to swoop in and save you," he chuckles.

"Oh, them? Well, duh. Of course they're coming for me. But you should be far more worried about *me* in the meantime. I will flay the skin away from your body and make myself a new cloak with it. That's a promise."

"You horrid bitch! No one else would dare speak to me in such a way. Do you know who I am?"

"A disgusted, wrinkled, old fool? Yes, I am well aware."

"You'll hold your tongue, girl, or I'll cut it out!"

I slowly stick out my tongue at him, smiling around it as his expression twists with disgust and frustration.

He stalks toward me, pulling a black cane from his robes and raising it with the intent to strike me, but then Cole's voice booms through the throne room behind me. "What is the meaning of this?"

The Umbra Mortis halts with his cane in midair. "Your Highness–"

"What are you doing?" Cole cuts in, his footsteps coming to a stop several feet behind me, just out of view.

"Interrogating our prisoners, Your Grace, of course."

"Who gave you permission to speak to the princess in my absence?"

"It doesn't matter," The Umbra Mortis says, lowering his cane. "She–"

"She will not, under any circumstances, be in your company, or the company of any other order members, when I'm not present. Am I understood?"

"Yes, but–"

"Am I understood?" he booms, calm fury lacing each word as he draws out the syllables.

The Umbra Mortis looks furious as he rests his cane and tucks it back in his cloak, bowing his head in submission. I don't miss the slight smirk on his withered lips, however, or the way he scowls at the king, who's slowly walking around me now.

I should probably lower my head in a bow. That would be the appropriate thing to do.

Instead, I glare at him as he comes into view. I do put my tongue back in my mouth.

"I apologize," he says quietly.

"You apologize? For what? Attacking my school? Killing my friends? Letting your men beat me into a fucking pulp?"

His jaw flexes, but he keeps his gray eyes locked on mine for several seconds, searching them. He breaks from my gaze and continues to walk across the room, looking at each man he passes. "No one goes near her without my approval. No one touches her. No one even breathes when she's near. Am I clear?"

A rush of the words, "Yes, Alpha," passes around the room.

He continues, pacing back in my direction, "The princess is our special guest and will be treated as such. If I hear that anyone, and I mean *anyone*, has touched a single hair on her head...." He drops his voice to a whisper meant for the Umbra Mortis, I'm sure. He stops in front of him, hissing the words directly into the old man's ear. "I won't be conservative in my punishments, am I understood?"

Nods. More rushed confirmations that the entire order is heeding his demands. But the Umbra Mortis is grinning. Cole sneers at him, stepping past him in my direction.

"Your Highness?" The Umbra Mortis asks, whipping his cane out again and tapping it against Cole's back.

I watch... pain... yes, that's pain, echoing through his otherwise steely expression as the cane presses against his middle back.

The Umbra Mortis lowers the cane, but Cole doesn't turn around to face him. His eyes are on mine.

"Her family has been made aware of her situation," the old man croons, entertained, apparently, by my predicament.

Cole ignores him, looking past me to the group of men standing in the archway. "Have her moved to her new quarters. The other girl, too," he says to them with less vibrato than the rest of the order members, like he trusts these three masked men more than the others.

New quarters?

"Your Highness, I'm speaking," Umbra Mortis snaps. Cole continues to ignore him, which seems to greatly annoy the leader of this fucked up society. "Your Highness, it's imperative that–"

"Enough," Cole cuts in, turning to face him as I'm hauled to my feet by more masked men in cloaks.

"If you're going to breed her," he sneers, "it must be done as soon as possible. The clock is ticking."

My heart nearly stops. I turn my shell-shocked gaze to Cole who's in a stare down contest with the Umbra Mortis. For the first time, I'm questioning who's actually in charge here.

"What the fuck did you just say?" I squeak.

"Has it not been mentioned?" The old man laughs, his eyes glowing with excitement. "Congratulations, Princess Misty. You're a breeder now. Just like your witch of a grandmother. Your spawn will be the next King of Tarsian. You should be honored–"

"Take her away, *now*," Cole rasps, refusing to look at me.

7

MY DEFENSE

Cole

She's exactly what I hoped she'd be.

Beautiful, sure. I knew she'd be beautiful. The soft, ocean blue of her eyes reminds me of the sky in the early mornings, when stars still dance toward the horizon until they're chased away by the sun. She's dainty and graceful. She's exactly what a princess should be, as long as she doesn't open her fucking mouth... but she needs to keep talking. She needs to keep pissing off the Umbra Mortis. She's the perfect distraction.

I hate that I need her.

I hate that she showed how useful she could be when she unleashed her powers in the library because she's just as trapped as I am now. But she might be our only hope. My only hope.

I sink behind the desk in the sliver of personal space I've managed to carve out for myself in this massive fortress built in the dead center of the desert. We're hundreds of miles away from the nearest cities—cities I now rule as Alpha King.

I look down at my hands, curling them into fists as footsteps echo

47

in my direction, cutting through the hallway that breaks my quarters into sections.

Declan appears, looking haggard. "Hey."

I nod in greeting, too exhausted to even open my mouth.

"Uh, the guy, Luke, is healing up fine. I thought I'd let you know. He got his shoulder damn near torn off, but the healer thinks he's going to be okay."

"I need to see him when he's had a few hours to recover," I murmur, reaching into a drawer and pulling out a bottle of whiskey. It's from the batch Alpha King Ryatt sent my father as a Solstice gift two years ago from a distillery in Crescent Falls. I pop the cork and drain the inch or two of golden liquid that remains, praying it dulls the pain shooting through my back.

"I'll bring him up—"

"Don't bother. I'll go to him."

"He's still in the dungeon," Declan winces. "I get moving the girls, but I don't think I can get him his own quarters without raising suspicions. Henry and I were already interrogated about why he's here while the rest of the prisoners are being held at headquarters."

I think of the catacombs stretching across the empty, endless desert. It's where the order should have stayed buried, hidden from the light of day. It's where at least a hundred college students are being kept as hostages, their families told to stay away if they want their children to live.

My mouth goes dry. I try to take another pull from the empty bottle. "You don't have to worry about it. The Umbra's attention is on me again now."

Declan grimaces, rolling his ankles before deciding to step into the room and sit on the arm of the faded, dusty chair in front of my desk. "I tried to stop her, you know," he begins, looking so fucking guilty it might be enough to break my heart—if I still had one to break. "I didn't know—I didn't know her boyfriend had—well—she was pissed that day. If I'd chased her down to give her the warning, she wouldn't have believed me."

"She wasn't going to listen, so it doesn't matter. She never does."

"What do you mean? Do you know her personally?"

"No," I reply after a moment, discarding the bottle and reaching for another full one, the last one.

"Look, man, you look beat. You need to sleep at some point. I got this handled. Misty and Georgia–"

"Princess Misty," I correct him, meeting his eyes. Gods, he looks like Adrian. The memory of my childhood friend, the man who was supposed to be my Beta one day, barrels through my mind and twists through my heart like a knife. Declan is his younger brother. Declan was never supposed to be here. He should be hundreds of miles away, in fact, seeking shelter with his family while I try to undo the mess my father inadvertently made.

"Yeah, I guess. I know her... differently. Not as a princess." Declan shrugs a shoulder. "Through school."

"She's still a princess. That's her title. You'll call her Princess Mystica from now on."

"She'll think it's weird. She already thinks I'm weird, Cole."

"You're not in college anymore, Declan," I say with more force than necessary. I cut myself off before adding that the university is gone. The social constructs that plague his shy brain don't mean a Goddess damned thing anymore.

He frowns. "So... what now?"

"I don't know," I reply, taking several gulps of whiskey before sliding the bottle in his direction. He looks me over, his eyebrows pinching with concern. Declan takes a drink, chokes, and sets the bottle down again, his eyes watering. He's young. I always forget he can't even shift yet. That was probably the first drink of hard liquor he's ever had.

I close my eyes and choke back a groan as bright pain licks up my spine before fizzing away.

"You know, she's got healing powers. She could take a look at... it." Declan rolls his lower lip between his teeth, shrugging helplessly.

I shift my weight in the chair, wincing as the backrest brushes against my back. "There's no point."

"But–"

"Declan, please." I close my eyes, hoping that's enough of a dismissal, but he doesn't know me that well yet. At twenty, he's six years my junior. He was the goofy, annoying little brother of my best friend who we bullied endlessly and he took it. Maybe even enjoyed it because it meant he was with us, and he worshiped the ground Adrian walked on. He's inexperienced and totally in over his head right now.

I owe it to Adrian to be nice to Declan. To protect him. He made me promise to watch out for him before dying in my arms.

"I just need something to do," he murmurs, looking down at where I'm sitting from his perch on the chair. "I'll do *anything*."

"Just keep an eye on the cryptology student. I need him. I'll find a way to get him out of the dungeon and somewhere more comfortable." Here, possibly, in my own quarters, where he'll live in secret. There's a few extra bedrooms. It would work, honestly, but only as long as the Umbra doesn't start getting suspicious and sends his loyal minions snooping around.

So far, the Umbra Mortis doesn't seem unnerved by the fact I'm keeping the princess close by saying I'm going to use her as a breeder. I even had word sent to her family about it. That was enough for the Umbra to believe it. It was easy enough to persuade him to see my line of thought in that regard. Her powers running through my bloodline was enticing to him. Maybe in any other circumstance, it would have been enticing to me, too.

"Can you just hear me out for a second, okay? That's all I need. I just know that Adrian—"

I hiss out a breath in warning.

Declan exhales deeply, nostrils flaring, and continues, "Adrian would've wanted you to at least try to heal, right? He'd be sitting here right now, calling you a fucking idiot, asking if you have some weird pain kink and that's why you're not doing something about it."

"This is more than a strained muscle, Declan," I growl, but he shrugs.

"She could do it. You know she can."

"She's too young. She's not even developing her wolf powers yet."

A late bloomer. Like me, apparently. I didn't have a wolf until a month after my twenty-first birthday. It was rather embarrassing, in retrospect.

"But she can shoot light out of her fingertips." He wiggles his fingers in emphasis. "Nathan told me she's got a weird thing about tears. She'd heal him whenever he had blisters on his ankles, for Goddess' sake."

The mention of Nathan has fire burning to life in my soul. I grip the bottle, but Declan hasn't noticed the rage slipping through the carefully crafted mask of disinterest I've been wearing for this entire exchange.

"How close are you with Nathan?"

"Uh, not so much. He's kind of a dick, honestly. I liked Rodney, that's how I ended up in that group to begin with. Rodney kinda took me under his wing when I joined the varsity track team." He looks down at his lap, pursuing his lips. "Fuckin' Rodney, man. I tried to get him out. His mom—gods." He runs a hand over his face, feeling the same kind of grief everyone on my side of things must be feeling right now.

We couldn't do anything to stop it. Nothing.

And I'm supposed to be the King of Tarsian.

But only with the Umbra Mortis pulling my strings.

"Bring me Luke when he's well enough to talk. Other than that, stand guard with Henry and… Gregory. Make sure no one goes into the suite the princess and her friend are sharing. No one but me, okay?"

He nods, blinking past emotion he's been trying to keep buried to the best of his ability.

I continue, "If they need anything, make sure it happens, but they can't leave their suite. They're safest there—with each other. I don't trust anyone else with them, but you, and your friends."

He rises, deciding that's enough of a dismissal to jolt back into action.

I lean over the desk, resting my weight on my elbows. The searing pain in my back is enough to make me sick to my stomach sometimes, but other times I'm so used to it that I don't think about it until someone touches me. Right now, it's excruciating. The Umbra Mortis saw to that when I stopped him from further hurting Misty.

I don't know how Dad went through this for two years.

I grip the bottle and rise, walking through my suite, balancing with my hand braced on doorways as the liquor hits my system and blooms into a warm, heavy haze. I reach the bedroom where a four poster bed I can't sleep in comfortably rises before me. Curtains sway in the desert breeze blowing sand across the stone window sill.

Once, long ago, before written memory, this entire desert was a lush paradise. This castle would have been beautiful then, but now it's a tomb, a gilded casket in a sea of nothingness.

I lift the mattress and pull a small, wooden box from a hole in the underside. I toss it on the bed and pace back and forth, hoping to slip into a stupor long enough to sleep without pain waking me up again. Hoping to pass the time before that cryptology student is well enough to translate the script and decipher the code lining the egg-shaped object within the box.

I open the lid, scowling down at the palm-sized, heavy, useless piece of iron.

I need to open it if I'm going to save my own life.

I need to open it if I'm going to stop the Umbra Mortis from unleashing hell on my kingdom–and beyond.

I need to open it if I'm going to save Misty's family–and her.

Otherwise, I'll go into death knowing I did I what I could… even if that's only turning the royal family, a family who were once allies–and friends–with my parents, against me… so they can rain their power down on Tarsian, ending the fight I couldn't finish and stopping the order before it's too late.

But I need their princess to do it.

I close the box, taking another drink, and stagger out of the room with no idea what I'm supposed to do next.

In my defense, I did try to warn her.

8

GETTING HIM BACK

Misty

I PACE IN FRONT OF A SET OF WOODEN DOUBLE DOORS. THEY'RE ETCHED with sweeping designs that're a near perfect match to the doors littered throughout the castle in Moonrise. This place–this apartment within the castle–it's beautiful. At least, it was likely very beautiful once. Everything is covered in dust as it stands. The glass vases scattered across nearly every surface probably held bouquets of tropical flowers at one point. Books used to line every shelf. Silk and satin draped over the massive canopy of the four poster bed in the main bedroom, I'm sure, and the bed was covered by silk sheets that smelled like rose oil, freshly cleaned.

Now, this apartment is a shell with ancient furniture and cheap, slightly ratty linens covering the beds, chairs, and old couches.

But I haven't really explored, not while my mind races. Where is Georgia? How do I get out and find her? I'll escape this place. I'll make it out. But I'm not leaving without her.

I bang my fists on the door, screaming at the top of my lungs like I'm a four year old girl again, and Dad just put me in time out for

53

kicking Sydney in the nuts for... well, normally there wasn't a reason to harass my brothers, I just enjoyed doing it.

The thought of Ryan and Sydney shatters my heart. I scream again and again, beating my fists until I feel bruises forming. My brothers will come for me. Their wives, too. My whole family will come, but I want a say in how we kill these motherfuckers. I want Cole's still beating heart in my hand. I want to crush the Umbra Mortis's face beneath my shoes–preferably my favorite heels. This castle will be painted red with blood when I leave.

Because *I will make it out.*

"GEORGIA!" I screech, yanking on the massive door knobs. "YOU BITCHES! YOU MOTHERFUCKERS!!!"

I kick the door. Dust floats down from the rafters as the room trembles under my fury.

"LET ME OUT!!!"

'*Please, shut up.*'

I freeze, slowly turning around like the voice came from behind me even though I know it's in my head.

'*Who are you? Tell me now. This isn't funny. This isn't some joke, you bastard. I've been taken, and I'm going to be forced to have sex with Prince Cole–*'

'*Alpha King Cole, actually.*'

'*You fucker,*' I hiss down whatever line is open between us. '*I need help. Whatever you are–whoever you are–you have to help me. You need to get in touch with my family somehow. You need to tell them where I am.*'

'*Please, just stop talking. I'm trying to sleep, and your screaming is driving me insane.*'

'*I'm driving YOU insane?!*'

I might actually snap. I might slip into a full psychosis and burn the castle with me inside of it.

Rapid footsteps echo toward the door. I jump back just as it swings open, revealing three order members in their black cloaks, hoods drawn, but no masks.

I tackle Declan to the ground, wailing on him, my fists meeting his jaw over and over. "Ow! OW! Fuck, okay! Get her off of me!"

His companions try to pull me off, but I grip his cloak and bite down on the side of his jaw, drawing blood. He screams.

'Did you just bite someone?'

I ignore the voice as the two other young men drag me off Declan, who scurries away with tears in his eyes as he clutches his face. I feel a sliver of regret when I notice the shock and pain twisting across his face. Tears actually drip down his cheeks, and his lower lip trembles. "I'm not going to hurt you, okay?" he says through tears.

I try to yank out of the grasp of his companions. I haven't given them a good, hard look yet. But through my haze of fury, curly black hair comes into view. "Misty, that was mean. You didn't have to bite him!"

"Oh, my Goddess–" I jerk out of the hold of the two men and launch myself at Georgia, who's standing in the doorway covered in bandages but otherwise whole. I press her face into my shoulder as tears erupt, and I sob until I can't breathe.

The men just watch us for a moment. Through my tears, I take in the faces of the two other men. More TU students. A grade below me, I believe. I can't remember their names, but their eyes are... damp. Damp with the same kind of grief and disbelief I've been feeling since the library was attacked.

"What the fuck is happening?" I voice out loud, unable to stop myself.

Declan, his cheek puffy and dripping blood from my bite, gets to his feet and limps toward us, herding us back into the apartment. "You have to stay here, both of you. We'll bring food up soon. Towels, clothes... whatever you need. There's running water in the bathroom if you want to shower."

Georgia and I just stare at the young man as he tries his best to explain the amenities, like we're on a vacation in a crappy hotel.

"Rats are kind of a problem, but we're taking care of it," he concludes with a wince then turns on his heel, followed by his minions, and the door slams shut behind them with a crack that echoes through the apartment.

I let go of Georgia and race to the door. Locked. Of course. I whirl toward her, buzzing with nervous energy. "Try every door and window."

She nods, bursting into action, and for the next ten minutes, we run from room to room, testing each door, finding nothing but closets and extra bedrooms. The windows are locked tight and made of thick, impenetrable glass. I go as far as picking up a chair and hurling it against one of the larger windows, but it bounces back into me, knocking me flat on my ass.

We're covered in dust and new bruises when one of the men from earlier comes back. He's a soft-voiced man of probably nineteen who blushes every time Georgia looks in his direction as he lays out a tray of bread, thin stew made of potatoes and… possibly chicken, and two jugs of water. He keeps his distance from me though–for good reason.

I'm too hungry to look past the food and think about taking him down, which would be easy with Georgia's help, stealing his keys and escaping this place.

He brought clothes for us. Nightgowns. They're basic and styled like long T-shirts made of gray and blue cotton. He leaves towels and fresh linens and then hurries away, locking the door behind him.

We eat like we're starving, which is probably true. Not a crumb is left when we're done. We take turns showering. I get a good look at Georgia's injuries and add my tears to her jug of water while she finishes her shower. I spend the next two hours watching her slowly, but surely, heal while we sit on the bed in the main bedroom, looking through the old books and treasures we found in the apartment.

Neither of us say much. I think she's in shock, honestly. She's flushed, and her eyes are wide and frazzled as she makes little jokes, acting like we're not in the fight of our lives.

I stay awake even after she falls asleep. I tuck her into bed and curl my body around hers. Only then do I cry. Not the furious, angry sobs from earlier. Not in relief over seeing my friend alive and well. I cry because my heart is broken–and because I'm terrified.

I want my mom. I want to go home, to Crescent Falls, and hug my mom.

My tears slip into Georgia's hair.

I close my eyes eventually, letting my body succumb to the darkness creeping in. Sleep... we'll both feel so much better with a good night's rest.

But instead, my dreams jolt me awake every ten minutes. In my dreams, I'm suddenly in Silverhide, watching Aviva walk toward Ryan, her gilded bow draped over her back as she grabs his hand, squeezing hard. He lowers his forehead to hers, murmuring something I can't hear and... the village, which I spent a week in before going to campus, shortly after they got married, isn't the sleepy, quaint space I remember. Now, it's a city of tents. Warriors from different armies mill about, blocking my view of my brother and his mate. Snow falls in heavy, unending clumps.

I open my eyes to darkness as the dream fades. Grandma told me all about her visions when she was my age, how she could find people in her dreams, how she could see them, clear as day. Maybe that's what I just saw—my family preparing for... war.

It makes sense. I know Ella wouldn't let something like an attack on a university slip by unattended. But wasn't she allied with Alpha King Jaxon of Tarsian?

Oh, right, he's probably dead, which is why Cole is now 'King Cole' instead of prince.

I realize with a start that when we saw him, when we were shopping for the party, he'd probably been planning the attack that happened the next day.

My stomach curls, and I know I won't be sleeping any more tonight.

A soft click echoes from the foyer to the bedroom we're sharing, then the main door opens with a gentle squeak.

I freeze, listening as footsteps— steps someone's obviously trying their best to hide—enter our apartment and stop, and the world goes silent again.

I fly out of bed, grabbing one of the old books off the chair by the door and rush through the darkness to the foyer, tossing the book as hard as I can at the tall, hooded figure standing near a dormant fireplace.

It bounces off the side of his face. He hisses, turning to me in the moonlight pouring through windows on the far wall.

Cole stares at me, looking me up and down, his gaze brushing over my bare legs and the thin nightgown before meeting my eyes again. "That was unnecessary."

"What are you doing in here?" I rush out, keeping my distance. I stand in the archway leading to the hallway that houses the bedroom I'm sharing with Georgia, guarding it. I will not let him pass, and he knows it.

"Why are you still awake?" he asks in a calm, monotone voice that sounds vaguely familiar. I suppose I might have heard him speaking in those weird mirrors Ryatt has. I've never met him or his family, but Kenna knows Cole, and every time she talked about him, she sneered.

She had good reason not to like him, apparently.

"Why are you here?" I repeat, ignoring his question.

"I'm doing my rounds."

"And that means barging into my room? Get out."

He turns for the door. That's when I notice his height. He's tall. Incredibly so. I've only seen him a few times, most of which were while kneeling on the floor in pain. His face is… gorgeous. He's a very handsome man, honestly. It's a fucking shame he's evil, and I have to kill him.

I pick up the book and throw it at him again. This time it hits him square in the back, and he chokes out a groan and doubles over.

Alarm bells ring in my head as he grips the doorframe, panting, damn near trembling in pain.

"I didn't hit you that hard," I rasp, swallowing against the lump in my throat. "You *fucking* pussy."

"Oh," he chokes on a laugh. "Are you always like this?" He's breathless as he turns his head to me, pale with pain, the ghost of a smile touching the corner of his mouth. Familiar. *Too familiar.*

"Always like what?"

"A *raging* bitch."

I scowl at him. "I'm going to kill you."

"I believe you," he breathes.

I take a few steps in his direction, furious, my hands balled into fists. "Did you come here to use me as your breeder, like planned?"

"No."

"Good. Because I'm not letting you touch me, ever."

"What makes you think I want to?"

Now, that confuses me. I narrow my eyes at him as he slowly straightens up. "But this is your decision, your plan. You attacked my school. You kidnapped me!"

"It's not kidnapping, Mystica, you're not a child. I *abducted* you."

"Are you trying to be funny?" I snap, and he smirks again, but that smile is gone in a flash. "You asshole! Get out!"

He rushes out a breath, turning his face to the door as he shuffles a single step, then has to brace himself on the wall again. "I will, just give me a moment."

"What's wrong with you?" I ask, not kindly, but I am curious.

He chuckles darkly. "If you're going to kill me, now would be a good time. It would be merciful, honestly. Just–Just grab that vase." He points to one of the tables along the wall. "Hit me over the head with it, *please*."

"You're joking."

He turns to me again. "I'm not."

"I didn't hurt you that bad."

"Are you in the habit of throwing books at people so often you can recognize the level of damage you're inflicting?"

"I have two older brothers." I tilt my chin upward. "But you know that."

"Are you saying you've thrown things at them?"

"Of course, I have, but you look like you're dying. The book barely touched you."

"I suppose you're going to tell me you only nibbled on Declan's face, too?"

I clench my jaw. I do feel bad about that, but he doesn't need to know it. "What's wrong with your back?"

"It's nothing."

"It doesn't seem like nothing."

"It's nothing that concerns you. Goodnight, Mystica." He pulls the door open and slips out. I hear him grunt with the effort of closing it again. Through the wood, I hear him curse under his breath, then walk steadily away.

I cross my arms beneath my chest, confused about that interaction and his familiarity. His voice especially. I huff a breath and sigh, tucking my hair behind my ears as I turn for the hallway, thinking maybe I could try to squeeze in a few extra minutes of sleep, but then a stack of... stuff... catches my attention.

My school books are on the coffee table between the two old couches. My backpack. My makeup bag. My shower stuff. Several changes of clothes–both my clothes and Georgia's. Her things. The blanket she slept with every night that I always gave her shit for because it has huge holes in it. It was hers as a baby.

Tears sting my eyes as I look back at the door. Did he bring this stuff here? Why would he do that? Why bother when we're his prisoners?

9
HE'S A DICK

Misty

THE NEXT MORNING, I'M SUMMONED BY DECLAN AND HIS CRONIES. Dressed in my favorite brand of athletic shorts and a tank top–my school uniform, basically–I walk steadily behind them, in iron chains over my silver manacles, and Declan keeps his distance.

I'm hungry and tired but curious about what comes next, especially after last night. Georgia seemed okay this morning–quiet, a little dazed–but that's expected. I'm sure reality hit her as we ate bland oatmeal together in the warm sunlight streaming through the windows that bathed the dust all over our apartment in gold.

I feel chipper and ready to commit murder, however. Which is my plan. I feel like I'll give Declan a pass, though, at least for now, since I damn near bit his cheek off yesterday. Still, I size up the two men standing at my sides. Gregory, an art history student, like Georgia, has dark skin and short, black hair. He's my age–tall, and strong. An athlete of some kind. He's the one I'll have to worry about, but I can take Henry, poor kid. He's mousy and quiet with pale blond hair and hazel eyes that nervously watch my every move.

Declan could kick my ass if he wanted to, but I don't think he does. I think he's the leader of this little trio. I think they might have been friends at school, actually. And, finally, I believe he works directly for Cole.

I switch my focus to the castle, trying to mentally map each corridor and staircase, but it becomes increasingly obvious that this place is a maze. I'll need a physical map somehow. I need to make one. I need to get out of our room and explore, at least a few times, so when the time comes, I can lead Georgia to freedom.

Before long, we start walking down staircase after staircase until the light of day disappears, and we're sucked into darkness. At first, I think I'm being taken to the dungeon again, which makes me think of Luke.

"Luke Abernathy," I say to men, the first words I've uttered since they fetched me and told me to get dressed. "Where is he? How is he?"

"He's just fine," Declan answers without so much as looking back at me.

"He was on death's door," I sneer. "I could have healed him, but your brethren ignored me."

"You could have, yeah. It would have been better in the long run for him, I think. His shoulder got dislocated, but it's fixed now." He mumbles under his breath, "He'll probably need surgery to correct it fully when this is over."

When this is over. A single dose of hope blooms through my heart. What a thought, indeed.

Declan opens a set of doors and leads us into a wide room with a low, stone ceiling. Order members in plain clothes look up at us, some bright-eyed with excitement, others... well, they just look weary and unimpressed.

I'm starting to notice, now that I've had a night of rest, a shower, food, and the wolfsbane is out of my system, that there's different factions within the order. Some members want to be here. They wanted to do the attack. They wanted to see us beaten. Others are forced, I think, to conform in order to stay within the ranks.

At least, that's what I think by the looks on their faces as I pass. Looks of hope and looks of disgust mingling.

"Ah, there she is." The Umbra Mortis turns to look at me as I'm guided to the center of the room. It smells like sweat and blood in here, and I'm jarred by the realization a duel might have just happened based on the bloody floor beneath my sneakers–which somehow, by some miracle, survived the attack. I love these fucking sneakers.

I look around, uneasy, at the faces again. The worn, dead look in their eyes. I spot a wolf against the far wall, and feel my stomach twist. It's dead.

A young man sits nearby, hanging his head in his bloody, bruised hands, silently sobbing as another member quietly comforts him.

My blood pressure rises as I turn back to the Umbra Mortis. "Why am I here?"

"To show everyone your powers, of course," he rasps, grinning like a madman. "We're training. The boys wanted you to join us. They could use some entertainment."

"Entertainment?" I glance around and freeze when I see Cole sitting on a set of stone steps along the wall. He's wearing all black–black suit, black cloak–the works. His eyes hold on mine. He obviously allowed this, didn't he? Didn't he tell everyone they weren't allowed in my presence unless he said it was okay?

I hold his gaze for a few more seconds before turning back to the Umbra, wondering, once again, who's really in charge.

"Lift your hands, girl," he snaps, walking toward me. I dig in my heels to stop myself from flinching away as he roughly grabs my wrists and... green light echoes from his touch as he unlocks the manacle on my left wrist. I look into his eyes, seeing the same power simmer there, turning them an even brighter green.

I yank my hand away. He chuckles.

"What are you?" I ask, baring my teeth at him.

"I think one manacle is enough. We wouldn't want you getting ahead of yourself." He strides away, his cloak billowing out behind him. "Very well. Let's begin."

"Begin what?" I shout, but then a tawny wolf trots into view. I watch it pad to a stop ten feet away from where I'm standing, rubbing my aching wrist. My healing powers whiz to life, quickly knitting the scrapes and bruises the twin manacles made it impossible to work past.

"Your objective is to kill," he tells the wolf. "Begin."

"What?" I croak, but the wolf barrels toward me, teeth bared and glowing green eyes wild with… more of that magic. I can't shift yet. I've had some warrior training, but not much. My main weapon is my mouth, my mind, and my… powers.

I stick my hand out, grimacing as my powers of light fizzle to life again, smoke puffing from the finger tips before bursting with blue mist that I send in a straight line toward the wolf. It darts out of the way, trying to gain ground by coming around my side.

I jump to the left, kicking my leg out to trip it, but it's faster than me. It clamps down on my right forearm and thrashes, dragging me to my knees.

I cry out in pain, my eyes briefly landing on Cole again. He has his eyes closed tight, that fucking bastard.

I grunt with pain and frustration, punching the wolf's head with my free, left hand, and blast it with my powers. It lets go of my arm and rolls away.

I scream as I blast it again, my light turning the dark, bloody room bright blue. The wolf whimpers, crawling backward away from me.

"Finish it," the Umbra Mortis says to me, grinning from ear to ear.

'Stop,' the voice in my head orders. The word works through my brain and echoes through every bone and every muscle. I go still, panting, my powers dying out.

"I said finish it," the Umbra Mortis firmly repeats, glowering at me. "Now!"

I want to. That's the worst part. I know this is an order member, this wolf. This wolf who has the blood of what could be hundreds of TU students on his hands. He deserves it, doesn't he? For me to kill him?

'Resist,' the voice says, softer this time.

"DO IT!" The Umbra stalks toward me, drawing his cane from his cloak.

I meet Cole's eyes again. He's looking right at me. Holding my gaze. My breath comes in sharp, shallow rasps as I raise my hand at the Umbra Mortis instead.

He halts then takes several steps back the way he came.

Dozens of eyes are on me. They watch me kneel, then crawl–exhausted–toward the wolf. I've injured him badly, I can tell. My light created a long, deep gash along his back and ribs that's bleeding profusely. He lowers his head and looks away from me as I reach his side and lay my shaking left hand on his wound.

He whimpers. The sound shatters my heart. I did this. I shouldn't have. It didn't feel right.

"I'm sorry," I whisper, gathering the wolf's head in my lap before lowering my face to his. "I'm so sorry."

Soft, gentle white light whispers from my fingertips, mingling with the tears I let flow freely down my cheeks. It's working. Even while still wearing one of the manacles, my healing powers ignite, glimmering between me and the wolf as his skin knits back together, and his heart starts beating properly again.

The room is totally quiet. I don't think anyone is breathing.

Even the Umbra Mortis has nothing to say. *Thank Goddess.*

But movement catches my eye as I lift my head. Cole stands, his brow knitted in confusion as he looks down at the wolf, down at its face.

"That's enough," the Umbra Mortis shouts, but my attention is fixed on the expression cracking over Cole's profile.

Shock. Pure, unfiltered shock. Then hope. Then... relief.

I look down at the wolf. I'm not sure what I'm expecting to see. Maybe I'd accidentally turned him into a toad or something, based on the shocked look on Cole's face only moments ago.

But then I see the green magic in his eyes flicker several times and go out, like blowing out a candle. He has hazel eyes now. Beautiful, kaleidoscope-like eyes. Normal eyes.

The wolf slumps in my lap, sighing with relief, then promptly falls asleep.

Silence. Utter, absolutely deafening, silence chokes the room..

'*Good girl,*' the voice rasps. For whatever reason, I look right at Cole.

He holds my gaze for what feels like an entirety before whirling and stalking toward the door, saying, "Take her back to her rooms, now."

"I am not done with her!" The Umbra Mortis slams his cane on the ground, the sound echoing through the room. "She is not going anywhere!"

But I'm being lifted up by Declan and... what was his name? Henry, right. Declan and Henry guide me away from the wolf, but my left wrist is still free of its manacle. I should... do something, right? Blast them all? Escape?

But as I look around the room at the few hopeful faces watching me in awe, I realize, deep down, that something sinister is afoot.

My gaze rests on the Umbra Mortis. I raise my free left wrist and blow him a kiss.

He sees red.

"You fucking, useless whore!" he thunders and points his cane at me. I feel like all the air is being sucked from the room. Electricity crackles, making my hair stand on end. Green light flares to light behind his eyes, but then he disappears from view.

Cole is standing in front of me, between me and the Umbra Mortis, facing him. I have the sudden urge to lay my hand over his back but stop.

"Lower your cane," Cole commands.

"She was brought here so we could use her–"

"I said," he growls, "lower your cane, Richard."

Richard? The sadistic leader of the Arcane Umbra is named *Richard?* Ha, ha. *What a Dick.*

I snort a laugh. Cole straightens. I'm sure he'd look over his shoulder and scowl down at me if he wasn't facing off with *Richard* right now.

"I will use her at my will, boy. She is the order's property now!"

"She is *mine*," Cole says with certainty.

With that, he whirls, grabbing my uninjured arm and yanking me out of the room. Declan and his friends follow closely behind.

None of us say a word until we're well above ground again, and daylight pours over us, highlighting my tattered arm. My healing powers are working but slowly. I'm exhausted from the powers I used during the fight and healing the wolf; I didn't leave enough for myself.

"Go to the infirmary and get bandages, now," Cole tells the trio, and they leave us, their footsteps moving in the opposite direction. I'm jogging alongside Cole to keep up with his incredible lengthy strides.

"Wait–" I puff out, my lungs burning. "You're walking really fast."

"You're bleeding all over the place."

"Oh, sorry," I drawl, "about getting blood on your fancy mosaic tiles–" I yelp in surprise when he pulls me to an abrupt halt in the center of a long corridor.

"Am I going to regret not putting that silver band back on your wrist?" he asks harshly, staring me down.

"Probably," I deadpan.

He frowns, closing his eyes to gather himself for a moment before sighing, "I need you to behave."

"I don't do that."

We start walking again. I don't question where we're going. I'm slightly curious. Is he taking me to his lair?

He is. He opens a plain-old wooden door, and I step inside a suite similar to mine but a little bigger.

I turn to him as he closes the door, locking it.

"Are you going to have sex with me now?" I ask wearily.

He runs his tongue along his lower lip, shaking his head. "Are you looking forward to it or something? You're rather obsessed with the idea."

I grit my teeth. "I hate you."

"Good," he breathes, seemingly relieved as he strides past me. "Let's fix that arm."

1 0

A WHOLE LOT OF BLOOD

Misty

I FOLLOW COLE THROUGH HIS… APARTMENT, I GUESS. THE LAYOUT OF these suites is remarkably like the Firestone castle in Moonrise where my family has their own apartments within the castle. But this place is practically empty. Dusty and stale. If he has personal objects, they're not here.

I creep behind him, careful to keep at least a few feet of distance between us as he leads me into a bedroom that… smells like him.

I hadn't noticed before–his scent. It's very clean and brisk. It's hard to describe. I don't dwell on it. Instead, I'm looking at his perfectly made bed–so perfect I wonder if he's ever even slept in it.

"Sit down," he commands… gently, at least.

"Why?"

"Because you need stitches, and you're very short. I don't want to have to bend down the whole time."

"I'll be completely healed in a few hours."

"That's long enough to catch an infection," he grumbles as he pulls open the top drawer of a dresser.

"Why do you even care?"

"Because I'd have to find another breeder, and that sounds like a hassle." He pulls a metal box out of the dresser and shuts the drawer, turning back to me. "Sit down, Mystica."

"No one calls me that," I grumble, walking to the edge of the bed and flopping down.

"It's your name."

"Yeah, but no one ever calls me that."

"Why not?" Alpha King Cole *kneels* beside the bed and takes my right arm. Shock flutters up my spine as he pushes his hood back and lets his cloak fall to the floor behind him in a tangle of black fabric. His hair is very short, like he doesn't want to fuss with it. It's blonde, a little darker than mine, and curly. In fact, I bet if he wore his hair long, spiral curls would dance around his ears and neck. It would take me hours with a curling iron to get the same effect.

"Is there something on the top of my head that you find fascinating?" he asks under his breath.

I look away from him, crossing my legs and staring through the window at the endless desert. I hear him open the metal box and start moving things around, then he grips my arm again, twisting it into position. "Yeah," he says after a moment. "You're going to need stitches."

"You're wasting your time and effort," I argue, but the words come out as a hiss as he starts cleaning the jagged, shredded teeth marks the wolf left. "Do you even know how to do stitches?"

"Yes," he says, his eyes focused on the wounds as he cleans my arm.

"How?"

His jaw tenses for a few seconds before he says quietly, "I'm a physician."

I snort a laugh. "Oh, please."

He arches a brow but doesn't look at me. "Is it that hard to believe?"

"Uh, yeah. You're an evil, kidnapping dictator. You're not a doctor."

"You were *abducted*, not kidnapped, but believe what you want," he breathes, rising to start laying out surgical thread and all kinds of other instruments I can't name. He does have a lot of medical equipment, I'll give him that. The box is the fanciest first aid kit I've ever seen.

"If you're a doctor, then why are you allowing members of your order to kill each other?"

He kneels again, sighing as he adjusts the placement of my arm. "This is going to hurt."

"What? The stitches or the truth? You're a monster."

"I've been called worse."

"You're being so casual about this–OW! That hurt–" I swat at him away right as he places the first suture, but he grabs my free hand I just sent flying for his head. Calmly, he presses my hand to my thigh.

"I can sedate you if that would make this more comfortable for you," he says, looking up into my eyes. "It's your choice."

"You're not sedating me."

"Okay, then." He looks away and starts stitching up the bite marks, one by one, while I squirm and curse his name over, and over again.

Declan appears carrying a plastic bag full of rolled up bandages, but glares at me, looking slightly smug that I'm the one sweating and almost in tears this time, not him. He has a bruise shaped like my teeth on the side of his jaw–black and blue.

"Make it hurt," he tells Cole. "For me."

"Go away, Declan," Cole murmurs, hyper focused as he works.

Declan tosses the bag on the bed and swaggers out of the room.

Cole murmurs something under his breath before rising up on his knees to reach for the bag in the center of the bed, his chest pressing into my knees. Our proximity is totally inappropriate and equally as overwhelming. I rear back, trying to lean out of his touch. He doesn't seem to realize how close we are. I'm just his patient right now, and one quick glance at the perfectly placed sutures has my mouth moving before I can stop it.

"Are you really a doctor?"

"I am."

"Why?"

"Because that's what I wanted to be when I grew up." He doesn't look at me as he rifles through the bag.

"You were going to grow up to be Alpha King, though?"

"When my older brother passed away, yeah, I became the heir."

I didn't know that. I honestly don't know much about his family at all, other than the fact his father was the King of Tarsian. "You had an older brother?"

"Yeah, Adam."

"What happened to him?"

"I don't see how that's your business–"

"Did you kill him, too?"

Wrong thing to say, Misty.

Cole exhales deeply, looking furious for a moment, but not toward me. His eyes fix on the far wall just above the headboard. They're a pale gray. Not dark, steely silver like Kenna's eyes. Softer than that.

"I'm sorry," I whisper.

"It's a valid question to ask a man who killed his father, I guess."

I chew my lip as he wraps a bandage around my arm. Minutes pass. He's meticulous, double checking everything he does. "Are you hurt anywhere else?"

"My wrists hurt."

"It's the silver. There isn't anything I can do about that. The barrier is enough to stop it from burning you, but it weakens the bones." He rises, taking his kit with him to discard the needles he used, but he takes several moments to check his supplies.

I sit awkwardly at the edge of his bed, unsure what to do next.

"Adam was in an accident when he was sixteen. He broke into one of the temples that came out of the sand when your aunt took her throne. It hadn't been explored yet, and the floor gave way. He fell, as did the friend that was with him. Broke his neck." He shuts the kit with a snap.

"I'm sorry."

"It's all right. It's not like you pushed him."

I frown at him as he tucks the box back in the dresser. He hesitates for several seconds before turning to me, tucking his hands in his pockets. "The stitches are dissolvable. They fade in a few days, maybe sooner if your healing powers catch up to the injury before then."

"Why don't you call yourself a healer?"

He chews the inside of his lower lip. "It's what they called me when I graduated from medical school. A physician."

I narrow my eyes at him. "Are you a witch, then?"

"No. Why would that matter?"

"The only medical school here is in Moonrise…" My eyes go wide. "You went to college in Crescent Falls?"

"For my medical degree, yes. I studied biology at TU first." He turns away again, fishing in another drawer for something.

Confusion blurs my senses. This can't be the same man who abducted me, blew up my college, and is going to use me as a breeder.

"Why are you doing this?"

"Because the likelihood that wolf had a clean mouth is low."

"Not the stitches." My voice sounds like gravel. "Why are you doing *this*?"

He grips the dresser with one hand, hanging his head.

"Cole?" I ask, forgoing his royal title… because I don't think he's in the habit of really using it.

I don't think he *wants* it.

"You need to stop asking questions. The less you know, the better."

"No," I say, standing, edging toward him. "No… you just killed so many people. You're keeping me, and several other students, here captive! You—you want to use me as a breeder! What's the reason? To go to war against my family? To try to take over Eastonia? If that's the case, then why bother helping me at all? Why bother keeping me alive?"

I reach for him, my fingertips grazing his back and he winces, flinching away from me. I *barely* touched him.

I draw my hand back, those same alarm bells I'd heard the other night ringing through my skull. He's wearing a black shirt, having discarded his cloak some time ago before he started mending my arm, but I see the fabric going damp and the smell of blood rising between us.

"What–What happened to you? You're bleeding!"

"You need to leave."

"Cole, your back is bleeding *a lot*," I grind out, shocked, my voice shaking.

"Declan!" he shouts, his eyes closed as he grips the dresser so hard it groans and cracks.

I ignore the rush of Declan's footsteps and step closer, reaching for him again. "Cole, what's the matter?"

Declan races into the room, panting.

"Cole!" I shout, watching the blood drain from his face.

"Get her out of here, right now," he pants, and Declan grabs my arm.

I allow him to yank me out of the room. Cole doesn't even shut the door, but I hear the dresser topple over. "Wait–stop–he's really hurt! What happened to him? Did he duel like those order members were doing today?"

Declan marches me through the suite, but his face is pale, too, his eyes wide with worry.

"Declan!" I wrench my arm from his iron grip. "What the fuck is going on around here?"

He grabs me again, shaking his head and murmuring curses under his breath. Finally, once the door to Cole's suite closes behind us, he whirls me to face him, pinning me against the wall.

"Listen to me," he whispers, looking around before continuing, "What else can you do?"

"What do you mean?"

"Powers wise. You can heal; you can shoot light out of your fingers. What else?"

"I don't know!" I shove him away, but he grabs me and pulls me down the hallway.

"Things are really bad right now, Misty. I'm not going to lie to you about that."

"Fucking obviously!"

"Shhh!" he growls, looking over his shoulder like we might be followed, or overheard.

"What's going on? What powers does *Richard* have? What's Cole's part in all of this?"

He chews his lips, his eyes frantic, like he's internally debating something.

"Declan!"

"Okay, fine. Fuck it!" He rips us to the side, through a door, and into a small, dusty, dark room that might be a coat closet.

I choke on the dust, wheezing painfully. He slaps a hand over my mouth. "Be very, very quiet."

Voices and footsteps sound beyond the door. I freeze.

He waits for the voices to recede, then says, "He's not letting anyone help him, but you have to. He's going to die if his injuries aren't treated."

"He's a doctor, right? Why doesn't he heal himself?"

"He won't. I don't think he can."

"Maybe that's a good thing," I sneer up at him. "He deserves to die for everything he's done."

Declan looks down at me, searching my eyes. His expression softens, filling with grief. "You have no idea what he's had to do, Misty."

"Then tell me," I beg.

He opens his mouth, surrendering, but then promptly snaps his lips closed. "I'm being summoned."

"By Cole?"

He shakes his head. "The Umbra Mortis. Hurry, I need to get you back to your room. Something's happening."

We run through the castle—well, he's dragging me, and I'm doing my best to keep up with him—and he practically tosses me into my suite before slamming the door closed and fumbling with the lock.

"What's going on?" Georgia asks from behind me, rushing into the room.

But I'm barely paying attention to her hurried questions when she notices my bandaged arm.

Declan jammed the door. It didn't lock properly.

I can get out.

RAN RIGHT INTO IT

Misty

"Wait, wait." Georgia smooths her hands through her hair, riling up her curls. She closes her eyes, takes a deep breath, and says, "Let me get this perfectly straight."

"Okay." I curl my legs beneath me as I sit across from her in our bed. It's been a few hours since Declan stupidly left the door jammed, but I haven't made any moves yet. Instead, I told Georgia *everything*. I figured if I leave tonight to map the castle and get caught or killed, she'll live on to at least tell my story.

"We've been kidnapped by an underground secret society, and they're responsible for the attack on TU," she begins, raising a finger. "Nathan not only cheated on you, but is part of the order." She raises a second finger.

"Yep."

She frowns. "You think the order is trying to start a war with your family."

I nod, and she raises a third finger.

"And you're being forced to be Prince–"

"Alpha King," I quickly correct. She scowls.

"Alpha King Cole's *breeder*?"

"Yeah, that's really it."

She shakes her head in disbelief. "Why the hell am I here then?"

"I have no idea!" I can't help but laugh. This whole situation is ridiculously... scary. Heartbreaking. Absolute, utterly fucked up. If I don't laugh, I'm going to break.

"His *breeder*?" She grabs my bandaged arm. "And he... did this to you?"

"He's a... doctor." I gently roll my arm out of her grasp and hug it to my chest. "He went to medical school in Crescent Falls." I don't understand why I feel suddenly defensive of this monster, but I do. I saw a different side of him today, and while it in no way makes up for his transgressions against an entire kingdom, at this point, I can't help but feel like he... isn't totally in control of this.

I decided to leave out the fact I'm starting to think good ol' Dick, a.k.a. the Umbra Mortis, has some type of power he's using on the order. The green eyed wolves remind me of the rogues Aviva and Ryan told me all about when Mom and I spent a week in Silverhide before the semester began.

Could the attack on TU and the battle in the Deadlands earlier this year be connected?

Georgia's still talking, but I've zoned out completely. My stomach growls loudly, and she frowns, flopping onto her back. "Do you think they forgot to bring us dinner tonight?"

"I think something's happening," I say, echoing Declan's sentiments to me hours ago when I'd had him convinced to just tell me the whole truth before we were so rudely interrupted.

My mind hovers between the present and the past. Georgia gets up to go take what she says will be the longest bath known to man while I sit in the center of the bed and pick through the memory of Cole gripping the dresser in pain I can't fathom.

His bloody back seeps into my mind. I thought, when he'd come into our room doing his "rounds" that he'd simply been... sore.

Maybe from all that pillaging and killing he'd been doing during the attack.

This is something else. He's wounded—badly.

I press my knees to my chest as I unwind my bandage. I'm completely healed but covered in thick, medical grade sutures. Just like I thought.

Just as I start to examine my stitches and memories of Cole's proximity start to drown out the burning questions about him, a pounding on the main door echoes through the room.

"Thank the Goddess!" Georgia chimes over the sound of running water. "They remembered to feed us!"

I swing my legs out of bed, unease licking up my spine and sending a chill over my skin. Declan and his little friends never knock. They just barge in with meals, or my summons, like this morning. It's also nearing the middle of the night, by my estimation. I have a feeling this isn't food.

I twist the single manacle I'm left wearing on my right hand as I near the door, worried about messing up my plan by opening it and whoever's behind it locking it tight again, like Declan failed to do. I make a snap decision and stuff a book as far as I can beneath the left door, knowing the right side is always the one that swings open. If the door remains unlevel, it won't lock properly. At least, I'm praying that's the case.

I listen as keys jingle on the other side of the door and stand back, my heart hammering.

The door opens a crack, then further, revealing...

No. This is the last person I want to see right now.

"What do you want?" I manage to say. My tongue feels like lead as Nathan shoves the door open and stares at me.

"I'm taking you to see the Umbra Mortis."

"Did Cole—The Alpha King allow you to fetch me? He seemed pretty serious about that aspect of things."

"It doesn't matter." He reaches for me, but I step out of his way. "Don't make this hard, Misty. I'm doing what I can–"

"What was her name?" I ask into the distance I'm trying to put between us.

"What?" His upper lip curls.

"Her name? The girl you probably got pregnant at the Arcane Umbra party. Remember? The night you told me you were going for drinks with the guys?" I smile cruelly at him. His face is cast in shadow, but I can see his life flashing behind his eyes. "I hope you at least got her off campus before the attack." I look down at my nails, smiling as I let the words settle in and spread through him like a virus. "It was the least you could have done."

He snatches me out of the room, slamming the door shut behind him.

"You have no idea what you're talking about. You've been dosed with drugs for days–"

"And that started the day you came to the dormitory, didn't it? What did you do, Nathan? Spike our drinking fountain? Georgia has no memories of that party, and the more I think about it, the more I think you might have done something to her during her shower. Dropped a few wolfsbane tablets in her shampoo." It sounds unlikely, but something happened to her, and I can tell, by the look on his face, that I'm right… at least about his participation.

He doesn't look at me for a long time. I walk steadily beside him as we weave through the castle, through the maze of identical hallways. I have no idea how to even get back to Cole's suite on my own.

It's going to take me forever to map this place, but I have to do it, even if it's just so I never have to see Nathan again.

He pulls us to a stop just before we're set to cross a stone bridge hovering several stories above a wasted, sand-swept courtyard. "Misty, look. I didn't want you getting sucked into this. I tried, okay? I tried to get you out of it–" He exhales deeply as he shoves me up against the wall, caging me in. "We have a way out. I'm going to make this better, okay? The Umbra Mortis promised that once Cole's done with you, I can have you again. He'll even give us our own territory–"

"What the actual fuck are you talking about?" I sneer, shoving him away.

He roughly grabs me and pins me to the wall again. "And just so you're aware, I had to cheat on you. It wasn't even about you, Misty. Fuck, I have needs, okay? We've been together for two years and never even made it past second-base."

My jaw literally drops. "Get away from me. This is over."

"No, baby," he whispers. "Don't be like that. Everything's going to be okay. I'm going to fix it."

I shove him, but he's leaning in, pressing me against the wall so hard I can't catch my breath. "Get off me, now!"

His hands grip my waist. "I hate the fact you have to sleep with him. I want you for myself. I could fucking kill that guy." He leans down, brushing the words over my neck. "I'm just going to take you right here so King Cole gets my scraps–"

I grunt with effort, using all of my strength to bust out from his hold and rake my nails across his cheek. He shouts, stumbling backward. "What the fuck, Misty?"

I'm already halfway across the bridge. I have no idea where I'm going, but wherever it is, it's far away from him, for sure. I whirl to face him, shouting, "If you ever even look in my direction again, I'll kill you. I'm being dead serious, Nathan. Don't ever touch me. Don't look at me, don't try to speak to me."

"But we're mates–"

"We are *not* mates," I grind out then continue stalking across the bridge. There's a single set of doors at the end. It's my only option. I throw them open and walk straight into a den of order members. "What?" I snarl at them as the doors close behind me. "What the fuck are you looking at?"

Several of them look away, hanging their heads. Others are giving me curious, somewhat entertained expressions as I float through the center of the room, right up to Richard.

Cole stands nearby, his arms crossed over his chest. His eyes follow my progress, one brow raised ever so slightly in curiosity about my foul mood, but I don't care.

His eyes dart to the door, however, when Nathan rushes in behind me, and I swear to the Goddess, Cole sees red when he notices my nail marks peppering Nathan's face.

I'm probably imagining that, though.

"What the fuck do you want now?" I snarl at Richard, the Umbra, whatever he's called. I point my finger at him, coming to a rest only six feet from where he's standing.

I'm sure this place is a ballroom or throne room or formal sitting room. It's big, with massive windows overlooking the desert and star filled sky. I don't care. My heart is racing, and I'm absolutely furious, ready to take that pent up anger out on this motherfucker instead of killing Nathan in front of all his little friends.

"Princess, thank you for joining us."

"It's not like I had a choice," I snarl. "What do you want? Do you want me to fight another wolf? Maybe do a little dance for your sick, twisted order's entertainment?"

He stalks toward me, smiling. I allow him to come close enough to me to smell the sharp, herbal scent of his robes. He grabs my arm, clapping the silver manacle back in place. "You forgot this. I'm only trying to keep my order safe from unruly witches and their untrained magic."

"I'm a wolf, not a witch." I try to yank my hand from his grasp, but his filthy fingernails dig into my still tender skin. "If this is all, I'm going to go back to bed. Bring us some food, you fucking monster."

He tightens his grip, staring down at my sutures. "Interesting."

Finally, he lightens up on his hold, and I pull my arm back as he briefly turns to Cole, staring him down. Cole gives him an equally serious stare, like he's challenging him to say something.

"As you all are aware," Richard booms, directing his words at the assembled crowd, "our dear, fearless leader must return to Oasis in the coming days to oversee the brewing conflict at the border."

My eyes flick to Cole. He's watching Richard like a hawk, though.

He continues, "In the meantime, we will be returning to headquarters to prepare for the next stage in my plan. I want you all to get to know the princess better from now on. Her room will be open for you to explore as you will—"

"She's coming to Oasis with me," Cole rasps, his eyes going dark and deadly.

"Oh." Richard turns on his heel to face Cole. "I thought you'd changed your mind about making her your breeder, based on the fact you've been playing *doctor* instead of bedding her. I think my men will enjoy her company more than you, anyway."

"She's mine," Cole reiterates. "That was our deal." He drops his voice so only the Umbra, and me, can hear.

Nervous shuffling sounds throughout the crowd, but I ignore everyone else and watch Cole, perplexed.

"Then do it," Richard hisses. "Like I said, the clock is ticking. Hold up your end of the bargain."

"I plan to."

"Tonight," he says, arching a brow.

"She's not in heat for another few days. I confirmed it." Cole briefly looks at me while I narrow my eyes at him.

That's not true. Plus, I don't have a wolf for another few weeks, and heat isn't really a thing I've had to deal with yet. I don't have a mate who could sense that in me through our bond. My moon cycles are regular, though. I find myself doing desperate internal math that feels impossible given I don't know the date or time.

Cole's *lying* to Richard… for my sake. Why?

"I don't care. Tomorrow then. Tomorrow night, you bed her. And I want witnesses in the room."

Cole lets go of a breath, obviously at an impasse. He looks so tired, so pale. I realize with a start that Richard has his hand curled around Cole's wrist, a ring glinting on his finger. It swirls with that same, green magic.

"I choose the witness."

"Not any of your loyalist little dogs. No."

Cole straightens, calmly removing Richard's hand from his arm. He walks toward me but doesn't look at me as he scans the crowd. "Him," he says, and I swear I see a sick kind of smile touching the corner of his mouth.

I whirl to see who he's looking at, and my heart skips a beat.

Nathan turns red with fury, grinding his teeth.

Suddenly, I'm all right with this breeder business.

1 2

DECODE

Cole

Late afternoon sunlight drifts through several open windows overlooking my desk. I scan the notes I took on Misty's injuries, written in untidy, looping scrawl. A physician's handwriting. My mom always said I was going to be a great doctor based on my handwriting alone.

Four two-inch lacerations just below the wrist on her right arm. Twenty sutures. I'd used 5ml of sanitizing solution, one roll of medical grade, sterile gauze. If she were an actual patient, I'd see her back in five days to remove any sutures that hadn't dissolved. And, based on the nature of the injury, I would have ordered antibiotics…. Yeah, antibiotics, a ten day round, just in case.

It hadn't mattered. When she'd burst into the meeting last night, snarling at everyone and going as far as to point her manicured nail at Richard like she was about to put a spell on him, her bandage was gone, and all twenty sutures were fixed on skin that had healed completely.

I close my notebook and slide it into the lower drawer in my desk just as the door opens, and Declan leads Luke Abernathy into my office.

"We've got two hours before the guards do their rounds in the dungeon," Declan says, his hood casting shadows over his profile.

Luke looks around the room with a mix of curiosity and fear lighting behind his eyes. I watch him grip the top of a chair with his good hand, the other arm fixed in a poorly wrapped sling. I sigh, standing and rounding my desk, motioning for him to sit.

"He won't be returning to the dungeon. If anyone mentions him to you, tell them it was by my decree. I'll deal with Richard."

Declan nods and leaves the room, closing the door firmly behind him.

Luke sits but says nothing as I walk around him, locking the door. "I'd like to examine your shoulder."

"I–the healer already did."

"She works for the order." I walk to his side and begin unwinding the sling. He doesn't move. I can sense his heartbeat rising, however. "Try to relax. I'm not going to hurt you."

"Why are you doing this?" he murmurs under his breath, his eyes briefly flicking to mine.

I exhale through my nose, leaving his gaze to look at his mangled shoulder. The injuries are completely internal. His shoulder popped out of joint, and based on the bruising, it took several people to try to jam it back into place before they gave up. "You're going to need surgery when we return to Oasia." I gently prod the swollen muscles, grimacing when he winces from pain. "Torn ligaments. This is a major rotator cuff injury, Luke. There's nothing I can do for it now, but with surgery, and a few months of physical therapy, you'll have normal function." I hope. I hope by the time I get him out of this hellscape, there's still time to fix the damage that's been done, mentally and physically.

Fear has a way of tearing people apart–slowly. Methodically. Until nothing is left but a shell of who they once were. I've seen it happen. I saw it rip apart a royal court until nothing was left.

I continue my examination of his shoulder, mentally mapping the injuries so I can jot them down later in preparation for when we return to Oasia. Misty could probably heal him if I can get the shoulder back in the joint. That would be the best case scenario. I saw first-hand what the powers of her grandmother could do while I studied medicine in Crescent Falls. Her tears were used infrequently, kept for the most horrific and hopeless situations.

If Misty has even an ounce of those powers, she could help Luke.

But not me.

He swallows hard and jerks his arm away from my touch. I ignore him, making quick work of putting his arm back in the sling–correctly this time. He has to be in so much pain right now.

I round my desk and sit down again, careful not to brush my back against the chair.

Luke's face is flushed from pain, but he does his best to hold my gaze as I give him a once over, checking for other injuries.

"My dad said you had to leave your residency," he says under his breath.

"Two years ago," I confirm, scanning his face before reaching into my desk. "My father was sick."

"But he wasn't actually sick, was he?"

I pause before reaching for the strange, egg-shaped piece of iron rolling around in the bottom drawer. It's the reason I brought Luke, the son of one of my father's commanders, here today. It's one of the reasons I've been able to keep him alive, and so far, out of Richard's clutches.

"He was very ill toward the end," I murmur in reply, setting the useless artifact on the desk between us. Luke doesn't even look at it. His eyes hold steadily on my face, trying to decipher the emotion behind my eyes. He won't find anything there, even if unlocking secrets is his specialty. I've had two years to hone the art of making myself look completely neutral even when the world is crashing down around us as we speak.

"There's a rumor that you killed him," Luke edges, his voice a whisper against the breeze coming through the window.

"I did," I confirm, meeting his gaze. This time, he looks away. "I brought you here to make sure your shoulder was at least on the mend. It's not, and I'm sorry for that. I should have seen to you myself when you arrived. Obviously, I've been unable to do that until now."

"Because you're working for the order?" There's a touch of a growl in his voice that doesn't go unnoticed.

"One faction, yes."

He narrows his eyes.

I continue. "Like I said, when I return to Oasia, you'll travel with me, and your shoulder will be mended. You'll be reunited with your parents, but you'll remain in the castle while you recover."

This surprises him. "Reunited with my parents?"

"Of course. Your father is beside himself with worry. I've made it clear that you'll be coming home."

Luke looks around the room. "What's going on around here?"

"A coup." It's the simple answer. The long answer is much, much more complicated. Instead of explaining the danger all of Eastonia is in, I flick the iron egg in his direction. It rolls across the desk and falls into his lap. "What is it?"

He jerks back, surprised by the shockingly heavy object falling onto his legs. "This?"

I nod, crossing my arms over my desk and resting my weight on my elbows as fresh pain flutters through the lacerations across every inch of my back. "Do you know what it is and where it came from?"

He shakes his head. I tilt mine toward the egg in a silent command to look at it a little closer. I watch him examine it, prodding the clefts and archaic buttons, smoothing his thumb over the symbols I can't interpret.

I studied medicine. Modern medicine. Not midwifery or witch medicine like Princess Kenna. I didn't study history or archeology like Misty. I know nothing about cryptology.

But it's Luke's specialty.

"Where did you find this?" he asks, shocked. "Do you realize how old this is?"

"What is it?" I grind out, already feeling impatient.

"It's a *cryptex*, obviously." He murmurs a remark under his breath like I should know this already. "These are Talisenne symbols. This language predates the Firestone language by over a thousand years."

"Well, open it."

"Open–open it?" he chokes, his eyes growing wide. "I can't open it. I can't read the symbols–"

"But you knew what they were–"

"I know they're Talisenne, but I don't have a lot of experience translating–" he sucks in a breath and holds it, then lets it out slowly, like he was getting overexciting and decided he needed to calm the fuck down to think rationally. "If the order hadn't destroyed the library in Serpentia, I could have deciphered this for you in a matter of hours. As it stands, I have nothing to reference."

"The royal library in Oasia might have something about the Rosetta people. Talisenne was their language, anyway," I murmur, dropping into thought as I mentally scan the shelves of a library hundreds of miles away. "But you could decipher it?"

"Yeah. It wouldn't be that hard. Uh, Misty could help." He straightens a bit, and I realize what he's about to do. "If you could like, I don't know, keep her alive for a while?"

"What makes you think I want to kill the princess of Crescent Falls?"

"Are you using her as bait or something?"

I clear my throat, keeping an eye on him. I can tell he's preparing to plead for her life, to offer his services to me in exchange for freeing her. Again, it's not that simple.

"Misty is safe with me and will remain so. She is not the property of the order. She is mine."

He chews his lower lip. "She's really smart. She's great, actually. A lot of people don't like her, but I don't think they get her, you know? Maybe you don't know what I'm talking about but…"

"She's loud and opinionated? Used to getting her way?" I add with a small smile.

Luke nods. "We were on an expedition together this summer. At that temple, the one they pulled us off of. It was supposed to be a three month long internship, but we made it a month before the administration nixed it and sent us home. She was furious. Her team had just uncovered an entrance into the temple and had plans to unseal it. Then we were pulled off, and last I heard, the entire place was paved over… for that highway project."

"That's not what happened." I lean back as far as I can without my back touching the seat.

Luke eyes me for a moment. "Something was found there, wasn't it?"

"How did you know?" I ask quietly, curious, more than anything.

"That place didn't feel right. All those old temples, you know, they're just creepy. Smelly…. Old. We joked sometimes about the temples being haunted but this one… it was more than that. Everything went wrong. Our instruments stopped working or gave us weird readings. It just had a vibe about it that set everyone off. Those who could shift said they felt the need to do so all the time while we camped around the temple, like they wanted to crawl out of their own skin and run away…." He tapers off, meeting my eyes again. "So, is this what was found?"

"No," I breathe, rising as Declan's voice echoes through my head in warning. Misty's being taken from her room. Nathan is leading her here.

I've been trying not to think about what tonight will be like. If I'm going to take her to Oasia with me, this is the only way. It's the only way, short of forcing her into marriage, that keeps her out of Richard's clutches and safely in mine.

"Does the word Baetyl ring a bell?" I ask Luke as I pull on my cloak.

He stares up at me in disbelief. "You're joking. The Baetyl is a myth."

"Unfortunately, it's not." I motion for him to rise. "Come. You have new quarters nearby."

"Wait–" he rushes out, standing and turning to follow me out of the office. "You can't be serious. The Gate of the Gods doesn't exist."

"It does, and TU students inadvertently led the order right to it." I look over my shoulder at him as I unlock the door. "Do not say a word about this conversation to anyone else. Do you understand?"

"If the order is somehow able to open the Baetyl, it would be disastrous. At least, based on the legends."

"I know," I grind out, motioning to the iron egg–cryptex still in his hand. "That's why you're going to figure that thing out for me, understand?"

He nods, but he's pale as he sets the cryptex back on my desk.

Within moments, Declan is shuffling Luke out of my quarters. I follow closely behind him until we reach a point where several hallways converge into one. Declan leads Luke down one corridor just as Nathan appears, his face red and puffy around the four nail marks Misty bestowed on him last night like the good girl she is.

In another life, I'd reward her for that.

Right now, though…

"You're late," I say, even though I had no idea when this was going to happen tonight. Nathan glares at me as another set of footsteps follow them down the hallway, echoing off the walls.

Richard appears, grinning like a madman.

"You're not invited to this show, Richard. Only him."

I don't dare look at Misty, but I can feel the pressure of Nathan's grasp on her forearm. He's squeezing her to the point of pain. I grit my teeth to stop from grinding them.

"I just wanted to ensure you're going to do this the right way, Your Highness. I told Brother Nathan if you fail, he can have her instead."

My blood boils as Misty flinches, but she turns and glares at Richard over her shoulder instead of cowering with her eyes on his feet.

"Can we get this over with?" she sneers.

THAT'S IT?

Misty

"YOU WILL WAIT HERE," COLE SAYS SHARPLY TO NATHAN, POINTING AT A wooden chair in what could be considered a living room.

I glance around the apartment. Cole's bedroom is at the very end of one of the hallways to the left. My blood rushes, and my heartbeat sounds in my ears as Nathan gives him a smug look and plops down on the chair, crossing his legs.

Cole stares him down for several seconds before snatching me down the hallway. Nathan laughs, shouting, "Don't worry. I warmed her up for you."

I wince as Cole slams the door shut behind us.

"He didn't touch me," I assert, but my voice wobbles. I clear my throat, looking up at Cole, who's staring at me like he doesn't believe me. "I swear, he didn't touch me on the way here. He wishes he had, I'm sure, but he's full of shit. He's just trying to get a rise out of you."

Cole grinds his teeth but turns away from me. "Sit on the bed."

Here we go. I remind myself it's just sex. Grandma had to do this at one point in time, and if she hadn't, I wouldn't have been born because my dad wouldn't exist, right? I'm only doing this to keep myself, and Georgia, safe. Cole needs me as a breeder, which means I have some leverage.

I pull off my shirt, slip out of my shorts, and leap onto the bed, lying flat on my back in its center. Cole has his back to me as he reaches into his dresser. I wonder what he's looking for? A blindfold, maybe? Maybe he's into some kinky stuff, and I'm about to either have the worst, or best, night of my life?

I reach behind my back to unclasp my bra.

"What the fuck are you doing?" he rasps.

I roll to face him, my arm crammed behind my back as I fumble for my bra clasp. He's holding a pair of medical grade scissors and some tweezers and making a valiant effort to not look down as my breasts bounce free of my bra. "Uh… what are you doing with those?"

"Taking out your stitches," he grinds out, his cheeks going red.

"Oh." I find it impossible to swallow. I blink once, then twice, then my brain connects to my body again. I rip the sheets around my nearly naked body. He turns away to give me privacy like he's not about to be *inside of me* tonight.

He sighs, glancing over his shoulder to make sure I'm decent, then approaches the bed and sits down. He's still wearing his cloak, his black shirt. He smells like… books. Like parchment, with an underlying hint of aftershave and… evergreen.

"You smell nice," I say under my breath.

He sighs again, snipping the first suture free. *How romantic*, I think sarcastically. Georgia did her best to prepare me for this. She told me point blank that Cole looked like the kind of guy who would *"Talk me through it,"* which made me blush and imagine exactly what she meant by that. I'm not a total newbie when it comes to men. I've kissed my fair share. I thought I was slick when I snuck my high school boyfriend into the old Silverhide territory in Crescent Falls to make out, but we were caught by Ryan and his Beta, James. Ryan dragged me back to the castle, to our parents, but he didn't snitch on me. I never saw that boyfriend again, though.

"What are you thinking about?" Cole asks under his breath.

"I think my brother might've killed my high school boyfriend," I murmur, my eyes fixed on the wall over the slope of his shoulder. His scent is all around me right now–overwhelming my senses in a *good way*. He smells really nice, and now it's all I can think about.

"Which brother?"

"Ryan."

"I doubt it's true, then. I've always heard Sydney is the one to watch out for."

"Sydney's more calculated," I reply with a smirk as he continues to remove the sutures one by one. "Ryan's just a barrel. He just rolls through every situation without a thought in the world. They're very different."

He says nothing for another minute. I feel a sting on my arm and look down to watch him drag a sterile rag across it. He rises from the bed and discards the sutures, rag, and other supplies. His silence is choking the room.

"Now what?" I ask.

He shrugs out of his cloak, letting it fall in a heap of black fabric at his feet. "I'll make this quick."

"Okay," I breathe, swallowing hard. He unbuttons his shirt as he strides across the room and turns off the light. I'm swallowed by darkness, but through the moonlight drifting in through the window, I see his profile pacing back toward the bed.

More fabric falls to the floor, then the bed shifts, and he's here, tugging the sheets down. "You didn't need to totally undress," he says hoarsely, like he has something stuck in his throat.

"It felt appropriate," I wince, letting go of the sheets to let them slip between us. His bare legs brush against mine, sending flutters of warmth over my skin.

His shirt is unbuttoned but he hasn't taken it off. In the moonlight, I catch glimpses of his muscled chest and torso. He's strong–tightly muscled, like he takes care of his body. He's built like a swimmer, honestly. Broad shoulders, broad chest, a trim waist...

"You don't have to look at me like that," he whispers, reaching between us to... to....

My lips part as his fingers slide between my thighs, over the fabric of my underwear and I'm... not sure it should feel this good. I barely know him. If anything, I have more questions about him and his motives than answers. Do I think he's a monster? I don't think so–not anymore. Should I be begging for him to touch me more, to slide his fingers through the wetness pooling through my underwear? Probably not, but here I am, arching into his touch.

I feel a tremor roll through his body. He lowers his head, holding himself up on one arm like he's trying to keep distance between our bodies.

He doesn't ask why I agreed to this, and I'm glad. I didn't have a choice. I don't think he has a choice. Part of me wants him to at least want this a little, though.

He doesn't ask if I'm ready. Every move he makes is methodical, medical–honestly. There's no love or desire in his touch as he ropes an arm beneath me and hauls me toward the top of the mattress so my head rests against the pillows. I'm just a vessel for his future child, and that's how he's going to treat me. I shouldn't expect to feel anything.

But my hands still settle on his shoulders as he dips his head, his forehead resting in the crook of my neck. I stifle a moan when I feel his cock for the first time resting against my inner thigh, teasing my entrance. He's big. Georgia teased me about how he might be big, but Georgia has no idea that I didn't go all the way with Nathan. I have no references. I have no idea what this is supposed to feel like, to be like.

I've never done this before.

My earlier confidence slips just enough for doubt to come rushing in. I grip his shoulders, squeezing my eyes shut as he thrusts into me in a sleek, calculated motion that simultaneously has my toes curling and legs locking in pain... at first. A breathy groan leaves his lips, tickling the skin just below my ear as he lowers his body against mine. He gives me a moment to adjust to him... or to adjust himself to me, based on the way he grits his teeth against my skin and begins to move in slow thrusts. He keeps his arm beneath me, his fingers gripping my waist as he rolls his hips against mine in a way that cuts through the pain, and surprise, of this almost-stranger taking my virginity.

Boy, my friends back home are going to have a field day with this story.

I bend my knees on instinct, clutching his waist between them. The feeling of him inside of me is the most insane sensation. A deep, aching feeling of need begins to thrum through me, spurred by the sound of his skin meeting mine. I scooch closer, arching my back. The smallest shift in position has even more of that delicious sensation throbbing between my legs. I make the smallest sound against my will, and his hand tightens on my hip.

I want him to throw the medical aspect of this out the window. I want him to throw me around, to show me what this could really be like if we knew and liked each other. If we wanted to be doing this together for real.

Another moan escapes my lips. One hand slides up his neck into his hair. He keeps his face in the crook of my neck, but I hear him inhale before groaning low in his throat, his movements becoming more erratic.

"Cole," I breathe, losing my sense of reality. "Cole–"

"Am I hurting you?" he rasps, dragging his cock out to the tip before burying himself so deep my eyes roll back in my head.

"No." I squeeze my eyes shut as I start to shake, my muscles locking up all over my body. My inner muscles clench around his cock, causing him to hiss out a breath and finally lift his head to look at me.

Nose to nose, he looks down at me while I snake my fingers through his hair, my breathing erratic and unsteady. "Do not come."

"What?" I gasp, looking up into his eyes.

He shakes his head, jerking into me again with enough force for the headboard to smack against the wall.

"Don't you dare come," he commands, his eyes wild and dark. "Misty, don't–"

My voice shatters in a moan as hot, unreal pleasure rips through my body. I spasm around his cock. He groans, clutching the sheets as he slams into me once, then twice, cursing under his breath as he starts to come undone at the seams.

He looks peaceful for a flash of a second and it… kills me. He's not a monster. He's just a man–trapped–going through ungodly things, and I see that written all over his face as he loses himself in my body.

And that makes it worth it. I gave him a moment of comfort. It was something he needed–maybe something that, deep down, I needed, too.

He rips himself out of bed. I'm not totally sure if he'd even finished, but now he's pulling on his pants, pacing around the room like he's ready to put a hole in the wall as he picks his socks up from the floor.

I sit up, trying to gather the sheets around me when he stops and stands perfectly still. I track his gaze to a spot on the bed just between my knees. Moonlight catches on the hint of blood.

His eyes meet mine with heartbreaking intensity. "You've never done that before?"

"N-No," I bite out, hating the way he's looking at me right now. He's furious. Shock and rage dances behind his eyes, followed by the worst of them all… guilt.

"I'm sorry," he whispers. "I didn't know."

"It's okay," I manage, giving him a watery smile. "I enjoyed it–"

He holds a hand up, disgusted. "Don't ever say that to me again."

I have all but three seconds to stand before he rips the sheets from the mattress so hard the sound of fabric tearing echoes around the room, pinging from wall to wall. I grab my clothes, but I'm barely dressed when he throws the door open and stomps into the hallway.

I pull my shirt over my head and peek around the doorframe just in time to see a murderous Cole shove the wadded up sheets against Nathan's chest. "Take these to your leader, you filthy, fucking animal."

Nathan pales at Cole's tone but hurries away. Cole can sound so scary when he wants to. I'm kind of into it….

But then Cole turns around, breathing hard. "Get out."

"Me?"

He nods, grabbing the top of the chair Nathan had been sitting in. "Please, go."

"I don't know how to get to my room." I shift from foot to foot, hating the look on his face, feeling a curling, twisting sensation in my stomach.

Is he that disgusted by me?

Was I really that bad?

"Declan will meet you in the hallway. Go."

"Cole?"

"*GO.*" His eyes meet mine–dark and stern.

"Asshole," I scoff as I brush past him. I let the door slam shut behind me, thankful to find Declan waiting for me nearby instead of Nathan. "Don't say a word to me, Declan."

"Wasn't planning on it," he grumbles, and a few minutes later, I'm tucked inside my room.

Georgia's asleep.

I don't think I could sleep if I tried.

I pace in front of the door for over an hour before I find my nerve again and grab my notebook out of my school bag and a pen.

I kick the book free from the door, and slide through it.

Let's find a way out of this hellhole.

14

WHO'S DYIN' NOW?

Misty

It's been two hours since I left the apartment I share with Georgia. I creep around another corner, sketching the sharp angles of what I believe might be the fourth floor of this Goddess-forsaken fortress, and I'm no closer to finding a way out than I was when I left my rooms.

Another foyer stretches ahead of me, followed by another staircase leading both up and down, splitting down the center. I sigh, tapping my pen on my lip as I ponder whether to take the stairs or keep walking to the exterior bridge that connects this area to another tower, I think.

Whoever built this place was a glutton for punishment. My legs are burning from the effort of navigating at least a dozen staircases already.

I lean against the wall for a moment to catch my breath, flipping through the four pages of notes and examining the crudely sketched map. I can get back to my room from here. I believe we're on the sixth or seventh floor up there, if my estimate about where I am now is correct. I haven't run into a single soul yet, and for that I'm exceedingly grateful.

I walk to a window overlooking the desert, seeing nothing but sweeping, endless sand that dances in the stiff, cool breeze. The moon is fading, which means morning is coming within the next few hours. It's probably the early hours of the morning now, and if I were smart, I'd be hightailing back to Georgia instead of moving in on the bridge.

But the tower… it's narrow. There's probably a staircase spiraling down it to its lowest level… and a door to the outside world.

My heart beats out of rhythm as I edge toward the archway leading outside then stops completely when I hear voices echoing in my direction.

I whirl toward the voices, desperately looking for a place to hide, but it's too late. Four men dressed in black cloaks stop at the end of one of the hallways leading into this foyer, staring at me, shocked.

I don't recognize them, which worries me. Of course, it wouldn't be Declan and his buddies finding me.

One of them steps forward, snickering. "What the hell are you doing out of your room?"

Oh, fuck, this is bad. I tuck my notebook behind my back. "What the hell are you doing out of your room?" I echo. "It's the middle of the night."

The man smiles faintly, clicking his tongue as his companions fall in line behind him. "You shouldn't be out, Princess. It's not safe out here for someone like you." The teasing edge to his voice burrows into my chest as he looks me up and down, smirking. A hungry look passes behind his eyes, and I decide I have no need to stick around to see what he has to say next.

I run. I run like my life depends on it, because I'm sure it does, and dart around the railing of the staircase, making it up three steps before one of the men grabs the back of my shirt and yanks me back so hard the fabric rips.

Panic blurs my senses. I'm not wearing a bra. I left it in Cole's room. That bastard probably threw it out the window to erase the evidence of me in his space. Asshole.

My brain jolts into fight or flight mode the second my back hits the stone floor and multiple sets of hands fly toward me, grabbing my legs, my arms, pinning me to the ground.

I fight. That's all I can do. My powers are useless in these stupid manacles.

"Screaming won't do you any good, Princess," their leader, I assume, growls, snickering again as he picks me up by my shirt and slams me into the ground, my head cracking against the foot of the stairs. White light erupts behind my eyes, then fades, revealing terribly blurred vision. My head swims with pain while they laugh at me.

"Help," I gasp, begging my powers to do what they were made for which is followed by more laughs.

I can't move. I hit my head unbelievably hard. I can feel the single glimmers of healing powers working desperately, trying to move past the manacles. It's not enough. *It's not enough.*

"No one's coming to help you, whore," another male voice sneers, followed by the sound of fabric ripping. I'm being jostled, like they're tugging me back and forth, fighting over who gets me first.

Tears sting my eyes. "Please—help me!" I grit my teeth, pushing past the pain and the sensation of passing out, forcing myself to stay awake. My ribs splinter. I'm being kicked—repeatedly. Laughing fills my ears, blurring the sound of my own erratically beating heart.

'Help me.' I reach for that stupid, annoying voice. My own voice sounds strained in my head, broken and bleeding like my body is now.

'Where are you?'

'I don't know. Help—'

'I'm coming.'

I close my eyes. It's useless. The owner of this voice is… nothing. A figment of my imagination. At the most, some wayward god hell bent on tormenting me. What is he going to do? Smite these dickheads for using me as a punching bag, or worse?

The thought of them touching me… oh, Goddess, it really pisses me off. So much so that I have a single spurt of rage that spirits me back into alertness. I swing an arm wildly, my knuckles meeting flesh. Some part of someone's body, at least.

"Hold her down, for fuck's sake!"

My arm is caught and twisted above my head. I scream in pain, rage, and sheer frustration, letting my voice echo from every wall in this prison. I feel it then—something new—something strange and beautiful. It's like a lightbulb deep inside my brain just turns on, and then I'm flooded by… power. Not like my light or healing powers. This is different. It feels different. It tastes different.

"Shit, her manacles—"

Metal clangs as it hits the ground. A hand claps around my throat and squeezes hard.

I'm too weak to move. I try to thrash, but it's useless. I'm bleeding a lot, I think. My back is wet. My hair sticks to my skin. There's a metallic smell in the air that has to be blood, and it's mine. No doubt about it.

I really didn't want to die this way.

A sharp, snarling growl funnels toward me, and everyone holding me to the bloody ground goes deathly still.

Claws rake the stone as something large and angry stalks toward us. I turn my head, blinking past tears, and see a massive wolf creeping out of the darkness, razor-sharp teeth gleaming in the fading moonlight.

The guys holding me down don't even have a chance to scream.

Golden fur blinds me. The sound of flesh tearing and guttural, rasping dying breaths sound around me. I lie there, stupidly prone, useless and frozen in a puddle of my own blood while a giant wolf leaps over me repeatedly, tearing all four order members to ribbons.

"I'm going to die now," I say out loud, unsure if the words actually leave my lips. "Tell Ryan I stole his video game counsel before he moved to the Deadlands. It's in my closet in Crescent Falls. I dropped it on accident, so it's broken but… I want him to… have it back." I take a shallow, rattling breath. My body goes numb as my healing powers ripple through me, trying to undo the damage. I already know it's too much. The powers aren't developed enough to handle something like this, but they're trying.

"Tell Aviva I liked her best," I rasp, choking on a sob. "Sarah's a close second. Sydney can suck it."

'You're not going to die,' the voice says sternly.

'I want to.'

'I don't want you to.'

"Why the fuck do you care?" I laugh, my mouth full of blood as I choke the words into existence, out loud.

The wolf is right above me now, panting, his face soaked with blood as his eyes—gray eyes—turn to meet mine.

"Cole?" I choke out, and the shock drags me under. Everything goes black.

* * *

I scream myself awake, jolting upright, surrounded by cotton sheets and deep golden sunlight. Sunset, actually. It warms the bed I'm lying in and highlights familiar surroundings.

I turn my head to find Cole sitting beside the bed, his legs crossed as he scribbles notes in a notebook bound in dark green leather. "That was very loud," he grumbles without looking in my direction. "Also very unnecessary. Lie back down, please."

"What the fuck happened?" My entire body trembles as I stare at him. He's wearing a plain ol' cotton T-shirt and black sweatpants, making him look more like a man than a villain from my nightmares. His cut biceps flex as he turns to face me fully, giving me an exceedingly calm and somewhat bored expression that instantly grinds my gears.

"You snuck out of your room against your better judgement and were viciously attacked by four order members who no longer exist," he says plainly, bluntly.

I lick my lips, still trembling. "You helped me."

"Obviously."

"You shifted and helped me."

"I did save your life, yes. You were badly hurt, worse than you were when TU was attacked, actually." I'm not sure he meant for his voice to dip lower than usual, to let a hint of emotion show. Raw emotion. Worry, concern, fury... the works. "Why did you do it?"

"Sneak out? Because I had to. I have to get out of here somehow!"

"What were you going to do, Misty? Traverse the fucking desert? Die of heat exhaustion and thirst?" He glowers.

I push the sheets down and hop out of bed, then promptly lose function of my legs. He's out of his chair in an instant, tossing me back in bed and tucking the sheets around my frame with fervor.

"Just stay in bed for a little longer–"

"You drugged me!" I grip his arm and dig my nails into his skin.

"I had to. You were bleeding out!"

"I would have healed–"

"Eventually? You didn't have the time, Misty, you were stabbed repeatedly, but you probably didn't feel a thing because of the massive head injury. A normal person would have died from that alone– instantaneously!" He's furious as he growls down at me. "You are lucky I got to you when I did."

Memories spirit back to me. "You're the voice in my head."

He rears back, stalking around the bed to his seat. I follow his process, noticing the untidy handwriting in his notebook. My name is all over it. My height, my *weight*. I narrow my eyes at him as he turns his chair to face the wall and sits.

"Hello?" I snap. "You're the voice in my head!"

"Unfortunately."

I lean forward, snatch a pillow, and toss it at his head. He dodges it.

"Are you going to explain why?"

"No."

I'm fuming. My hands curl into fists, insults of epic proportions dancing on the tip of my tongue, when the door opens and Georgia flutters into the room, her face washes with relief. "Oh, thank the Goddess. I thought you'd wake up a completely different person. You look just as pissed off as you normally do!" She races toward the bed, but my eyes are still drilling holes in the back of Cole's big, stupid skull.

"Georgia, a few moments, please," Cole says without a lick of emotion. Georgia frowns and pads toward the door, giving me a look over her shoulder.

"When you're well, you can fill me on last night," she smirks with a wink. Cole shifts his weight in his chair, choosing to ignore that statement, but it obviously made him very uncomfortable.

"Why is she here?" I say under my breath when the door closes again.

"It's safer here, with me. Neither of you are leaving these rooms until we leave for Oasia in three days."

I sit up a little straighter. "What happened while I was *drugged?*" I drag the word in an accusatory fashion.

He stays facing the wall, hunched so his back doesn't touch the chair. "I dragged the pieces of those order members to the Umbra Mortis and gave the order a clear picture of what happens when they touch you, then I came back and have been listening to Declan and Georgia flirt incessantly for several hours while you slept, peacefully, *quietly.*"

"That's it? You won't face repercussions?"

"I'm in charge."

"But are you *really?*"

15

CURSED AND SCARRED

Misty

COLE RISES, TURNS HIS CHAIR TO FACE THE BED, AND SITS, HIS EYES holding mine. "I am still the king. The rest is out of my control."

"Including using me as a breeder? It wasn't your decision, was it? You were being forced–"

"I'm doing what's necessary." He has no plans to elaborate based on the look on his face.

"You hated it, though. You looked… disgusted by me."

His steely, carefully crafted expression of neutrality cracks. "No–"

"But you were."

"Misty, I wasn't disgusted by you at all. The opposite." His eyes glow with emotion. I'm sure if I knew him better, I'd be able to see the pain there, the regret. "I didn't know you were a virgin and I was rough."

"You coulda been rougher." I arch a brow, and to my relief, the corner of his mouth ticks into a smile before it fades away again. He probably has a beautiful smile. He's probably one of those guys whose

109

laugh lights up a room. I wonder how long it's been since he's done either.

"That's not funny."

"You almost smiled." I should keep pushing him just for the entertainment factor. Being a captive is dreadfully boring.

"That wasn't a smile."

"I'm pretty sure it was."

"You need rest," he says, cutting me off, ending this line of conversation. He stands and turns, giving me a glimpse of his back. Blood creeps through the fabric of his shirt again.

"It looks like it hurts," I say, leaning forward and knitting my fingers together to stop the impulse to touch him. That's when I notice I'm no longer wearing the manacles. I lift my wrists to eye level in shock. "You took them off?"

"You got out of them somehow," he corrects, pulling a fresh shirt from his dresser. He turns to face me, hesitating with the shirt in his hands.

Instead of blasting him with my light, which is what my brain is begging me to do, I sweep my legs under me, kneeling in the bed. I ignore the fact I'm wearing one of his shirts and not much else. That's a conversation for another time.

"Can I see your back?"

He chews his lower lip, holding my gaze. "I don't want you to waste your powers. You're still weak. You should conserve them for yourself."

"It wouldn't be a waste. Whatever it is, it really bothers you. It bleeds all the time, doesn't it?"

He tosses the fresh shirt on the bed and pulls his shirt over his head with a resigned sigh. I give his body a thorough, somewhat greedy once over. I can't help it. He's a very good-looking guy. If we were in any other situation, I'd allow him to hit on me, maybe even ask me out. I'd even consider saying yes.

I remind myself that this man is possibly a father-killing, princess abducting, madman, but it doesn't stick the same way it used to. Right now, he's just Cole, and when he turns around, sitting on the edge of his bed with his back straight, perfectly still, I stifle a gasp of alarm.

"Oh, my Goddess." I can't breathe. My entire body shudders as I scooch toward him, my eyes wide in horror.

Horrifically deep, infected lacerations pepper nearly every inch of his back. His skin is red and mottled, furiously inflamed. It's ugly and terrible. The marks are… symbols. Words, maybe, in a different language. Whirls and jagged, roping interconnecting images.

Tears roll down my cheeks. I ignore them, edging forward, not daring to touch him. I'm correct. It's symbols carved into his back.

"What the fuck?" I manage to gasp, my throat closing in on itself. "Who did this to you?"

"Who do you think?"

"Fucking Richard?! Why? Why would you let him do this?"

"I didn't have a choice." He arches away the second my fingertips brush the single piece of unbroken skin between his shoulder blades.

"What is it?" I'm desperate. I can feel his pain like it's my own. A burning, sharp ache through my back that pinches and curls as I move closer until my knees settle on either side of his hips.

"A curse."

The floor could have dropped from beneath the bed, and I wouldn't have noticed.

"I'm going to heal you, okay?" My voice shakes as fresh tendrils of blood spill from the wounds.

"You can't."

"*I can.*"

He shakes his head, his body going slack with defeat, but I'm determined, angry, and fucking over this nightmare. I'm not sure how he's still alive, let alone functioning. How did he shift with his back like this?

"Please lie down," I rush out, moving away to give him room. He doesn't move. "Cole, please. Let me try."

He sits there in silence for several minutes, all while I hold my breath and pray, before moving toward me and lying in the center of the bed, turning his head as he places it on one of the pillows. He wraps his arm around the pillow, his eyes focused on the far wall.

I can't fail, can I? When Aviva was hurt, I'd come to Maatua to help my Grandma patch her up. My healing powers are stronger than Kenna and Sydney combined, but against a curse?

Where do I even begin?

"You should talk to me while I do this." I straddle his hips, sitting on top of him. It's an odd position, but I need to work fast once I start. "It'll distract you."

"What do you want to know?"

I could ask him about why he's doing all of this—working with the order. Get the details I need.

But I don't ask those questions. Instead, I ask, laying my hands flat over the injuries, "You had an older brother?"

He winces as faint light pours from the palms of my heads. "Yeah. I'm the middle child."

"You have a younger sibling?"

"My sister, Annabel." He sucks in a breath as I move my hands up. Tears slide from my cheeks and fall onto his skin, sizzling into the lacerations. "She's your age. Twenty." He grits his teeth. He's in pain. I'm sitting on him and practically roasting him like a chicken with my powers, but if he could live with these wounds, he can live through this.

"I had no idea you had a sister."

"You wouldn't have. My father kept us out of the public eye until I was old enough for him to announce me as his heir." His voice is laced with pain, but my powers are doing something, at least. The gnarled, jagged lacerations start to smooth out, the infection fading.

"Why?"

"It was my mom's idea. She—She was a maid when they met. They were mates, but Tarsian was still under the yoke of King Kane's influence. Kane was forcing Alphas on this side of the river between here and the Roguelands to marry for breeding and alliances to better his kingdom. Dad kept her hidden, refused to marry Kane's choice for him, and had the three of us. I grew up in one of the villages surrounding Oasia instead of in the capital."

His voice starts to lose the undercurrent of pain as I continue to work. I'm shocked at my progress. The wounds stop bleeding, and the infection goes away completely… but that's it. The symbols somewhat knit together but leave horrible, painful scars. The curse is still there. I can feel it through my powers. It's deep enough that I can't reach it. I worry the scars will reopen. In fact, I can already tell they will.

This curse is meant to spread.

"Where's your sister now?"

"She's with my mom in Crescent falls, in hiding."

I still my movements on his back. "Crescent Falls?"

"I can't tell you exactly where."

"I understand." I swallow back the onslaught of questions plaguing my mind. "How long have they been in hiding?"

"Almost two years."

"What?" My heart lurches. "Why?"

"The same reason your family hid you. To keep you away from someone who wanted to use you, like Gabriel."

My brows knit. Gabriel? How does he factor into this? "What?"

He turns his head to look at me over his shoulder. "Who do you think gave Gabriel his special blade? Who do you think funded him, gave him the tools he needed to try to overthrow your family?"

"The order?"

He nods, laying his head back down.

"He was part of the order?"

"It's complicated," he says, his eyes growing heavy. I can feel his muscles relaxing as I smooth out the wounds along his shoulder blades.

"Why did Richard want your mom and sister?"

"He wanted to use them as a reason to get my father to join him. Gabriel and his coven had been defeated by then, and Richard was falling out of my dad's favor, so he started making threats. Dad sent them away when he realized Richard had been involved with the Draven coven but couldn't banish him from court at that point; he had his talons in everyone. None of us realized how long we'd be apart, but... he didn't have a choice. In the end, I guess it didn't matter."

I lick my lips, my powers nearly drained and my tears already drying, but I keep working, watching his wounds knit together under my touch.

"What happened to your dad?"

Cole's quiet for several moments. I start to think he's asleep, but his eyes are still open, and his expression is shadowed–dark. "The Order of Arcane Umbra didn't used to be what it is now," he begins, taking a deep breath as I heal the last of the symbols. "It was a fraternity, honestly. It's been around for centuries, aligning Alphas, creating a brotherhood that tightened kingdom bonds…. Dad was part of it, so I was, too. I joined as a freshman."

I work on his back from the beginning, doing all of the work over again for good measure.

He continues, "The Umbra Mortis is a position held until death. The last Umbra Mortis died, and Richard came in as the new leader. I'd already graduated from TU and was in Crescent Falls by then, far enough away I didn't learn about what was happening until Dad sent my mom and sister to me, telling me I needed to return. He was... ill."

"He was like you. Cursed?"

He nods, wincing when my powers drift over a stubborn laceration. "He downplayed what was happening. Only his inner circle–his head commander and his Beta–knew what was happening, and by the time I came home, it was far too late."

"How did he get cursed to begin with?"

"He let Richard into his ranks. Richard had big ideas about modernizing Tarsian–like agreeing to the road system that would link us to the Roguelands. When Dad started pulling away, he threatened our family. I think by then Richard had already found the Book of Whispers."

My heart stops. "He has the Book of Whispers?"

My powers die out, leaving me feeling empty. I don't think Cole's noticed, though, because he says sleepily, "He's responsible for what happened in the Deadlands this summer. It was a test."

"He's going to build an army?" My blood runs cold.

"He already has."

"He's going to try to take over Eastonia, isn't he?"

Cole swallows hard, struggling to keep his eyes open. "Your family has to stay out of Tarsian, no matter what."

"They're going to come for me," I argue.

"I made it very clear," he breathes, "that I'd kill you if they stepped foot over the border."

"Would you?" My mouth goes dry.

"I would kill you if it meant Richard couldn't use you like he wanted to. Doing to you what he did to me."

"You told him you wanted me as a breeder–"

"Because it was the only way I could keep him away from you."

He's been playing Richard this whole time. Pretending to be on the same team. Saying he wanted to use me to add my family's power into his bloodline when really he needed a reason to keep me close and away from the order.

"It wasn't your idea to attack the campus."

"I couldn't stop it. I couldn't stop them from taking you. This was the only option I had."

"Why does he want me?"

"For the power you used to take off your manacles last night. You can unlock anything, just like your dad."

I blink at him, shocked. Can I really? I look down at my hands, curling them into fists.

"You can open the Gate of the Gods for him." He meets my eyes for the last time before he closes them again.

My heart quakes as I slide off him. He doesn't notice. He's asleep–falling into a total stupor. I watch his face for several seconds, lost in thought, before I let my gaze roam to his back. It looks so much better than before. Mostly healed but heavily scarred. I did my best. He probably hasn't been able to sleep in… what could be months.

I have more questions than answers, but I know one thing for sure–we're fucked. Wholly, utterly fucked. If Richard has an army of cursed wolves waiting in the wings, the Book of Whispers, and the Gate of the Gods at his disposal, we are doomed.

So, I do what anyone in my situation would do–completely disassociate until the person who can answer my questions wakes up again.

I sit in his chair. I grab his notebook. I click his pen. I scribble the same notes he'd been taking on me only an hour ago, my hand shaking so badly I can't read my own handwriting.

My family could help him out of this.

Cole is taking the brunt of Richard's violence to try to save his own kingdom, isn't he? Trying to unravel the order from the inside out before it's too late?

He saved me, didn't he? This whole time, he's been trying to save me?

Why would he even bother?

I lay the notebook down on the bed beside Cole and listen to Declan and Georgia flirt outside the door late into the night, until I fall asleep face down, my arm draped over Cole's back.

16

GREEN-EYED MONSTER

AVIVA

"I HAVE HER."

Ryan and I turn to look at Sarah. We've been avoiding looking at her because, quite frankly, she looks terrifying right now. Her eyes are glowing and totally, completely violet. Her hair floats around her head as she stands with her hands on either side of what Ryan called a "bird bath."

It's not a bird bath. It's some weird bowl that an even stranger, tiny man brought here all the way from Veiled Valley. Apparently, Arthur, the royal historian, has a collection of useful objects in his treasure trove in Veiled Valley's library, and a scrying bowl hadn't been hard at all to acquire.

Still, Sarah has been bent over this bowl for almost a week, whether it's snowing, blowing, or sunny and absolutely frigid.

The tip of her nose is bright red as her glowing eyes widen and her mouth pulls into a smile. "I have her. Guys, I found her!"

Several people rush toward her, but Ryan and I hang back. All around us, a city of tents clogs the Silverhide valley with hundreds of warriors milling about, huddled around fires. I watch Ryatt move toward Sarah, his arms crossed over his chest and eyes set on her face as her powers whirl around her, casting her in a pale violet glow that reflects off the snow.

Neither of us speak. We wait, breathless, and watch Sarah's powers dim.

She gasps as her powers hit their limit, cut off like someone blowing out a candle.

"Where?" Ryatt asks, tapping his fingers on his upper arm.

"She's on the move," Sarah pants, bending with her hands braced on her knees to catch her breath. "I need to drop back in–I didn't get a look look–"

"You need a break," Ryatt cuts in, shaking his head as he chews his lower lip. He's grown so impatient over the last week–dropping in on Silverhide every other day to check on Sarah, to try to gauge if Sarah has picked up on anything yet–anything at all.

A week after the attack, we've done nothing more than fill our territory with troops. Thankfully, they brought their own supplies because we just spent the entire summer ensuring we had enough food stowed away for our own pack, not for close to a thousand warriors.

Tent cities like this one are stationed all over the Deadlands at this point. We're closest to Tarsian here. It's roughly six-hundred miles south from here to Oasia, compared to what Ryatt said was over a thousand in the Roguelands. Don't ask me how the math works because I'm just a girl from Endova who got swept into this madness when Ryan gave my father a golden elk pelt.

We're just waiting on Sarah. Once we know where Misty is, we can reach her, get her to safety, and then Ella and Isaac can do their worst.

My stomach turns at the thought of war, but here we are.

"You need to rest," Ryan whispers into my hair.

I lean into him, trying to steal his warmth. "I'm fine."

"You've been on your feet for hours," he argues, his hand sliding against my lower back under my coat.

I almost say I'll be on my feet for a lot longer than that soon if Sarah's truly found Misty. My eyes dart to Evander, who stands stoically and emotionlessly nearby, his gaze locked on Sarah and Ryatt.

Evander and I are the chosen ones. The fools who will be traveling into Tarsian to rescue the princess.

I close my eyes against a wave of nausea and turn to bury my face in Ryan's chest. His scent is the only thing that doesn't make me want to throw up right now.

Ryan exhales deeply, wrapping his arms around me to shield me from the bitter cold wind whipping around us.

"I don't feel well," I admit. It's the first time I've voiced it out loud. Ryan knows I've been struggling the past few days. I keep telling myself it's stress and not the baby. The baby our family doesn't know about yet.

"Let's go home. Just for a little bit." His heavy, heartbroken tone speaks volumes.

If they've found Misty, I have a few days… maybe even just a few hours until I need to leave for the border.

And I'm sick.

I don't know if I'm going to be able to do this… and I don't know if Ryan's going to even let me try at this point.

We don't have a choice, though.

* * *

Misty

I jolt to awareness when I feel a hand tapping lightly on my shoulder. It's pitch black in Cole's room—dark, and warm. Stars fill the night sky beyond the window. I straighten, turning to face Georgia, who looks down at me with concern shining behind her eyes. "You okay? You've been in here for hours," she whispers, motioning toward Cole. "Is he dead?"

I blink several times before smoothing my hand over my face. I could have sworn I'd just been standing in Silverhide, listening to Aviva's... inner thoughts. Is she pregnant? That's what it sounded like. And what the hell is Sarah up to? She looked scary as hell.

It was a dream. I shake it away, trying to clear my head as I stretch my aching back. I fell asleep sitting in Cole's chair, slumped over the mattress. My legs tingle as I stand and reach for Georgia. "I don't think he's dead."

"Well, that's good," she whispers, reaching to poke him in the ribs just to be sure. I grab her hand.

"Don't. His back, see?" I point to the scars covering every inch of his skin.

"What is that?" she hisses, her voice just above a whisper.

How do I even begin? "Uhm, he's cursed, I think. Actually, I know he's cursed. I healed him as best I could but...." But the scars are already reopening–puffy and an angry red that makes my stomach hurt just to look at them. I gently lay my hand on his back, my powers igniting on impulse. He jerks ever so slightly but stays asleep as my powers knit him back together... again.

But this time... something feels different. An electric current rips up my arm. I yank my arm back in pain.

"Are you okay?"

"I don't know," I murmur, examining my tingling fingers. I lay my hand on his back again, igniting my powers, and feel... *it*. The curse.

"Georgia–" Declan slides through the door and halts when he sees us standing over a still totally asleep Cole–with my glowing hand on his back. "Are you healing him? Is that what you've been doing all night?"

"I'm healing him *again*," I hiss. "Now *shut up*. I'm trying to focus!"

If Declan were a good boy, he would have turned and left the room, preferably taking Georgia with him so I could focus, but now both are flanking either side of my body as I lay a second hand on Cole's back and push my powers forward with all of my strength.

A few of the symbols fade completely. Several reopen and close again. My pale blue light starts to turn an... eerie *green*.

"Stop," Declan rushes out, grabbing my arm. "Stop, now!" He shouts the words loud enough that Cole jerks, then groans in pain. "STOP! MISTY, STOP!"

"What?!" I shout, but then I'm being tossed across the room by Declan, my back meeting the wall with a crunch. The air leaves my lungs in a strangled gasp.

But now Declan is the one being thrown... *to the ground*. Cole is up and out of bed, pressing Declan to the floor by his neck while Georgia screams for him to stop.

I gasp for breath, trying to find enough air to scream at Cole to get off of Declan, but then Cole lifts his face, and his eyes come into view.

Green. That same swirling, sparkling green of the wolf that Richard made me fight a few days ago.

No. No, no, no.

"Cole!" I scream, extending my hand. "Don't make me do it, you fucking bastard! Cole, you need to fight it! COLE!"

"WHAT THE HELL IS HAPPENING?!" Georgia screams over my voice.

"Get–her–out–of–here–" Declan chokes, his eyes nearly popping out of his head because of the pressure Cole's putting on his neck.

I scream Cole's name again. He bares his teeth at me. If he shifts, Declan's dead.

I don't want to hurt him, but I have to.

I send my light through the room. It rips through Cole in a blast that sends fractals of light bouncing from wall to wall. Cole slams into the window, falling in a heap on the ground just out of view behind the bed.

"Declan!" Georgia drops to her knees and tugs on Declan's arm while he gasps for breath, a horrible bruise already forming around his throat.

"Get out," I tell Georgia, my voice sharp as a knife. "Get out of this room, now."

"I'm not leaving you in here with him!" she shouts, pointing to Cole, who's wobbling to his feet, trying to pull himself upright using the bed for support. His eyes flicker with that strange, green magic as he spots our group huddled around Declan.

"Declan, get up," I hiss, nudging him with my foot. I extend my hands toward Cole again, arching a brow in challenge. Cole bares his teeth at me again. He's an animal right now. Totally, completely lost within himself. Oh, Goddess, *What did I do?* What exactly did I do to cause this?

Declan scurries to his feet and scoops a still screaming Georgia into his arms and flees. He doesn't bother to shut the door. Why would he? He's running for his life right now while *I* deal with *his* Alpha.

"Are you going to bite me?" I taunt, nothing but the bed separating me from Cole. "Shift, then. Do it like a wolf, you cursed beast!"

The green magic flickers again. How do I fix this? I obviously did something to him with my healing powers. I found the curse, wherever it is, and caused it to ignite. I was able to heal that wolf, wasn't I? Didn't Cole see the way the power dimmed in its eyes while my healing powers went to work?

A realization dawns on me the moment Cole lunges, still in his human form but on the cusp of shifting.

I hadn't used my healing powers on that wolf.

I'd used something else.

Dad can unlock anything–break into anything–whether it be a lock, or a *mind*.

I have a single second to dig deep and beg for those untrained powers to show themselves before Cole throws his entire body against me, and we slam into the wall together.

I muffle a curse but keep my hands on him as he drags me to the ground. He's blind with... rage. Animalistic rage that reminds me of the stories that Ryan and Aviva told me about the battle this summer.

This isn't just a curse. Cole is being turned into a rogue. This curse is eating away at him slowly, picking him apart, and he's been fighting it for... Goddess knows how long. But I found its source, I think. Somewhere, deep inside, beneath the scars....

"Look at me," I say in a strained voice, clutching either side of his face. "Look at me, Cole. I'm here. It's me."

We're nose to nose. He's not fighting me, not really. He's fighting against whatever's trying to take over inside–those powers I weakened by healing his back. I can tell he's still here, trying not to hurt me, trying to regain his body, but the curse is stronger. It's desperate to hang on, like it's aware, which is really fucking terrifying to think about.

'Look at me. I'm here,' I say to Cole, to the voice in my head that shouldn't be there, unless he's... unless he's more than just some random guy I'm stuck in this shitty situation with. I'll ask him about that later, when I cure him. *'I'm here.'*

My hands glow a pale silver. The green power in his eyes dims until it flickers out completely.

Just like the wolf from the duel, he sighs, trembling as he slumps into a dead kind of sleep.

My heart shatters. Tears spill down my cheeks as I sob uncontrollably.

"M-Misty?" Georgia shrieks, running back toward the room. She and Declan slide to a stop in the doorway. I turn to look at them, stuck beneath Cole, whose entire weight is pressing me to the floorboards.

"Declan, how do we get out of this fucking castle?" I cry out.

17

PREPARATIONS

Cole

I STAND IN THE DOORWAY OF THE BEDROOM. DUST HANGS IN THE AIR, dancing around the absolutely mangled four poster bed and the over-turned dresser. Splintered wood coats the floor. It's a mess. A huge, dusty mess.

I first woke up what must've been hours ago–face down on the floor, alone. I'd stumbled out of the bedroom thinking something had happened–an attack, perhaps. Maybe Richard had made good on his threats to lash me with his powers again, this time, for good.

But three very concerned figures were holding court well into the night. Misty healed my back. The second I made my first appearance after her ministrations, she'd been giddy with delight and pride over 'breaking my curse,' and telling me she'd already forgiven me for almost killing her and Declan in the process.

I have no recollection of anything past the conversation I had with her… yesterday. Last night? Yeah, it's morning again. The sun is still rising along the horizon. I've been out again for hours… asleep. I can't remember the last time I slept.

I blink several times, turning to face the hallway, where Georgia's voice is lifted in displeasure while she accuses Misty of cheating in their card game for a third time. Misty already admitted she's a cheat. She can count cards. Georgia keeps agreeing to play with her like she stands a chance.

Part of me thinks I might be dead. I've felt this way since I woke up on the floor, my wrists tied to one corner of the bed, with Misty slumped–asleep–in one corner of the room. This easy feeling in my body, in my mind, doesn't feel real. I wonder if I'll blink and the world will go back to being dull, gray, and painful, but I step back into the foyer and the color remains.

I'm not getting my hopes up that the curse is gone but... her powers did something.

Richard can't find out yet. This will undo everything he's been working for for years.

Hopefully.

Georgia's too afraid to meet my eyes, but Misty looks up at me, giving me a tight smile as I walk past them.

I need to get them out–today. Preferably within the next few hours. That means I need to meet with Richard.

I grind my teeth as I walk into my office. I close the door, sit down, and let my head fall to the desk with a thud.

I almost killed her last night, just hours after she healed my wounds the first time. I almost ripped her to shreds against my will. Still, she remained by my side all night, watching her own powers take apart the curse until it faded to almost nothing.

I should be happy. I should be plotting to use the princess to take down the order.

In reality, I have to get her far, far away from here–from Richard– before he finds out what she's done.

Declan enters the room without knocking. "It's set up," he begins, closing the door against the voices drifting in from the foyer. "The order is meeting in an hour."

"Thank you." I eye his neck. My handprint is totally visible on his skin in a deep, black bruise. "Why didn't you let her heal you?"

"She didn't offer," he frowns, flopping onto the chair in front of my desk. "Should I ask...?"

"She'll say no." I want to smile, but I've forgotten how.

"It might be best for me to keep looking like this. You can spin some story about how I made a move on *your girl*, how you have to take me back to Oasia to execute me publicly, or something, for touching your breeder."

I roll my lower lip between my teeth, considering. "That's actually not a bad idea."

"Georgia thinks I'm smart," he says with a shy sort of grin. He actually blushes–deeply. "She said she likes intelligent guys." He shrugs as he twirls a lock of his hair around his finger.

"Well," I breathe. "Hopefully she finds one."

"Was that a joke?" he snorts. "It really did work, then. You're healed. See, I told you she could do it–"

"She just made herself invaluable to the order. We need to leave." I start packing up my desk, organizing my notes. I ignore Declan, who's waiting for me to say something else, to give him an order, a plan. Right now, my mind is clogged by the "what ifs" of Misty's situation. I shouldn't have let her heal me. I regret it immensely. I should have kept her in the dark until I found a way to get her back to her family.

Now, I have a feeling she's going to fight me the entire time to *stay*.

From the moment I saw her for the first time in Serpentia, I knew that staying in her life could never be part of the plan, regardless of what the Goddess thinks is best.

"Go get Luke; bring him here." I rise with every intention of packing the rest of my things in my absolutely wrecked bedroom. "Make sure our faction of the order knows what's about to happen."

I walk past him, nudging the door open with my foot. I don't look at Misty when I pass by her perch on the couch. I can feel her gaze boring holes in the back of my head, however.

I step into my room again with a sigh, closing the door.

"So, what's next?"

"Goddess—" I nearly jump out of my skin. Misty blinks up at me, looking totally innocent as she bats her eyelashes, smiling. "I'm going to put a bell around your neck so I know where you are at all times. You scared the hell out of me."

"You'd be light on your feet too if you didn't stalk around all the time. I can hear you coming from a mile away."

I'm not sure what to say to her, especially after everything that's happened. "Are you okay?"

"Me? Yeah, I'm fine." She crosses her arms under her chest. We stare at each other for several seconds before she adds, "How are you?"

"I feel a little odd."

"I mean, yeah. That's totally understandable after having a curse pulled out of your body."

"You shouldn't have done that."

"Why not?" She impatiently taps her foot, frowning.

"Think about it," I edge, looking into her eyes. Gods, she's beautiful. Like a little doll. Clear, bright skin and those eyes that… I wish I would have looked into the other night when we'd… slept together, if we can even call it that. "Mystica, Princess of Crescent Falls, the curse breaker. Now Richard won't want to give you up."

She narrows her eyes at me. "Are you teasing me? I just saved your life. A thank you would be nice, but no." She twirls like she's going to leave, which would be a blessing, but flutters to the window instead.

I exhale deeply, fighting the urge to just tell her the truth, but I can't. It wouldn't do either of us any good.

"We're going to Oasia. Tonight."

"How do we get there?"

"The order has some vehicles. It's how you got here, actually. You were drugged and put in a car."

She looks at me over her shoulder, still glaring. "Cars can't drive on sand like this."

"They can, and they will. If they don't, we walk. If you could shift, that would be helpful."

"Well, I can't."

"Not for another few weeks, right?"

She arches a brow, turning ever so slightly to face me. "How do you know my birthday?"

Fuck. "Your school records."

She mulls this over for a moment, deciding to accept that answer, when the truth is far more complicated. "I don't even know what day it is."

"Once we're in Oasia, you'll have access to a calendar– and a clock. I promise."

"You know what I'd kill for?" she says, sliding down the wall into a seated position on the floor.

"What?" I murmur, unpacking the meager belongings I've been keeping in the dresser.

"My phone." She blows out her breath.

"Ah," I smile, and it feels… foreign. "You're one of those."

"What do you mean by that?"

"Always glued to your phone, texting… posting selfies…."

"I'm very popular, Cole," she huffs, hugging her knees. "I have a lot of friends who are probably wondering what the hell happened to me, seeing as I'm kidnapped–"

"*Abducted.*"

"Oh, my Goddess, you're *really* annoying. Maybe I should have kept you cursed. You would have turned into a rogue and run off into the sunset or whatever."

"A rogue?" I turn to her, narrowing my eyes. "Why do you think that?"

"Because that same power in your eyes was what was controlling the rogues in the Deadlands," she replies matter-of-factly.

"You're close, but that's not really what the curse was doing."

"What was it doing then?"

"Killing me, making me reliant on Richard. Making it possible for him to control me, at least, he tried. I fought it, every day."

"Can I ask you something?"

"Can I say no?" I mumble under my breath, but she barrels forward.

"Did you kill your dad because you wanted to—or because you had to?"

My hands freeze while reaching for my medical kit. The memory of those last moments with my dad blur my senses. I refuse to see it, to let the moment I drove a knife through his heart while he curled his hand around mine and pressed down... I can't. I can't think about it.

"I didn't want to," I tell her, and it's the truth.

"I didn't think you did."

"Can I ask you something?"

"Yeah?"

Are you ever going to forgive me? I close my eyes, my back to her. A few seconds later, I ask, "When we reach Oasia, will you help Luke with some research I have him working on?"

"Yeah, of course." She sounds slightly disappointed that that was my question and not something personal. "Uh, my turn now. Do you have a mate back home?"

Fuck my life. "Uhm, no."

"A wife?"

"Misty—"

"A girlfriend?"

"No, I don't."

"Oh, that's a relief. I was worried I'd be walking into some drama when we got to your house--castle, whatever it is."

I turn to her and notice her cheeks are blood red. I wonder if she struggles to stop her internal thoughts from falling from her lips on a regular basis. "I don't have anyone back home as it stands."

She holds my gaze, nodding, her blush creeping down her neck.

"What's going to happen when we get to Oasia?" I can hear the nerves in her voice.

"Not everyone is on my side," I admit. "Not everyone knows what my father went through, and they see me as the tyrant Richard wants Eastonia to believe I am. So, we are... walking into hell."

"Fun," she says weakly, trying to smile. I know the feeling.

"I have a plan. I have allies. You'll be safely returned to your family."

"But I can help, can't I? My powers–they broke your curse–"

"I'm not involving you further."

"Then, what? You just... let the order start a war with the rest of Eastonia? Crescent Falls is involved now, too, aren't they? Because I was taken?"

"My objective is to get as many people out of Tarsian as I can before Richard enacts his plans. He knows better than to fully trust me. He has friends and allies within my court that I need to investigate. We're going to Oasia, and you're going to be... kept away from court until I can get you out."

"I don't like this plan. I can help–"

"I don't want you to help."

"But–"

"You've done enough," I whisper.

"I cured you! I broke the curse."

I don't have the heart to tell her it isn't that simple. That the curse is still there, lurking under my skin. That's something that even she, with her powers, can't eradicate.

It's still there–waiting for a spark. A spark Richard has, and will eventually use, to finally bring me to my knees.

She needs to be very far away when that happens.

I can't allow her to be this close for much longer... for a multitude of reasons.

"In Oasia, you will continue to be my breeder."

Misty glares at me. "What?"

"In name only, which is part of the reason I have to keep you hidden away. Like I said, Richard has friends in my court. Spies, especially. You are not safe there. You're not safe at all until I find a way to get you across the border."

She purses her lips, giving me that cat-like glare that makes me feel things I can't put into words. Maybe in another life we'd have a chance. Maybe the Goddess will give me that–another shot–maybe centuries or millennia from now when Misty and I wake through the same timeline again… I'll find her. I'll do this the right way.

"Why is your voice in my head?" she asks with heartbreaking softness. I can't give her an answer. When I say nothing, she asks with that same choked tone, "Was it you who kissed me at the party?"

Memories of that night spirit back into existence. My hands tighten to fists. "Yeah."

"Why?"

"Because I needed to," I admit, holding her gaze.

She just nods, her eyes dropping to her knees.

Declan rushes into the room, breathlessly bracing himself on the doorframe. "Richard's summoning us. This is happening now. If we're leaving, we need to be prepared."

I pull on my cloak and follow him out of the room.

18

THESE DREAMS REMAIN

Misty

EVERYTHING THAT HAPPENED OVER THE LAST FORTY-EIGHT HOURS IS A blur. One moment, I was sitting on the floor of Cole's trashed bedroom, talking in low tones as he packed his meager belongings into a worn backpack. The next, he donned his cloak and left, and almost nine hours later, returned to me and Georgia passed out cold in one of the apartment's guest rooms. Georgia didn't stir when Declan picked her up and carried her out of the room, but Cole woke me gently, telling me it was time to *go*.

I didn't have time to ask how he'd managed to get us out of the fortress claimed by the order. The few personal items he'd retrieved from my dorm room were already packed away in a car, he'd said. He offered me a sweatshirt that smelled like him and guided me, Georgia, and Luke–with an entourage of over twenty exhausted order members in their black cloaks, through the fortress I failed to map.

There was one way out. Maybe at one point in time it would have been a grand foyer, something beautiful and heavily decorated–warm and welcoming. But when we reached the end of a long, twisting

133

staircase, there was nothing but a broken front door and a space full of sand.

I didn't see Richard at all. That's a blessing. It was sheer luck, honestly. I'm no longer wearing my manacles... I was the one who got them off.

Cole made it clear enough that Richard couldn't know that.

But as we sped away, driving over leagues of sand and dunes, I fell back asleep to the sucking, twisting feeling that this is far from over. I'll see the Umbra Mortis again.

I just hope it's on my terms... with his decapitated head squished under my shoe.

I always fall asleep in cars. Cars, airplanes, boats—it doesn't matter. Engine noise is my lullaby, so I slept with my cheek pressed against the chilled window, ignoring the brightly lit, star-filled night sky, and dreamt like I was flipping pages in one of our family's extensive photo albums.

In Crescent Falls, Sarah lands with a thud on the front walkway to the castle, breaking through the magical ward. Light fans in a dome shape, surprising the guards, but she's frantic, her coat billowing out behind her as she sprints through the ankle-deep snow to the front door. Silver tears streak her cheeks as she tears up the grand staircase. The castle's decorated for Solstice—greens and blues and silvers—but it blurs as I follow her progress to the darkened upper levels of our family home.

I see Mom stepping out of the nursery, tucking her robe around her stomach, her eyes wide with shock. I can't hear what they're saying to each other, but Sarah motions wildly, then grips Mom's hands, smashing an envelope between them before turning into the room Mom just exited. My dream splits, giving me a glimpse of Sarah shedding her coat and tearfully, silently, crawling into bed between her sons and pulling the sleeping boys close. Tears run down her cheeks as they settle against her. Then, I'm back with Mom. Cosette approaches wearing a bathrobe. It must be early morning in Crescent Falls because I can actually smell the coffee wafting through the air as Cosette ropes an arm around

Mom's shoulder and dips her head to read the letter in Mom's hand.

My dream spins, and I'm looking over my dad's shoulder at a war camp somewhere in the Roguelands. He scribbles the letter while Sydney checks his watch. I can feel Sydney's nerves. He's wondering if Sarah made it home to the boys, her services dismissed... for now.

"We know where Misty is. She's in Oasia and safe. An influx of people have been moving over the border into the Roguelands sharing news about what's happening in Tarsian, coming here to seek shelter. We're now under the impression there may have been a coup in Oasia. Misty's caught in the middle, but she's with Cole. Everyone's getting a break for a week or two while Ryatt, Sydney, and I adjust our strategies..."

I wake up, blinking into the first glimpses of daylight. Something happened, obviously, for my family to suddenly start thinking I'm safe with the new Alpha King. I rub my eyes to prevent being pulled back into sleep, but it's useless. One minute, I'm looking at the back of Cole's head as he reads... a book... in the front seat, and then I'm in the Deadlands, in Ryan and Aviva's bathroom.

I can hear them. Aviva's sniffling as she leans her back against the inside of the huge copper bathtub, her face pale and streaked with tears. Ryan's fussing over the bathwater, his eyes sweeping over his mate with concern as he forgoes any scented soaps and oils.

"The midwife said it's perfectly normal," Aviva gulps, her face gaunt and eyes cloudy with tears. *"Some people just get more sick than others."*

Ryan's speechless, shaking his head over and over again. *"You haven't been able to keep anything down for days, Aviva."*

Aviva gives him a watery smile that doesn't reach her eyes.

"I'm sending you to Veiled Valley, to Kenna."

"You can't. They're going to send me to Tarsian soon with Evander—"

"You're not doing this. I'm putting an end to it. You're sick, Aviva. You're pregnant, and sick, and I'm not going to sit here and allow my wife to go into battle. I shouldn't have been okay with it from the beginning. This is over."

She sits up, reaching for him, her wet hand curling around his forearm. *"I was given the Gilded Bow for a reason. What if this is the reason? This is Misty—"*

"Misty is fine. Misty has always been fine. Wherever she is, she's giving them hell. Trust me. I'll talk to Ryatt. He'll be here tomorrow with an update on the situation at the border..."

They fade, replaced by Ella in her office in Moonrise, tiredly speaking to commanders. Then I'm in Veiled Valley, where Kenna sits in her steamy bathroom, painting Brie's nails. Both turn as the door opens, and Evander appears, exhausted, and the steam scrabbles around their bodies as the family collides after a long time apart.

Finally, I'm standing on a ship, looking out over the ocean beside my grandma. Grandpa Maddox paces as he talks on his cell phone just out of range, but Grandma turns to me, tucking a lock of hair behind my ear. *"I'll see you soon, okay? You're doing everything correctly."*

"Are you really here?" I ask. She nods, smiling softly as the wind whips through her nearly white hair.

"I can see you, Misty. We share this gift, remember?"

"I tried to heal him, but I don't think it worked. I'm missing something, aren't I?"

"Some things can't be undone."

I wake again with a start, my head lolling, noticing Cole leaning back, his eyes heavy with sleep as the sunrise rips over the endless sand dunes. We close our eyes at the same time, and it's quiet for a while. Peaceful, and empty.

But then I'm in his head. I don't want to be here. I don't want to be seeing the scene playing out in front of me.

There's blood soaking the white tiles around a young woman's body. Her limp hand is outstretched toward a young man being forced into a kneeling position, his face washed with rage and anguish as green-eyed guards in black roughly hold him to the ground.

Cole's heart beats out of rhythm as he watches in horror. He's shouting at... Richard. Richard stands beside the kneeling man, pointing his cane at the dead woman. Somewhere in a distant part of Cole's nightmare, I hear a baby crying.

"Cole," the man begs, frantically shaking his head. *"Don't do it. Don't do it! Don't give in to him!"*

I can't hear what Richard is saying to Cole, but I can feel Cole's emotions like they're my own. He's in pieces. His friend is dead on the floor just a few feet away, her dark hair fanning out, covering her face. Her mate, his best friend, is begging him to resist, to fight, to not give in.

But Cole has blood staining his hands already. His father's blood. He looks down at his hands and back at Adrian, his life-long friend. The brother of his heart.

"Look at me, Cole," Adrian begs, tears streaming down his face. *"Get Dec out of this. Get Marcella out of this. Protect them. Promise me you'll protect them."*

Richard is screaming at Cole over Adrian's voice. Adrian reaches for his dead mate, straining his fingers just to touch her…

Richard rips his cane from his cloak and points it at Adrian. *"Make your choice, Alpha King."*

"Cole, no!" Adrian screams, tears flying as he shakes his head. *"Don't. Don't do this. Let me go, Cole. Let me go–with her. Please. Don't let him do this to us. Don't let him do this to Tarsian!"*

Richard strikes Adrian with his cane across the face. Blood sprays.

"I'll do it!" Cole screams, edging toward Richard with his hands outstretched in surrender. He's terrified. He's breaking, piece by piece, as Adrian spits blood and groans in pain. *"Please, I'll do it. Don't– don't hurt him. Don't hurt anyone else."*

"I want you to swear your allegiance. Take a knee, Alpha King, to me."

Just as Cole begins to kneel, Richard grins maliciously, raking the head of his cane across Adrian's face. This time, green magic bursts from the silver snakes, and Adrain's scream of pain splits Cole's world in two.

I watch as if in slow motion as Cole runs to Adrian, holding him to his chest as the man dies a horribly painful death as he's consumed by dark magic.

Richard jabs his cane against Cole's back.

This is the moment he was cursed. The same moment he lost nearly everyone he loved.

I jolt awake, breathless, as the car bumps out of the sand onto an endless, smooth… highway.

I lean forward and reach between the seats, gripping Cole's shoulder on impulse. He turns to me, his eyes glazed by sleep, by the nightmare I just lived with him, and holds my gaze for several seconds before placing his hand over mine.

The driver—a man I don't know or even recognize—doesn't look at us. He stares ahead at the massive highway, at the sand on either side, and the distant mountains beginning to fade into view. This is the range that separates the desert of Tarsian from its mountainous region, and the border to the Roguelands and the Deadlands beyond.

I keep gripping his shoulder even when his hand falls away. Georgia has her head in my lap, her fist tucked under her cheek. Luke and Declan snore in the third row behind us. We've been driving all night—for countless hours.

I've never been to Oasia, but I've heard the stories. Ella loves it here. It's one of her favorite places to visit, for vacation, especially. I know she was close with Jaxon, but she never mentioned anything about the late Alpha King's family. But the city begins to fan out around us…. She mentioned *that*.

It's the most beautiful place I've ever seen. Buildings of pure white begin to come into view, blue roofs glinting in the morning sunlight. Sand gives way to grass and tall palm trees. Parks and shining neighborhoods surround oases, the pools the capital city is named for. But an undercurrent of darkness cuts through the beauty. Men in black cloaks move like shadows as the car leaves the highway and begins driving through the city center. Very few people are out on the streets, but the few that are stop to watch our caravan pass toward the golden castle rising on the horizon.

Not gold, I realize upon further inspection.

Alabaster walls and foundation… but at least half of the castle is made of glass.

We roll through a heavily armed gate. To my relief, the guards don't have glowing green eyes. Maybe the castle is safe. It's wishful thinking, because as the car passes beneath the castle itself, driving into a wide underground room, and the driver cuts the engine, Cole turns to me, his expression stern and serious.

"Don't talk to anyone from this moment forward. Don't trust anyone but Georgia, Declan, and Luke. Not the maids who will be tending to you. Not the people you'll meet in my court. No one. Understand?"

I nod, swallowing past the lump forming in my throat. He searches my eyes, his expression cracking to show me a sliver of his real feelings. He's nervous.

"I won't talk to anyone," I echo, and he nods sharply, turning toward the windshield. A figure appears, stepping out of a nondescript door with a shocked, then relieved, expression on his face.

Suddenly, Declan is climbing over the seat in his haste to get out. His elbow smacks me on the side of my face as he clammers for the door I've been sleeping against for hours.

"Get off!" I growl, shoving him. He steps on my feet as he opens the door and rolls off my lap onto the ground.

But then he's up and sprinting toward the finely dressed man who's likely my dad's age, maybe a few years old.

Declan throws himself in the man's waiting arms.

Adrian's face floods my mind as the man turns to look through the windshield at the rest of us.

This guy is their father, isn't he? The late king's Beta?

Cole gathers himself before getting out of the car. Georgia, who's been asleep up until Declan pummeled us, sits up, confused. I slide out of the car without waiting for Cole's instruction and hurry to his side, having to jog to keep up with him.

"Orion, we have things to discuss," Cole says dryly, trying to shrug me off as I grip his arm.

Orion keeps his arms around Declan as he nods, his eyes sliding to mine. "Princess Mystica," he says with a nod. "Welcome to… Hell."

19

THIS ISN'T OVER YET

Misty

I KEEP MY HEAD DOWN AS COLE BRISKLY LEADS GEORGIA AND ME INTO the depths of the castle. I can tell we're in an area dedicated to maids and servants. The hallways are narrow and connect to a massive kitchen, a huge laundry room, and several rooms I'm sure are used for mending or to house supplies.

Maids scurry out of our way as Orion stalks ahead of us. Cole keeps his hand firmly fixed on my upper arm. There's nothing gentle about his touch. I don't turn to look into the eyes of the curious staff peeking their heads through doorways, trying to catch a glimpse of the king and his... entourage? No, captives. Still, captives. Especially based on the way he's dragging me up a flight of stairs. He wants it to look rough.

So, I squirm a bit. He doesn't tell me to stop. If anything, he tightens his grip in encouragement.

Orion says under his breath, "We decided it would be best to house her in your rooms. Her friend–"

"Mind-link, Orion," Cole says flatly, ripping me around a sharp corner.

I get a single glimpse of what I'd consider the main area of the castle before we pass into another narrow back hallway. White marble. Intricate craftsmanship. It's like this palace was carved by a master sculptor. It's a work of art.

But the hurried footsteps of Georgia, Luke, and Declan disappear behind me when we reach the top of another staircase. I turn and see nothing but shadows. "Where'd they go?"

Cole shushes me, saying into my head, *'Outside of our rooms, do not speak directly to me.'*

I chew my lower lip, glaring up at him as he yanks me back and forth, around corners, down more narrow hallways that form a spider's web of connections behind the gilded walls of his palace.

This is his home. His domain. And he's just as tense and cold as he'd been in the order's fortress in the middle of the desert.

We pass several inconspicuous doors before Orion stops at the very end of the hallway. He pulls a massive set of keys from the pocket of his tailored jacket and slides one into a narrow wooden door. He pushes it open, the new air carrying the scent of lilies and salt as Orion steps into the darkness. We follow.

Another tight room. Another key. Then, we're standing in a hallway bathed in sunlight that dances across white floral wallpaper and warm-tone hardwood flooring.

Dainty tables line the walls on either side. Cole's hand drops from my arm. He pushes the hood of his cloak back before shrugging out of the length of fabric completely, tossing it into Orion's waiting arms. "Burn it."

I stand with Orion while Cole stalks down the hallway, turning to the left. I glance at Orion, taking in his details–his short light brown hair, the lines beside his eyes and mouth, the scruffy beard and light blue eyes–then follow my *fake future baby daddy* into what I believe is his private apartment in the castle.

The space erupts around me. Cole's standing near the far wall of a large sitting room that's open to the rest of the apartment. Several doors are open, showcasing two bathrooms, two bedrooms, an office, and a small, personal library.

I wouldn't expect Cole to live in a place like this. It's very feminine, honestly. The wallpaper is light and floral, and the place is absolutely spotless.

Then I remember the fact that he's likely spent very little time in this place. He didn't grow up here. He went to college in Serpentia then moved to Crescent Falls for the rest of his schooling.

I find myself slightly disappointed I'm not seeing a glimpse of who he really is right now.

"Are we alone?" Cole asks, turning to Orion, who nods. Cole licks his lips, his body totally, completely rigid. "I don't want any maids in here unless I'm present. No one comes through those doors–" he points to a set of massive white double doors nearby, presumably the main entrance to the apartment, "--unless I'm already here. Otherwise, Mystica's unbothered. No one comes in or out, and she doesn't leave without a vetted escort."

"Misty," I correct under my breath. Both men glance at me.

"I want guards outside the door," Cole continues.

"We have a few left," Orion says, his jaw clenched. "It hasn't spread to everyone."

Spread. The word bounces through my skull looking for a place to land, but I don't let it. I refuse to think about Cole's curse, or why some guards have glowing eyes and others don't. Later. I'll think about it later.

"I need updates, numbers," Cole continues, pacing back in the direction we came. "I need to meet with any commanders who still have their minds to themselves."

"We're prepared to meet with you," Orion says, but his tone has a hint of… something. There's a crack, like his real emotions are trying to choke him.

"What's happening on the border?" Cole asks, turning around when he reaches a row of tall, arching windows overlooking what might be a huge courtyard.

I'm not sure what to do right now, so I tuck my arms behind my back and decide to explore. I already know what's happening at the border because I had dreams of my family pulling back, taking a break, and giving themselves time to regroup.

My visions are confirmed when Orion says, "The Allied Kings have their armies camping out at the border. We've been sending as many people through to their side as we can, but Richard has his own forces trying to undo our progress. He has his army scattered across the border at this point. We've been finding breaks where we can, pushing townsfolk through. Only a few Alphas have agreed to leave, however. Those that have left with their packs agreed to carry information. They're on our side."

My stomach turns as I step into one of the bedrooms. It's empty. Not a lick of furniture. I move onto the second.

"What are our chances of getting the princess out unseen?"

"Highly unlikely. Richard's army… they know what to do if she's seen, if she tries to escape. Their hivemind…." Orion trails off, presumably having the rest of the conversation over the mind-link as I step into the main bedroom.

Our bedroom, obviously, because I'm still his breeder.

It's a south facing room. Sunlight pours over a massive four-poster bed, baking the clean white sheets and silken duvet.

That's really it. It's not overly decorated. It smells like… cleaning solution. It doesn't smell like Cole at all.

I flip on the light in the bathroom as their conversation carries through the air.

"She needs clothes. Everything. We're coming here with nothing."

"Lavender has already started a wardrobe for her. She just needs her measurements."

"Can Lavender still be trusted?"

"Yes, she's unscathed. She has maids who–"

I turn on the shower, drowning out their voices for good. Steam rises, billowing over the smooth, white and emerald tiles. I catch a glimpse of my reflection in the mirror and wince.

I'm a mess. I drown in Cole's sweatshirt, and my skin is gaunt and pale from exhaustion and stress. My hair is a disaster, but my appearance is one thing I can fix. The only thing I have control over, honestly.

I find some big, fluffy towels and some unlabeled bottles of what I hope are shampoo and conditioner, then I strip out of my grubby clothes, kicking them into the corner of the room.

The water feels amazing–not stale and barely warm like at the fortress. I scrub the hell out of my hair, raking my fingers through it, then coat my body in so much soap the suds gather ankle deep at my feet.

I stay in the shower longer than I need to, my forehead leaning on the tiles, and when I finally decide to emerge and wrap myself in a towel, I walk into the bedroom to find Cole walking out of the closet with several items of clothing draped over his arm. Orion is gone. We're alone. Totally alone.

We stare at each other for a moment. I resist the urge to ask, "What now?" and waltz to the bed instead, with a bottle of lotion in my hand, and plop down.

I can feel Cole watching me but keep my eyes on my legs as I use the lotion. It smells fine–like vanilla and maybe… apricots.

The bed shifts beside me. Cole sits on the edge near the pillows, untying his shoes, the clothing he fetched from the closet resting between us.

"Can I see your back?" I ask into the deafening silence.

"I think we have a lot to discuss–"

"I don't care," I say softly, under my breath. "I don't care about your rules, what I need to do and *be* while I'm here. I get it. I understand. I saw–" I catch myself before telling him I'd shared his nightmare while we were in the car. "I saw how tense you were when we were walking through the castle to this… place. I get it. I'm in danger. We're all in danger."

"I'm still the king."

I turn to look at him over my shoulder, my wet hair sticking to my skin. "Yeah, I guess you are." I try to give him a smile, but it falls flat. "*The rebel king*. Wolf King of the Resistance"

He… smiles. Finally, actually, *smiles*. But he looks down at his lap while he does it, refusing to look me in the eyes. "That sounds like the title of a bad movie."

"Well, our lives are a bad movie right now," I quip, edging closer to him. "I need to see your back–now."

"It's fine. It feels–"

I smooth my fingers over the back of his neck where a new symbol is already forming. My stomach tightens. I thought I'd cured him with my new, special powers but….

He reaches up to grip my fingers. "Misty–it's okay. You've done enough."

"I can just–just keep healing you," I say, my voice full of gravel as I desperately try to keep my wits about me. "I'll heal you when you need it, so you're not in pain."

He lets my fingers drop and allows me to roll up his shirt. His muscled back shines in the sunlight, highlighting the scars littering his skin. It looks so much better than it had when I first saw it. Some symbols are completely gone, and others are raised and silver, but new, smaller, deeper cuts have started to spread and I… failed.

I press my hands to his back and let my healing powers flair. He lets me do it for a few seconds before arching away. "I can't let you keep doing this."

"I have to."

"No," he says under his breath, rising from the bed and turning toward me, fisting his shirt.

I kneel on the bed, still only wearing a towel. "Why not?"

He arches his brow. "Because I don't want you to."

"Why?"

"Don't–don't argue with me about this–"

"I'm stuck in this too, Cole. For Goddess' sake–" I slide off the bed and grab a button down shirt he'd laid on the sheets, obviously for himself, then pad to the bathroom.

"Misty."

"What?" I shout, turning to face him. "What do you want? What am I supposed to be doing right now? Huh? Sitting around, by myself, cloistered here, while you do *what*? Let this curse eat you, and your court, alive? That's what's happening, right? The curse gives Richard some kind of power over you? He cursed your father and turned him into his puppet, didn't he? He cursed you after you killed your dad, then used Adrian and his mate to get you to surrender to him? You were never given a choice in any of this, were you?"

Cole stares at me, his jaw ticking with words unsaid.

I nod to myself, chuckling darkly. "How do I factor into this? My powers? Richard needs me for something, right? Well, so do you, and I'm not going to sit by and watch you slowly die while you–"

"While I what?" That smooth, carefully crafted patience that radiates from him finally snaps. He stalks toward me, a brow raised. "While I *what*, Misty?"

"Keep me locked up here like a precious trophy you plan to dangle in front of Richard!"

"That's not what I'm doing," he growls, bracing his hands on either side of the doorframe. "It wasn't my decision to ever involve you. I fought to keep you out of this!"

"Why? I'm not your responsibility. You owe me *nothing*."

"I owe it to your family to see you to safety."

"They can handle their own business!" I stand on my toes, trying to look harder, maybe more menacing. "I can handle *my* own business. I'm in control of my powers, and I can use them as I wish, and I will continue to heal you, and you'll continue to let me!"

His eyes are dark as he looks down at me, barely an inch of distance between us. My heart beats out of rhythm as we continue to glower at each other.

I go to push him away, but I clap my hand against his chest instead, sending my healing powers bursting forward. He winces but holds my gaze.

"Stop."

"No."

He grabs me, clutching me close, leaning down so we're nose to nose. "I said *stop*."

"I said *no*."

"You need to stay away from me, Misty."

"Why?"

His lips brush against mine. He takes a ragged breath, closing his eyes as my powers sweep over his skin.

Another sensation takes over. A sensation that's been making me entirely insane since the moment I began to think he wasn't the monster he portrayed himself as.

I want him to live. I need him to be okay.

Because I *want* him. I want to know him beyond this fucked up mess we're stuck in.

I rise up on my toes and kiss him soundly.

THIS TIME IS DIFFERENT

Misty

COLE BACKS ME AGAINST THE DOORFRAME, HIS BODY CURLING OVER mine to chase my mouth as I lower my feet to the floor. The memory of our kiss from the party weeks ago clogs my brain for several delicious seconds. He tastes the same. Warm and minty. His lips are soft but demanding as his tongue slides over my lower lip, beckoning for me to open for him.

The towel covering my body is holding on by a thread as I wrap my arms around his neck. He lifts me up, pinning me against the doorframe and pressing his body to mine. My hand drags down his back, leaving a trail of my healing powers. He trembles, and the kiss turns to something hungry and... wild.

"Stop healing me," he breathlessly commands.

"No," I counter, but his mouth steals the word from my lips.

It doesn't strike me that we should stop. There's no reason for this. This attraction, this bone-shattering *need* I've felt since we slept together for the first time–as quick and cold as that was. Maybe it's morbid curiosity. Maybe it's my utter desire to know everything–to pick him apart until I find what makes him tick–who he used to be, before the order stole those parts of him away.

But this is the perfect distraction from our crumbling worlds. Right now, there's no war. Right now, a curse isn't eating away at him. Right now, I'm not separated from my family and hidden away in a kingdom I don't know, chased by a dictator who wants me for my powers.

Right now, I'm warmed through and seeking solace in *him*.

All while he's losing himself in *me*.

He holds me up by my thighs, my legs wrapped around his waist. He pushes my wet hair away from my neck, one hand cupping my throat to keep me where he wants me.

His scent overwhelms my senses. When his free hand leaves my neck to caress my cheek, the motion followed by a soft, tender kiss, I… fold. The world around us fades to nothing but the taste of him on my tongue and the feeling of his strong arms carrying me to the bed. He lays me down in its center, climbing over me and pulling the towel loose. He's out of his pants in moments, but there's nothing cold and medical about this. Not this time.

I've never been kissed like this. Every sweep of his tongue–every hard, hungry press and soft, tender stroke has my heart skipping beats. A sensation of warmth fills my chest, making it hard to catch my breath. Or, maybe that's just because we're kissing so much and so hard I haven't given myself a moment to breathe.

The sheets are warm from the sun as his mouth travels to my neck, sucking bruises across my collarbone, and lower, to my breasts. He draws his tongue across one of my nipples, stopping to suck it into his hot, hungry mouth. I arch into the sensation, exhaling sharply in a moan.

Cole hums with desire. His hands glide down my sides, one hand resting on the swell of my hip while the other cups my opposite breast, kneading and squeezing while I writhe beneath him.

Every part of this is new to me. This… worship. This sudden obsession on his end. The look in his eyes when he finally rises to kiss my mouth again is heavy and hooded, like he's completely lost his mind, and he's more than happy about it. That warmth in my chest brightens with... relief.

I'm not sure why I have this overwhelming sense that I can comfort this man I barely know, and only know because of horrible circumstances, but that knowledge trips something in my brain, igniting the growing sense that... something else is going on here.

Focus, Misty, I tell myself, taking a deep breath between kisses. That dull, throbbing ache between my legs starts to steal my rational mind, and I'm more than okay with it. I'll *think* later. Much, *much* later.

His legs are tangled with mine now, his arms wrapped around me, holding me against him. I rake my fingers through his short, soft hair–soft like silk. I want him to grow it out for me. I want to ask that of him. I want to lie in bed with him and ask him about his life, his interests, his desires and....

He goes still, holding himself up on an elbow.

"What is it?" I whisper, turning his cheek to look at me. "Cole?"

His free hand strokes down my hip. His cock is rigid against my inner thigh. I want him to just–to just do what he did the other night. I rock my hips against his in emphasis.

His mouth moves like he's trying to say something, to tell me something, but thinks better of it.

"Please," I whisper, sounding needy... whiny, actually. He doesn't seem to mind, though. The corner of his mouth ticks into what I'd consider a smile. A small one, but it was there. I saw it. "You smiled again," I whisper, stroking my thumb across his lower lip until I reach the corner of his mouth.

"I'm trying," he admits, and that crushes me.

Oh, Cole, I think, running my fingertips over his profile. He's been through so much. He's been carrying too much. Taking care of everyone but himself.

I promise myself at that very moment that I will be the one taking care of him from now on.

So, I throw my weight against him. He huffs in surprise as he lands on his back in the center of the bed, looking up at me with a startled, confused expression lighting behind those lovely gray eyes. I straddle him, panting, unsure what I'm supposed to do next, but the need bouncing through my body seems to know *exactly* what to do.

I reach between us, sliding my fingers down the length of his cock and back up again. His chest heaves, but his eyes don't leave mine, not until I guide the head of his cock through the slickness between my thighs, through my folds, pausing on my clit.

My toes curl. He groans softly, arching his hips on impulse. I do the motion again, and again, teasing us both until we're both panting and trembling.

Even in my anger over his abrupt dismissal, I understood why he'd been so furious after we'd done this for the first time.

He felt like he'd taken something from me.

"I want this," I say in a voice that sounds wholly unfamiliar. Normally, I'm confident. Steadfast and sure. Now, my voice wobbles, edged with guilt over how this happened for us the first time, and how I thought his behavior afterward had been because of *me*. "Do you?"

"Yes," he says, his voice low and rasping. "I do."

I slide onto his cock with more effort than I anticipated. He grits his teeth as I slowly move my hips, begging my body to adjust to his size, but I'm struggling. His hands rest on the curve of my waist, trying to guide my movements but I'm... not very good. I hate not being great at something the very first time I try it.

Suddenly, he's pulling me down, taking my mouth in another heated kiss that nearly breaks me out of my own spiral of self-doubt, then promptly flips me over onto my back.

He kisses me as his cock parts my folds. He buries himself deep, groaning against my mouth, the sound of his pleasure causing my inner muscles to throb and tighten around him in anticipation.

"I hurt you the last time, didn't I?" he whispers against my cheek. He ropes his arm around my leg, guiding my knee up. He slowly presses into me again, hitting a new depth—a new spot deep inside that has me gasping and moaning his name.

Cole smiles–with teeth. A real smile. It's nearly enough to push me over the edge into sweet oblivion, but he's not done with me yet.

"Move with me," he commands, rocking his hips into mine. "Match my tempo. Yeah, just like–just like that."

His other arm slides between my back and the sheets, his hand resting on the back of my neck as he presses our bodies together, thrusting into me in deep, measured strokes. He kisses me over and over again, deciding the speed and depth of his thrusts based on the needy sounds I make as the ache ghosting through my body turns to molten need.

"Cole–" I gasp, arching my back as he slows his movements, grinding his hips into mine.

He kisses my breasts, groaning as he drags in, and out, savoring the feeling of my muscles clamping down around him.

This is not like last time. His hands are everywhere–touching me, exploring my body with fervor that edges on obsession..

I'm into it. My inhibitions slip away completely, and it's just me and him, our bodies open to each other, and I'm going to come… right now.

I arch off the bed, chasing that delicious friction, but Cole slows his movements and presses me against the mattress.

Nose to nose, he looks down at me, slightly shaking his head. "Don't come."

"But–you said that last time!" I bare my teeth in frustration when he stops moving completely, still buried to the hilt. I writhe, pouting and about to start begging when he kisses me softly, tenderly.

He pulls away, tracing kisses across my jaw, down my neck.

"Cole, please," I whimper, raking my nails down his back. I'm sure he's thankful he allowed me to heal him again. He pulls out of me, groaning under his breath before trailing kissing down my stomach.

My inhibitions are suddenly on high alert. I try to squeeze my thighs together but his head is… in the way.

"Relax," he breathes, then he's kissing my inner thigh, gently dragging his teeth over the sensitive, heated skin toward my center.

I clap my hand over my mouth in disbelief, and to stop myself from screaming in sheer, unhinged ecstasy when his tongue parts my folds.

I knew this was a thing. Fia and Darby had a spirited argument about it once—when Darby's current fling said he hated it, that it was dirty, and Fia and Georgia told her to dump him immediately. I'd laughed along with them, acting like I knew what they were talking about, but in reality, I'd barely let Nathan touch me beneath my bra and now... now Cole's spreading my legs wide and groaning, lapping my clit, his fingers sliding into of me and hooking, which makes me instantly see stars.

But there's something in the way. My own stupid, raging thoughts. My memory of the night he ripped the bloody sheets from the bed and stuffed them in Nathan's arm. Cole's face had been so broken—so beyond regretful. So *sorry*.

"Misty," he breathes against my thigh. I open my eyes and look down at him, a tear sliding free from my lashes and rolling down my temple. He keeps his eyes on me as he kisses my knee, then moves up to me again, wrapping his arms around me.

"I'm sorry—"

"Don't," he rasps, kissing me again—softly, brushing my tear away with his thumb.

I reach between us, stroking his cock before guiding him back inside of me. I feel a pinch of soreness, of heat, before he settles and begins to move in slow, easy strokes.

There's something about his weight on me that does the trick. He's everywhere, blurring my senses, stealing my thoughts, making my powers simmer beneath my skin. I feel those tingles again—like electricity building at the base of my spine. My thighs tighten, my muscles coiling with delicious tension. I'm so focused on the way Cole's making me feel that I haven't noticed that he's buried his face in the crook of my neck and fisting the sheets on either side of me, his body tightening like he's desperately trying to hold something back.

I rake my fingers through his hair again, whimpering from sheer pleasure into his shoulder. When my teeth graze his skin, he shudders, murmuring something I can't decipher.

The orgasm is softer than the first time we were together. It moves through me in slow, unhurried waves. I gasp, then sigh as pleasure rocks through my body, beating in time with my racing heart. Cole lifts his head, kissing me through it, riding out wave after wave of release until I'm limp in his arms and warmed to the bone.

He grunts, tightening his grip, then drops to the side and drags me against his chest.

We lie there for several minutes trying to catch our breath.

My eyes feel heavy as I blink into the sunlight. I have no idea what time it is, but being next to Cole has me feeling the safest I've ever felt. I could sleep. Slip into that dead kind of sleep where even visions won't wake me.

I close my eyes.

A string I've never noticed before plucks in my chest.

21

A BABY

Misty

A FREAKIN' WEEK HAS PASSED IN MY CONFINEMENT. TO SAY I'M LOSING my mind is the least of it. On the first day in Oasia, I lost my mind and body to Cole, spending the night beside him—learning the secrets of his body until the sheets smelled like us, and we slumped into a dead kind of sleep.

But that was a week ago. In between, I've been pacing the apartment, slowly fading into the wallpaper, watching wolves dart around the courtyard a few stories below. Every day is the same. I wake up—alone. I eat breakfast by myself. Lavender—a pretty, middle-aged woman—comes to dress me in beautiful dresses that cover nearly every inch of my skin—not that I'm going anywhere, though. She hasn't spoken a word to me, and she barely looks me in the eye.

Yesterday, Georgia finally came to see me. Apparently, she's been hoarded away as well, but Declan keeps her company. Luke is in the same boat. Alone, well fed and well dressed, but otherwise occupied with a special project Cole bestowed upon him, but I haven't seen Luke since we arrived.

Cole... well, admittedly I haven't seen him much, either. He leaves in the early hours of the morning to do... Alpha King things, I assume. Juggling a broken kingdom on the edge of war can't be easy because he stumbles back into our room long after the sun's gone down, and I've gone to bed. Most nights, I don't even notice his arrival. Last night, however, I felt him slide into bed. He rolled over on the very edge of the mattress, trying not to wake me. I think, in reality, he'd been trying to keep a great distance between us.

But I'm lonely. I miss my family. I miss someone else's touch, and he is the only person I... think about, in general. It's an overwhelming feeling–this desire that won't die out, even now that I'm somewhat safe. When I arrived in Oasia, and we slept together again, I chalked it up to basic, primal, animalistic instincts. I wanted to have sex, and he was a willing participant. I wanted to be touched, to feel a moment's love and comfort. So did he. We needed it and used each other to fulfill that need.

I'm lying to myself every day, convincing myself it's not more.

I think we both know it is.

So, last night, I rolled across the mattress and wrapped my arm around him, squeezing my chest to his back, letting my healing powers drift between us. He hadn't rolled over to face me, but he didn't push me away, either. We'd fallen asleep like that–spooning–which was incredibly difficult for me, being the big spoon, because my face was jammed against his back, and I could barely breathe but... his scent was calming–beautiful–everything I love in one.

But now I'm sitting on the edge of my bed in a silken nightgown that drapes around my ankles, waiting for Lavender to come with my breakfast, do my hair, and dress me.

Another day... waiting? I have no idea what's going on anymore.

The servants' entrance opens like clockwork at 8:00 A.M..

Lavender–with her black hair neatly swept in a bun at the base of neck–arrives in a dress of pale yellow that covers her chest, arms, and back. Everyone here dresses the same. Long sleeves–thin, breezy fabrics in soft, muted colors. It's to beat the heat of the day, I've come to realize. To shield our skin from the unforgiving sun of the desert that surrounds the city.

But today, she's not alone.

A one-year-old girl with dark brown hair sticking straight up on the top of her head clutches Lavender's gown, wrinkling the fabric as Lavender balances the baby on her hip. Lavender looks flustered, her cheeks pink and eyes heavy with stress as she pushes the breakfast cart into the room with one hand, knocking it into a table.

I jump out of bed and hurry to help her, my eyes holding on the baby who stares at me with wide, dark blue eyes.

"I can do it," I assure Lavender with a tight smile.

Lavender sighs as the baby continues to clutch her dress, whining a bit. Lavender, who hasn't spoken to me at all over the past week, says softly, "Thank you, Your Highness. I've had a bit of a morning."

I glance between her and the baby, who has tears dried on her cheeks. "I can see that."

"She's teething." Lavender breathes, following behind me as I steer the cart toward the little bistro table near the windows overlooking the courtyard. Coffee scents the air–thank the Goddess. I've been dying for a cup more than usual this morning.

I set out my plate and mug then start opening the platters of eggs and fruit–the usual assortment. The baby jumps in Lavender's arm, pointing a chubby finger toward a bowl of strawberries.

"You've already had your breakfast. And a snack… and second breakfast," Lavender grumbles, trying to set the baby down on the floor. "I need to lay out a dress for the princess now, pet."

The baby squawks, her face going red with sudden fury.

"I'll hold her," I say with a smile.

Lavender stares at me. "Oh, no. Princess. It's all right. Eat and I'll– figure something out–"

The baby starts to scream with rage as Lavender turns with her in her arms.

"Actually, I insist. She can share my strawberries."

Lavender turns back around, looking conflicted.

"I won't hurt her," I try to say, my voice wobbling. "If that's what you're worried about. I have so many nephews... and second cousins... the works."

"Oh, Your Highness, that's not what I was worried about." Lavender smiles softly, her dark eyes creasing as she looks down at the baby. She sighs with resignation and thrusts the baby into my waiting arms. The girl leans away from me at first, but I sit down, settling her into my lap and pulling the bowl of strawberries in front of her.

She instantly snatches a handful of chopped strawberries and stuffs them in her mouth, sighing around the bite. "Oh, honey, you don't have enough teeth for all that," I laugh. She looks up at me, her cheeks round and full of fruit, and gives me a watery smile.

Lavender returns from the closet with a few dresses for me to choose from, smiling wistfully at the scene playing out in front of her.

"Strawberries are her favorite," she smiles, but the smile doesn't reach her eyes. "They were her mother's favorite, too. She ate them all through her pregnancy. We could barely keep up with demand." Her eyes shine with unshed tears–tears she's refusing to cry.

"Who's her mother?" I ask, and to my dismay, a flicker of jealousy ripples through my chest. This isn't... Cole's baby, is it?

"Elsbeth... Lady Elsbeth, of course. She's, uhm... she's dead."

Lavender turns around before I can see the expression of utter dismay playing across the dainty features.

I remember the dream I shared with Cole–the nightmare of his friends getting killed. The faint cry of an infant somewhere in the background that I'd noticed when the dead woman came into view.

"She's Adrian's daughter, isn't she?"

"Uhm, yes. Marcella is her name. We call her Marrie for short."

"Marrie," I smile, trying to stop my eyes from watering. Marrie reaches for the eggs. I pull the plate forward, having lost my appetite at the memory of the dream of her dead parents.

Lavender looks pained as she watches us, sitting down in a chair nearby but giving me, and Marrie, space. I get a few bites of eggs before Marrie finishes them off, and there's no hope for the strawberries. They're gone, and now the baby is reaching for my coffee.

"Oh, you don't want that," I giggle, and she grins up at me, showing me only two teeth.

She's perfect. A beautiful reminder of a future I'm not sure she's going to have. That kills me.

I turn my teary eyes to Lavender, noticing the same look of resignation in her gaze.

Marrie lets out a big yawn as I continue to pick at my breakfast in silence, sipping my coffee, which honestly starts to turn my stomach in a way it never has. Lavender goes about her duties—laying out hair pins and brushes, tidying up the room, and eventually I feel Marrie slump in my arms, her cheek pressed to my chest.

I rise like I'm holding a live bomb and gently dab strawberry juice from her face with a napkin before laying her in the center of my bed and arranging a barrier of pillows around her so she can't roll off.

"You do have experience with little ones, don't you?" Lavender asks as we stand near the bed and watch Marrie sleep for a moment.

"I have two nephews," I tell her. "And three second cousins... and I think I might have a niece on the way." I sigh heavily, my heart lurching. Will I ever see them again?

Lavender wordlessly leads me to the vanity next to the far wall. I sit in silence while she brushes my hair, occasionally looking over our shoulders at the bed to make sure Marrie isn't awake and trying to escape.

"So, what's on my agenda today?" I ask wryly.

"Uhm... lunch and dinner. Here."

"Of course," I murmur, exhaling deeply. "Is Cole busy today?"

"Yes, very." Her sigh of frustration is evident as it weaves through the words.

"Could you send him a message for me?"

Lavender raises her brows but doesn't stop braiding my hair. "Of course, I can try."

"Tell him I'll start speaking in tongues and ripping wallpaper from the walls if he doesn't find some way to keep me entertained... preferably his own company?"

She tries to hide her smile. "I will. I'm sorry he's keeping you here, locked up like this. I hope he told you why."

"The castle isn't safe?"

"We have a large court," she says quietly. "Unfortunately, we have no idea who we can trust anymore."

"Who do you trust?" I ask, meeting her gaze in the mirror.

She thinks about it for a long time. "Cole," she says, forgoing formalities. "Cole, and Orion, and his family. They're so far... mostly untouched by the curse, those that are still alive." She swallows hard against the memory of Adrian and his mate, Elsbeth. "Elsie–Elsbeth was my daughter, so Marcella is–she's my granddaughter. She's with me more often than not these days, as Orion is quite busy. His mate is ill."

Ill. The word worms through my body. "She's cursed, right?"

Lavender's jaw tightens. "Yes, she is."

I turn around to face her, "I can fix that–at least, make it more comfortable for her. I was able to help Cole, and I still do. I'd have to keep doing it, but if she's in pain—please let me help?"

Lavender holds my gaze for a long time. "I'll ask," she whispers, tears in her eyes. "I will ask, and I'll let you know. Uhm... it's very bad, Your Highness, I should warn you–she's in the later stages–"

"Misty is fine," I tell her, squeezing her hand. "And I don't care. Just let me help."

She nods, a single tear rolling free before she wipes it away and sniffles back a sob. "Oh, I meant to ask days ago, but when are you expecting your courses? So I can have supplies prepared?"

"Courses?"

"Your–your moon cycle," she says under her breath.

"Oh, that." I turn back to the mirror, whizzing through some internal math. Cole did make good on his promise to give me a calendar and a clock. My birthday is in a week. Winter Solstice is the week after that, and my moon cycle...

"Oh, it's a week late, at least," I grumble, staring at my reflection in the mirror.

"Oh," Lavender echoes, clearing her throat. "It's the stress, I'm sure."

"Yeah," I grind out, still staring at my reflection. There's no way I'm pregnant, right? My cycles are always on time, without fail. Of course, I know how babies come to be, but… it's only happened *twice*, and I'm not certain Cole finished… inside of me, seeing as I'm his fake breeder, and he's not actually trying to get me pregnant.

I grip the edge of the vanity. Lavender must notice my sudden stillness because she lays a timid hand on my shoulder and says, "It's far too soon to tell."

I whip around. "Don't tell Cole. It would kill him."

She nods but looks pale. "It's just stress. That's why it's late."

I want my mom. *Holy fuck, I need my mom right now.* "Yes. Stress."

"Stress," she echoes, but neither of us look convinced.

"He didn't want to do this to me."

"I know," she rushes out, looking pained.

"We had to–" my voice cracks painfully.

"I've been told," she whispers, "about how he managed to get you out from under the order. Your parents have been informed of your whereabouts, Princess."

"Just Misty, *please*." I'm on the cusp of breaking, for real this time.

"Misty," she swallows, nodding. "Cole is going to get you out of this. He's working on it."

I don't tell her I can't leave until this is finished. Until I know he's going to be okay, and the curse is broken. I won't leave until then.

Marrie huffs from the bed and sits up with a confused sigh. "Baba–baba baba baba–"

Lavender hurries to her, scooping her up and patting her back. "That was barely a nap, my darling girl. Go back to sleep."

Lavender gives me a slight nod in goodbye, and begins to walk away, but stops. "Would you like to take a walk with us?"

"Am I allowed?"

"I wouldn't want you ripping the wallpaper," she says with a smile.

22
LET ME HELP

Cole

ORION PACES ACROSS THE ROW OF WINDOWS OVERLOOKING THE CITY. Sun bathes the blue roofs, but in the distance, storm clouds gather on the horizon. Storms aren't uncommon this time of year. They're vicious, though. Flooding is common–something we need to count on.

So on top of... on top of pretending to be a war lord while simultaneously trying to force the Alphas in my kingdom to get their people out, and to the border, before I start a real war with Richard... I have to deal with the people who won't leave and ensure they're safe when the rain starts.

"I want warriors in the city center ready to rescue those who're ignoring the warnings to evacuate to higher ground tonight," I murmur, running my hand down my face.

Orion watches the storm, sighing, "It might not be as bad as we're anticipating."

"It always is," Commander Abernathy, Luke's father, says from his perch on a couch nearby. "Maybe the flood will wash away Richard's forces lingering in the city. You know none of those men have their heads to themselves, anyway. I doubt they know what's coming tonight."

"That's wishful thinking," I gripe, staring at the commander before flicking my gaze to Orion. "Lock the castle down. No one leaves after dusk. All maids and servants will be housed in the servants' quarters on the second floor tonight."

He nods, tucking his hands in his pockets.

"A word?" Commander Abernathy says as he rises, glancing at Orion before settling his gaze on me.

This is all I have left. These two men. Everyone else is either cursed or I've managed to get them out and into hiding.

"Sure," I say to the commander as he sidles up to my desk and leans against it. "What is it?"

"I need to get Luke out," he says in a low, scraping voice. "As soon as possible. I know you have him working on something but… we're running out of time."

I nod, feeling the crushing weight of my life in general shoving down on my shoulders. "I understand. When the storm passes, we'll work on getting him and his mother to the border. With Georgia–the other student. They'll go together."

Orion purses his lips as he moves toward my desk. "Declan will be heartbroken. He doesn't stop talking about that girl."

"Declan should go, too," I tell him, meeting his eyes. "And Marcella and Lavender. Everyone who's able needs to prepare to leave while we still have a chance to get through Richard's lines at the border."

"Lavender won't leave you," he says quietly. "She won't leave the maids, either."

I look between the two men, the two holdouts. "All of you need to leave Tarsian."

They look at each other, then shake their heads. "No," Commander Abernathy says. "We're in this fight, Cole. You know what I promised your dad. I mean to keep it. I'm not leaving you behind." He reaches across my desk to squeeze my hand. The commander has always been a stubborn bastard, but Orion?

"I can't leave her behind. You know that," he says in a near whisper. I nod. That's all I can do. "You should take the day, Cole. Get some rest. Spend time with Misty–"

I hold my hand up to silence him. "I have work to do." I rise and push in my chair then turn for the door, effectively dismissing both men. Commander Abernathy heads in the direction of the library where Luke basically lives right now as he tries to translate the cryptex, but Orion falls in step with me.

"Does she know?" he asks quietly.

"No."

"Her birthday's next week. You should talk to her about it. Don't let it be a surprise."

"She'll be over the border before then."

"We're not going to be able to get her over the border without help, and you know that."

"It doesn't matter at this point. We have to try." The letter on my desk from Richard burns through my mind. He's in Serpentia again, preparing for his next phase of his grand plan. I have to go there to stop him. How, I'm not sure. I'm hoping Luke figures out the cryptex because it was found with the *Book of Whispers*. I need to understand its significance, if it's something I can use to not only break this curse, but stop Richard from opening the Gate of the Gods, unleashing hell on our world.

He's close to doing it, too.

He just needs Misty, but he's biding his time for some reason.

"Cole," Orion says, grabbing my arm and pulling me to a stop. "You need to tell her."

"No."

"You'll live with regret for the rest of your life–"

"I have only a few weeks of life left, Orion."

"You're in better shape than you were when you left with Richard to go to Serpentia a few weeks ago. She has healing powers, doesn't she? Like her family?"

"She can't undo the curse."

"Then *live*, Cole, for a few fucking days at least!"

I yank my arm out of his grasp. "I'm not doing this to her. She's going home, to her family, and then her parents and her aunt and uncle can invade, as planned."

"And where will you be when that happens?"

"Here, with the rest of those who won't make it out regardless of the outcome of the war," I snarl. "With the *cursed*. You go, take your family, and go."

"Cole–"

"It's done, Orion." I hold up my hand, dismissing him, but then Lavender's voice carries in our direction.

The beautiful, open air corridor overlooking the courtyard smells like rain already even though the storm is still dozens of miles away. I walk to the railing, looking down at the figures below.

"She likes you," Lavender says to… Misty, who's out of her room and holding–holding Marcella.

My chest lurches at the sight. Pockets of sunlight dance through Misty's golden hair as she turns with Marcella in her arms. Misty's dressed in muted blue. She looks… like a queen as she lifts her face to the sun, smiling.

Heartbreak ghosts through my chest. In another life, this would have been our home–our kingdom. The baby in her arms would have been *ours*.

"Cole," Orion says softly. "You deserve–"

"Don't," I cut in, shaking my head and turning away from the scene. "Please."

I close my eyes as Misty's laugh echoes through the corridor, brought here by the breeze. I try to resist it, to turn away and walk back to my office to sit in silence, or to the library to hound Luke about his progress like we still have time to act, but find myself walking down a staircase and turning toward the women.

Misty beams in my presence. I try to smile back at her but fail.

"Cole!" she grins, her eyes wide and bright. "What are you doing out here?"

"What are you doing out of your room?" I ask, and her smile fades instantly. I glance at Lavender, who looks guilty as hell as she steps toward me.

"It was my idea, Your Grace. She needed some air."

"It's fine," I say softly, looking back at Misty as Orion approaches, trying to convince Marcella to give up her new friend.

"Let's go see Grandma for a minute," he says, but the baby doesn't care. She clutches Misty tight, shaking her head.

"Do you think that's a good idea?" Lavender says to Orion. "Lacey hasn't been–" She cuts herself off, shaking her head as her eyes meet mine.

Lacey, Orion's mate and the mother of Declan and Adrian, was cursed a year ago. She's still alive because Orion can't do what I'd done to my father.

"Is Lacey your mate?" Misty asks, turning to Orion. "She's Declan's mother, isn't she?"

Orion shoots Lavender a glare. "Yes, she is. She's unwell–"

"She's cursed," Misty corrects, her eyes scanning our small group. "Lavender told me. I can help."

Lavender clears her throat, throwing me an apologetic glance, but then refuses to meet my eyes again.

Orion shakes his head. "Princess Misty, I understand you were able to give Cole some... relief, but my mate is... Cole has only been cursed for a few weeks. Lacey was one of the first. She's beyond help."

"You don't know that," Misty says with a scoff, scanning the group again. "Let me try." She holds my gaze. "Please, let me try."

I look at Orion, who isn't at all happy with the idea. He wants Lacey left alone. I know he goes to the temple and prays for the Goddess to take her, soon, to put her out of her misery. "It's up to you, Orion. Do you want Lacey to be able to see Declan and Marcella again before they leave?"

Orion looks down at his boots, closing his eyes. "She doesn't know about Adrian and Elsbeth."

"She doesn't need to know, Orion," Lavender says with heart-breaking calm. "Give her this gift. Let the princess give her some comfort before–before she goes to the Goddess."

I look at Misty, who pats Marcella's back as she glances from Lavender to Orion.

"Fine," Orion says, his eyes still closed. "Let's do this now, then, before the storm. She's always loved the rain. She'll want to see it."

Marcella allows Lavender to take her from Misty's arms. "I'll bring her by if Lacey is well enough to see her."

Without further conversation, Orion turns on his heel, stalking back to the stairwell. Lavender sits with Marcella on a bench, letting the baby play with her necklace, and I gently tuck Misty's hand in the crook of my elbow, following Orion.

"I need to warn you about what you're about to see," I tell her, walking slowly to put distance between us and Orion. "Lacey's case is advanced. She's not lucid anymore."

I can feel Misty looking up at me as we reach the top of the stairs and walk side by side down another long, open corridor. We're alone. No guards or servants lurk in the shadows, and Orion has already walked out of sight.

"How did she get cursed? How did it happen in this court?"

I shake my head. "I was in Crescent Falls when it began. My father was trying to oust Richard from our court, the city, Tarsian, in general, actually, after finding out he'd been working with the Draven Coven. From what Orion and others have told me, he quietly cursed a few high ranking individuals, making it seem like an illness, and convinced everyone he had the antidote because he cured one of them, one of the commanders' wives. It was enough for him to weasel his way back into my father's good graces, for a few weeks, at least."

"Did he actually cure her?"

I shake my head. "No, she died a few months ago, but he was able to make it look like the curse was gone."

"The curse is from the *Book of Whispers*, isn't it?"

"Yeah, it is. That's what he's using to do all of this."

We round a corner together, passing the throne room, a ballroom, and a formal dining room before I lead her through a door and up another set of steps. At the top of the stairs, I pause, turning to face her. "If you can't do this, we'd all understand."

"Of course, I can do this. I healed you, didn't I? It doesn't hurt as much?" Her voice has lost that sharp, teasing edge completely. Now, it's soft. Tender. Full of feeling that makes me want to take her into my arms and….

Misty wraps her arms around me, doing what I couldn't. Holding me in the shadow cast by alabaster columns that stretch to the glass ceiling.

"Do you trust me?" I whisper. I'm not sure why I say it. Of course, she doesn't trust me. I'm one of the villains in her narrative. I have to be. I wish I'd tried harder to be because it will make this… unraveling so much easier when it happens.

"I do," she says, her chin resting on my chest as she looks up at me. "I'm pissed you locked me in our room all week and barely said a word to me, though."

"I'm sorry about that. It's been… busy."

"You can make it up to me tonight. We'll have dinner together, and we can talk and… hangout."

"Are you asking me out?"

She balks, but her eyes are playful as she lets me go and inspects her nails. "I don't ask out men. They ask *me* out. And, I rarely say yes, so you should be flattered and jumping at the opportunity."

"We'll hang out tonight."

She smiles, and it's radiant. She takes my hand, tugging on it to get me moving again. I lead her through the castle, toward the rear, where the walls are shadowed and out of the sun's embrace. A chill snakes through the air when Orion comes back into view, waiting by a door, his face cast in doubt.

He looks up as we approach. "Did you warn her about what she's about to see?"

"I think I've probably seen worse," Misty cuts in before I can reply.

She has no idea what she's walking into, and I don't have the stomach to go into detail.

"How bad is it now, Orion?" I ask.

Orion pulls his keys from his pocket, unlocking the door.

A BLADE OF BLUE

Misty

THE ROOM IS DARK BUT CLEAN. IN FACT, THE CURTAINS ARE DRAWN against the sun, and Orion has to turn on a lamp, which barely floods the room in muted light.

There's a single bed in the corner, the blankets bunched around a... woman.

Chains rustle as she sits up, turning sightless green eyes in my direction, and I...

I turn away, bracing my hands on the wall as nausea drags me under.

Cole's behind me, leaning down as his hand rests on my lower belly, splayed wide. "You don't have to do this."

"Why is she wearing a *muzzle*?" I bite out, my eyes watering from the effort of trying to stop myself from throwing up out of rage.

The chains rattle as the woman begins to keen.

"Lacey, it's all right. I've brought a friend to see you. She might make you feel better." Orion's footsteps sound somewhere behind us. Lacey cries out in a mutated voice that sounds like talons being dragged across a chalkboard. My body lurches with nausea again, my healing powers already buzzing over my skin, sensing something is very, very wrong.

Cole remains behind me, his head lowered, his voice in my ear, "You don't have to do this," he repeats. "She doesn't have much longer. I'm not sure it's even worth it to try."

"Is she… aware?"

"Not anymore, no."

He keeps his hand on my belly. It's comforting–warm and… it grounds me. I'm not in this alone. He's here, supportive of whatever I choose to do.

I slowly turn around. Cole's hand drops as he steps to the side, giving me a view of Orion gripping his mate's shoulder and trying to ease her back onto the pillow, but she's thrashing, her eyes a wild, solid green.

Her nightgown is clean like she's taken care of regularly, but the smell of blood is so thick in the air I can't breathe past it. Symbols of all sizes and depth cover her entire body from what I can tell. Her face, her arms, her fingers…

Patches of hair are gone completely. Open symbols cover her scalp.

Thank the Goddess she doesn't know who she is anymore. Thank the Goddess… she isn't aware of the pain she must be feeling.

"How long exactly?" I gulp, my hands trembling as I try to will my legs to move.

"A little over a year."

"How long was your dad sick?"

"Two."

I look up at Cole, noticing the way he struggles to swallow against the words. His dad was like this? He saw his own father like *this*?

I want to ask why he didn't reach out to my family for help, but I'm starting to understand. Richard has the *Book of Whispers*. He has, at his fingertips, unlimited power.

He could have done this to my family. I'm not sure our powers are enough to stop him.

He's *going* to do this to my family, using the war to bait them in….

I find the nerve to step up to the bed, deciding to push the image of the woman, so hurt and sick she's nearly falling to pieces under Orion's hold, into the recesses of my mind and just focus on one thing.

Making her better. Taking the pain away.

I kneel, gripping her hand, feeling the symbols between us. Orion holds her down as she thrashes and screams like she's been taken over by some kind of demon, tears in her eyes.

Can he still feel their bond? Can he speak to whoever, or whatever, she is now, through that same bond?

Is she gone? Or are there pieces still there, begging for help?

"I'm so sorry," I tell her then close my eyes and let my powers flow.

All of the hair on my head stands on end as my powers thrum to life. I send them forward, through our clasped hands. My heartbeat sounds in my ears, drowning out Orion's shocked gasp and hurried questions toward Cole.

But I can feel Cole walking up behind me, laying his hand on my shoulder and squeezing.

'*You're doing it,*' he says into my mind.

I open my eyes, watching the symbols on her arm knit together, the ghastly gray color of the unbroken skin turning a soft peach.

She shakes with pain, but I don't stop. I can't. My powers hone in on her body, locked on their purpose. They know what to do.

I reach to lay my other hand on the side of her head.

Orion nearly grabs my arm before Cole grabs him.

"She bites, remember?" Orion hisses, terror in his eyes. "You know what happens when they bite!"

"Let her work." Cole edges away from the bed, herding an increasingly agitated Orion back.

When Lacey's keening shrieks turn to human-like whimpers, Orion thrashes in Cole's arms. "Lacey? Lacey!"

"Help–" Lacey's voice, rattling from lack of use, echoes through the room.

I can't stop now. It's working. It's really working.

My powers are only growing stronger instead of fading. I don't understand? Normally, at this point, like when I healed Cole's back for the first time, they'd fizzle... growing weak until they go out....

Cole's by my side again, his eyes wide in disbelief as I rise on shaking legs and pull my hands away, but my powers keep flowing, connected to Lacey by unending beams of light.

"What is this, Misty?" Cole asks breathlessly, shocked.

"I don't know," I rasp, looking past the light to the woman still lying in the bed, her skin... clearing of the symbols, completely. They're fading *completely*.

"Oh, my Goddess," Orion gasps, stumbling toward the bed. "Oh, Goddess—"

"Misty," Cole pants, his hand on the small of my back. "You–you ignited the curse in my body. How did you do it?"

"I don't know–"

"You unlocked it with your powers," he rushes out, watching as Lacey's back arches off the bed, her trembling growing so extreme the entire room starts to shake. The green magic in her eyes flickers. "Misty, I want you to try something for me. I want you to draw out the curse."

"I can't," I gasp as my powers reach a peak–so strong I can barely handle it.

"You can. I want you to try."

"I don't know how—"

'Focus,' he says into my head. '*Breathe, and focus.*'

I close my eyes, sending every power I have funneling into the woman at once.

Two white wolves in a clearing. Two white wolves face the sunrise. Two white wolves look out over scorched earth. A great war. A war... won.

A swiftly moving chill sweeps through my body. I gasp in pain as the cold bites into me like needles.

My eyes open to silts. The room spins. Cole's holding me upright, shouting in my ear not to stop, that I can do this.

The green magic in Lacey's eyes fades completely. Her eyes are a soft hazel. She's lovely. She looks like she's my mom's age. She's here—with us. Her eyes meet mine, pleading. *Help me. Help me, help me.*

My light turns… green.

"Misty!" Cole shouts.

I know what I did wrong last time. I had the curse by the fucking balls, but I quit—I quit before I pulled it out and destroyed it.

I won't quit this time, even though I'm being screamed at by two men, and the woman on the bed is shrieking in pain.

I scream. My voice carries, bouncing from wall to wall as my powers burst forward, drawing out the curse until its… its….

Here. In the room with us.

I stumble back into Cole's arms as green light flares right in front of my eyes. I lift my hands as the magic barrels toward me, reaching for me like a hand with gnarled, twisted fingers.

But suddenly there's a blade in my hand. A blade of pure, blue… mist?

I wield it, slicing through the curse at the very last second. The magic shatters.

The results are immediate. The room pretty much explodes. The green magic erupts like splintering glass, showering over us as Cole and I hit the ground with a crunch.

The lamp explodes, sending sparks whizzing through the air.

Then it goes totally, utterly still.

I can't breathe. My lungs collapse as I curl into myself, shaking in pain and the bitter cold sensation of completely exhausting my powers.

I'm so, so cold.

"Misty? Misty?" Cole rolls over, rising on top of me, my face clutched between his hands.

Somewhere behind us, Orion is coughing, gasping for breath as he fumbles for his mate through the ash hanging heavy in the air. I hear an unfamiliar female voice raised in alarm, and then I start to pass out.

"Misty? What's wrong? Look at me!"

"I just need a little nap," I gasp, choking on ash and smoke. "Just for a minute–I'll close my eyes for a–for a minute. A short minute…."

I'm scooped up like an infant. The dark room is replaced by vivid sunlight. Cole's voice fades in and out as he shouts at Orion, but I have no idea what they're saying to each other. Cole's sprinting, and the castle around us is a total blur.

"Where's my knife?" I rasp, fighting the growing darkness clogging my vision. I know what this is. I've been taught how to handle this–exhausting my powers, and the hangover that happens afterward.

"The knife you *made*?" Cole rasps, his voice low and stern.

Made?

I hear a door splinter like he's kicking it open, and then we're back in our room.

"Bath," I croak, shivering so violently my teeth click together. My skin feels like it's freezing over. I can taste frost on my tongue.

Cole is breathless as he slides into the bathroom with me in his arms. I hear the water, I feel the hot steam rising as he lowers me to the ground and rips off my dress. "What is this? What's wrong with you? The curse–"

"No," I breathe, gritting my teeth against the cold and the black nothingness blinding me. "I'm–my powers are gone. I need–warmth–and sleep–" I moan in pain, my bones aching so badly I want to scream, but I fight it.

I remember being told about Ella and Sarah's experiences with this phenomenon. Sarah had been out for days. Ella was mum about how Ryatt brought her back to life, though. They just spoke about being so cold and empty it was painful–worse than giving birth, in their shared opinion.

My dress rips. Cole tosses the fabric away and jumps into the tub with me pressed to his chest. Water soaks my thin, lacy bra and matching panties. He hisses at the temperature, but to me it's bliss.

I decide I'm going to be the one to get through this… depletion… without passing out. I'll brag about it when I see my family again. I won't shut up about it, honestly, rubbing it in everyone's faces.

"You did it," he says, over and over. "You broke the curse."

My head lolls as I fight the feeling of being dragged into unconsciousness. I refuse, straight up. I'll rest when I'm dead. I'll rest when the man holding me to his chest and pressing desperate kisses into my hair is cured, when I've broken his curse.

Because he's mine.

I'm not giving him up.

"Cole," I say shakily. "Cole–"

"I'm here."

"I think I'm pregnant."

He's quiet for the space of a heartbeat.

"You're not," he whispers.

"I could be, couldn't I?"

"You're delirious." His voice shakes with disappointment–grief.

"Probably," I mouth, then lay my head back but keep my eyes open. It takes all of my strength.

But now he's standing with me still clutched to his chest–sopping wet, his clothes leaving puddles of hot water on the bathroom floor as he leaves the room, covering me with a towel.

"Get her in bed, now," he says to someone I can't see.

Lavender stutters over whatever she's trying to say.

Cole repeats himself, "I need your help getting her dressed and in bed–"

"He's here. The Umbra Mortis is here," Lavender chokes out, desperation heavy in each word.

TIME RUNS OUT

Cole

Misty shivers in my arms as I stare at Lavender. "What did you just say?"

"The Umbra Mortis just arrived," she says slowly, her eyes wide with panic. "He's coming here–to the castle. Any minute now."

My life flashes before my eyes. He can't see Misty like this. He can't find out Misty just broke the curse in Lacey, either.

"Fuck. Fuck, fuck–" It takes all of my strength to lay Misty in the bed gently instead of tossing her like a rag doll. Lavender quickly takes over redressing her in a nightgown while I run around the room, opening closets and pulling drawers from the dresser, searching for anything to throw over her nearly frozen body. I rush into the bathroom and swiftly change into dry clothes.

"What happened?" Lavender hisses as we hurriedly tuck several blankets around Misty. Misty shivers uncontrollably, her teeth chattering so loud I'm worried they'll break. I fish in the blankets for her arm and take a deep breath before going completely still, my fingers locked on her pulse.

If she were in a hospital right now, I'd be running into her room, chasing down a nurse with a crash cart. Anyone else would be dead with a heart rate this low.

I grip her wrist, watching her eyes as she fights a dead kind of sleep trying to pull her under.

Then I crash back to reality. "She cured Lacey. Completely."

"What?" Lavender whispers, stepping to my side. "How is that possible?"

I tuck Misty's arm against her side and stuff the covers around her, laying the back of my hand over her freezing cold forehead. Her breath puffs with frost, and her eyes are totally glazed as she looks at my arm, going a bit cross eyed.

I ignore Lavender's murmured question and command, "Bring Georgia and Luke here, immediately. To say goodbye."

"Is Misty dying?"

"No, I don't believe so, but Georgia, Luke, Orion, and his family are leaving now. For the border. You, too."

She grabs my arm. "I'm not leaving you, Cole."

"I'm not giving you a choice. You have to go, right now. Don't pack anything. Don't bother with goodbyes. Take Marcella–and go."

Lavender's jaw works, but no words leave her lips. She straightens her spine and brushes a few tears from her eyes before giving me a curt nod.

I send commands to Orion through the mind-link. I have no idea where he is, or where he's taken his mate, but Lacey can't be seen by anyone right now.

I sit on the edge of the bed and hang my head in my hands as Lavender leaves the room, her rapid footsteps echoing until the door shuts with a firm snap. After a few seconds, I turn to look at Misty, leaning over her body to rest my hand on her forehead again.

Her eyelids flutter.

"Why are you fighting it?" I ask softly, as gently as I'm able to despite the nerves ricocheting through my body. "Just sleep."

"I cured her, didn't I? I broke the curse."

"You did."

She licks her lips, sucking in a shallow breath. "I'll cure you next. In a little bit."

"No, not when this is what happens to you–"

"I can't let you live with it anymore. It hurts me, too. I feel–I feel like it's in my own body." Her eyes meet mine in a haze. "Alarm bells in my head. That's what I heard the night you kissed me at the party, and I accidentally touched your back. I heard it–again, when you brought us our things at the fortress, and I threw that book at you. It was my healing powers telling me something was wrong."

Close. She's close to the truth.

"I will help you."

"No, Misty. I have to get you out of this."

"So you'll just–what? Die?"

"An Alpha doesn't leave his pack behind." I smooth my hand over her forehead, into her hair. I can't tell if she's warming up, but she sighs under my touch, her eyelids fluttering again.

"My family could help."

I nod, chewing the inside of my cheek as she slowly submits to the darkness pulling her under. I run my fingers through her hair until she stops leaning into my touch–asleep.

She's right. Her family could have helped–years ago, when Richard first started coming into power. It's far too late now, now that he has the *Book of Whispers* and has unlocked the magic he's wielding–turning my homeland to a barren, cursed underworld. Turning my people into monsters. Using those monsters as his puppets, his army.

And his army is coming. The attack on TU was the last phase of his plan. Now, he has Serpentia, and Serpentia has the Gate of the Gods.

If he gets it open without Misty's help... it's over.

I listen to the mind-link as I walk through the castle. Orion has Lacey hidden. Lavender just brought Georgia and Luke to say goodbye to Misty, who's dead asleep and has no idea I'm separating her from her friends. Luke is going to take the cryptex with him when he crosses the border into the Deadlands with instructions to find someone in the royal family and hand it off.

He couldn't figure it out. I don't blame him for that. It's disappointing, but that's just the way it is.

Minute by minute, the last wave of my people are moving toward the border. My warriors—those who're still untouched by the curse—are herding the last holdouts—the last Alphas who'd refused to leave—toward safety. Then, my meager forces, my loyal warriors untouched by Richard's magic, will return to Oasia and we will... fight until there's none of us left. We'll beat Richard down until he's weak, and Misty's family can sweep through with their massive armies and unlimited power, ending what I couldn't.

There will be nothing left of Tarsian when it's over.

But I can't just abandon it. My home, my people....

I locate Orion a few minutes later, stepping into his family's private quarters in the castle. Lacey's shivering, barely awake, on a couch with Declan kneeling beside her, talking in low tones.

Orion turns to me, pale and flustered. "Is Richard here yet?"

"No, but I'm sure he's on his way." I glance at Lacey before stepping closer to Orion. "Get them out, now. Don't wait. Use the tunnels."

The tunnels date back to King Kane's era—when people were escaping his wrath, trying to reach the Roguelands, to reach freedom.

Funny how things never change.

"Declan and Luke are going to carry her," he says under his breath, motioning to his mate.

"You're going—"

"I'm not. Neither is Commander Abernathy. Neither is Lavender." He holds my gaze, daring me to argue.

"You realize this is a death sentence, right?"

"I promised your father I'd have your back through this."

"I'm the king now," I remind him, but he shakes his head.

"I made a promise to my friend to protect his son."

A tingling sensation coasts through my brain, similar to the mind-link–but painful. A deep ache spreads through my body, making the scarred symbols roar to life. I resist the urge to pitch forward, to brace my hands on my knees.

"Richard's here." I hold Orion's gaze. "Get them out, now. We're out of time. I'll make sure he stays busy."

I go on to tell him Declan, Luke, and Georgia will be traveling with at least six maids making their escape tonight during the storm. Flooding in the tunnels is going to be a problem if the rain is torrential, but we're out of options.

They'll swim to the border before I let more people fall into Richard's hands.

I head to the throne room. Like clockwork, the high ranking court members funnel out of their lairs, their eyes glowing green–summoned by Richard's magic.

These men and women were once friends of my parents. People we could trust, who we loved.

Now they... simply don't exist anymore. They stare at me with blank, green stares as I pass them, refusing to look into their familiar, yet wholly changed, faces.

I reach the throne room in a haze. Blood stains cover the once white mosaic tiles. I imagine Lavender on her knees scrubbing her own daughter's blood from the floor like it's happening again, right now.

But I'm alone, left with only memories of that horrific day.

I sit on my father's throne–my throne–and wait.

The room begins to fill with green-eyed monsters. Alphas trapped here, their Lunas, their adult children and heirs. Maids and male servants. Warriors who hadn't been able to escape Richard's clutches. They stare, and wait, in silence.

Several cloaked figures appear. Richard leads his pack–his order of demons–his loyal few with their normal, uncursed eyes flanking him.

Nathan has the audacity to smirk as he stands a few feet behind Richard when the monster comes to a stop below my throne.

"I thought you were in Serpentia," I drawl in a bored, uninterested tone that betrays my rapidly thundering heart.

Richard smiles, chuckling under his breath. "I had some business to take care of here before sending my forces to Serpentia. I'm sure you understand why."

I tilt my head. "Would you care to explain?"

Richard doesn't fully trust me. He shouldn't. I don't blame him for hesitating before he admits, "You've put me in a bind, *Alpha King* Cole. You have something I need."

"Well, I'm using *her*, so your master plan is going to have to wait until my heir is born."

"You think the Allied Kings are going to wait to attack?"

"I think they want their princess protected, especially since she's with child." I smile cruelly even though my heart is shattering in my chest. I haven't given myself a single second to accept, let alone think about what Misty told me in her power haze. The idea that she's actually pregnant is horrifying. I tried–I tried to stop this from happening but… I'm out of control around her.

"Then you've succeeded," he says with marked disappointment.

My fake smile widens. "Yes."

Richard purses his lips, motioning Nathan forward. "Well, now that that's done, you can come to Serpentia with me as planned."

I watch Nathan step beside Richard. My blood simmers, my vision filling with red.

Richard continues, "Brother Nathan will ensure the little witch is *taken care of* in your absence."

Nathan smirks again, and I rise. "If you think I'm allowing the princess out of my sight, you're delusional. She's carrying my heir."

"Don't worry, Your Highness. You have a few days to continue playing with your little pet. It's her birthday soon. I've already started planning her… *party*."

"What?" I growl under my breath.

"Her birthday party. She's turning twenty-one!" Richard barks a laugh, looking at Nathan, who nervously returns it with his own laugh. "I'm dying to see what kind of wolf she becomes. Brother Nathan had the honor of meeting her family last spring and learned so, so much about them. Did you know they come into their powers in full at twenty-one?" His smile is sick–twisting his gnarled old face. "I wonder, King Cole, if you've seen what else she can do? Especially since you've been the one holding her down.... I wonder, does she fight it? Or does she writhe when you're between her pretty little legs?"

"Enough," I snarl.

"What can she do, Cole?"

I walk toward him, balling my hands into fists. He pulls his cane from his cloak, pointing it at me in warning.

"You're not allowed to remain in the castle. You know you're unwelcome here," I growl. I look at Nathan, edging toward him with every intention of tearing his head from his body. "And you," I snarl, leaning down so we're face to face, "you had the honor of meeting her family–the possibility of joining their ranks. Was it worth it, I wonder, to break her heart like you did?"

Nathan pales, leaning away.

"Oh, don't tell me you've caught feelings for that stupid whore," Richard chuckles.

I turn my wrath on him. "Get out of my castle. Get out of my city. You camp on your precious highway."

He smirks, tapping Nathan with his cane.

I look down, noticing the outline of symbols beginning to fade into view on Nathan's hands.

"You fool," I tell Nathan, knowing that he asked for this, to be cursed, to be part of whatever world Richard promised him.

Richard begins to turn away. "We'll be back in a few days for the party."

"There will be no party."

"Let's not forget who's in charge here, boy," Richard grins.

I hold Nathan's gaze until he finally turns away, and the group falls out of sight. The rest of the cursed onlookers fade into the shadows, going back to pacing their rooms, trying to think past the curse to remember who they are and why they're here.

The rain starts to fall when I find Orion again. He tries to ask me what happened, but I silence him with a hand, saying, "I need Declan to carry a message for me to the border. I have an idea about how to get Misty out."

25

WHO HE REALLY IS

Misty

I'm dreaming. I know this is a vision—a glimpse into life happening far, far away. I think I love this power the most.

I think I'm somewhere on the far northern coast of Crescent Falls, near the border with Celestoria. It's definitely one of the fog-soaked islands—an obscure, rural pack territory.

I stand on a hill overlooking a cottage. Yellow, winter grass hugs the little house, smoke rising from its chimney. A young woman with mousy-brown hair steps outside, bundled in a coat, hiking a messenger bag over her shoulder as she turns back to the door and smiles, saying something to the woman standing just out of view within.

Then, I'm following the young woman as she walks toward the village. She smiles at a few people and wolves she passes. Her eyes are a soft gray—Cole's eyes.

This is his sister, Annabel. This is where she lives now.

I watch as she steps into the yard of a single story stone building. Children dart in the brisk, cool winter air, chasing a ball around.

189

Other's funnel into the building carrying backpacks, mingling with each other.

Annabel stops in the courtyard, kicking the ball back to the group of seven or eight-year-old boys, and says something to them I can't hear, tapping her watch.

She follows their progress with her gaze as they dart into the school where she teaches.

But a group of men walking by catch her attention. They're packed for a journey—duffle bags hanging over their shoulders as they turn toward the road leading toward the port where a boat awaits to take them… to war.

I watch as Annabel stares longingly at one man in particular. He stops to look at her. He's handsome in a rugged way. Tall and strong. Likely my brothers' age. He gives her a sad kind of a smile, raising a hand to her.

She waves sadly at him in response, but her eyes tell me everything I need to know.

She loves this man, and based on the broken look on his face, he loves her back.

He disappears into the mist with his group, and Annabel dabs tears from her eyes as she turns to the school entrance and walks inside.

I expect to be torn from the vision now, to find myself in someone else's living room, watching another scene play out, but Annabel pauses in the doorway.

She turns slowly, her eyes scanning the courtyard before she looks directly at me.

"How is he?" she asks in a dreamy, far away voice.

I look over my shoulder, thinking she's talking to someone else, but everyone else has faded from view.

I turn back to her, confused and more than surprised. I remind myself this is just a dream, but she says, *"Cole? Is he all right? Is he taking care of himself?"*

"As best he can," I answer. *"He—He tends to take care of everyone else more than himself."*

"I know," she says with a soft smile. *"He's always been like that. He'll be a great king."*

We stare at each other. She starts to turn back to the door but thinks better of it, saying, *"He's not the monster he wants you to think he is."*

"I know."

"He–He's been waiting for you. He wanted nothing more. It was his dream."

"What dream?"

"You," she says, matter-of-factly. *"His–"*

I'm yanked from the vision. Gasping, I blink into hazy, gray light that fills my eyes and burns for a moment before Cole's face comes into view.

He sighs, laying his hand over my forehead. "You talk in your sleep," he mumbles.

"What time is it? What day? How long–"

"You've only been out for most of a day. It's past midnight now." He leans out of view and returns with a... blood pressure cuff?

"I don't need that," I groan, closing my eyes against the light of what I realize is a lamp. The room around us is cast in soft light, but the sound of thundering, ceaseless rain howls throughout the room as the dead sleep loosens its grip on my body and mind.

Cole bunches it in his hands, pursing his lips as he sets it back in a giant bag resting on the edge of the bed. I sit up, scowling at the bag. "What've you been up to?"

"Checking your vitals." His cheeks go a little pink as he stuffs a stethoscope back in the bag. "I just gave you a shot of adrenaline to wake you up. You need to eat."

A slight, pinching pain flares to light in my upper arm. I rub the spot, frowning at him. "I have healing powers, remember?"

"Yes, and I'm a physician. While you laid here like you were dead, I did what I needed to do to make sure you were going to wake up again... eventually."

He rises and gives me his back as he packs the rest of the bag and leaves it on a table across the room, his body cast in shadow. I watch him lift his head to look out the windows, at the rain, and decide that Cole is a sensitive, big-hearted *softy*.

I continue watching him with interest as he fixes a plate for me, choosing the best pieces of fruit, the crispiest pieces of bread. He wordlessly fluffs the pillows behind me and tucks me in tight before handing me the food and taking a seat in the little sitting area across the room.

I nibble on the food, watching him instead, watching the way he crosses his legs and rests his head in his hand as he pours over a page in his notebook.

I wonder what he was like during his school years. Was he popular at TU? Did he play sports, hangout at the bar and party with his friends… or was he quiet? Did he spend his days, and nights, in the library? Did he prefer the quiet solitude of the study hall over the busy, noisy common rooms in the dorms?

I bite into a grape and watch him scribble notes–notes I'm sure are about me.

"You have a habit of staring at me," he says under his breath.

I frown, stuffing another strawberry into my mouth to stop some smart-ass remark from leaving my lips.

"If you're still hungry, I can try to cook you something… I dismissed the kitchen staff and the maids earlier today." He closes his notebook and rises, walking toward the bed. He looks slightly guilty right now as he taps the spine of the notebook against his palm, his eyes meeting mine. "You likely don't remember, but Georgia left today. She came to say goodbye. I have it on good authority that she'll reach the border by tomorrow morning."

I swallow my food but feel an emptiness creeping in. "She's safe, then?"

He nods, sitting on the edge of the bed with a sigh. "Declan and Luke left as well, as did Orion's mate… Lacey."

"Is she okay?"

"She will be. You did, in fact, break the curse." His eyes hold mine–soft, and…warm. Something about Cole in general is comforting. His presence rewires my brain, honestly. I tend to get lost in my own head, burdened by my tangled thoughts. I mask that part of me—the anxious part, the part that likes to slip into doubt—by being sharp and commanding. By talking over everyone, butting into business I have no reason to be in…. I constantly find distractions to keep myself busy so I never have to feel too deeply into my own head.

And then there's Cole who I think enjoys being in his head. I think he enjoys being alone—craves it, actually.

We couldn't be more different. He couldn't be more different than any man I've ever known.

I'm not sure I deserve his kindness, honestly.

I doubt, had our situation been different, I would have given Cole the time of day.

And that fact makes me feel horrible.

"How are you feeling?" he asks quietly.

I blink, wondering how long I've been sitting here in silence. "I'm fine, really."

"Are you feeling… pain, anywhere?"

My heart. My heart feels heavy and broken as I try to work through the feelings creeping through my body.

"No," I lie, and he gives me a look.

"Something's wrong," he whispers, arching a brow. "You're not arguing with me, so you must be in pain."

"I'm not in pain," I assert, dragging my knees to my chest beneath the thick blankets covering my body. "I'm just thinking."

Cole holds space for me in silence. He doesn't pry. He doesn't nudge my shoulder and tell me to chill, like Nathan would have done. In fact, Cole just… waits. He waits for me to be ready to talk to him about what's going on in my head if I want to.

"I don't get you at all," I say, dropping my eyes to my fingers as I knit them around my knees.

"You don't get… me?"

"You're not what I expected you'd be. Kenna—my cousin?"

"Yes, I know Kenna."

"She doesn't like you. She never really explained why, but when you kidnapped me, it made more sense that you're some kind of monster than knowing that you're actually *this*–" I wave a hand at him for emphasis, not that my words make sense.

"Kenna doesn't like me because we went into the same kind of study," he says softly. "At least, that's what I think happened. In truth, I never got a chance to really know anyone in your family, so I can't be sure what the reason is, but I assume it's because I became a doctor, and she also studies medicine."

Kenna can be rather competitive, so that makes sense to me.

"What did you expect me to be like?" he asks, genuinely curious.

"A typical Alpha male," I groan, leaning against the pillows. "Full of yourself. Cocky and arrogant."

"I'm sure I can be like that–"

"When you need to be. That's the difference." I lean forward again, reaching for his hand, toying with his fingers instead of picking at my nails like I want to. "You're really nice. I'm not used to that."

His fingers curl around mine.

"It's not fair that you're going through this," I say softly, lifting my eyes to his. "Alone."

"I can handle it."

"I don't think you can." I hold his gaze, seeing the first hints of raw emotion behind his carefully crafted expression. "You're really good at this–pretending. Being all stoic and emotionless. It's probably what makes you a good doctor."

"I never said I was a good doctor–"

"You've been fussing over me since we met," I say in a strained voice. "You care about me. But I'm... I'm in your way here, aren't I?"

"No," he breathes, shaking his head as he leans toward me. "Misty, that's not–"

"You should hate me," I tell him with a trembling voice.

"No," he murmurs, reaching for me. "Stop. Hating you will never be an option."

"But all of this is because of me. The attack on TU–"

"That wasn't your fault."

"My friends getting roped into this–you being stuck with me, having to use me as a breeder just to–just to try and protect me–"

He leans his forehead against mine as I start to come apart at the seams. "That's not how I feel, Misty. I don't hate you. I'm not–I'm not taking care of you because I have to. I'm here. I'm here with you, beside you. I'm here for you."

I close my eyes. He cups my cheek, tilting my face to his.

"I saw you for the first time the day before the attack. Do you remember?"

I nod, imagining the moment in my mind when he'd passed with a group of order members flanking him. He'd paused to look at me a second time, smirking ever so slightly while I'd glowered at him instead of bowing like Georgia.

"You glared at me," he laughs, his eyes narrowed and heavy with emotion I can't describe. "And I was so thankful for it because, at the moment, I knew you'd be okay. Whatever I was forced to throw at you, you'd handle it."

He rises over me, lowering his body against mine, balancing on his elbows as he presses his weight into me and I... relax. The way this man's touch can ease my anxious mind and heart needs to be studied.

For a moment, Cole's expression relaxes, too, replaced by a dark, heady look in his eyes, and I thrum to life beneath him. I arch my neck, chasing his mouth with mine, but he doesn't lean down to kiss me.

He snaps out of whatever came over him and asks, "Do you remember making that blade with your powers?"

"No," I answer honestly, but my tone is weak and needy. My lips part as he drags his thumb over my lower lip. He watches the movement, his eyes locked on my mouth.

"You're incredible," he whispers, finally meeting my gaze again.

"I'm not the one sacrificing everything for my kingdom," I say hoarsely and instantly regret it.

Cole's eyes change. His mouth briefly brushes over mine before he pulls away, clearing his throat as he leaves the bed. He paces a few steps away while I lie here feeling empty–and cold.

"Richard is here, in Oasia."

I blink, spurred back to reality. "Why?"

"He's throwing you a party," he breathes, tucking his hands in his pant pockets. "For your birthday."

I sit up, shaking my head. "Why would he do that?"

"He's under the assumption you'll come into the powers he suspects you have–the powers he needs to open the Gate of the Gods. You've already developed those powers, though, judging by what you did for Lacey." He turns to me looking apologetic–and a bit nervous. "Can you shift yet, Misty?"

"I don't think so," I tell him, unsure what exactly he wants from me right now. "I haven't felt anything–wolfish, yet."

"Do you want to try?"

26

VISITING THE PAST

Cole

MISTY SLIDES OUT OF BED, UNEASY ON HER FEET. SHE PACES A FEW
steps, stretching her arms over her head with a sigh.

I watch, and wait, for her answer. I'm not totally sure why I asked
if she wanted to try to shift. Maybe it's because I'm actively plotting a
way to get her out, and if my plan fails, she's going to need to *run*.

"I'm not ready," she says, matter-of-factly.

"That's fine."

She looks down at her hands. "I don't feel any changes yet. Nothing. Is that normal?"

I sit on the edge of the bed. "Yeah, that's perfectly normal. Most
wolves don't come into their shifter powers until the day of their
twenty-first birthday, sometimes a few days before, or a few days
after," I remind her.

She sighs, picking at the fabric of her pale cream nightgown. It
hugs her body in a way that has my mouth going dry, but I force
myself to ignore those feelings and focus on our conversation instead.

My wolf has other priorities, however. She turns into the lamplight, which highlights her naked figure behind the gown, and I feel the urge to grab her and pin her to the bed–or shift.

I close my eyes, desperate to calm down, when she says, "Both of my brothers came into their wolves as teenagers. So did my dad."

"What about your mom?"

She sighs, shrugging. "I think she was… normal, but she lost her wolf for a while."

"Do you feel anything like–urges?"

"What kind of urges?"

I open my eyes to Misty closing in on me with short, timid steps, still clutching her nightgown.

Where do I begin? I almost ask if she feels what I feel. That pull. That tingling, overwhelming sensation all throughout my body when she's near, but I… can't.

Not when she's looking at me like this, her pupils widening and cheeks going rosy.

I rise, clearing my throat. I can be stronger than this. I can fight the thoughts screaming at me to keep her, to turn this fight against Richard into a fight for her, for not just her future, but ours.

That's not fair to even consider.

She reaches for me, but I edge past her, heading for the door.

"Where are you going?"

"For a walk."

"Can–can I come?"

I nod, motioning her forward. Barefoot, she pads toward me, looking unsure and a little confused as I grip her fingers and lead her through my apartment and into the quiet, darkened hallways of what was once a busy castle.

Misty's footsteps beside me are silent, but mine echo through the darkened corridors.

"Where are we going?" she whispers.

I shrug. "You haven't had a formal tour. We could do that now."

"Is it safe?"

I sigh. That's a very good question with a complicated answer. "Right now, it's just me and you, so it's about as safe as it could be."

"Did Georgia really leave?" She swallows hard.

I glance down at her. I wonder how much she remembers from the night she healed Lacey, broke her curse, and then slipped into a frozen stupor.

Memories of what she'd said to me in the bathtub sprint through my mind. *I think I'm pregnant.*

She hasn't said a word about it since.

I walk her through the ball room, which is dark and bathed in blue light as lightning cracks through the sky, illuminating the ceiling height windows and domed, glass ceiling.

"Georgia, Luke, Declan, and his mother left a few hours ago. Marcella, as well."

She nods like she's internally digesting this news, but her eyes shine with mingled grief and understanding. "How did you get them out?"

"You mentioned catacombs," I begin, leading her into the formal dining hall where a sweeping mural replaces the glass ceiling. "You're right about them. They exist, and they connect the major cities in Tarsian. Georgia is traveling through them right now, I suspect." I explain that the catacombs beneath Oasia connect to a crude tunnel system that stretches for nearly forty miles, with an even cruder rail system to shorten the trip.

She's well versed in the history of Eastonia being not only a proto-history major but a member of one of the royal families. Still, her eyes shine with unease as we cross into the kitchen, which is empty and sterile.

"Are you hungry?" I ask.

"Can you even cook?"

I roll my lower lip between my teeth, shaking my head. "Never learned."

She leans on the massive kitchen island, giving me the softest of smiles. "Me neither. I guess, since you dismissed your entire staff, or they're cursed, we'll just have to starve."

"Lavender's still here. She wouldn't let that happen to us."

"Why didn't she leave with Marcella?"

I motion for her to follow. We leave the kitchen, maneuver through a network of servants' hallways, and reach a set of large, ornate doors.

I hesitate, my hand curled around the door knob.

Her hand rests on my back. I feel the slight pinch of her healing powers fluttering over my skin beneath my shirt.

"I'm all right, Misty."

She pulls her hand away, tucking it behind her back. "I can't control it. Whenever I touch you, my powers ignite. I can't help it."

"You need to train those powers so you have full control over them."

"Well, maybe if I hadn't been so rudely kidnapped, I would have had a chance over Solstice break," she murmurs.

I look down at her, fighting a smile. "Abducted."

She rolls her eyes but gives me a cat-eyed smirk, for whatever reason, I feel the strength to open the door into the throne room.

Lightning splits the sky overhead, showering light through the glass ceiling. Misty follows me, looking skyward, her lips parted in amazement.

But then her gaze falls on the twin thrones on the far side of the room and the once-white tiles now stained a dark brown only a few feet away.

She stops walking. I keep going, turning around after I've put a sizable distance between us.

"This is where it happened, isn't it?" Her voice carries through a crash of thunder. "Adrian and Elsbeth died here."

"They did." My voice echoes as rain pounds against the glass, sending a hum through the throne room.

"I—I saw that moment. You had a nightmare in the car. I was there with you."

I'm not sure what to say. She steps toward me, her hands outstretched.

"It was the worst day of my life," I admit, curling my hands into fists to stop from feeling the blood on them like I'm still kneeling here, holding Adrian to my chest. But my grip loosens when Misty's eyes flicker with faint light, her hands still outstretched. "What are you doing? Misty?"

Light flows from her fingertips–gentle and mist like, curling in steady streams that illuminate the room.

Figures appear from the mist, thrumming with sparkling light. Elsbeth and Adrian standing side by side, their voices muffled and dreamlike as a third figure approaches.

It's me.

I step out of my way, watching as my likeness approaches my friends. I remember this moment. Adrian and Elsbeth tell me that they're having a baby. Marcella is on the way.

My likeness picks Elsbeth up and spins her in a circle, light flying through the air in glimmering sparks.

I slowly turn to Misty. Tears stain her cheeks, but she gives me a weak smile before grimacing, sending her powers flaring across the room.

Children of mist and light dart across the tiles. Trees made of the same magic appear as me–when I was a child–chasing my older brother through the woods toward the village I grew up in the mountains outside Tarsian.

I whirl as more memories ignite. Me, graduating from TU. Me, stepping into the hospital in Crescent City for my first shift during my residency. Me, kneeling by the fire and handing Annabel a solstice present–that leather messenger bag I bought when she started her schooling to become a teacher.

Me, walking past Misty, seeing her for the first time, feeling the mate bond snap into place.

Me, finding her again at the Arcane Umbra party, kissing her, feeling so desperate and broken knowing it was too late to save her.

Me, desperate to get her out. Me, losing my mind trying to heal her after those order members nearly killed her.

Overwhelmed, I turn to Misty, tears in my eyes. Her eyes glow with power.

The magic images fade, turning to specks of light that bounce around my feet.

"I don't—don't know how I did that," she stammers, sucking back a sob. "I'm sorry—I'm so sorry, Cole, I shouldn't have."

I run to her, scooping her into my arms. Thunder booms over-head, followed by crackling lightning that bathes us in blue as I kneel with her in my arms.

She caresses my face, pressing her nose to mine. "I hate this."

"I know." I have to fight for the words. "Misty, I'm sorry."

She runs her fingers through my hair, choking back a sob before pressing her mouth to mine. "Let's leave. Right now," she says against my lips, desperation lacing each word. "Both of us."

"I can't," I rasp, closing my eyes against the pain spreading through my chest. "I can't leave my kingdom behind."

"But you've done enough!" Her voice sounds so broken.

"I'm the Alpha King."

"You never wanted to be!"

"Misty," I breathe against her cheek, pressing her body against mine. Her trembling kiss shatters my heart.

I'll never forgive the Goddess for this—for thrusting us together when I was already on borrowed time. For giving me her for so little time.

Misty deepens the kiss. My body answers, a groan leaving my lips as she grinds her hips against mine.

That other force takes over. That need I haven't been able to control. My wolf begs to mark her, to knot her, to claim her as mine.

Her nails claw the back of my neck before drifting into my hair. My hands drop from her hips to her thighs, bunching up her dress until I feel her warm, soft skin under my touch and squeeze.

She lets out a soft, needy moan that rewires my brain, and I'm instantly lost to the need to be inside of her.

I lay her against the tiles, covering her body with mine.

She breathes sharply as she fumbles with my belt and zipper, but in a matter of seconds I'm nudging her legs apart, my pants and boxers pooling around my knees, and pulling her panties to the side.

She arches off the floor, my name leaving her lips in a sharp gasp as I bury myself to the hilt, her inner muscles squeezing me so tight I lose the ability to breathe.

"Gods," I pant, groaning sharply as I thrust into her again, slipping an arm under her lower back to tilt her hips toward me.

The new angle has me coming unglued immediately.

She pulls me down, her mouth crushed against mine. I pin her leg against my hip and grind into her until she gasps and moans, taking shallow breaths. Noises I'll dream about later, when she's long gone, safe again with her family.

Her orgasm rips through her, leaving her trembling and shuddering in my arms. I pull her close, forcing myself to savor this moment, this feeling, the way she's undoing the horrible memories of the throne room and giving me a sense of peace I haven't felt since the day my world fell to pieces.

I come undone with her arms wrapped around my neck.

Those fine threads binding us, threads she can't feel yet, sing with both satisfaction and the crushing heartbreak of knowing this is the last time I'll be with my mate like this.

She's limp and panting in my arms when I pull out, reaching down to right her nightgown. I mouth three words into her hair before kissing her, long and slow.

She's leaving in a few days. Her—and our child.

I failed to protect her from that.

I can't let her stay. It was never an option.

Neither is me going with her.

This is it. This is all we get.

I carry my mate to bed.

27
JUST DO IT

Misty

I FELL ASLEEP CURLED AROUND COLE IN THE LATE HOURS OF THE NIGHT. He'd laid me in bed, and I'd immediately pulled him back to me, not ready to give him up just yet.

I can't tell myself this doesn't mean anything anymore. This feeling–this overwhelming ache–isn't growing weaker, and I'm desperate for a way to keep him.

I drew lines over his chest and stomach as we fell asleep in each other's arms, the sheets tangled and pushed to the edge of the bed, listening to the rain pour over Oasia.

But I wake up to Cole sitting straight up in bed.

I rub my eyes, blinking into the darkness. "What's wrong?"

He shushes me, his body rigid as he scans the room.

Fear creeps through my body. My heart skips a beat as he slowly, silently, slides out of bed and pulls on his discarded pants, fastening his belt. Still, he looks around, his eyes narrowing as somewhere in the depths of the apartment, a door clicks shut.

I shoot upright. He heard it, too, and holds out a hand in a motion that tells me to stay still, to stay here.

He edges toward the door, which is slightly ajar, and waits.

My heart bounces up my throat as terror blinds my senses. Seeing Cole like this–rigid and… worried… it does something I don't like to my brain. Anxiety rushes in, followed by adrenaline, and my ears start to ring in warning when Cole slowly opens the door a little further.

"Cole," I hiss as he steps out of the room, my heart thundering.

He ignores me, standing stoically in the doorway, his back muscles flexing while he scans the living room.

It happens fast. One second, he's here, and the next, a figure in black is tackling him to the ground back into our room.

I scream as the figure brandishes a blade and tries to jab it into Cole's neck, but Cole rolls with the man toward the bed.

I jump to my feet, running to the end of the mattress. "Cole!"

A second figure enters the room in a black cloak with his hood covering his face. He looks at Cole before turning his head in my direction, his profile catching the faint, dreary morning light coming through the windows.

Nathan narrows his eyes at me then stalks in my direction.

I hold my hand out in warning. "Don't come any closer," I snap.

He pulls a long blade from his cloak, the curved metal barely visible in the darkness. Cole, meanwhile, gets on top of the first man and snatches his knife from him, lodging it in the stranger's throat. A sharp gasp of pain echoes around the room, but Cole's already on his feet and barreling toward Nathan.

"Stop!" I shout, worried I'll hit Cole with my powers instead of my intended target–my disgusting ex-boyfriend.

I'm not sure what to do. I gape as Cole sends a fist flying, his knuckles splintering against Nathan's jaw. But Nathan is… different. Cole's normally much stronger than him. Cole's built, and fast, and Nathan is more a "gym rat" than the man I love–

Love. The word tangles through my head at the most inopportune moment. Stupidly, I leap off the bed and crash into the men just as they collide.

Cole grunts in pain when my elbow collides with his collarbone. The three of us hit the ground–hard–falling through a dainty little table.

Nathan doesn't make a single sound. He rises, quick on his feet, and grabs my leg.

I kick wildly, my toes meeting his groin with a crunch, but he doesn't so much as flinch.

That's when I notice the faint green light creeping through his eyes.

Panic drowns my senses. "Cole!"

Nathan drags me across the floor. Cole is on all fours, trying to catch his breath. I turn to look back at him at the same moment he pulls Nathan's blade from his side, blood spraying. Nathan stabbed him right in the ribs.

Fear clouds my senses. I go slack, unable to tear my gaze from Cole as he sways, trying to catch up to us, but he has to brace himself on the doorframe while Nathan continues to drag me away. "COLE!!"

I reach for him, begging my powers to activate, and send a beam of what I hope are my healing powers toward him.

Something hits me over the head–hard.

My vision blurs. I choke on my own breath, fighting the sharp, throbbing pain echoing from my left temple. Pressure builds behind my eyes while I'm pressed into the tiles and quickly realize Nathan is stepping on my head as hard as he can.

It hurts so bad. I grit my teeth, my eyes water as I watch Cole struggling to stay upright–fighting his way toward me while blood gushes from his side. His eyes shine like he's trying to shift. He's too hurt. I can see it in his gaze as desperation whispers over his face.

I reach for him again, crying out as I send my healing powers toward him. Just as my light fans over Cole, and Nathan lifts his foot to no doubt crunch his boot through my skull, Cole shifts.

There's blood everywhere. His gaping, open chest wound erupts but doesn't stop him from careening toward Nathan in all his wolfish-glory. Cole is a massive wolf. Huge, and fast, he leaps off his claws and collides with Nathan.

I roll away, landing back on my belly, and watch in horror as Cole tackles Nathan to the ground, busting through the bistro table where I would have been having breakfast a few hours from now.

Nathan writhes, trying to kick out from Cole's hold, but Cole rips into Nathan's chest with a massive golden claw.

Blood gurgles through Nathan's scream. I feel a pinch of regret for him. A single sliver of the feelings I used to have for him flare to life.

That hesitation–the sudden need to call out to Cole to tell him to stop–must show in my face because Cole says into my mind, *'If you want him to live, tell me now. You can heal him, but you need to know that he asked for this. He wants to work with Richard, and he likely asked to be cursed.'*

My mouth goes dry. I think of all our good times. Introducing Nathan to my family. Flirting and giggling at the bar in Serpentia. Kissing in shadowed corners of the university. Watching his track meets...

But then I think of my Grandpa Maddox and his concerns, his doubts. I think of Nathan's lying. His affair. His lying, again.

How he would have killed me just now if Cole hadn't stopped him.

I nod, but close my eyes as Cole bites through Nathan's neck.

I hear the sound of flesh tearing and... and Nathan's head rolling across the tiles...

I pinch my eyes shut, stifling a horrified sob as a larger thud echoes through our sleepy, normally quiet and totally spotless apartment–now wet and crimson with blood.

A scream tears the air. Lavender's shrill, terrified voice breaks as she cries, "Oh, my Goddess! Where are they?!"

Three sets of hurried footsteps rush in my direction, but I can't look away from the scene in front of me, not now that I've opened my eyes.

Cole is bleeding profusely, lying limp in his wolf form next to what's left of Nathan's mangled, headless body.

I crawl, ignoring Orion's shouts, ignoring Lavender bellowing as she sobs. I ignore the third male voice, lifted in alarm. I imagine it's Cole's commander, Abernathy, whatever his first name is. I reach Cole's side and flatten my hands over his chest, sending my healing powers ripping into his body, stitching him back together again, piece by piece.

But then Orion kneels beside me, his hand on my back. "Do it. Cure him."

"Richard will know." My voice doesn't sound like my own. It's far away, dreamy, and nearly lifeless. I'm so tired of this. I just want to wake up beside Cole. I want to eat breakfast and go for a walk, to go to the store to buy groceries and get distracted by Solstice decorations like a normal couple. I want to bicker over our Solstice plans. I want to take him to see my family and vice versa. I want to fall asleep with him in our bed, in a home we share and made *ours*. I want a future where he slides a ring on my finger and calls me his wife. I want to cry with him in our car when we drop our kids off at kindergarten for the first time. I want to watch his hair turn gray and the creases around his eyes grow with age.

I want a different life with him.

I want a shot at that.

But that isn't what fate had in store for us, is it?

Tears cloud my eyes, roaring down my cheeks and falling onto his fur. Orion rubs my back like I'm one of his children that he's comforting, his fingers curling around my shoulder in solidarity. "Leave the scars but kill the curse. You can do it. I've seen you do it."

I meet his eyes. They're pleading, filling with tears. "He won't leave, even if I break the curse."

"But he won't be Richard's puppet anymore. Give him this. Do this for him."

"He doesn't want it."

"He will never admit that he'd lost his will to live–to even try– until he found you. Do this for him. Give him a chance–"

My powers surge against my will. My wants, hopes, and dreams blur my actions. Maybe it's selfish. Maybe he'll look back on this moment and hate me, but I won't let him die like this. If he wants to die in a blaze of glory fighting for his kingdom, fine. Be my fucking guest, Cole. But I won't let a curse spun by a madman take him.

I'll kill him myself before I let Richard hurt him anymore.

Isn't that what Cole said he'd do for me? Kill me so Richard couldn't have me?

I close my eyes as the first wave of the curse fights back. I know the feeling now. I know the push and pull of my powers fighting something ancient and terribly strong—something that doesn't want to give him up.

But, he's mine. No one else—nothing else—gets to have him. Just me.

Orion stays by my side as my powers untangle the curse. I don't need a blade of mist this time. I take it apart, fractal by fractal, turning green light to ash, turning the bloody room around us to a cloud of smoke so thick I can't breathe, but I don't give up.

Cole's curse runs deep, and it takes all of my strength—all of my power—to erase it. But, I leave the scars. They'll be there forever—a constant reminder of what he had to do for his kingdom and for me.

Maybe Richard won't notice it's gone with the scars still in place. That's my hope as my body starts to freeze, my powers shuddering until they flicker out.

I'm barely aware of Lavender behind me, her shaking hands cupping my face so I have to look into her teary eyes.

"You did it, sweet girl," she hums, giving me a sad smile.

I don't feel Commander Abernathy trying to scoop me into his arms and barely register him telling Orion he's going to put me in the tower for safe keeping.

But then Cole's voice echoes around us. I blink, and he's here, his body draped in a robe someone must have thrown onto him when he transformed back into his human form. He takes my face in his bloody hands and kisses me deeply, ignoring the eyes watching our every mood.

"Thank you," he murmurs against my lips.

I feel myself slipping, falling into that dark, endless sleep. I can't fight it this time. I used my powers to their breaking point repeatedly, over and over, for weeks now. Healing him, healing others, fighting for my life against the terrors of our situation.

I slip in and out of consciousness for the next two days. Cole is always here–with me. I'm not sure he's left my side. I pick up bits and pieces of the conversations he has with whoever visits our apartment in the castle–which has been cleaned of blood and the bodies removed. I heard mention of a dress. Cole wants it to be pink, a specific shade. Bubble gum. My favorite color.

But he's sad and stressed. He knits his fingers in mine when we're alone and tells me stories about his childhood, his brother, and Annabel.

On the second day of my second power haze, I hear Lavender's voice drifting through the room, and something strange on my belly–cold, and firm.

"There's a heartbeat," she whispers, softly, her voice a drifting flicker of noise in my numb brain.

"Have they confirmed they'll come? It's been days," Cole replies in a broken voice.

"Not yet, but this is her only chance to get out. Both of them."

I slip back into the darkness with Cole's fingers squeezing mine.

2 8

MESSAGE FROM THE ENEMY

Ryan

THERE'S A RIVER THAT RUNS THROUGH THE DEADLANDS. THE SAME river that splits Eastonia in two. On the other side, mountains hug the horizon, blurring the view of Tarsian beyond. In the Deadlands, the river is… wide, but still. A large, lumbering stretch of clear water that weaves through the plains.

Here, in the Roguelands, in what used to be a city called Twin Rivers, now nothing but a husk of what it was twenty or so years ago when Ryatt and Ella were young, that same river is angry and narrow, full of rapids and rock.

Sydney stands beside me as I watch the water—the shattered ruins of bridges running across it at several points.

And the rowboat fighting the rapids.

Sydney straightens, narrowing his eyes at the group of warriors shouting at the few men inside the boat who are shouting back for help as the rapids send the boat lurching in a circle. The women on board scream—shrill and terrified.

"There's a child on that boat," Sydney growls under his breath, gripping my arm for a moment before we rush toward the water's edge, splitting through the group of Rogueland warriors.

"Throw them ropes!" I shout. "Now!"

Freezing rain pelts my face, turning the once snowy ground to slush and pockets of pure, glare ice. It's nearly pitch black, save for the light of lanterns hung on posts, highlighting sunken pathways used by warriors taking their meal breaks along the water's edge. My boots slip over the frosty river bank as I watch the warriors toss a rope to the boat as it passes–and miss.

Sydney and a few of the warriors rush down the bank, shouting commands at the frantic people inside the boat.

I run to Sydney, snatch the rope from one of the warriors and throw it myself.

A young man with light brown hair, wearing a black cloak, catches it. His soft blue eyes meet mine, terrified and exhausted, but he winds the rope around his forearm as the boat careens toward another set of absolutely gnarly rapids before the river takes an abrupt turn out of my sight.

It's the middle of the night. If the boat is full of refugees from Tarsian, like we believe, we'll lose them around that curve.

I hold the young man's gaze as the water rips the boat away. He's going to break his arm in half once the rope goes taunt. He knows it, too, based on the look on his face. He grimaces with determination and bites down on his scream as the rope snaps straight, and the little boat careens toward our shore.

We've been doing this for days… catching boats. Herding terrified, soaking wet refugees to shore. They're coming from all over. Small pack territories in the mountains. Desert territories. Some come from as far as the southern sea surrounding Serpentia.

But most of the people rushing to the river these days are from Oasia, and this group is no exception.

A young woman with dark skin and curly black hair sobs as she tries to untangle the rope from their hero's mangled arm. He's pale white, biting his lip so hard blood drips down his chin. Another man stumbles onto the rocky shore, followed by six or so young women dressed in tattered uniforms. Everyone is crying. Everyone is battered and exhausted, covered in grime.

The older woman being lifted from the boat with a baby who can't be much older than Maeve is—she's—

"Get a healer down here, now," I snarl to one of our warriors, giving him a shove as I step past him to the woman's side.

She's covered in scars. On her face, her wrists... even her fingertips. She's wearing a hat but I can tell the scars continue into her hair. She shies away from me when I reach for the infant in her arms, the baby bundled against the cold. She clutches the baby, terror in her eyes while I physically pry the baby from her hands. "I'm not going to hurt her. You need help—"

"You're her brother."

I turn with the baby in my arms—who squawks in panic at being held against the chest of a stranger.

The young woman is staring at me, tears in her eyes, her dark curls sticking to her cheeks.

"Oh, my Goddess," she sobs, trembling in the cold. "You're one of the twins, aren't you?"

Sydney approaches, narrowing his eyes as he scans the woman's face.

"You're—you're Sydney," she says to me, her lips parting in a sad, desperate smile. "You're Sydney—"

"Ryan," I correct, juggling the now screaming, absolutely terrified baby. Out of the corner of my eye I see Sarah and Aviva making their way toward us through the gloom, both wearing identical expressions of confusion. "Who are you?"

"Georgia," Sydney says under his breath. "You're Georgia, aren't you?"

Tears of relief fill Georgia's large, brown eyes. She nods, sucking in a breath. "I—I am. Misty—Misty's still there—"

Sydney takes Georgia by the shoulder, sweeping her to the side, toward the muddy track leading to the rows of tents and open fires of the warrior camp. "I'm taking her to see Ryatt."

Georgia curls in on herself, reduced to shuddering sobs. Behind me, the rest of the people from the boat are being tended to.

The baby slaps me in the mouth and screams.

"Goddess, let me take her," Sarah rushes out, snatching the baby from my arms. "Where's her mother?"

I blink, shaking my head. "I have–I have no idea."

Aviva steps to my side as Sarah rushes away with the baby. I watch her go, my head spinning as Aviva turns, her hand gripping mine, to the rest of the people from the boat. They're being herded away to be interviewed, warmed up, and tended to, but one of the young men is arguing with a warrior.

"I'm supposed to–"

"I don't care what you're supposed to do. I said, get in line!"

"I was commanded by the Alpha King of Tarsian to–"

"That makes you an enemy!"

I let go of Aviva's hand as the warrior shoves the man, no older than nineteen, to the muddy ground. Whatever the young man was holding falls from his hands and bounces across the rocks, hurtling toward the water.

"Hey!" I shout, snarling at the warrior–one of Sydney's warriors from Crescent Falls. I storm toward them, yanking the young Tarsian man upright while Aviva runs to the river bank to fetch his fallen object.

"Get off!" he shouts, shoving against my chest.

"Who are you? Where did this group come from?"

"Oasia," he snarls.

"Obviously," I bite out, dragging him toward the camp, but he digs in his heels, turning to look over his shoulder at Aviva.

"Stop–Look, I was told–I swore I'd give that to someone in the royal family!"

"Well, I'm the royal family, and so is the Alpha King of Crescent Falls, and the Alpha King of the Roguelands. They're here, too, so it's your lucky day–"

"Declan has a message from Cole for Misty's dad," the man chokes out, still fighting my hold. "It's imperative it's delivered!"

"Cole?" I look down at the man, letting him go.

"Alpha King Cole," he rushes out, trying to catch his breath as he rubs his arm. "Cole. He–He has a way to get Misty out of Oasia. He sent us–he sent us away and made us promise to get the message–"

"Which man had the message?"

"The guy who just broke his fucking arm!" he shouts, throwing his hands in the air. "You have–gods, you have no idea what we had to do to get here. The tunnels–" He runs a filthy hand over his face, dragging fresh tears over his cheeks. "My dad–my dad's still there. He wouldn't leave. He wouldn't leave Cole."

Aviva reaches my side carrying a muddy, oval hunk of what looks like stone at first glance.

It's been weeks of this–this waiting. This stressing over whatever details are brought over the border. Tales of groups of refugees being caught and separated by Alpha King Cole's warriors on his side of the border merge and distort with accounts regarding what sounds like a coup–like Tarsian is being completely overrun by an unknown enemy and what's left of Tarsian's ruling class is trapped inside, the king included.

All we know, based on what little intel we've received, is that Misty is alive, and presumably safe, but in the Alpha King's company.

This kid makes it sound like Alpha King Cole is a fucking buddy, not a ruthless dictator who killed his own father to take over an entire kingdom... and then straight up kidnapped my baby sister.

I grab the man by the arm and start dragging him into the camp again while Aviva tries to wipe the dirt off his–whatever the hell it is.

"What's your name?"

"Luke Abernathy," he chokes out.

"Where is Misty right now?" I rip around a corner, dragging him through the mud, his tattered sneakers sliding as a city of canvas comes into view. Wolves and warriors mingle around fires. Generals carry out commands as I escort Luke toward the edge of the encampment.

"She's at the castle in Oasia, under Cole's protection."

"Oh, is that right?" My tone is cutting and dripping with sarcasm.

"The same guy who told our parents he'd be using her as a breeder, and if they made any moves to invade, he'd kill her?"

Luke squeaks in pain when my grip tightens on his upper arm. I catch up to the warrior leading the other guy, Declan, I guess, to the commanders' tent on the far side of camp.

"Ryan!" Aviva's voice carries in my direction at the same moment I snatch Declan out of another warrior's grasp and start dragging both men toward the tent.

I ignore her, which I rarely do. Normally, Aviva is the only thing on my mind. Actually, she's always the only thing on my mind... until what feels like our entire world went to war. A week ago, when refugees began showing up in the Roguelands from Oasia and carrying news that Misty was there, we'd been called here. The whole fucking family–stuck here, in tents.

Enjoying my pregnant wife's body while knee deep in mud, slush, and Goddess knows whatever filth hasn't been on my radar since we arrived.

Aviva's voice fades completely when I toss both men into the commander's tent. My dad looks up from the rickety desk at its center where a map of the Roguelands is splayed before him.

"Give it to him," I snarl, pointing at Declan. "Now."

"Give me what?" Dad rounds the desk as Declan rises and fishes in his jacket, pulling out a crumpled letter. He gives it to Dad with a trembling hand, refusing to look him in the eye. Dad takes it, his eyes meeting mine for a moment before he turns his back to us and opens the letter.

"Up," I say to Luke, snapping my fingers.

"Ryan–" Aviva shouts, sliding into the tent with a huff.

But Dad goes rigid. "Get Ryatt."

Sydney follows Aviva into the tent. "Georgia's with the healer. She can confirm Misty's okay, and the baby belongs to–"

"Get Ryatt, *now*!" Dad bellows, crumpling the letter in his hand. He doesn't look at us but motions to a trio of warriors standing near the entrance of the tent, the letter crumpled between his fingers. "Get these two something to eat, put them up in one of the tents. They're going to Moonrise in an hour."

Moonrise? I step out of the way as they usher Luke and Declan out, leaving just the family. Me, my mate, and my twin brother.

Sydney shoots me a look dripping with both concern and confusion as he excuses himself to find our uncle in the muddy chaos beyond the tent.

"You and Aviva will be returning to the Deadlands within the hour," Dad says under his breath, flattening a map of Tarsian on the desk, his forefinger brushing over Oasia, then tapping. His eyes meet mine, heavy with an emotion I've never seen cross his face. Vengeance. Murderous, furious vengeance. "Have your army ready to invade Tarsian."

"When?"

29

BUBBLE GUM PINK

Misty

LAVENDER FANS OUT THE SKIRT OF AN IMPOSSIBLY PINK GOWN. I STARE at my reflection in the mirror as she kneels, adjusting the hem.

I'm swimming in a sea of bubble gum. It's not even my best color. It does nothing for my skin tone, or my hair, or my eyes.

But this color has always been *mine*. And somehow, Cole knew.

I smooth my hands over the tight waist, the boning, the satin fabric that flares out at my hips. It's a real ball gown–fluffy and extravagant. I'm already a princess, but right now, I actually feel like one.

"My mom would flip if she saw me in this," I say with a huff, my throat closing around the words. How many times have I promised myself I'd stop crying? A hundred? A thousand?

"In a good way, or a bad way?" Lavender asks, rising to adjust the poofy sleeves that taper at my wrists.

"A good way." I blink back tears. "She's going to hate that she's missing my birthday. Probably more than she hates the idea of our family being at war over Solstice. It's her favorite holiday."

221

Lavender swallows hard, nodding, but obviously unsure what to say to comfort me right now. It's useless. We both know any kind, reassuring words are absolutely pointless right now. Last night, three days after being nearly killed, watching Cole get stabbed, listening to Cole literally rip my cheating ex-boyfriend's head off, and then healing Cole and breaking a vicious, ancient curse... I woke up to the news that Richard is here, in the castle, setting up camp with over a hundred of his order minions. Apparently, he has my birthday wrong–because the party is tonight.

My birthday is tomorrow.

"Where's Cole today?" I ask, my mouth going dry. I haven't seen him in days. He'd been around when I was in my second power-coma in the course of a week, of course. I have fractured memories of him fussing over me.

But ever since I woke up last night, I've been alone.

"He's had his hands very full," Lavender says quietly.

Yeah, no shit. Still, I want to see him. I want to talk to him, to ask if he has a plan for this party. I also want to just... be with him, for a moment. See him without knowing the curse is still in his body, his blood.

"Let's finish your hair now," Lavender says under her breath, motioning for me to move to the vanity where she's set up a station full of hair pins and makeup.

I let her paint me like a porcelain doll. She twists my hair into an updo, pinning meticulously crafted curls on the top of my head with gem-encrusted clips and pins.

I ignore my reflection, staring down at my nails instead, lost in my tangled thoughts.

"Cole's avoiding me, isn't he?"

"No, sweetheart," she whispers, giving me a sad smile in the mirror. "He's...." She bites down on her lip.

"It's because I'm pregnant, isn't it?"

She pales. "No–"

"I remember. You did something. A scan, or something."

"I confirmed it, yes," she says under her breath, her cheeks flaring with heat. "I–I shouldn't have, without your permission, but Cole was worried… for both of you, after your latest power… surge?"

I bite back a smile. "So, I'm pregnant, then?"

"There's no longer a midwife here, seeing as she's cursed and lurking downstairs somewhere in the servants quarters, but we had what we needed to confirm that, yes, you're pregnant."

I finally meet my eyes in the mirror. Cole must be so… so….

She squeezes my shoulder. "He loves you."

"Don't say that." I turn from her and rise, striding across the moonlit bedroom to where a pair of heels have been laid out on the bed–just as pink as the dress.

"Misty. We should talk about this–"

"There's nothing to talk about, especially tonight." Especially about the idea of Cole loving me. The idea of Cole choosing me over this war with Richard.

Lavender huffs a breath before storming in my direction. She stops short, however, as I throw her a look and sink onto the edge of the bed to strap my heels around my ankles.

"Cole never wanted this."

"I know that–"

"I don't think you understand," she grinds out.

"Who wants a war, Lavender?" I snap.

"That's not what this is about–"

"I don't know what *this* is!" I start to break–again. My heart is on the verge of shattering. I'm not sure the incredibly tight bodice squeezing my breasts is enough to hold it together.

"Cole loves you. You are everything he's ever wanted. You should know that, before whatever tonight brings our way. This would have been easier on him had you not been involved–"

I scoff; she winces. "That didn't come out like I meant it to."

"It doesn't matter," I rush out, blinking rapidly to stop fresh tears from ruining my makeup.

"It does matter," she asserts, her hands on her hips. The look on her face screams she's made up her mind about something, and I remember that this woman is a mother—was a mother—and had a daughter, like me, at one point.

I know I'm supposed to just shut up and listen right now, even if her opinion about Cole's feelings for me is the last thing I want to hear.

"I've known him since he was a child. His mother and I grew up together. I worked in this castle with her when we were new maids. I was there when Jaxon fell in love with her, when she found out he was her mate. I helped get her out, into hiding, so King Kane wouldn't find out she was pregnant with Adam. I was there when Cole was born," she says with a sad smile. "And he wasn't born to be a king."

I look up at her. She gives me a very sad, but knowing, smile as she continues, "He never wanted this. I'm not talking about a war, or a curse…. He never wanted to be king. He still doesn't."

"Then why is he fighting so hard to keep it?"

"That's not what he's fighting for." She sits beside me. "He's fighting for you. To give you a chance to get out, to be free, to have a life, even if it means he loses you."

"I've only known him for a few weeks. He can't feel that way about me yet."

"I think you know he's felt this way about you since the moment he saw you."

I bite the inside of my cheek.

Her hand rests on my lower back. "Cole and his father didn't get along. It started after Adam's death, of course. Cole became the heir by law, and Jaxon required him to leave the village where he was raised and come here to finish his schooling, to train to be a warrior, to be a king. Cole fought him the whole time. At one point, Cole hated Jaxon. They… couldn't be in the same room together without screaming at each other. His mother and I chalked it up to Cole being a surly teenager."

"Why did they hate each other so much?"

She shakes her head. "Cole made it clear he had no intentions of being Alpha King. Jaxon wasn't giving him a choice in the matter.

When your aunt, Queen Ella, rose to power... Tarsian was nothing. It was a desert full of rogue packs, Alphas living in the shadow of the rebellion against Kane. Jaxon was one of those rebels. His pack was the largest, the most organized. He was charming and sharp—exactly what your aunt needed to control this area of Eastonia, so she made him Alpha King, and Cole, as he grew up, had different ideas about what Tarsian should be."

She rises, pacing away from the bed as she continues, "Cole grew up looking toward the future, while Jaxon only saw the past. Cole believed more than one Alpha King was necessary for our kingdom. It's the largest, by far. The most geographically challenging. We have deserts, mountains, and coastlines... hundreds of miles between the largest packs.... Cole knew it was already too much for Jaxon, who barely saw his mate and children."

"And Cole wanted to be a doctor."

"Yes," she says weakly. "He did." She sighs heavily, shaking her head. "He believes Ella should take over Tarsian, expand her powers here, choose her favorite Alphas and have multiple Alpha Kings."

"Cole would dismantle his own kingdom?"

"He doesn't see it that way, no," she replies. "He saw the way it was killing his father. He didn't want that for himself. Maybe, had Adam lived, Adam would have kept the kingdom intact and ruled, starting a family dynasty, but Cole... no. He wanted quiet. A little house in some cute neighborhood in Crescent Falls where he could drive a car to an even cuter clinic somewhere downtown. He wasn't a child of Tarsian, even though he was born here. He never belonged here. He wanted more."

"A clinic? Not the hospital?" I find myself lost in Lavender's vision of what kind of life Cole would have chosen for himself, had he had the option.

"He was halfway through his residency in pediatrics when he was called back to Tarsian," she says softly, sadly.

"He wanted to work with kids?" My heart cracks, threatening to shatter into tiny shards with no chance of mending them back together again.

She nods. "He'd come home from TU, when he was studying his undergrad in biology, with sketchbooks full of blueprints for his future clinic. How he'd paint the walls with murals like a circus and…" She trails off, heartbroken. "When he was accepted to medical school in Crescent Falls, Jaxon knew Cole wasn't coming back. That was it. He'd lost his heir, and I believe that might have been the reason he allowed Richard to sweep in with his grand vision and design for Tarsian. I think Jaxon believed he could tempt Cole to come back, and I know… I know it killed him when that failed, when Richard got the best of him, and Cole returned to Tarsian to clean up his father's mess. Cole wanted… a wife. Kids. The family he didn't have growing up, and even though Jaxon died by Cole's blade… the fact that he killed his son's dreams is what actually took his life."

Silence chokes the room. She paces toward the windows, looking out at the full moon. "Cole is a good man."

"I know," I reply hoarsely.

"You gave him a few weeks of… the life he should have had, and I will be forever grateful to you for that."

I chew my lower lip, closing my eyes as I fight for the words I'm looking for. How do I say that I'm not ready to give him up this easily? That my entire heart is here, lost to him? I'll never be the same after this is said and done. Whether he's my mate, or not. I would have felt that by now, right?

I'll know tomorrow, I guess. Probably. If I ever come into my wolf.

Footsteps sound in the depths of our rooms. I turn to Cole, my heart lifting with excitement but… It's not Cole.

Commander Orion approaches wearing a tuxedo. He looks stiff and uncomfortable as he clears his throat, bobs his head at me, and slides his gaze to Lavender. "It's time."

"She's ready," Lavender replies, nerves and heartache clear in her tone.

I turn to Orion. "Where's Cole?"

"He'll be there," Orion replies, but I shake my head.

"What's going on? He's planning something, isn't he?"

Orion purses his lips and glances at Lavender. "Did he tell her?"

"No," she echoes, and now I'm getting pissed.

"Tell me what?"

Orion gently takes my arm, tucking my hand in the crook of his elbow. "It's time for your party, Princess. Our guests are waiting."

3 0

YOU KNEW THE TRUTH

Misty

"Do not speak to anyone," Orion says as we walk through empty, entirely too quiet halls. "Do not look any of *them* in the eyes, and do not, under any circumstances, use your powers. Any of them."

My grip on the crook of his arm tightens as soft, slightly off-key music starts to sound through the hall, mingling with our footsteps.

"Them, as in, Richard and the order?"

"No," he replies, his voice like gravel. We turn a sharp corner, and the grand foyer erupts into view–undecorated and cold… and full of green eyed members of this court, this castle.

Maids and servants. Alphas, and their Lunas. High ranking warriors and commanders.

They funnel into the ballroom as if in a trance, their eyes glowing green and bodies covered in open, bleeding symbols.

My stomach pitches and turns. My dress feels too tight. I can barely breathe.

One man stops walking. He slowly turns his head, that green light flickering several times–like he's fighting for control–before the

229

single sliver of self he has left is yanked from him, taken over by the curse once again.

Orion flinches, grinding his teeth.

"Do you know him?"

"He was one of King Jaxon's commanders." He quickly motions at a trio of young women passing into the ballroom behind him. "His daughters—triplets."

"They can't be more—more than thirteen! Richard is cursing children?!" My voice is a low hiss, my eyes locked on Orion's to stop myself from staring at the monsters passing us by.

"We got most of the kids out before it got bad. But... the curse spreads." He starts guiding me along, edging into the ballroom. "We had a few biting incidents, only when the curse had spread to the point the afflicted were no longer aware of who they were. That's how Richard got to the families, especially here, in the castle. Families didn't want to be separated, and at first, refused to leave. Cole put an end to that, pushing everyone out. This is who's left." He motions to the ballroom—to the green eyed zombies standing still as stone.

But a group of men in black cloaks zooms past us. I nearly jump out of my skin in alarm but notice Orion eyeing one of the young men in particular. This group doesn't have green eyes. No scars mar their fingers, necks, or faces—the only parts of their bodies visible. The man holds Orion's gaze, nods, and to my great surprise, winks.

Oh, shit. I was right. Something's happening tonight. That's why Cole isn't here. I watch the order members weave through the crowd. I turn and spot more men in black cloaks, recognizing a few as order members who left the fortress and traveled with us to Oasia.

I was right about Cole being part of a different faction of the order. He has people on his side, people who are... going to fight. Tonight.

This is happening tonight.

My heart beats out of rhythm as the crowd parts, and Richard appears, cackling menacingly as he claps his hands. "Princess Mystica. What a vision you are."

Orion grinds to a halt, tugging me close. I hold onto him for dear life.

Do not use your powers. Do not use your powers. Don't, Misty. The words bounce through my skull as power prickles in my fingertips. I curl my nails into Orion's suit jacket and glare at Richard as he walks toward us, inspecting me like I'm a prized mare.

"What a gods awful color," he snorts, his eyes narrowing as he walks a tight circle around us. "I suppose not everyone can have good taste."

"My skin-tone is far too warm for black," I fire back as he rounds us, coming to a stop in front of me and way too close for comfort. "If I were more sallow and lifeless, like you, I might be able to pull it off."

I smile as his lips thin. He checks his watch, smirking. "It's nearly the end of the night. So, show us this wolf. I've been dying to see it all day."

"You got my birthday wrong," I grin, giving him a practiced, princessy giggle. "I'm not twenty-one until tomorrow, but thank you for the… party? It's rather dull, isn't it? No one's even dancing."

His eyes glow with faint power, and suddenly the music erupts, and several green-eyed couples swing onto the dance floor and dance like they're being pulled by strings.

Richard is the puppeteer, after all.

My heart races. I steal a glance at Orion as Richard whirls and walks away. "So," Richard snarls, "We wait."

The dancers swirl around me and Orion, but my eyes are on Richard as he moves toward his posse–his loyal order members. Cole's faction blends in with their black cloaks, hoods drawn over their heads.

Orion takes my hand and leads me into a dance. "Princess Mystica," he whispers, his eyes tracking Richard as we spin, and spin, barely aware of our steps. "You're going to come into your wolf in ten minutes."

"I'm a late bloomer, apparently. I feel nothing."

Orion heaves a breath, his eyes scanning the far side of the ballroom as we waltz, careful to put a good bit of distance between us and Richard's monsters. "Still, Richard isn't going to leave you alone once the clock strikes midnight. You need to be prepared."

"Prepared for what, exactly?"

A hush falls through the room as the dancers come to an abrupt stop. Orion turns with me in his arms as heavy, steady footsteps sound, echoing through the room. Overhead, moonlight streams through the glass ceiling, highlighting the ghastly, scarred faces of Cole's trapped court… and Cole, himself.

He's dressed in all black–an insanely well-fitted tuxedo. His dark blond hair is swept back away from his face–longer than it used to be, when we first met. His eyes are stern and cold as his gaze sweeps the room.

But then his eyes meet mine and hold. His gaze softens to something edged with heartbreak.

My heart stops beating as he makes his way to us and extends a hand.

"I owe you a dance."

I slide my hand into his. "Why?"

"Because I was very late to your birthday party."

For some reason, the look in his eyes makes me wonder if he planned to show up at all, but before I can think too deeply, he sweeps me into a dance.

No one else is dancing, and there's no music, but his heartbeat leads the way, timing our steps.

"You are high bred, aren't you?" I tease.

His hand slides down my back, tugging me closer. "One of us needs to be able to dance. You're lucky I know the steps, otherwise your party guests would be laughing at us."

"If they could laugh," I whisper, and make the impulsive decision to lay my cheek on his chest.

We couldn't be closer if we tried. Several minutes tick by like this– us swaying in silence, dancing to the sound of our mingled heart- beats. It's crushing. This… horrific sadness. This sudden, blinding knowledge that whatever we had is coming to an end… right now.

"I love you," he says so softly it shatters my heart.

"I know. I love you, too."

"I'm so sorry–"

"Don't, please–just–just stay with me. Let me–let me help you, somehow. Let me fight by your side."

He tilts my chin so I have to look at him. Our dance draws to a close in the deafening silence.

"I love you," he repeats, firmer this time, like he wants me to know–*needs* me to hear him say it. He pulls me close, clasping my face between his hands as he lowers his head to mine, brushing a tender kiss over my forehead. I grip his jacket until my knuckles turn white. Something's supposed to happen any second now, right? I turn into a fluffy, furry wolf? Richard attacks us? Whatever Cole's plotting comes to fruition?

"Promise me something," he whispers, dipping his head, his lips barely brushing my cheek.

"Anything."

"Don't tell the baby who I was."

Shock runs wild through my body. I grip him harder, unsure if I heard him correctly. "Cole–"

"Promise me. Don't tell him who his father was. The kind of man I had to be. *Please.*"

I look up at him as the clock strikes midnight. I feel the change. It's an unfamiliar pull that skitters through my body, settling deep, deep in my bones.

Cole kisses me in a way that's both familiar and shockingly new. My entire body thrums to life like I've just been struck by lightning. Cole's scent overwhelms my senses as his tongue slides over mine, deepening the kiss to something so intense I feel the sudden need to–to mark him.

My mate. My mate. My mate. My mate.

He stumbles away, panting. I stand, shell shocked and shattered.

"Cole," I rasp. "This whole time? You knew, this whole time?"

Richard's shocked, cackling laugh erupts all around us, echoed by his puppets who's eyes cast us in an eerie green glow as they move closer, but I'm looking at Cole as he shakes his head.

I'm looking at my mate while the world topples, shattering like glass.

Richard's muffled voice echoes all around us, "What an interesting development! Our fearless leader's little pet is actually his mate. How devastating–"

"I couldn't tell you. I thought I'd have you out of this by now. Misty, I am so, so sorry."

"You knew we were mates since the attack, didn't you?"

"Before," he admits.

"Cole," I squeak, stunned.

"The moment I saw you. That's why this is so fucking complicated, Misty. I had to use my own *mate* as a breeder." He paces back in my direction but his eyes are on Richard, his voice lifting in volume for the entire room to hear. "I had to watch *my* mate be beaten and dragged," he snarls, then his eyes meet mine again, softening. "That night you got attacked by those order members, you nearly died in my arms. I promised I'd never tell you after that. I couldn't put you through anything else–"

"You fucking asshole," I weep, my voice breaking over the words. Part of me wants to rage, to slap him, but only because he wasted so much time. Precious time. Time we could have had together knowing we were mates. But my words are lost to a thundering jolt of energy that explodes through the room. The glass ceiling cracks as black mist funnels all around us, drifting between me and Cole.

My eyes go wide as two men come into view.

"*Dad?*" I choke, my heart leaping out of my chest.

Dad starts to run toward me, but Uncle Ryatt grabs his shoulder.

Cole looks at them, panting, looking both relieved and heartbroken. "You're late," he growls, baring his teeth.

I look wildly to Richard, on the far side of the room. His eyes are as big as teacup saucers as he fumbles with his cloak, drawing out his cane.

Ryatt's silver eyes blaze with power as he arches a brow at Richard.

"Go," Cole shouts. "Take her, now. And go!"

"Cole–" I grab his arm. "Cole, come with me. Please. Please come with me!"

"I can't," he says hurriedly as Richard starts screaming orders.

I sink my nails into his jacket, my other hand flat on his chest. "Please. Don't do this. Just leave. Stay with me. *Please!*"

He holds my gaze, shaking his head.

"Misty," Dad's voice is hoarse, choked with emotion.

"You asked them to come, didn't you? You invited them to this party knowing he'd be distracted."

Cole just stares at me, his chest rising and falling with shallow breaths as he shakes his head.

"I'm not leaving without you," I push, gripping his arm. "I won't. You're my mate, Cole. I love you–"

He rips his arm out of my grasp and takes several wide steps away from me, moving closer to Richard.

"Cole?" My voice trembles. "Cole–" Dad runs up behind me, grabbing my arm. "COLE!"

"Princess Mystica of Crescent Falls," Cole thunders, his eyes filling with furious tears, "With the Goddess as my witness, I reject you as my mate."

Pain. Blinding, roaring pain burns through my body, my soul. Threads in my chest that bind me to Cole–threads I hadn't known were there–pluck loose, fizzling to ash.

I scream his name as he turns his murderous gaze on Ryatt. "Ready your forces."

Suddenly, the room bursts in chaos. Cole's warriors attack, and then Richard's monsters–

Dad snatches me around the waist.

Cole turning to Richard and shifting is the last thing I see before I'm pulled apart by my dad's and uncle's magic.

31

WHY THEY TOOK HER

AVIVA

A SHIFT IN THE AIR WAKES ME UP WITH A START. I SIT UP, REACHING TO peek through the blinds. Snow falls in lazy spirals, blurring the tents rising in the pastures just outside the Silverhide village in the Deadlands.

Nothing seems amiss, but...

Ryan lifts his head from his pillow, blinking into the darkness.

"Did you feel that, too?" I whisper.

He groans with the effort of leaving our warm bed, stumbling in the darkness as he pulls on a pair of sweatpants. "Stay here, okay? I'm gonna check it out."

We've grown used to the noise of having several hundred warriors sharing our space—our village—but this wasn't a *sound*. It was a feeling that's still lodged in my chest as I ignore Ryan's command to stay in bed and follow him through the quiet house.

This feels like deja vu. Weeks ago, when Misty had been taken, this exact same thing happened. We felt a shift—like the air in the village parted—and then received earth-shattering news.

Ryan's thinking the same thing I am. It's been a rough night. One marred by stress and the uncertainty of Ryatt and Isaac having gone to Tarsian and Ryan having just returned from Navvan, where most of our army is located at this point, after delivering the news we could be going to battle by daybreak. We found solace in each other, closed away in our room, tangled together under our sheets, ignoring the what ifs.

Now, we're staring them in the face.

A blood-curdling scream echoes through the village before we even step out onto our front deck. Ryan takes off in a sprint as the scream tapers off, replaced by bone-shattering sobs.

My heart quakes as I tie my bathrobe around my waist and tear after my mate, wearing nothing but the robe and pair of slippers. Black mist settles all around the center of the village as three figures come into view.

Misty's golden hair falls loose from an intricate updo as she pushes against Isaac's chest. He's holding her, wrapping his arms around her as he crushes her to his body like she's a child having a total breakdown.

"TAKE ME BACK!" she screams, her voice full of pain. "TAKE ME BACK! YOU DON'T UNDERSTAND!"

Isaac's shushing her gently, calmly, like she's still his baby. His eyes are glassy with tears as he struggles to keep a hold of her.

Ryan stands totally still several feet away, watching with marked concern as Misty–wearing an amazing pink ball gown–doubles over their father's arm and sobs so hard she can't breathe.

"T-take me back!" she chokes, sucking in a shattering breath before screaming again with so much sorrow my own eyes sting with tears. "Take me back to him. Please! *Please*, I'm begging you! He'll die. *He'll die there–*"

Ryatt turns to her, taking her face in his hands. "Listen to me, Misty–"

"YOU!" She bursts out of Isaac's hold and sends her hand flying, racking her nails over Ryatt's cheek.

He takes it. Closing his eyes against the pain as Misty screams at him, calling him horrible names.

"YOU COULD HAVE TAKEN HIM!" she bellows with heartbreaking clarity. "YOU COULD HAVE FORCED HIM TO COME WITH US! WHY DID YOU LEAVE HIM BEHIND? WHY!?"

"What the fuck is happening?" Ryan says under his breath.

Misty's sobs wake the village. People look out of windows, drawing back curtains, gathering in their doorways as the Princess of Crescent Falls breaks into pieces in her father's arms.

For a moment, she seems to be calming down, sucking in deep breaths, blinking away her tears, but... I taste metal on my tongue, and electricity crackles around my feet.

Misty shifts for the first time, tearing out of her ballgown. Isaac shouts a curse as he struggles to keep his grip on his daughter-turned-wolf. She claws the hell out of him in what I think might be fear, or surprise. It's her birthday. This is probably the first time she's ever shifted, and I doubt it was voluntary.

"Fuck," Ryan murmurs, watching with wide eyes as Misty leaps out of Isaac's arms and sprints on unsteady legs into the snowy night, her golden coat disappearing into the darkness.

We whirl to Isaac and Ryatt, who stare at each other for a moment before getting in each other's faces and arguing–shouting over each other's words. Isaac shoves Ryatt, seething, "You fucking knew, didn't you? You knew they were mates!"

"I didn't know," Ryatt snarls, shoving him back and then grabbing his jacket.

"Mates?" Ryan shouts over the chaos brewing between the other two Alpha Kings. "What the fuck are you talking about?"

I turn from the men, who have been at each other's throats for weeks. Ryan and I talked about it in length last night, when we heard they left for Tarsian together. He mentioned how this war is opening old wounds, reminding his dad, and his uncle, of a time when they were enemies–when they hated each other. Now, we're at war again, but they don't have their wives around as buffers.

They're just two alpha males fighting over who has the better idea, the better solution.

"She's my fucking daughter!" Isaac screams in Ryatt's face.

Ryan squeezes my arm before edging toward the men to try to defuse whatever's happening, and I… shift. I shift, and tear through my favorite robe, kicking off my slippers, and slink away unseen.

Poor Misty. I follow her tracks, noticing how she struggled to get her legs under her. Shifting for the first time can be tough. Sometimes, the transition can be painful, especially in the legs, on the paws.

I lift my snout to try to catch her scent then turn and sprint to the left, toward the towering mountains fanning each side of our precious valley.

It takes me a few minutes to reach her, still sprinting as fast as she can like she's running from whatever just happened. She doesn't look at me. She keeps her big, glowing blue eyes locked on the ridge line.

I can't do more than follow, keeping a few feet of space between us. We reach the ridge line, but she doesn't stop. She runs along it for a mile before dropping down again, near the hot springs and the lake below.

She slows when she reaches the lake, babying her paws like they hurt, which I'm sure they do. She pads toward the dock, her feet leaving deep paw prints in the snow, and lets loose a sharp, painful whimper before slumping to the dock.

I edge toward her, stopping a few feet from where she's lying. Her body shakes with wolfish sobs, pained whimpers echoing across the frozen lake.

'*Oh, Misty,*' I say, more to myself than through the mind-link. I have questions, of course. I'm sure everyone does. But instead of pestering her, demanding answers, I lie down beside her, laying my head over the back of her neck.

'*I missed you,*' I tell her quietly, gently.

She whines like she's in pain, and I think she might actually be in great pain, and it's not from shifting and running over ten miles first thing.

I press my weight against her, cuddling close, watching the snow gather on the ice as she cries, and cries.

* * *

"THEY WERE SUPPOSED TO TAKE HER DIRECTLY TO MOONRISE," RYAN says in a near whisper as he pours two cups of coffee at the kitchen table, and one mug of tea, for me, of course. It's the bitter, nasty stuff Kenna has me taking for my morning sickness. She's the only one who knows about our baby so far.

He glances at Misty, who's sitting silently on the couch in our living room, her legs tucked beneath her and body wrapped in a thick blanket.

The jewels in her hair glint in the frosty daylight coming through the windows, but her eyes are on the fire.

"Why didn't they?"

Ryan shakes his head. "I'm not sure. I think they just needed to get her out, to anywhere. While you were gone, I separated them. Ryatt disappeared in a puff of smoke, and Dad is somewhere blowing off some steam, I hope. I have no idea what happened."

Neither do I. I sat on that dock with Misty until she rose and shook me off, padding back to the village. She came here, to our house, and locked herself in the bathroom for over an hour before emerging in a pair of my pajamas, her face dry but gaunt.

Now, her eyes are red, and her face is so white she could blend with the snow gathering on the windowsills. She hasn't said a word.

Ryan sighs heavily and gives me a look before creeping toward his sister and extending a cup of coffee, but she doesn't look at him. She doesn't acknowledge him at all. He rolls his lower lip between his teeth and sets the mug on the coffee table.

I watch with bated breath as he turns from her, running his fingers through his hair as he makes his way back to me. "I'm going to go find Dad and make him tell me what the hell happened."

I nod, keeping my eye on Misty as Ryan shrugs into a jacket and leaves the house.

241

The second the door closes, Misty says in a broken voice, "He rejected me."

I lean my hip on the kitchen table, curling my hands around my mug of tea. "Why?" I already know it's Cole she's speaking about. I mean, *it has to be*. The fight between Ryatt and Isaac would make sense if that's the case.

Misty heaves a breath, her voice rattling as she replies, "Because he's going to die, and he... he didn't believe I could make a difference in that outcome. He did it to force me to leave." She shakes her head, her face contorting with pain. "I thought–he knows–" She pinches her eyes shut, sucking back a sob.

I'm at her side in an instant, sinking beside her on the couch.

"I'm pregnant," she whispers, her puffy, red eyes meeting mine. "I'm pregnant, Aviva."

"It's going to be okay," I urge, but inside, I'm spiraling.

"He told me–he told me to–to not tell the baby who he was. Cole is so... he's so broken. I thought I could heal that part of him. I thought I had. I healed his body, but the damage was done. He's been through too much and he–he doesn't see a future anymore. He gave up." She hangs her head, fisting her hair as she squeezes her eyes shut. "He's going to die out there like he planned. He turned on Richard. He told Uncle Ryatt to ready his forces, to get me out, and then he–he attacked. I don't know if he made it out. How could he have? I could have helped him. I could have saved him, but he wouldn't let me."

My hand ghosts down her back, steady and unyielding. She leans into my touch, her body moving toward mine on impulse. "It hurts to breathe," she whispers, choking on another sob. "I have a hole in my chest where our bond should be. I got–I got to feel it for a *moment*." Her tears soak into my shirt as she presses her face against my shoulder. "Now it's gone. He's gone. I knew when the sun rose, he'd be dead. He's gotta be dead now. There's no–no other way–"

"I'm so sorry," I whisper, the words barely audible over her choked cries.

"What am I going to do? What do I do without my mate? I held on," she says through gritted teeth, her grief turning to sudden fury.

"When he rejected me, I held on. I refused. I still feel—feel just a glimmer of what was there. How do I move forward? I can't accept this! I can't accept that he's going to die, and I did nothing."

Her words settle in my chest. The memory of storming back to Endova when I got the news that Ryan was dying rushes back, clouding my senses.

I know how she feels because I felt that same fury. That same hurt and desperation.

Mercy walks through the door without knocking, Freya close behind. I silently nod for them to come in, having called them through the mind-link for backup a few minutes ago.

But Mercy's face is pale and wan as she allows Freya to skirt past her, carrying an armful of precious handmade clothing and little treats to try to cheer Misty up.

"What's wrong, Mercy?" I ask as Freya kneels in front of us, laying a supportive hand on Misty's thigh.

Mercy swallows hard, shaking her head. "We just received the first reports from the border. It's begun."

Misty lifts her head, blinking at my sister.

"The battles have begun. We're officially at war with Tarsian."

32
NO GIRLS ALLOWED

Misty

It's morning. Early morning—still too early for the sun to breach the mountains and send light spilling over the village of Silverhide.

I roll over on the couch, wrapped in a thick blanket, and stare at the dying embers in the stone fireplace across the room.

I haven't slept. Pain echoes through my body, settling deep in my bones. It's not a sharp, bright pain. It's the kind that aches and throbs—a dull thrum of noise that makes it impossible to focus, let alone close my eyes and rest.

I feel empty. Empty, and alone.

'Why did you do this to me?' I ask through the sliver of bond I still share with Cole… I hope. I hung on so tight when he rejected me, refusing to let him do it.

But his voice is no longer in my head.

My eyes are dry and rimmed red as I watch the embers flicker like stars against a sea of darkness. I have no tears left to cry. I used them up. They're gone.

Ryan and Aviva's bedroom door opens nearby, a shadowed figure ducking as Ryan steps out of his room and pauses in the doorframe. His eyes scan my nest of blankets before settling on my face. He closes the door as quietly as possible when he notices I'm awake.

"Morning," he says under his breath.

My lips part, but no sound comes out. I feel boneless–unable to sit up. Too weak and depressed to even move.

He walks over to the couch and sits down with a groan near my feet, fisting a pair of thick socks that he wordlessly pulls on. He's dressed for... a journey. It's an Endovian outfit with all those weird loops and leather strings that can stretch to fit his wolf form, keeping him fully dressed when he shifts back to his usual form.

My stomach turns. He's going to the border right now, isn't he? His eyes–just a shade darker than mine–flick to meet mine as he straightens, huffing out a breath. "Sleep okay?"

"I don't think I slept."

"Yeah... me neither." He glances at his bedroom door with eyes full of regret. "Want to talk?"

"No–I don't. Not right now."

He rises from the couch, patting me hard on the thigh, before walking toward the worktable in their kitchen. I rise enough to peek at him, watching him tuck knives and long blades into a weapon belt and secure it around his waist. Ryan looks... not necessarily exhausted, but his eyes are glazed and heavy as he packs his things.

"Sydney's forces crossed the river in the Roguelands last night, a few hours after you arrived," he says into the silence. "The border in the Roguelands is secure now–under the control of warriors from Crescent Falls and the Roguelands. They're moving their armies over in preparation to invade. I'm heading to Navvan to do the same on our edge of the map." He murmurs the last words as he shrugs into a thick wool jacket, stuffing a pair of gloves in his pocket.

"Have you heard..." I trail off, my throat closing around the words. A dry, strangled sob works through my chest, painfully trying to crawl up my throat, but I force it down. Cole's face dances through my mind. The memory of his twisted, pained expression as he'd rejected me will forever haunt my dreams.

Ryan sighs, shaking his head. "Ryatt and Evander are in Oasia."

"What?" I sit straight up. "Uncle Ryatt–he went back?"

Ryan scans my face, his eyes going dark. "They brought Evander's Ghost army with them to do some reconnaissance while the rest of our forces move into the desert." He slides his thumb along the edge of one of his blades, lost in thought, then asks, "What happened, Misty?"

"I don't know where to begin," I admit, tugging my knees to my chest. "Ryan, I don't know what to even say."

"Then I'll help," he says under his breath, turning to face me. "Who's in charge in Tarsian?"

"Not Cole."

"So there was a coup?"

I nod, my lower lip trembling.

Before I can explain, he says, "This... Richard guy Dad keeps talking about... he retaliated against Cole for killing King Jaxon?"

"No," I rush out, sliding to my feet. "No, that's wrong. That's wrong, that's not what happened."

"I need to know," he says firmly. "I get you're not ready to talk about this, but we're sending thousands of warriors into Tarsian today, with more flooding in tomorrow, and the next day. Who is our enemy?"

"Richard. The Umbra Mortis. Cole didn't–King Jaxon was cursed by Richard. Richard has magic, Ryan. He has the *Book of Whispers*, and he used it to curse Cole's dad, and the Arcane Umbra society, and Cole's entire court... his pack..."

Ryan stares in disbelief. "This Richard person has the *Book of Whispers?*"

I hold his gaze, knowing exactly what's going through his head right now. His mate almost died this past summer because of that damn book, and now I have to confirm it.

"Richard used the book in the Deadlands, in Navvan. It was a test.

Thinking back on it, now that I've seen what he can do with those powers... he was able to curse that guy from Navvan."

"Hardan."

"Yeah," I murmur, picking at my nails. "And through Hardan, controlled the Rogues. I don't know how he did it, exactly, but Cole told me it was a test. A test of Richard's powers. And it wasn't a failure even though... your people prevailed. Cole told me Richard has an army. I don't know how many warriors he has, but if he spread this curse throughout Tarsian, it could be tens of thousands of people."

Ryan's seeing red. I watch the way he grips his blade before sliding it into a holster.

"What side is Cole on?"

"Ours. He's just trying to protect his people from this monster. He... was trying to protect me, and everything he's done... everything he had to do... was to try to protect me from Richard. He never wanted to use me as a breeder, but we had to. Ryan, I–"

The bedroom door opens abruptly. Aviva steps out looking a little green as she braces herself on the doorframe, hanging her head. Ryan stiffens, then says softly under his breath–so softly I almost miss it, "Fuck."

Aviva looks up, blinking into the dimly lit room and scans her mate's outfit and weapons. "Ryan?"

"Aviva, you should go back to bed. Sarah's going to be here any minute."

I look between the mates, trying to read their expressions. Aviva looks like she's slowly putting pieces of a puzzle together while Ryan looks guilty as fuck.

"Why is Sarah coming here?" Aviva glances at me. "Oh, to take Misty to Moonrise."

"And... you." Ryan meets his mate's large, coppery-brown eyes.

"What the fuck did you just say?" She shakes her head, laughing. "Goddess, this morning sickness... I hallucinated–"

"You're not going with me to the border, Aviva–"

"Yeah, I'm not," she confirms, giving him a confused look. "I'm going to Oasia with Evander."

Oh, shit. I take a slow step backward toward the couch as Ryan hangs his head.

Last night had been madness for everyone but me. I'd slipped into numbness, barely listening to the hurried conversation between Aviva and her sister, Mercy. Aviva left at one point, coming back to the house with Ryan, but I'd been pretending to be asleep on the couch. I couldn't hear their muffled conversation behind their bedroom door, but if the first battles on the border began last night, I assumed Aviva, our family's best warrior... much to Evander's annoyance at having been toppled from his podium... would be going to war, as well.

She wants to. This is what she's good at. What she was made for. Why the Goddess gave her that big-ass golden bow.

But now I'm realizing what I missed from the conversation, especially when Ryan says, "Evander and the Ghosts are already in Oasia."

"What?" Aviva gasps. "I–I overslept. They left without me–"

"No," he breathes, meeting her eyes. "Aviva, you're not going. You're not going to battle. You're going to Moonrise with the rest of the women in our family–your sisters, all of them, will be going, too. Freya and Dahlia–"

"Ryan!" she shouts, her eyes wide with confusion. "What are you talking about?"

"You're sick, baby," he says softly, painfully. "I can't let you come. I can't lose you–and our baby."

Aviva looks like she's about ready to rip my brother into pieces, and honestly, rightfully so. But... Aviva's *pregnant*. I saw that in a vision–her being so sick she couldn't eat, and Ryan so beside himself about how to help her–all while the family seemed to be counting on her to be the one rescuing me with Evander's help.

"You're leaving me behind," she whispers, hurt lacing each word. "No–"

"It's not up to me anymore," he asserts. "My dad–and Ryatt–know about that pregnancy now."

"You promised we wouldn't tell anyone until–"

"Until we were ready, I know. But I'm your mate. I'm your husband, and it's my duty to protect you. Both of you, so you're leaving. You're going somewhere safe until this is over."

Aviva looks shattered as she glances at me, shaking her head. "I'm going with you, Ryan."

"I can't let you do that."

Aviva pants, curling her hands into fists, just as Sarah walks through the door, bundled against the cold.

Ryan steps toward Aviva, but she turns from him.

Sarah goes a little pink when she senses the thick tension in the room and skirts past them to me, throwing her arms around me in a very tight embrace.

But over her shoulder, I watch as Ryan pulls Aviva against his chest, against her will. He murmurs something into her hair that's obviously meant for just them, and she goes slack, burying her face in his chest.

Tears finally sting my eyes again. Maybe I do have some left.

Sarah pulls out of the hug, clasping my face between her hands. "Goddess, I missed you. I knew you'd be okay." Her eyes betray her words, though. She takes in my thinness, my gaunt, exhausted features. "Everyone's in Moonrise. Your mom, too. She's very excited to see you. Hannah and Beta Cassian are staying in Crescent Falls, running things in her absence."

I hear the door to the deck click shut. We turn to see who left—finding Aviva standing in her pajamas, her hair loose and wild, tears glistening in her eyes before she wipes them away and turns toward their bedroom.

"We'll give her a moment to pack, I think."

I'm not sure what to say to her. I'm not sure what to say to anyone. The only person I have words for is Cole, and he's so very far away. Is he still in Oasia, I wonder? Did he make it out, or is Evander going to find his lifeless body in the castle he hated, in the court where he felt no ties, yet fought so hard to protect?

I think of Lavender and Orion, wondering if they made it out. Lavender, especially. Goddess, I'm going to miss her.

But then I remember Annabel, and Cole's mother.... Do they keep in contact with Cole, somehow? Do they know how bad things are in Tarsian?

Are they protected?

Aviva drags a duffle bag toward Sarah, refusing to meet our eyes.

Sarah's mouth pinches in a straight line as Aviva steps to her side.

"Are we ready?" Sarah asks.

I look down at my borrowed pajamas. I dig deep, wondering if now that I'm able to shift, I'll have access to those strange teleportation powers some of us inherited... so I can jump to Cole, instead.

But I feel nothing but that empty pain of his loss–of our shattered mate bond.

Aviva says weakly, "Get me out of here before I change my mind."

Sarah squeezes her shoulder and extends a hand to me, saying, "Next stop, Moonrise. I made Isla promise to save some breakfast for us."

I grip her hand, and close my eyes.

'Stay alive,' I beg Cole, praying these are the words that stick, that travel down that single thread I'm hanging onto.

33
CONVINCING THE QUEEN

Misty

BEFORE MY BODY EVEN CATCHES UP TO ITSELF, MOM HAS HER ARMS around me, pulling me into the tightest hug possible as Sarah's powers shudder away, falling like ash that covers the ornate red carpet in one of the upper wings of Aunt Ella's palace in Moonrise.

Golden finishes blur my vision. My senses go haywire for a fraction of a second before familiar scents and voices bring me back to reality.

I slowly fold my arms around Mom's back and squeeze.

Neither of us says anything for a long, long time. I stand on my tiptoes and rest my chin on her shoulder, closing my eyes and breathing in her sweet, floral scent. She's been wearing the same perfume for decades. She always smells the same—the smell of my childhood.

"Mama," I whisper into her strawberry scented hair.

She trembles with silent sobs, cupping the back of my head as she pulls away. Her big, dark blue eyes—eyes she shares with Sydney and

Ryan—sweep over my face, over the new lines of exhaustion and heartbreak.

I feel a pang of regret... for Lavender. Looking into my own mom's eyes and seeing her joyous relief over having her daughter back, and whole, makes me imagine what losing Elsbeth must have been like.

What scrubbing her blood from the floor must have been like.

It all comes rushing back to me. The attack on TU... watching the books in the library suspend in midair before they fell, and the screams that followed. Being caught with a silver net and unable to do anything while Georgia was brutalized and dragged away. Luke's mangled shoulder. That odd look in Cole's eyes the first time I saw him without his order mask, how angry he'd been with me—and now I know why.

He warned me repeatedly to leave campus.

But I would never have known him if I had. I would have missed my chance at the few precious, though absolutely traumatizing, weeks we had together.

I wouldn't have had *him*. Our baby.

Mom pulls away to inspect me further and notices the hand I have pressed against my lower belly. It's a reflex. I can't help it. I know she can see the pain behind my gaze when her eyes meet mine again.

"Oh, Misty," she whispers against the onrush of conversation beginning to funnel around us. "Oh, honey–"

"I should see Kenna, shouldn't I?" Kenna, my cousin, the midwife. She'd be able to help me. Help me through this pregnancy, on my own. By myself. Mateless.

Mom smooths her hand through my hair as the sounds of the palace reach their normal pitch. Excited children bounce through the room. Sarah presses quick kisses to her sons' heads before mentioning she has a few more people to pick up, followed by Cosette asking if she's feeling all right, if her powers are dimming, if she needs food, and rest.

But Sarah disappears in a flash of violet light, sending a slight chill through the room as her powers waft over us.

The children go on playing like nothing happened.

They're used to this now, which is… gut wrenching. Being separated from their parents.

Aviva disappears around a corner, her head hanging, just as Ella stalks into the room, pausing to watch my sister-in-law move swiftly down to what I assume is the private apartment Ryan keeps in the castle.

Ella's eyes soften, her mouth working despite staying silent, but then she turns her attention to me. "We need to talk."

"Can it wait, Ella, please? She needs to eat something." My mom holds Ella's gaze, but I already know the answer.

This conversation can't wait. Ella is the Queen of Eastonia. Every Alpha King bends the knee to her, and her alone.

I step out of Mom's embrace and walk to my aunt but brush past her, walking down a familiar hallway, down a familiar set of steps, another hallway, and finally, into her massive, golden office.

The silence surrounds me in a warm embrace. I sink into a luxurious leather armchair and hang my head in my hands, listening to my own thundering heartbeat. Waves of anguish run through me, sharp and throbbing, before receding like the tide.

I don't feel like myself. Maybe it's because… today is still my birthday. I think…. Has it only been a few hours since the ball? I'm changed. I have my wolf. I should have my mate, too.

My body convulses with a sob that makes my bones knock together. I have no will to eat, let alone breathe. I want to crawl in bed and hide, let myself wither away.

We've all heard the stories about what rejection does to a wolf. It's painful and jarring. Some people go mad. Some people lose their ability to shift, at least, temporarily.

Going insane doesn't sound so bad, especially after what happened to me over the past several weeks. Losing that rational part of my mind would be a blessing right now. All I want to do is lean into the part of me that's already scheming about how to get back to the man that rejected me, so I can save his life, or die trying… beside him.

The door clicks shut somewhere behind me, followed by Ella's soft footsteps. I lift my head as she leans on the corner of her desk, dressed in fitted cream trousers and a matching blouse. Her hair is swept in her usual bun—right on the top of her head, and messy—with rogue waves falling around her sculpted face.

I've always thought of Ella as the family beauty. But when she opens her mouth, her sharp tongue twists that beauty into something so fierce I've seen grown men cower in her presence.

But at one point, she was like me. Almost exactly. Stuck in a foreign place with a mate she thought was her enemy but grew to love so deeply she'd move mountains for him.

"Did our family ever truly forgive Uncle Ryatt?" I ask without meaning to even open my mouth.

She sighs heavily, crossing her arms under her chest. "I didn't really give them a choice in the matter. Your grandma can attest to that, seeing as she met him for the first time because I burned a hole through the center of their house in order to save his life." She unwinds her arms and thumbs a piece of paper hanging off her slightly unorganized desk, her eyes distant and dreamy. "But yes, he was forgiven. He was never their enemy to begin with."

"But he tried to be. To push you away."

"To keep me at arm's length," she replies, smiling wistfully around some memory. "You can obviously see how that turned out."

"So it's possible, then."

Her eyes meet mine and hold as she sits in the armchair beside mine, slouching and crossing her legs. She looks exhausted and worn. "Start from the beginning, Misty. I need to know everything that happened to you."

So, I begin. I paint her my story in vivid color. I bring to life the memories I hope to one day forget. I show her the Cole I once knew as a monster, a murderer, a tyrant, and then show her the man I fell in love with. My mate.

Talking about Richard and the order is harder than anticipated. I don't leave out a single detail, no matter how small and insignificant.

How they dress, who I recognized within their ranks, their manner of speaking, walking, and fighting.

I name names. I tell her who I believe was fighting for Cole within the order and who sided with Richard. I describe the fortress and how to find it, if possible.

Hours must have passed. The sunlight coming through the massive windows in her office spills across the shallow carpet, signaling midday. More time wasted, in my opinion. More time I could have spent fighting beside my mate.

Ella sits quietly beside me the entire time. She doesn't ask questions, or prod me for more details.

But when I tell her that Cole and I did, in fact, sleep together... her eyes meet mine.

"Richard had to know Cole was using me as intended," I whisper, shame ripe in every word. "And Cole... I think he was running out of ways to keep Richard away from me, so we.... He did what he needed to do, and I was a willing participant." My throat closes, but I edge forward, pushing past the memory of that first time together and how Cole nearly fell apart. "But it wasn't the only time. And... I fell in love with him. He's my mate. He–he was."

"Ryatt told me what happened," she says softly, her eyes holding on her fingers. "That he rejected you."

"Yeah. Uhm... I don't know what to say, other than he's not the monster he had to pretend to be. He's not the enemy of your kingdom. He's been trying to unravel the order from within, and I think he made progress, because he attacked Richard just as Dad and Uncle Ryatt took me away."

"His father was a good friend of ours.... I have a hard time believing Jaxon wouldn't have reached out for help."

"You don't know Richard," I croak. "He would have... he has the *Book of Whispers*."

Ella's gaze flicks to mine, her face going pale.

"He says he has the location of the Gate of the Gods, and that's why he needed me. Because he thought I had the power that Dad has—the ability to unlock anything. Cole used me as a breeder to keep me safe and away from him, but he ran out of ways to do it."

Ella's at a loss for words. She rises, dusting her suddenly clammy hands on her pants. "Can you unlock anything, Misty?"

"I don't know." I rise, letting my powers flow free, turning the palm of my hand toward her and showing her my newest little trick. My powers of mist form a perfect, basic key in the palm of my hand. She watches as the mist shifts, turning to a blade, then a silly, little bird. Random things. Stupid things. Useless… things.

Her eyes meet mine full of an emotion I can't decipher. "And you believe Richard, the book, and the Gate are in Serpentia?"

"Cole believed so."

"Has he ever seen the Gate?"

"No. I don't even know what it's supposed to be or what it looks like."

She nods, pacing. "I still have access to the mind-link with Ryatt. Our powers allow us a… larger distance, so to speak. Cole was not in Oasia when they arrived earlier this morning. In fact, the castle was on fire."

A chill snakes up my spine. "Did he make it out?"

"We have Evander's Ghosts heading to Serpentia as we speak to do some spying on the order, and to locate Prince–Alpha King Cole. If he's located, you'll be the first to know."

"So what's the plan?" I wring my hands, growing desperate.

Ella clicks her tongue. "Right now, our allied armies are storming Tarsian. Serpentia is several days' journey from the border, but we're hoping Richard and his forces back down when they see us coming. I'm sure we'll outnumber him by the thousands–"

"That's not going to matter," I argue. "The magic he has–"

"I understand your concerns," she cuts in.

"Our family should be there, fighting! All of our combined powers–"

"This isn't just about our family, or your mate. I have my people to think about. I have Tarsian to think about. A long, drawn out, bloody war–"

"There will be a war, Ella. I've seen it." I point to my head. "I've seen it. I see visions, like grandma. I've seen the battlefield. The green magic everywhere. We need to go, or everyone is going to die. My brothers, Evander, my dad…" I step toward her. "Ryatt will die."

"Ryatt is a Shadowsynger."

"Richard's curse doesn't discriminate. I've seen it. I've healed it. I've broken it, and unless I'm back in Tarsian to stop him myself, it's over."

Ella swallows hard, her eyes searching mine. I want to shake her. I want to ask what happened to her to make her so weak. Anger flares like it's never flared before, raging through me like a disease.

"You and Ryatt have the ability to wipe out an entire kingdom with the snap of your fingers," I hiss, feeling her power settle around me, thrumming with its own heartbeat. "If you don't do something… if you don't let me do something… you're going to have to, and it'll be the end of Eastonia as we know it, won't it? You using your powers in full?"

"Misty, you're young," she snaps, but her eyes are sad and glossy. "I can't fault you for having romantic notions about running into battle to save this man's life, but it's more complicated than that. Hundreds of thousands of lives are at stake if this curse spreads the way that you've said it does. Our warriors are at stake, and this needs to be handled delicately, diplomatically."

"We're past that," I rasp, shaking my head. "You know it. Once our forces reach Serpentia, it's over."

"You don't know that," she says softly. "Plus, he needed you to open the gate, didn't he? You cannot return to Tarsian for that very reason, Misty. I think you know that."

"Mom," Kenna's voice rings through the room as she slides through the door and comes to an abrupt stop, noticing how close Ella and I are standing. The tension is thick enough to cut with a knife. Kenna clears her throat, saying, "Arthur is here."

Ella takes a breath, turning from me. "Send Luke in with his Cryptex. Arthur will know what to do with it."

"Luke's here?" I gasp, turning to Kenna.

3 4

OVER OUR HEADS

Misty

I wait in the hallway for Luke, not believing he's actually here, in Moonrise, in the same place I currently am. Eventually, he's escorted around a corner by two of Ella's royal guards. His eyes go wide when he sees me, his cheeks flushing. "Misty–"

"Luke," I whisper, trying to smile at him, but my heart is skittering out of my chest. He glances at the guards before taking several swift steps ahead of them to reach my side. I pull him across the hallway to a set of windows and benches overlooking the city of Moonrise, now bathed in afternoon light.

"You got out," he says in disbelief. "I heard that you had, but I didn't believe it–"

"Is Georgia safe?"

"Yes, she's with her family. Her father's fighting, but she and her mother went to Crescent Falls–"

"What did Cole have you working on in the castle?" I rush out. "I was supposed to help you with it but never got the chance."

He pulls a small, oval object out of his jacket pocket and hands it to me. "It's a cryptex. He said it was found with the *Book of Whispers*. I'm not sure how he got his hands on it. He never gave me the details, but he wanted me to open it. I think it's from the time of the Rosetta people–"

"It's not." I stare down at the symbols. I'd been studying the Rosetta people when all of this started. "This is Firestone."

"What? It can't be. The symbols."

"It's–it's their early language." My feet are moving before my mind has a chance to catch up. I leave Luke behind, gaping, as I break into a sprint, tearing through the castle as fast as my feet can carry me. I leap down a staircase, nearly missing the landing entirely and crashing into the wall, but adrenaline carries me forward as I rush toward Ryan and Aviva's suite.

The door is locked. I slam my fist against it over, and over. "AVIVA! Open the–"

The door swings open revealing a frazzled Aviva dressed in a silky robe, her hair pulled back in a very messy bun on the top of her head. Her face is silver with tear stains and her eyes are dark and furious. "What," she breathes, "do you want?"

I ignore her tone and push past her into the snug foyer of the suite. I jerk to a stop when I see Grandma Isla sitting in one of the armchairs, her dainty legs crossed as she balances a cup of tea on her knee.

"Grandma!" I shout, swallowing back my shock.

"Hi, sweetheart. I heard you were back." Something about her smile and the almost mischievous look in her eyes confuses me, but I don't have a second to waste. I whirl to Aviva, who stalks past me and slowly settles back into the chair she claimed for this–this evening tea party.

"Dinner's soon," Grandma says, tilting her head toward Aviva.

Aviva shakes her head, going a little green at the mention of food.

"We need to talk," I gasp. "Right now. Aviva, you can read Firestone, right?"

Aviva nods, but she looks like she's on the verge of throwing up. She sips her tea, grimaces, and locks her eyes on mine. "Why?"

"Tell me these symbols are Firestone." I thrust the cryptex into her arms. She almost spills her tea, throwing me a dirty look. I fire one right back. "Look, I know you're pissed at Ryan right now, but I need your help."

She looks down at the object and sighs, but her eyes undergo a great change. "Where did you get this?"

"Cole–Cole gave it to Luke. He said it was found with the *Book of Whispers.*"

Aviva stares at me, hard. "Who has the *Book of Whispers?*"

"It's a long story," I tell her, swallowing hard against the lump forming in my throat. "I don't have time to explain, but Cole wanted to open this. He thought this could help him–help his people, some-way. Please–please tell me you know what those symbols mean and how to open it."

Aviva holds my gaze, her eyes softening and her face going slack in resignation. She swipes her thumb across the strange stone buttons. Grandma Isla leans in as Aviva starts pressing the buttons, which unlocks new buttons with new symbols.

"What are you doing?" I ask, sudden worry spinning through my brain. "Aviva?"

"It's just math," she murmurs under her breath. "These are numbers, not words or letters. It's a numerical puzzle."

I glance at Grandma, who gives me a, "I have no idea what's going on," shrug.

A sharp crunch echoes through the room when Aviva pushes one last button, and the cryptex cracks open, the stone crumbling in the palm of Aviva's hand.

Grandma's gasp cuts through my own shout of surprise, and then my... utter disappointment.

"A moonstone?" My words wobble. "That's it?"

"It's not a moonstone," Grandma says with marked surprise. She plucks the stone from Aviva's hand and stares at it in sheer disbelief.

"What is it, Isla?" Aviva asks softly.

"It's a Diamond of Faith," she whispers, her eyes glowing with sudden... power.

I feel a tug toward the diamond as well, like it's calling to me, my powers answering.

Grandma shakes her head, rising to her feet. "This is impossible. Maddox put the Diamond of Faith back–he put it back decades ago."

"Then there's more than one," Aviva counters, walking toward her. "What does this mean? What could it possibly be used for?"

"Ella mentioned the historian from Veiled Valley is here, in Moon-rise," Grandma says hurriedly. "Where is he?"

"In Ella's office," I reply, trying to get a grip on my roiling powers. My fingers teem with blue mist against my will. I tuck them in the pockets of the pajamas I've yet to change out of.

Aviva and I follow Grandma, matching her hurried pace as she stalks through the castle. Ella's office door is open, but Grandma pulls it open wide, fisting the diamond as the smallest man I've ever seen in my life comes into view.

Arthur is… not a shifter. No one knows exactly what he is, but he's definitely not one of us. His head barely reaches my belly button, and he has sharply pointed ears and an ancient, withered face. He was very old when Ryatt and Ella were young. Apparently, he's… simply ageless, which is perfect, since he's in charge of keeping the history of Eastonia. His bright eyes fall on our group, then the diamond, going wide and round.

"Well, where did you find that?" Arthur asks us.

Luke lingers in a corner looking pale in the presence of my aunt, who rises from her desk chair. "Mom, what is that?"

"A Diamond of Faith," Grandma chokes out, looking… angry. I don't understand. "Tell us everything you know about them and why this was found with the *Book of Whispers*."

Arthur purses his lips. He pinches the bridge of his nose, mumbling under his breath, "I was worried about this."

"About what?!" My heart is beating out of my chest. I don't have time for any of this. I need to get back to Cole, especially if this can help him defeat Richard.

"It was rumored there was more than one diamond, but no one was able to confirm it after the Firestone empire fell. The Firestone witches killed their forges, wiped their magic away, before pulling their cities underground."

"We know the legends," Ella snaps, her own power flaring in the presence of the diamond. "Why would it have been with the *Book of Whispers?*"

"The *Book of Whispers* wasn't a good thing. It wasn't created to be used for good. It's dark magic," Arthur begins. "The same dark magic only very specific witches are allowed to learn about. Curses, afflictions, the works. It could create, and open, realms. It also spoke of other worlds outside of our own. Worlds of danger, of evil... and how to open portals to... possibly the afterlife and beyond. It predates the Firestone witches by a millennia, at least, and no one knows where it came from or why it was created. When the Firestone witches discovered it, they hid it away in one of their temples, believing it was a book belonging to the oldest of the gods, the most vicious and vengeful, gods who used the book to leave our world."

"The Gate of the Gods," I whisper, turning to Ella. "It's not actually a gate, is it? It's not a–a tangible thing. It's a *spell.*"

Arthur nods. "It's *the* spell. The reason the Firestone witches hid the book."

My heart leaps out of my chest entirely. "Can anyone say the spell?"

"If they have a vector, yes."

"A vector?" Ella asks, her eyes meeting mine.

"Another person to draw power from."

"Richard wanted me for this. He believed I could open the gate. He needed my magic." I stare at the assembled group, my eyes watering.

Ella looks at Arthur. "What happens if he opens the gate?"

"No one knows. There's a legend about the gate opening, letting in a curse that turned Tarsian to sand and ash.... But my interpretation of the legend is different and long disputed by other historians." He looks a little smug as he continues, "Whoever tried opening it the first time failed miserably. It backfired, and the effect was catastrophic. The spells in the *Book of Whispers* are desperately complicated, and each carries a risk. Mess up and die. Read the words out of order, and curse your entire realm, so on and so forth."

My heart is on the floor between my feet. "But someone who can read the book… who can say the spells needed to activate them… they could open the gate?"

"Yes," Arthur says in conclusion.

I whip my head to Ella. "Richard's able to read the book. He's already used it. The curse."

"I know," Ella pants, looking wildly around the room. Her gaze lands on Arthur. "What's the significance of the diamond?"

"Diamonds of Faith were considered a… counterweight, so to speak. The owner of the diamond could break a curse, heal a body, so on–"

My mind reels over Arthurs words. Cole needs the diamond. There's no way to stop Richard without it.

"I have to go," I whisper, backing out of the room. I dig deep, trying to ignite those powers to jump, but I don't feel them. I don't have that ability, and it crushes me.

A ripple of power skitters across the sky, visible through the windows. A rush of awe and concern sounds from Ella's office as dark mist fans across the sky, blurring the sunset. It pulls away, falling like stars of pure shadow.

Ella rushes into the hallway. "No–what is he doing?"

"Aunt Ella?" I edge toward the window as the power fizzles away.

"Ryatt dropped his wards around Moonrise–"

A blast of dark, shadowy power rushes around us, sending sparks whizzing through the air. The windows flex, nearly splintering, as Ryatt appears in a cloud of his dark mist, holding a battered woman around the waist.

"Lavender?!" I scream, running toward them but slide to a stop when I notice the sheer amount of blood covering Ryatt from head to toe.

Ryatt drops her, struggling to catch his breath. He stares past me at his wife, his mate.

"Ella," he rasps, "drop your wards. I need your magic. *All of it.*"

"What happened?" Ella's voice is shattered as she stares at her bloody, battered mate.

"Tell Kenna to drop the wards around Veiled Valley. Then, send in your witches. All witches need to come to either fight or help heal."

"Ryatt–" Ella grinds out, but Ryatt shakes his head.

"Ryan's forces reached the desert. It's…" His eyes shine with an emotion I can only describe as… broken. Terrified, maybe. "We're in over our heads."

"What?" Ella steps toward him, but he holds out a hand, shaking his head.

"Drop all of the wards. Now."

Ryatt disappears. Ella rushes toward him a second too late. I sprint to Lavender, pulling her upright. She's hurt, badly. Blood seeps from wounds on her hands, her arms. Gashes from blades.

"Are you cursed?" I shout, biting through a cry of anguish as her face pales.

"N–No." She shoves something against my chest, leaving a bloody handprint. "Cole–he–"

"What about Cole? Lavender? Help–somebody help!"

Maids rush toward us as my healing powers ignite, drifting over her skin as I struggle to hold her up right.

But Aviva's standing shell shocked with Ella only feet away. She's looking at Ella with determination set across her features. "Take me there."

"No," Ella bites out, struggling to gain her composure. "Not until I know what's going on–"

"TAKE ME THERE!" Aviva screams. "MY MATE IS THERE!"

I can't catch my breath. My head spins as I sink to the floor with Lavender in my arms. Grandma is at my side, tears falling down her cheeks and landing in Lavender's hair. Her powers of healing are so much stronger than mine. Lavender's wounds knit together quickly, fully, but Lavender's exhausted. Something crinkles when the maids pull Lavender away. Six pages worth of a letter land in my lap.

It's Cole's handwriting.

I CHOOSE YOU

Misty

EVERYTHING ELSE IS A BLUR. AVIVA'S SCREAMED WORDS. ELLA'S RUSHED explanations. Grandma taking me by the shoulders and leading me away, tucking me in a sitting room somewhere in the depths of the castle. I barely feel her arm on my shoulder. I barely register sitting down in a chair, holding the bloody pages in my lap and watching the firelight dance over the untidy scrawl I know so well.

I sit there for what could be hours. Eventually, I'm joined by Sarah and Kenna… and then Aviva.

Still, I haven't read the letter. I've read my name, addressed at the top of the first page, over and over again. This is his final goodbye, and I'm not ready to accept that.

"What are we supposed to do?" Kenna grinds out. "The reports coming out of Tarsian are–"

"I don't fucking care what they are!" Sarah's voice pitches with fury. "The father of my sons is fighting for his fucking life right now, Kenna."

"My mate, too!" Kenna shouts. "But we've been told to stay, to be prepared to defend Moonrise!"

"I don't give a shit about Moonrise!"

"Well, if they fail in Tarsian, Crescent Falls is going to fall, so I hope you at least give a shit about that!"

Aviva stands in silence by the window with her golden bow, her eyes heavy with grief, watching the skyline as if she can see the battle taking place hundreds of miles south of here.

Kenna and Sarah's argument bounces through the room. Sarah wants to leave–now. She wants to go to Sydney and wants Kenna to come with her, both of them using their powers to try to stop this threat.

Kenna's argument is sound, however, which makes me feel absolutely hopeless. "If my father is struggling to advance the armies into Serpentia, our powers won't make a difference." She gets in Sarah's face, nose to nose. "If my father has to drop his wards here, and in the Roguelands, to use that reserve of powers... Sarah, you have to know–"

"I can't stand here and accept that we're losing this war before it's even begun," Sarah rages, her eyes going glassy and bright with tears. "We need to go–"

"If we go, and fail, there's no one left to protect the rest of the Allied Kingdoms. Your sons will not only lose their parents but the kingdom they were meant to rule!"

"Do you not care about Evander at all?" Sarah snaps.

I close my eyes, waiting for Kenna's scary shadow powers to erupt, but a calm stillness settles through the room... and Kenna bursts into tears.

I glance at them just as Sarah wraps Kenna in her arms and embraces her tightly.

My hands tremble as I turn and look at Aviva, who's still silently watching the inky black horizon. Even the stars are hiding from this war.

Then, I look down at the letter, reading the first pages.

"I can still feel you. I should have known you'd fight my rejection."

My lips twitch into a smile I can't stop, even as tears blur my vision.

"There wasn't any debate about my need to write this. I don't care about giving you closure, because that's not something either of us can hope for. What happened to us is horrifically unfair. The moment I saw you, Misty, was both the best, and worst, moment of my life."

"Asshole," I whisper under my breath.

"I wish I could go back to that moment when I passed you in the street. I wish I could have told you then, held you, just for a second more."

Tears slip free, sliding down my cheeks.

"I miss your voice in my head. I miss the way you used to watch me read, or write my notes. Your presence filled the silence in my life. You took up space, kept me whole, and when I had chances to just be with you, I felt like I had something to fight for, even if I didn't get to keep you in the end."

I feel Kenna and Sarah gathering around me. Kenna kneels near the fire, wiping her tears on the back of her hand, but Sarah perches on the armrest, resting her arm over my shoulder.

"If you're reading this, I'm in the thick of it. The battles in the desert have begun. I've followed Richard and his forces to Serpentia. That's where he's keeping the book—where he plans on opening the Gate. He's going to escape through it, we believe, after using the book to unleash hell on Eastonia and beyond. His desire for power knows no bounds, and my only consolation is that you're safe and with your family."

My chest rattles as I try to fill my lungs with air. I flip the page, noticing the writing growing more frantic as his words turn from the war, to what's in his heart.

"I told you I loved you, and I meant it with every fiber of my being. That will never change, and nothing has ever been more true. You were the future I wanted. You're the future I want, even if I'm not in it."

I grip the pages as my body thrums with despair.

"Being mates was out of our control. It wasn't something we got to decide—it never is. But I tell myself that I willed you into existence. That this feeling in my chest—this overwhelming love—was of my design. That I knit the threads of fate that bind us together, not the Goddess. That I choose you, every day, every second, and will continue to do so until I take

my dying breath because I love you, and I always will, mate bond be damned."

My chest heaves as I force myself to breathe, the letter crackling between my trembling hands.

"I hope that one day you'll forgive me for this. For breaking your heart, for severing the strings between us–but they were nothing in comparison to what I built. For what I feel–Misty, I need you to know that. I need you to know that you hang the stars in the very sky I'll die beneath on that battlefield, and when that happens, your name will be the last word on my tongue. I love you. I loved you then, the moment I saw you, and it had nothing to do with fate. I loved you before I heard your voice in my head and felt your touch on my skin. I loved you, and I got to choose to. I loved you intentionally. Fervently. Wholly, and completely. It's the only thing I've ever been able to choose on my own, and I will never regret the time we had. Not for a second. My only regret is that we didn't have more."

"Misty," Sarah whispers, wiping my tears away with her thumbs.

"I can't do this," I sob, looking up at her through a barrage of tears. But there's more.

"One day, when you're gray and tired, I'll find you. When you've lived a life of sunshine and ease, I'll reach your side again, and I'll guide you home. I promise. But you need to live, Misty. If you make me one promise–one vow you can keep–let it be that. Do it for me, and for what we could have been, had fate not intervened. Live, and love again, and I swear on the Goddess Herself...I will find you, and we will have our chance."

A painful sob tears through my body. I curl around it, biting down on my lip to stop from screaming. Sarah kneels beside me, wrapping her arms around my back and crushing me to her chest. Kenna moves in on me slowly, her fingers raking through my hair as I cry into Sarah's shoulder.

Aviva speaks from the window, however, her voice as firm and cold as ice. "Are we really going to let this happen?"

"Aviva," Sarah whispers, shaking her head. "Not now."

"Then when?"

I lift my head as Aviva stands on unsteady legs, her face washed with grief. "When everyone is dead? When our mates–the fathers of our children–are dead?"

Kenna gulps back whatever her reply to that might have been. Even Sarah stills, her eyes holding on Aviva.

But Aviva looks at me with so much conviction in her eyes, they glow. "Get up. Chin up, Misty. This isn't over."

"Of course, it's over," Kenna croaks. "It's done. The Gate is open. We have hours–"

"Exactly," Aviva hisses, her eyes leaving Kenna's face to hold on mine. "Wars have been won in less time."

"What are you suggesting?" Sarah turns but keeps an arm roped over my shoulder in solidarity. "Are you suggesting we go to battle? Die beside our men? Leave our children behind?"

"There won't be anything left for our children if we don't act, and you know it, Sarah."

Sarah pales. Aviva's right. Nowhere is safe. Even the furthest reaches of Celestoria will be affected. The curse will spread until it eats our kingdoms whole, leaving nothing but bones behind.

Silence hugs the room. Snow falls in steady puffs of white and silver beyond the frosted window–calm, and peaceful–a heavy contrast to the weight of the air in this room.

I look down at the letter, and the very last words Cole wrote in obvious haste. He's in Serpentia. He has to be.

I know where he is… which means I can find him and stop this before it's too late.

"You are the only thing that has ever made sense to me. You were the greatest gift, the only light in my world. When I die, I wonder if She'll send me back to those quiet moments–because lying beside you in bed while you slept in my arms... that was heaven. What is heaven really, when I already had you?"

There's only one thought in my mind. It's irrational and brash. It's furious, wild, and all-consuming.

"I'm not letting him do this without me," I whisper. "I'm not letting him go alone."

"Then we go." Aviva swings her bow off her back, the gold

catching the light of the fire. Her eyes sweep the room as Kenna rises, her shadows curling around her fingers.

"Then we go," Kenna echoes, resigning herself to the fact we're not going without her. "To Serpentia. To Evander."

Sarah closes her eyes as she lays her head on my shoulder, but when her eyes open again, they're that strange violet–all light. Violent, vengeful light. "To Sydney."

"To Ryan," Aviva echoes, and then her eyes are on mine. "To *Cole*."

"To Cole," I whisper, breathing his name back into existence.

I will kill anyone in my way.

That's a promise.

But a shadow in the doorway catches all of our attention. I rise, turning with Sarah as my aunt Ella steps into the room, her eyes shining like sea glass.

For a moment, I think this is already over before it began, but Ella looks into our faces, holding our gaze as she sweeps the room. "We'll need armor," she says softly. "We'll leave in ten minutes, girls. Be ready."

3 6

COATED IN ARMOR

Misty

"Forgive me, please," I say to Mom as we walk side by side to the war room, which is really just a massive training area at the very base of the castle. "I know I just got back…hours ago…."

"Bring them back for me," she replies sadly, her hand ghosting down my back. She stops at the staircase leading to the furthest depths of the castle. I turn to face her, and she tucks a lock of my hair behind my ear. "I'm okay here. I'll keep the kids happy and comfortable."

That's my mom's power. Being the leader of this family. She has a knack for bringing everyone together, keeping everyone loved and… whole.

I pull her into a hug and squeeze. "I'll come home again, I promise. I'll be bringing my mate home with me in time for Solstice, I promise."

Her tears fall into my hair. I reluctantly let her go and turn for the stairs, refusing to look back. I have to look forward–only forward–if I'm going to get through this.

Ella's already in the armory, sorting weapons, her eyes locked on her task. A huge map of Tarsian fans out on a wide, circular table.

On instinct, I sweep my powers over the map. Tens of thousands of tiny figures made of mist appear, moving in on Serpentia, colliding with Richard's... *massive* army.

My throat closes up as Ella looks at the map, at my power. Her eyes slowly meet mine. "That's a very useful power, indeed."

"Show me Cole," I say, and swipe my hand through the air again. Most of the figures disappear save for a small faction of warriors battling on the edge of Serpentia. He made it, and based on what I'm seeing on the map, he's gaining ground on Richard. A small group of order members, distinguishable by their inky, dark mist, races toward the campus with Cole's faction not far behind.

I hope Cole kills him. I really hope he just rips Richard's head off and crushes it between his jaws.

Aviva arrives wearing her typical leather armor. Her hair is braided tightly down the back of her skull, and her face is clear and dry. She's done crying, that's obvious.

Ella watches her approach the map. Aviva's gilded bow rests on her back, and the strange halter and belt she wears is full of weapons of every shape and size.

I'm not going to lie. I'm looking forward to seeing her in battle.

"Neat," she says, looking at my powers at work. "What's our plan?"

"No plan," I tell her with a shrug. "We're dropping in here, just outside of the city. Everyone will find their mates and fight as a unit. I'll be going to Cole, immediately."

My heart quakes with both nerves and utter excitement.

"Who are these people?" Aviva says, pointing at a group of warriors mingling with the Allied Kingdom forces. Instead of blue mist, they're a sandy brown as they race toward Richard's front lines.

My heart squeezes. "Those are... Tarsian warriors." I swipe my powers over the map, giving everyone a glimpse of the army–the packs–Cole sent over the border for their own protection. "They came back. To fight for Cole."

Ella sighs, pulling on a pair of crimson gloves. "Misty, you need armor."

I look down at the basic tank top and shorts I'm wearing–that I put on while braiding my hair and getting ready for whatever the rest of the night brings. "I want to be able to shift back and forth, like Aviva."

"I only have this armor," Aviva says apologetically.

An idea strikes me as Kenna and Sarah arrive, their eyes lined with dark circles and stress. The four of us parted ways to prepare, with them tucking in their children for the night, looking toward an uncertain future.

I let my powers flow over my body. If I can create a key, a bird, and a blade with my powers... Why not armor?

My mist swirls around me, casting me in tough, hard armor in a soft blue that hugs my body like a glove. When the mist settles, I'm totally covered up to the chin.

I take a few steps away from the table, crossing through the door of the armory into the wide, open training area. I break into a jog, then a sprint, leaping and shifting mid-flight. The armor made of mist shifts with me, turning to armor that covers my wolf.

"Very cool," Aviva beams somewhere behind me.

I stay in my wolf form for a few moments to test the armor, then shift back, praying I'm not totally naked. The armor remains, still hugging my usual form. I huff a breath in relief.

"I won't be shifting," Kenna says, smoothing her hands over her dark cloak. "I don't need to. I'm going to try to get to Serpentia's hospital and set up an infirmary with the rest of the nurses."

"We'll team up on that, Kenna. Once I find Sydney, we'll make you a path into the city," Sarah says, swallowing hard. Sarah has the most complicated and untamable powers out of all of us, Ella included. This battle will be a test of her powers, and skills, for sure.

But right now, there's only one thing on my mind.

Finding my mate, before it's too late.

"You and I are sticking together," Aviva says. I nod in agreement before she turns to examine Ella's weapons, but then Grandma walks into the room. "I have a score to settle with Richard, too," Aviva reminds us.

Everyone goes back to preparing. Grandma edges toward me, motioning for me to follow her to a quiet corner of the room.

"Here," she whispers, pulling the diamond—now hanging from a golden chain—from her pocket. She drapes it over my head, settling the diamond against my chest. "It's yours."

"It's—It's not mine."

"It called to you and your powers. You're meant to have it."

"Why?"

"I think we're going to find that out very soon." Her eyes—identical to mine—crease as she smooths a loving hand over my cheek.

"Take care of Mom for me," I tell her, but she gives me a sad smile.

"I'm going with you. All of you."

"What?" I back out of her touch, confused and concerned. "Why?"

"Your grandfather is already there," she admits.

Shock burns through my body. "Grandpa Maddox is in Tarsian?"

"Yes. He... went to fight with your father and your brothers. He insisted." Something in her eyes gives me pause. Grief shines there, but it's not edged with the kind of concern I expected.

"Is he... okay?"

She sighs, taking my hand. "Don't repeat this, all right? Your parents, aunt and uncle, already have so much to worry about right now."

I nod, an uneasy feeling twisting my stomach in knots.

"Grandpa has been sick for a while now. It's his heart. We've seen some healers, and physicians, but there's not much that can be done."

I furrow my brows. "But you could heal him."

"Possibly, yes, but he... doesn't want me to. Grandpa's an old man, Misty. I think he's tired. I think, in a way, he's ready. But he wanted to know the family would be okay without him, so he followed them to war with the intent on bringing his children and grandchild home to us."

I step closer to her. "Is he dying, Grandma?"

She closes her eyes for a moment then nods. Her hand squeezes mine.

"But you could—you should heal him!"

"You and I have the same powers, honey. If Cole came to you a lifetime from now and told you he was tired and ready to go to the Goddess, would you force him to hang on?"

I think about the sacrifices he's made for me and know the answer, even if it hurts.

"No. I couldn't do that to him."

"Then you understand how I feel. But—" She smiles at me. "I get one last adventure with him. It's been such a long time since we've done something like this."

I watch her walk away in disbelief, shaking my head.

I'll deal with that later, once this war is won.

* * *

Cole

Early moonlight drapes the city of Serpentia in shadow. It's a full moon—bright and beautiful, casting light all over the city.

Behind us, in the endless desert, a battle of epic proportions rages. I hadn't anticipated this level of violence. The ground quakes as armies collide. Richard had tens of thousands of enslaved, cursed people and wolves at his disposal… including all of the TU student's he abducted.

He let the curse spread to every pack, every town, and every city in Tarsian without remorse.

I could only get so many out in time.

A small faction of order members follows me through the empty city of rubble. Everyone who lived here is gone. Either escaped, or turned to cursed monsters that are now fighting to the death less than a mile away, trying to stop the tens of thousands of Allied Kingdom warriors from reaching Serpentia.

I hold my hand out and motion for five of the men to split from our group of… ten. Ten is all I have left. Ten men against ten-thousand, but I'm not here to defeat Richard's army. I'm here to kill him before he can finish this battle and leave… because that's what he intends to do. I'm almost positive that's what he intends to do.

The five order warriors split from our group and race into the city center, toward campus. I motion the other five to sweep along the edge of the city. Their mission is simple and clear. Secure the city. Push any of Richard's order members out.

I walk back out to the battlefield, alone.

My father had a sword. It's basic, slim and easy to handle. It has no power, no frills, but it belonged to his father–a grandfather I've never known–long dead. It comes from a time when Tarsian was nothing more than a slave state–everyone at the mercy of King Kane. This land has never been tamed or organized. I'm ready to let it burn if it means my people–the packs I managed to get out in time–have a chance of a life elsewhere, letting the sordid history of this place blur with time and turn to ash.

I sheath the sword. I'm dressed in traditional Tarsian armor that allows for shifting. It blends with the sand as I step over dunes, following the sound of chaos.

From the top of one dune, I can finally see the battle–the droves of warriors rushing toward the city. Wolves. All of them. They run toward the sea of cursed bodies not knowing there's little they can do to stop this.

Moonlight bathes the battlefield in an eerie silver glow while I wait, and wait, for the man that started this.

Richard is a coward, but he's a smart man. He knows he lost his opportunity to use the *Book of Whispers* to open his precious gate to another world, another hell where he plans to be a god, reborn. Now, this war means more to him than just a distraction. He needs to win, to overpower the royals and their powers, which means he's more desperate than ever.

I give myself a single second to think about Misty before locking her memory away, somewhere so deep I can't reach it. That single thread she refused to let go of quakes in my chest, desperately holding on.

"Come on, you fucking bastard," I rasp into the night air, looking around. A figure in a black cloak stands twenty yards away on another sand dune, his back to me.

With a book in his hands.

His eyes glow green as he whispers some ancient, dead language. He slowly turns his head to the side as I approach, unsheathing my sword.

He didn't kill my father. No, my dad died at my hands.

But Richard struck the match that toppled the pack my grandfather—my ancestors—built. I plan to kill him with the sword cherished by those people.

He closes the book and turns to me, giving me a grisly smile. Every time he uses the book, he grows uglier, if that's possible, like he barters his own life for the magic he summons.

"Come to the watch party?" he grins, motioning toward the battle. Green magic flares around the cursed warriors, bringing their fallen back from the dead. "It's practically over before it's begun. That's the nice thing about these magical wars—they're quick. It'll be over by morning."

I grip the hilt of my father's sword. I've been imagining this moment for months—debating how I'd do it. There were plenty of times I could have killed this man. Torn him to shreds. But he kept the book hidden, and I'd be damned if I killed him without knowing its location.

The only reason he's alive right now is because he's holding the book, and I'm going to give him a single chance to undo this mess before finally, *finally*, killing him.

THE GATE OF THE GODS

Cole

"Undo it," I tell him. "Take the curse back and reinstate order."

He purses his lips to a thin line, confused. "But, Cole, I can't. It's not something you can just… stop. Think about it. Use that big brain of yours. Do you see this place? Tarsian is so much bigger than the rest of Eastonia. Riches beyond belief lay below the sand. There used to be mines and forges here, mines that pulled silver and moonstone from the ground and forges that turned that into magic. Yet, in our time, the magic is hoarded by the royals–the Allied Kings." He sweeps his hand toward the battle. "But not anymore. Once I open the gate, it's over. This world will be no more. You can come with me, Cole. Be a god instead of a king."

"You can't, Richard. You failed. Misty is safe, with her family. You needed her to do this."

He smiles a bit sadly, but his eyes flare with mischief. "Yes, she is. Such a shame, really. It would have been easier to do it with her help. Quicker, less leg work for me." He opens the book as his eyes flare with magic like never before. I swear his very soul is sucked from his body as the pages flip to its very center. The text brightens with green magic, highlighting a specific, very lengthy spell.

"You did a fine job of hiding your bond with the princess," he says in a voice that sounds so unlike his own. It's deeper, and crackles as his words are pulled into the book.

I raise my sword, glancing at his army, which has... stilled, completely. Confusion echoes through the advancing armies as Richard's forces fall silent and stiff as stone.

"But she messed up during your aptly timed rejection," he cackles. "You're still bound to her. You have an echo of her soul inside your chest."

I resist the urge to back away. I raise my sword higher, prepared to strike, but something feels... wrong.

"I can simply... use your mate bond to open the gate. It's the most powerful magic of all, of course."

His army turns toward us and races over the sand at an impossible rate of speed. The sound of the armies bursting back into action deafens me, but it's not the noise forcing me to my knees. Richard begins the spell. Something cruel and powerful that I immediately feel in my bones.

Flashes of light catch my attention. I try to break from Richard's hold and look toward the battle, where another bright, furious light erupts.

I feel her.

She's here, running toward me.

Something sharp splits my chest in two. It's not my heart break-ing. It's not our bond snapping back in place.

It's a massive knife glowing with green power piercing my armor.

I nearly drop my sword as the sand starts to lift all around me, and I'm sucked into a sudden void appearing just beyond my body.

"COLE!" Misty screams, sprinting in my direction, shifting mid-step.

My arm trembles as I raise my sword, screaming as I try to send it slashing toward Richard.

* * *

COLE'S SWORD SPLITS THE AIR. MOONLIGHT FANS AROUND HIM, highlighting the massive blade sticking out of the middle of his chest. I'm sprinting in my wolf form, watching in desperation as he tries to send his sword toward Richard, but Richard's reading from the *Book of Whispers,* his magic flaring through the air, through the battle taking place all around us. Cole's arm gives out, dropping the sword.

I shift back to my usual form, my armor of mist surrounding my body, and create twin blades with that same magic, swinging my arms out as cursed warriors charge me from the sides.

I can't look away from Cole. He's fighting hard, trying to stay on his feet and retrieve his sword. He sways, gripping the blade sticking in his chest. I scream in terror when he pulls it free, blood spraying, but Richard is still reading from the book and...

The Gate of the Gods starts to rise like a swirling black vortex. It's nothing but aether–a shadow, blocking out the moonlight.

My powers rage in answer–sensing something wholly wrong.

I'm distracted and knocked to the ground by another cursed warrior, a young woman wearing a tattered dress. She's stuck between her human and wolf form, her teeth and claws elongated and her legs and arms bent at odd angles. She snaps her jaws at me, spraying drool, as I fight to hold her off. She pins me to the ground with unbelievable strength. My twin blades dissolve nearby, reabsorbed by my powers.

A golden arrow slices through her head.

I gape, screaming in disgust when her dead body falls on top of mine. The arrow whizzes back in the direction it came. I follow it, watching as Aviva leaps in the air and catches it. She's coated in blood, a furious, murderous look on her face. "Get up, Misty!"

She darts ahead of me, screaming Ryan's name while sending her arrow flying, and while she waits for it to return to her, brought back by its magic, she wields blades and slices through the stampede of cursed wolves storming in our direction.

I'm up on my feet and running in an instant, shifting as I leap off a fallen body and race toward Cole again.

He picks up his sword, but Richard's magic brings him to his knees again.

My heart lurches as Cole clutches his chest, trying to push past the power radiating between him and Richard, and rise.

I scream his name down the sliver of mate bond we have left as I weave through the battle in my wolf form.

I'm knocked down, tossed to the side. I shift back to my human form on instinct, landing on my back and rolling across the sand. Four cursed sets of eyes land on me, racing in my direction.

A large, brown wolf with dark blue eyes tackles them all to the ground like dominos.

"Sydney!" I rasp as he disappears over the edge of a sand dune, falling out of sight. I scramble to my feet, swarmed by more cursed wolves.

This is impossible. There're so many of them. They don't stay down, either. Tears blur my vision as I'm pushed further away from Cole and the... the fucking portal Richard's opening. Panic and doubt blur my senses. I'm knocked to the ground again. Teeth yank on my arm, trying to bite through my armor. My power flickers, dissolving some of the armor.

"No," I tell myself, bitter rage flaring to life. "No!"

My magic erupts in a rush of bright life. Wolves scatter, shoved away as my powers sizzle the sand–so hot it turns to glass.

"Nice," I whisper, hopping to my feet. I'll add that trick to my arsenal.

But the mind-link erupts. Sydney's badly hurt. Sarah's desperately looking for him. Ryan found Aviva, and they're looking for me.

Ryatt and Ella are separated, trying to use their powers against the curse–which is now spreading into their armies.

My dad, and my grandpa, are totally silent, though.

"Where's Grandma?" I shout through the mind-link, but my voice is lost in a sea of noise.

My light gave me a path—a way out of the fray. I shift, sprinting as fast as I can toward Cole. He's a quarter mile away. That's too far. I don't have enough time to reach him.

I skirt past enemies racing toward me. I shift back and forth, brandishing weapons of mist, slicing through cursed bodies without a hint of remorse.

I tell myself not to feel any of this yet. Not the guilt. Not the pain from shifting and my lack of training. Nothing.

I feel nothing but rage as I gain ground on Cole. He's crumpled over, kneeling in front of Richard while Richard—uses him to open the gate.

Something insanely large and dark as night charges toward me in the distance. It bursts through a swarm of cursed warriors, sending them flying through the air.

And at its side is Aviva in her wolf form.

I watch in awe as Aviva leaps in her wolf, shifting mid-flight. She grabs the shoulder of the beast racing toward me and soars off his back, sending her arrow flying before pulling her blades and disappearing in the center of a massive horde of cursed warriors.

The beast charges through it, and within seconds, Aviva appears again as her wolf, her bow attached to her back halter.

My heart races as the beast and the greatest warrior in our history turn to fall in step with me.

'We gave you some room to get to him. You gotta get there, now!' Aviva's voice bounces through my head.

'Is that my brother?!' I shout back through the mind-link as the big, terrifying… hellhound type beast races away from us, charging over a group of cursed wolves.

'We'll talk about it later,' Aviva rasps. *'Stay with me!'*

She careens to the side. I follow, my lungs begging for me to stop. My muscles scream in agony but I don't listen. We're so, so close.

'COLE!' I scream. *'Don't give up. Please, don't give up! I'm here!'*

He slowly turns his face. I wonder if he can see us racing toward him. He's never seen my wolf, but I like to think that he's looking at me now, and it's the reason he screams against what must be excruciating pain and grabs his sword. He sways as we gain ground, only a hundred yards away. The power coming from the portal is so intense. I can feel it in my powers, my very bones. My soul. Goddess, it hurts.

Cole swings his sword with all of the strength he has left.

It slices through Richard's shoulder, through his chest, at the same moment a golden arrow pierces Richard's skull.

Oh, my Goddess, he's dead.

A new found urgency tears me forward, the pain in my body dissolving to nothing but adrenaline. I topple out of my wolf form as Cole kneels, doubling over his knees. Richard erupts in green light, the book falling to the ground in a puff of sand.

But the gate is still swirling, still roaring with magic that shouldn't exist. It's beckoning me. Voices erupt in my ears. Images I can't decipher rip through my vision, momentarily blinding me.

But my legs are still moving. I'm running as fast as I can.

Cole needs to—to destroy the book. I feel it in my soul. That's what happens next.

Call it instinct, but I yank the diamond free from the neck, sending it flying in his direction. My powers lock the diamond in the hilt of a blade of blue mist.

I scream his name to get his attention.

Cole's beautiful, gray eyes meet mine. Blood coats his sandy armor. Too much blood.

"DO IT!" I scream, falling to my knees and quickly rising, racing for him.

He catches the blade and in one single action, stabs the book. The diamond flares with pale power. A boom shakes the ground. The gate quakes, ripples of dark power distorting the moonlight, but it remains—sucking the power from my body like it's pulling me toward it.

Cole falls face first in the sand, limp.

A scream rips out of my soul.

I leap the last few to him but feel myself… drifting.

Aviva screams my name, but I'm pulled into the void, the sounds of battle fading to nothing but soul-crushing silence.

3 8
THE ULTIMATE SACRIFICE

Misty

I LAND ON MY FEET IN A SEA OF MIST. SILVER FOG SNAKES AROUND MY ankles, around my glimmering armor made of pure light.

For a moment, I think I'm... lost within the aether–in the misty, shadowed undercurrent that separates our realm from the Goddess's kingdom.

But wet grass squishes beneath my boots as I stumble forward, breathless, damn near in pieces. Rain pelts the top of my head as I grope for anything to grab onto before I careen toward the ground.

I yelp as my body lands with a thud.

Thunder booms, followed by its rolling echo as it bounces toward me. The rain fizzles to a gentle whisper as the mist begins to part.

A great stone wall comes into view, and then two voices carry toward me, lifted in alarm.

I sit up with great effort, kneeling as I gasp for breath that won't fill my lungs. I slowly lift my head and see two women–one young and... stunning, with long, blonde hair and ocean blue eyes that seem to glow as she holds my gaze, her lips parted in surprise.

The second woman is older–beautiful and obviously royal. She wears a crimson cloak with a hood covering most of her rich, dark brown hair, but her eyes–the color of sparkling, polished jade, focus on my face in alarm.

A child hugs her leg, burying his face in her cloak, but he peeks at me with eyes that match hers, but his hair...it's just as blonde as the young woman reaching for him. His mother, obviously.

And his grandmother, in her red cloak.

"Help me," I croak, my voice cracking and trembling. Blood slips down my face. "I need help. Where am I? My mate–" My voice shudders out as a sob lifts up my throat, breaking the words into pieces. "Where am I?"

They stare at me. The older woman steps forward, extending a hand. Her mouth moves, but I don't understand what she's saying. Her words make no sense. She's speaking a language that's not even remotely familiar.

"I went through the Gate. Where am I now? Please, my mate–he's dying, and I need to get back–I need to close the Gate, and I'm–where am I?"

She shakes her head, her brow furrowing as the young blonde woman lifts her son into her arms and argues with her. The blonde woman hands the child to the woman in the red cloak, turning to face me.

My head pounds. Blood drips down my forehead, into my eyes, dripping down my jaw. I didn't realize how injured I was. I didn't know. I'd been so focused on–on getting to Cole.

"Please! Please, tell me where I am? We need help–my people– we're at war and I–"

The blonde woman steps forward, baring her teeth at me and they're...all wrong. Her canine teeth are elongated in a way that...she has *fangs*.

Any blood left in my body races to my head to try to process this. She's not–she's not a shifter. She's not a witch. She's something else entirely.

I hold my hands out in surrender. "Help me–I'm not here to hurt you!"

She keeps her teeth barred, her hands extended like she's preparing to defend herself, but she edges closer, the murderous look in her eyes softening as she closes the distance between us. "P-Please, I need to get back. Where is the Gate? Where am I? Please–"

She tilts her head, kneels in front of me, and reaches out to brush my blood soaked hair away from my face. I instinctively lean into her touch, and she's…cold. Cold as ice.

"Faye," the other woman says, followed by a string of words in their strange language.

Faye looks back at the woman, another string of unfamiliar words leaving her lips, but she says, "Emory," and that sounds like a name.

Faye and Emory. It sounds odd on my tongue when I repeat it in a pleading note that has her eyes softening further. It's their names, based on the look on her face when she hears me say it.

"M-Misty," I stammer, pounding my chest as if to keep my own heart beating. "My name is Misty. I'm the p-princess of Crescent Falls and we're under attack–I'm hurt–My mate–" I suck in a breath as her fingers work through my hair, pulling it back to reveal a gash running from my temple all the way to the back of my head. I have no idea how I got it. My powers are exhausted.

She exhales, her cheeks flushed as she turns and fires off a string of words to–to Emory. Hurried words. Words laced with desperation.

Then a whizzing sound cuts through the air. Something lands with a crunch nearby. I turn toward the noise.

A golden arrow sticks out of the grass, connected to a single, minuscule, golden thread.

Aviva.

My heart leaps, working again, as I jump toward the arrow. It trembles, tugging free of the ground like someone on the other end is pulling the thread. I grab the arrow just as it erupts from soil, and then I'm… hurtling back, through the mist, the women disappearing and replaced by that same, empty, nothingness.

Quiet. It's so incredibly quiet here. Just darkness. No stars to light my way. No sound. No voices.

But noise erupts. Screams and shouts of pain and frustration. The smell of smoke and death.

I feel it—hear it before the darkness fades.

And then I'm back, sucked into battle, into Eastonia, and rolling across the ground away from the Gate.

"MISTYYY!" Aviva roars my name over the sound of war, her voice a keening cry—a warning. "CLOSE IT! CLOSE IT NOWWW!"

I roll onto my back and blindly send the last of my powers racing toward the swirling, endless nightmare of aether in front of me, screaming as it yanks my powers from me, absorbing them.

Green power seeps through the ground around me, throbbing and thrumming like it has its own heartbeat. Richard cursed the world just to watch it burn. The Gate was his escape. His escape to a place where a simple, lowly, broken man like him could play *god*.

Not on my watch.

My scream can be heard in the heavens.

My powers—this moment—historians millennia from now…they'll write about it. They'll say how a little girl from Crescent Falls died beside her mate, exhausting her powers to the last drop so that everyone who came after that horrible, devastating war, would remember *his* name. *Their* names.

Misty and Cole.

Aviva and Ryan.

Sarah and Sydney.

Kenna and Evander.

Ella and Ryatt.

Isaac and Maddy.

Brie. Blake. Aris. Liam. Maeve.

And finally, Isla and Maddox—*the ones who started it all.*

My light burns a bright, unending blue—like dawn has come, chasing away the night. It flows gently despite the force of it leaving my body. It curls and drifts into the gate, turning the whirling aether a pale silver.

The Gate shrinks piece by piece, fractal by fractal, as my heart slows, and my vision blurs.

I don't see it close. I squeeze my eyes shut against the pain of exhausting my powers. My body turns to pure ice as the Gate closes and shatters over me like glass.

The ground rolls—thundering and shaking like the sand beneath me is being pulled apart.

I'm blown backward by a sonic wave that steals the air from my lungs. My eardrums burst. My bones nearly snap.

It's over.

A hand grips mine, squeezing tight. At first, I think it's Aviva clutching me, but when I turn my head, Cole's there, beside me, holding on by a thread.

I look into his eyes as he pulls me close with the last of his strength until my body's flush with his. We lie there in the middle of the battlefield, the desert wet with blood. The sounds of the last battles wane, replaced by a crushing, deafening silence...

And then the soft chirping of birds, and waves crashing against the nearby shore.

"Look at us," I whisper, holding his gaze. "We're dying. I hate that for us."

His lips part, but he's quiet, letting go of a breath as the corner of his mouth ticks into the softest, smallest of smiles.

"I love you," he whispers, squeezing my hand. His last words.

"I know," I breathe, smiling painfully. "I love you, too."

My healing powers simmer, shoving past the ice in my veins, beginning to slowly knit me together against my will. I want to go with him. I want to slip into death holding his hand but... it's not just me in this broken body.

"If it's a boy," I say, my voice fractured as the taste of blood fades from my tongue, "I'll name him Adrian. He'll be just like you. Kind and wonderful and brave."

Cole's eyes shine as the first inklings of morning fade the stars overhead. I don't dare blink. I look at him—my mate. The love of my life. Our baby's father.

I'm losing him. Every second that passes… it's all I have left with him.

"We'll–we'll live in a little cottage somewhere. He'll run around all day, in the woods, picking flowers and chasing birds, just like you did."

His mouth ticks into a smile again, but his eyes are growing heavy. My heart breaks, but I keep talking. "And he'll know who you were. What you did for us–for me. So I could live, and he could live. And he'll love you. Every night, when I kiss his cheek as I tuck him into bed, he'll feel you there…in every hug. In every silly little book–he'll know you, Cole. I won't let him ever forget you. I'll *never* forget you."

Tears slip down his bloody cheeks, but he doesn't blink them away. He holds my gaze as the light starts to dim behind his eyes, death coming in a slow, gentle wave. Painless and warm.

"I'll see you in his face." A sob chokes the words. "And–and I'll be reminded, constantly, of you. I know you wanted me to move on, to love again, but you are *it* for me. My only mate. My love–the love of my heart, and I chose you, Cole. I'll always choose you. My heart–it's yours until the day I die and we–we can be together again. I love you–Goddess, *I love you so much.*"

Cole dies with his fingers knitted in mine.

I bite back sobs as I look at him, memorizing his face. I reach for him with my free hand, smoothing my fingertips over his cheek, his jaw. I roll, keeping my other hand locked in his, and press one last kiss to his lips, tears spilling down my cheeks.

My healing powers are weak from use. My tears roll off his skin–useless.

It's done. It's over. We've won but at such an egregious cost.

One day, I'll accept that he's gone. Not today, though. Not now. Honestly, maybe not ever.

I curl into him, my tears soaking the ground between us, pressing his other hand against my belly where our child rests.

I don't know that miles away, Sarah and Sydney lie side by side. Sydney whispers into Sarah's hair as he tries to heal her, forgoing his own terrible wounds. He can't live without her. The boys–they need her. He needs her. But she's slipping through his fingers.

Somewhere in the ebbing chaos, Evander fights his way to Kenna, screaming her name. They spot each other, running, desperate and wide eyed, surprised to see each other alive. They collide and fall to the ground in an embrace. They made it out.

Ryan lies beside Aviva, her hand still gripping her golden bow. Both are injured beyond repair. He slides his hand over her belly, whispering a silent prayer before telling her he loves her, loves them. Maybe this death is a blessing for them. They're going together, as a family.

In Moonrise, Mom sits by the window, silently sobbing into her hand as her grandchildren sleep in a bed behind her. The last thread binding her to Dad snaps, and the pain she feels over his loss is enough to bring her to her knees. The sun rises on Moonrise, casting shadows over the faces of her grandchildren, of Ella's grandchildren. What can she tell them? How can she possibly convey the bravery of their parents? Parents who might not be coming home?

Ella screams Ryatt's name over, and over. She can't find him. She can't feel him anymore. She fights the urge to fall to her knees, screaming in pain and heartbreak.

I don't know that in a clearing, nestled in a crop of tangled, tropical trees, Grandma Isla rises to her knees beside her mate, who is lying lifeless beside her. Grandpa Maddox was right–he'd die in a blaze of glory for his family–for the future of the lives he built. He died happily, looking into his mate's eyes, and she let him go.

But Grandma had no intention of living without him. They promised this. Spoke of it in quiet, stolen moments. In darkened corners. When only the stars lit their way. *We will go together. I will not let you go into death alone.*

She raises her hand toward the sky, and from her fingers, a great, sweeping light ignites, reaching toward the heavens like a beacon, an offering, a sacrifice–her, for us.

Two white wolves look out over scorched earth, at a war, won. At her powers knitting the bodies of every fallen, desperate soul back together, destroying the curse.

Two white wolves look out at their family–the family they built–as their children and grandchildren open their eyes again, taking a breath, then another, then… another.

And as morning dawns, and the stars fade completely, a great white light is the last thing I see before I submit to the darkness thrumming through my body.

Two white wolves say goodbye, and join their ranks among the last of the fading stars.

Cole squeezes my hand.

3 9

NOT QUITE ENOUGH

Cole

I CHOKE MYSELF AWAKE. SMOKE FILLS MY LUNGS, SMOTHERING MY senses for precious seconds I quickly realize I don't have. Muffled voices fill my ears–a few shouts of pain, of surprise. People are calling out for friends and comrades.

I'm not in the afterlife. I know that immediately. Pain echoes through my body like waves, driven by the tide of my heartbeat as my body claws back to life, my chest wounds knitting together in real time.

But my hand is freezing. I squeeze the fingers tangled in mine and jolt back to reality, rolling with effort to curl my body around Misty.

"No," I breathe into her hair. "Come–Come back." I can't feel her anymore. My hand slides up to her neck, my fingers trembling as I feel for her pulse. It's there, but barely. A weak thump that pauses for several heartbreaking seconds. "H-Help!" I try to shout the word into existence, but my voice cracks painfully, turning into a scream. "HELP!"

Figures rush toward us in a blur. The battlefield erupts into view,

299

sharp with noise and bodies rising from blood-stained sand. Through the smoke, Serpentia rises in the distance–crumbling.

I push myself up on my elbows as the first people appear around us, crouching in a blur of tattered black robes and Deadland armor.

I jerk away from a trio of Arcane Umbra members, holding my hand out to prevent them from coming any closer, but then I look into their eyes.

Their eyes don't swirl with green magic. Their skin is clear of the curse. They look panicked and confused as they shout over each other, asking what happened, asking why they're here.

They don't remember.

My heart beats out of rhythm as a crowd gathers around us.

A sharp female voice cuts through the rest of the noise, and Queen Ella appears. Her dark brown hair is wild, and her face is covered in soot, but her sea-green eyes shine like polished turquoise as she drops to her knees beside Misty and takes her face in her hands.

Ella shakes her head, eyes wide with panic. Her gaze slowly rises to meet mine.

"Mark her," she rasps, holding my gaze with an intensity that sends tremors skittering up my spine.

"Mark her?" My voice is broken and distant, barely audible over the chaos awaking all around us.

She reaches for me, grabbing the back of my neck. "You need to mark her. She needs you. She used all of her power and is dying, Cole."

"I–I know," I rasp. "I rejected her–we're not mates–"

"You are. Always." Her expression shatters, tears filling her eyes. A rush of air roars over us, tiny thrums of light blue magic following in its wake. She looks to the sky, a tear falling free down her cheek. Other's notice, yelping and shouting in surprise as the magic soaks into the ground, waking more of the fallen warriors on both sides of the battle.

I look down at my mate. "Stop, Misty, you have to stop–"

"That's not her powers," Ella murmurs, still searching the sky for its source.

I shake uncontrollable as I watch the queen and look toward the source, her eyes glassy and rimmed red with soul-shattering sadness.

"Who is it?"

"My mom," she replies hoarsely, her hands gripping Misty's tattered armor. Her eyes meet mine again, resigned and determined. "Mark her. *Please*. We can't lose her, too."

I wasn't supposed to get to this point. Surviving this. Guilt rips through my system, paralyzing my body. I pushed Misty away. I rejected her. I gave her up.

This act should be her decision… not mine.

"Do it!" Ella screams.

I gather Misty in my arms, lowering my face against her neck. "I'm sorry," I whisper against her frozen skin. My tears fall into her hair as I rake my teeth over her skin, then bite down. Hard.

I've felt this feeling before. This otherworldly yank, this pull. Everything that I am is bound to her, to Misty, the woman I've loved since the moment I saw her.

I gave her away, forgoing everything I knew to be real, and true. I had to. I want to think she knew I had to do it. I want to think she's forgiven me.

I want to think she'll forgive me for this, too, as I pull on our bond, dragging her back from the brink of death.

My bite breaks her skin. The effect is immediate. I feel the bond erupt through us both, those broken threads snapping back in place, and the single string that still bound us, the string she refused to let go of, sings in satisfaction.

My wolf roars in triumph, trying to claw to the surface despite the pure exhaustion weakening my body.

I pull away with a wince as a sob chokes me nearly to death, my entire chest rattling with the effort to silence it.

"Up, now," Ella rasps with urgency. Another wave of Isla's magic coasts over us, weaker this time. It pushes the smoke away completely, revealing a bright blue morning sky. "There's an infirmary on the outskirts of the city. Find Kenna immediately. She'll know to go there."

Ella rises, her eyes on the distant tropical forest, and disappears in a rush of crimson mist.

I rise on unsteady legs, cradling Misty's limp body in arms. The order members surround me, talking over each other, begging for answers.

"Prince Cole–where are we? What happened?" an older man asks, gripping the black robes he doesn't recognize. He's one of my father's commanders. He's been cursed from the beginning, but now, he's… completely healed.

Terror and confusion clouds his dark eyes as I fight for words. "Gather the men you recognize, and anyone in black robes, and wait outside of the city for my command."

I turn away before he can reply and stalk toward the city where smoke still funnels into the sky, active fires being staunched. Bodies that should be dead wake up, encouraged by warriors from every kingdom. I watch two Arcane Umbra soldiers help a warrior from Crescent Falls to his feet. I see warriors from the Deadlands and Arcane Umbra assisting a trio of witches from Moonrise.

I pick my way toward the city in a haze, my heart beating out of rhythm. None of this makes sense. We should all be dead.

Imagines of Misty running toward me, throwing me that blade forged by her magic, cloud my mind. I reimagine the moment I sunk the blade into the *Book of Whispers*. I see Richard in full color, screaming in pain as he dissolves into ash with my sword and Aviva's arrow piercing his body. I watch my mate running toward me as I fall to the side, welcoming death, and then her disappearing into the void of the Gate of the Gods.

I turn around only once. Just once, to look at the place where Richard opened the Gate…. It's nothing but a stain of black on the golden sand.

I tell myself I don't care. That the questions in my mind don't matter. Not now. Not yet.

I nearly step on Ryan and his wife.

I back up, shocked, and look down at the couple. Ryan's lying on his stomach with an arm draped across her body. She's breathing rapidly, trying to open her eyes. I haul Misty over my shoulder and crouch, throwing Ryan's arm off Aviva's body and picking her up by the tattered leather armor covering her frame, tossing her over the opposite shoulder, just as Prince Sydney and a white-haired woman sprint toward me, screaming in alarm.

"I can't carry all three of them!" I shout. "I'm taking them to the infirmary!"

Sydney looks murderous as he charges forward, fumbling with his empty knife belt, but the woman yanks on his arm, forcing him to stop. Based on the look she's giving him, that's his wife. The one rumored to be a Mystic. Sarah, I believe, is her name.

"We'll meet you there," she assures me, digging her nails into Sydney's arm.

"The Arcane Umbra warriors have been told to gather at the edge of the city. I will deal with them once Misty and Aviva are settled and tended to." My eyes flick to Sydney, whose murderous expression is cracking with confusion. "They were cursed," I assert, holding his gaze. "They didn't know what they were doing. They don't understand what's happening now." I look at the couple, scanning their bodies. "Are you all right?"

Sarah gives me a smile, but her eyes water with disbelief. "We're fine."

"We'll help gather your warriors," Sydney says with an edge of bitterness.

Aviva moans, "Misty?"

"She's unconscious," I rasp, turning back to the city with heightened desperation. The women's weight bears down on my shoulders, and it takes all of my strength to carry them to the city's edge, ignoring everyone I pass.

The infirmary is nothing more than a square of rubble. Warriors from the Roguelands are trying to stretch a massive length of canvas to cover the area and shield it from the already unforgiving sunlight. Witches in cream colored uniforms dart around like mice, setting up cots, carrying buckets of water and towels. I spot Kenna in the crowd, and she turns to me, her silver eyes going wide in alarm.

She runs toward me as I step into the makeshift infirmary, struggling with my hold on both women.

"Aviva's fine but Misty–"

"Just lay them down," she rushes out, panicked as she scans her family members. I drop Aviva onto a cot.

She grimaces, opening her eyes to slits. "Ryan–where's Ryan?"

"He's alive. He's going to be fine," I tell her, and she looks up at me, shocked to see me standing and in one piece. I remember her from the battle. Her and her golden bow. A true warrior of the Goddess, this one. "Thank you for bringing her back to me."

Aviva blinks, then smiles, before slumping onto the cot.

I sit with Misty in my arms while Kenna examines Aviva, deeming her in one piece, and hands her care to the two unfamiliar witches who've been hovering nearby.

Then, she turns to me.

"You need to lay her down."

I shake my head. "I–I can't. Not right now. Just give me a moment–"

She lays a hand on my thigh, the other trailing over my chest, where the wounds inflicted by Richard are still knitting back together. "I need to take a look at you, too."

"I'm fine. I had to mark her. Your mom–she was there."

"It's okay," she says, swallowing hard. "But you can let her go, just for a minute. We have medicine for her to help her through this."

I shake my head, holding Misty tighter than necessary.

Kenna pinches her lips into a tight line and turns to her assistant, barking orders. The infirmary is being swarmed by those needing extra tending. Whatever healing magic spread through the battlefield had been enough to bring... *everyone* back from the dead, but not enough to mend broken bones and deep gashes. The smell of blood is nearly overwhelming.

I look around. No green eyes. No symbols. No curse.

It's gone.

A man parts the crowd, silver eyes scanning the area until they land on mine.

I lay Misty down, bracing myself for impact as Alpha King Ryatt stalks in my direction.

"Dad!" Kenna shouts. "Mom is looking everywhere for you!"

He ignores his daughter, making a beeline for me. I rise, knowing this is it, for real this time. It's time to face my fate.

But instead of his Shadow Sword piercing through my chest, King Ryatt grabs my shoulder and pulls me against him.

"Gods, Cole. You should have told us in the beginning–"

"Dad didn't want–he wouldn't–"

"You're fine," he says with fatherly affection. "You're fine now. Your mom's okay. We've been in contact with her."

"Misty–she used all of her powers, and I–"

"Dad, seriously!" Kenna hisses, tugging us apart. "Mom's in pieces. She thinks you're dead!"

"I was," Ryatt grinds out, giving us both a sharp look. "Where's your grandma? Grandpa?"

"No one knows," she replies, swallowing hard. "Mom and Uncle Isaac are looking for them now."

Ryatt looks at me, inspecting me for damage. "Stay with Misty. I'll deal with the warriors from Tarsian."

"They didn't know–"

"I know," he says. "I'll handle it."

Ryatt walks away with determination, disappearing through the crowd. I sit on the end of Misty's cot, hanging my head. I run my fingers through my filthy hair, shaking ashes free. Then, I lie down, curling my body against Misty and holding her to my chest, my fingers resting on her pulse.

Her hand snakes up my chest, resting on my heart.

I close my eyes.

It's over. It's done.

Now what?

40

STEPPING ASIDE

Ryan

Three Days Later

Tarsian is gone.

That's the only way to describe it. The cities, the packs... it's nothing but endless, blood-stained desert now. Even the sea lapping against the shores of Serpentia is stained a dark red, but I watch it fade as I stand on what's left of a deck overlooking the ocean.

Behind me, the incessant chatter of the injured and healing overwhelm the sound of the waves. A few people walk along the sand—warriors of different ranks and alliances. A young man in tattered Arcane Umbra armor talks to a group of men in armor from the Roguelands, reunited with old friends.

The curse is gone. The soldiers the Umbra Mortis turned into his puppets, his monsters, well... so far, they have no memory of the war, which is a blessing.

The rest of us remember, though. How could we ever forget what happened here? How are we possibly going to move on?

"Ryan?"

I turn toward Kenna's voice as she steps toward me, edging around a group of nurses from Moonrise here to help treat those still healing.

She huffs a breath and pushes her hair out of her face as she reaches my side, breathless. "Aviva and the baby are just fine. She just had another exam. I wanted to be the one to tell you."

A bit of the tightness in my chest eases. I lean my arms on the railing, bowing my head as I take a much needed breath, filling my lungs. "Good. Thank the Goddess."

"Thank the Goddess, indeed," Kenna echoes, leaning her hip against the railing. She looks out over the water, at the flawless blue sky. It's nearly sunset again, marking the end of the third day since the battle ended.

"How's everyone else?" I ask, glancing at her.

She keeps her eyes on the water. "Sarah's having a rough go of it, but she's just in shock. Sydney hasn't left her side, and he's been talking about taking her to Moonrise as soon as dawn tomorrow morning. I agree. I think she needs to see her boys to really grasp that this is over, that we won." Kenna's voice is like gravel—lined with exhaustion. "My mom and dad are doing okay. I don't think either of them has slept… at all. Your dad is still out looking for Grandma and Grandpa." She sighs, closing her eyes for a moment.

We all saw the light. No one could have missed it. It swept through the battlefield, through Tarsian as a whole. There were reports of it reaching the Roguelands. Even in Moonrise, the light lit the night sky for several seconds before fading.

Grandma's light. Her healing powers.

Kenna looks down at her hands. "I think Grandma's dead."

I chew my lower lip, nodding. "She did it, didn't she? Broke the curse?"

"She flooded Eastonia with her healing powers," she says softly, nodding. "All of us should be dead. But every warrior that fell on the battleground is alive and well. The curse is gone. The amount of power needed to do something like that... it doesn't make any sense. The only thing that makes sense... is...." She can't finish. Tears glisten on her lower lashes as she glances at me, barely able to hold my gaze. "Your dad, and my mom, are still holding out hope that they'll find them. I don't think they will. Not... not alive. It would have taken every ounce of her power–and then some."

"Once Aviva's cleared to travel, we'll join the search."

Kenna nods, smiling weakly. "I think you should just take your mate home, Ryan."

The lump that's been stuck in my throat since I woke up three days ago, baking in the sun without my mate, thinking I'd been whisked to the Goddess's kingdom only to find that somehow, we'd survived... I can't swallow past it. My head isn't on straight, and I'm grasping for anything that makes sense right now. Going home to the Deadlands, to my pack, to my house and curling up in my bed with my wife...that's all I want.

But there's work to do.

"Where's Sydney? I need to talk to him." I push off the railing, but Kenna makes no move to follow me.

"Last I saw, he was with Sarah in the infirmary, but the Alphas of Tarsian are meeting tonight to discuss what happens next. Sydney wanted to be there."

"What do you mean?"

She grinds her teeth. "Alpha King Cole called the meeting. I don't know what it's about, but he spoke with my parents recently about something."

I check my watch. "What time were they planning on meeting?"

"I don't know, a couple hours from now? Sydney told Evander it was at nightfall." Kenna looks down at her hands–raw and red. While everyone seems to be alive and doing well, she's been treating minor bumps and bruises, I'm sure. Still, I lay a hand over her shoulder and squeeze.

"You need to rest."

"I have work to do, too," she argues, but I shake my head.

"You look like shit, Kenna."

She smirks, giving me a cat-like glare. "Thanks, Ryan. You, too."

I give her shoulder another squeeze before wading through the crowd. Serpentia—what's left of it—has become a city of warriors from every kingdom, every pack, no matter what side of the war they fell on. I step over sleeping warriors slumped against what remains of a fountain. I pass a group of warriors from Crescent Falls talking with a group of warriors from Arcane Umbra. It's odd, really. Watching these groups converge when just three days ago they were fighting to the death.

My warriors from the Deadlands carved out a space for themselves just outside the city center in a three story building with a large courtyard. They're fine. I've checked in with everyone already, and they're all waiting to get home... but enjoying the heat, for sure. It's been snowing like mad in the Deadlands, so this is almost like a vacation... a morbid one, but still. It'll be months before we feel warmth like this again.

"Where's my wife?" Evander asks as he passes me, neither of us stopping. I point in her general direction, and he barely gives me a nod in hello, or goodbye, before running off to find her.

Chaos. Calm chaos. Like war—everything is just noise, color, and movement.

But instead of the sound of death, the air is full of laughter. The smell of blood is replaced by food being grilled over open pits where warriors are burning whatever they can get their hands on. Warriors of all ranks, all allegiances, share meals together under the sunset.

I click my tongue, nodding in hello to people I recognize, saying things like, "*Glad to see you're not dead,*" and "*What a fucking mess, am I right?*" While inside, I'm hanging on by a thread, especially as I reach the infirmary, housed in what used to be a dormitory on TU's campus, and spot my mate.

Aviva sits up in bed as I approach, smiling. But a man sitting on the edge of a bed a few rows away steals my attention from my wife.

Misty runs her fingers over Alpha King Cole's hand as he leans toward her, their foreheads touching.

I can hear my heartbeat in my ears, drowning out the rest of the noise all around me. Misty looks beaten—exhausted and worn thin. The Alpha King doesn't look much better. He actually looks far worse.

"Ryan!" Aviva grabs my hand, tugging me toward her bed. "Don't stare at them like that."

I run my tongue along the edge of my upper teeth, feeling... uneasy. I watch Misty lift her head, her lower lip quivering as he brushes a kiss over her cheek bone, and she closes her eyes. His mark is still raw and red on her neck.

Mates... again. I'm not sure I'm ready to accept this man into the family.

But then Cole's looking in my direction, and the soft, loving look he'd shared with my baby sister hardens to something fierce and deadly.

I arch my brows at him in a silent command to *fucking* try me. Let's talk. *Outside.*

I tilt my head toward the entrance of the infirmary, and he rises from Misty's bed.

"Be nice to him," Aviva hisses, squeezing my fingers.

My eyes slide to Misty, noticing her glare. I arch my brows at her. She can try me, too, if she wants.

I turn from the women and follow Cole out of the infirmary, but he doesn't stop walking. He's a tall guy—my height, actually—but I have weight on him for sure. It wouldn't take much to get him to the ground if he makes any snide-ass remarks.

"I would've done everything the same if I had to do it over again," he says the second I catch up to his side.

I halt, processing his words. Slowly, he turns to face me.

"I'm not sorry," he says, "if that's what you're expecting me to say. I'm sorry Misty got caught up in my family's mess, yeah, and that I couldn't stop it from happening, but I'm not sorry for anything else."

"You're gonna stand by that?"

He steps into me, only a few inches of distance between us. He might be the only man I can look directly in the eye, nose to nose. "Yes."

"You rejected her."

"What would you have done? If you had one shot to save your wife but not yourself? Would you have let her suffer through losing a mate by death? Or let her go?"

I grit my teeth. That's a good fucking question that I already know the answer to, and I hate it. I hate that I'm realizing Cole and I aren't that different.

I would have done the same. Over and over again.

He backs off and starts walking. I'm not done, even though I'm not exactly sure what to say to convey how I feel about this whole fucking mess, but I follow.

"So, what now? You marry my sister and live happily ever after in your pretty glass castle?" I press. Aviva told me to be nice. I probably could be nice, if I wanted to.

He licks his lips, shaking his head, but says nothing further as we walk toward another university building that might have been stunning at one point, before it was touched by war.

He holds the door to an athletic center open for me but doesn't look at me as we stride inside.

Several familiar faces turn to us when we walk into a cavernous space holding what remains of a swimming pool. The indoor track and balcony above it hang at odd angles, debris covering the ground, the pool, and blocking what look like locker rooms.

But several Alphas stand as Cole stops in the center of the space, tucking his hands behind his back.

I spot Sydney and Evander, who give me equally curious looks as their gaze sweeps from me to Cole and back again. I shrug, falling in line with them.

"Getting to know the new brother-in-law?" Evander says under his breath.

"He's not an in-law yet," I grumble, which amuses Sydney. To Evander, I ask, "Is this the Alpha meeting Kenna mentioned? Why was I not invited?"

"These are just the Alphas of Tarsian. Cole met with Ella and Ryatt two hours ago," Evander drawls, his eyes holding on Cole's profile.

"About what?" I murmur, but Cole begins to speak, his voice clear and echoing.

"I'm sure you've heard rumors today about what this meeting is about," he booms, and all eyes turn to him. "I wanted to gather you together to thank you for your service to my father's crown, and for trusting me with Tarsian when I... forced you and your packs to leave. And for coming back to my aid to fight for your kingdom. Your loyalty and sacrifice hasn't gone unnoticed."

A few of the younger Alphas nod, but the older ones... they watch Cole with interest, stealing glances at each other. Hardened Alphas. Alphas with decades of experience on their current king.

"My father wasn't born to be Alpha King. He was *made.*" He takes a breath, his eyes scanning the room, stopping on me, my brother, and Evander. "I've already spoken to the queen of Eastonia, but I wanted you to hear this from me before word spreads any further. I am stepping down as Alpha King of Tarsian. I abdicated the throne, officially, a few hours ago. Queen Ella plans to meet with the Alphas of the packs of Tarsian individually before announcing the future of our kingdom–led by many Alphas instead of just one king."

No one speaks to argue, but the older Alphas frown.

Finally, one speaks up. "Your father fought hard for that title."

Cole argues. "For his title, yes, but not for the family that would carry it forward. I want a different life for my mate than our Luna–my mother–had."

Sydney straightens beside me, folding his arms over his chest.

"Tarsian is too large for one king to handle. We all know it. All of your packs have different needs. When I spoke to the queen, I mentioned a council should be formed to discuss post-war recon-struction, but when it comes to establishing a new monarchy... I'm out. Queen Ella's current recommendation is splitting Tarsian into thirds–three kings. The king of the desert, of the mountains, and of the coast."

He's so casual about it, too. But the fatigue in his expression is… extreme.

"This could cause a civil war," one of the younger Alphas pipes up, but the older Alphas turn and glare at the men, immediately cutting off that notion in its infancy.

"I will be in Tarsian to oversee the transition," Cole clarifies. "For at least six months, at least, until the new kings have been decided. It's up to our queen. There will be no wars."

One of the older Alpha's walks toward Cole and bows. Others follow, quietly thanking him for his service in leading their kingdom through what I now understand was absolute hell and back.

After several minutes, there's no one else in the area but us.

Cole turns to us, his eyes on his shoes before he lifts them to the men who will have to consider him family–our opinions on the matter aside.

"You're giving up your title, just like that?" Sydney asks.

"I have an exhausted, traumatized, and pregnant mate lying on a cot across town. That's my only concern at this point. She's my only concern." He starts to step past us, but I… I'm the one who reaches out, clapping him on the shoulder.

His lips barely lift into what could be considered a relieved smile, but Kenna rushes through the doors, her face white and washed in heartbreaking resignation.

I immediately know what she's about to tell us.

I think we all do.

"They found Grandma and Grandpa," she croaks, sucking back a sob.

"Are they… okay?" Sydney steps forward.

She looks to Cole, then back to us, and shakes her head.

41

MAKING PEACE WITH THE PAST

Misty

COLE DOESN'T LET GO OF MY HAND. HE HASN'T SINCE WE LEFT THE infirmary, and I walked on unsteady legs for the first time in days, my healing powers finally reigniting to speed through the damage done by using every ounce of my powers to close the portal.

He didn't let go of my hand when Sydney whisked us through space and time to the tropical forest that hugs Serpentia, where the trees are so thick it blocks the moonlight on the forest floor.

His fingers are knitted between mine, holding tight, as I follow Sydney, Ryan, and Aviva down a fresh wolf trail and into a clearing on a bluff with a view of Serpentia, and the battlefield.

Ella's kneeling at the edge of the bluff, Ryatt standing beside her, leaning down with a hand on her shoulder.

Dad stands nearby, his head lowered as he runs his fingers through his hair repeatedly, his eyes locked on… on the clothing in the clearing.

Cole lets go of my hand, falling in step with Ryan and Aviva, while I step forward with Sydney in shock.

Kenna kneels next to the clothing, picking up Grandpa Maddox's favorite watch. Long ago, when we were kids, we'd painted him a picture, and our parents had it sized down to fit on the watch face.

He's been wearing it for… fifteen years, at least.

My stomach hollows out as I look at where Ella is kneeling at the edge of the bluff and walk to her side.

The sand stretches for miles before reaching the battlefield. It's endless, flawless, covered in golden waves from the rushing wind.

But two sets of paw prints lead away from the bluff before disappearing completely.

"They might just be lost in their wolf forms," Dad says somewhere behind me.

I turn back to the clearing, my heart in my throat as I look at the shadowed eyes of my family members. Sarah wrings her hands, glancing around. "I could–I could turn back time?"

Sydney gives his wife a look and shakes his head. "It would take us back through the battle."

She licks her lips. "Just to the end of the battle, when she used her powers. I could see where they went."

Dad stares at her, unsure. Ryatt and Ella continue to look out over the desert, neither of them speaking.

Aviva wraps her arm around Ryan's back, leaning her head against his chest. Sydney and Sarah look like they're debating Sarah's offer through the mind-link, but Cole… he's looking at me.

'*You could show them,*' he says sadly through the mind-link.

'*I know. I'm not sure I want to.*'

'*I think it would give them the same kind of peace it gave me.*'

I hold his gaze. I think he knows that deep down, I'd rather stay ignorant to what happened to my grandparents, but he's right. It's not about me, or my feelings. I glance at my Dad, who just lost his mom and dad. I look at my aunt, who's still looking out at the sand, waiting for them to return.

I extend my hands and let my powers flow.

Figures of mist appear in the woods. Wolves darting through the trees–warriors of all crowns, all kingdoms.

Grandpa Maddox is alone in the clearing. He's been fighting in his human form, wearing a button down shirt and trousers like he was just at a meeting with King Anthony in Maatua rather than racing through a battle ground. Why he didn't shift… I don't think we'll ever know, but the look in his mist-filled eyes tells me the truth.

Grandma mentioned to me that he was sick. He refused her healing powers, her tears. He was ready, I realize, to pass on his torch to my dad… to go to the Goddess, who had been calling him home for a while now.

So, he fought for his family, going out in a blaze of glory, just like he wanted.

His figure of mist whirls with wolves and warriors in their human forms. Decades of experience keep him on his feet longer than the others. My family turns to watch in shock as my powers dance around the clearing, and in the distance, my powers paint the moment I closed the Gate.

I watch in awe as the Gate fractures into mist, sending an echo of power through the battlefield, just as Grandpa falls to the ground.

He grips his chest, his body untouched by bite marks and weapons.

He died of a broken heart knowing his children, and his grandchild, were lying on the battlefield in pieces. His heart simply gave out.

Tears stream down my face as Grandma appears. Her clothes are tattered as she reaches his side, helping him to the ground. Their conversation is nearly silently–muffled whispers I have to strain to hear.

'Isla, let me go. I'll go with them. I'll keep them safe.'

'We promised we'd go together.'

My heart shatters as Grandpa Maddox reaches up to cup her cheek. She leans into his touch, her tears starting to fall, but he says, *'Save those beautiful tears, my flower. I love you.'*

'I love you.'

Grandpa Maddox dies in her arms. She doesn't scream and curse the Goddess for taking him. She thanks Her, running her fingers through his hair, kissing her mate goodbye.

Several minutes pass before she rises, resigned and plotting. In the distant battlefield, all of us are dying. I'm saying goodbye to Cole, somewhere, believing this is the end. The bitter end.

But Grandma knew that Grandpa fought, knowing his heart was weakening, to save his kids. His family.

And she'd be damned if she didn't finish that fight for him.

The look on her mist-filled likeness is set with determination as she raises her hands and lets her powers thunder. A burst of light so fierce it blinds us erupts through the clearing.

"Misty," Ella bellows nearby, but I push forward, showing my family what Grandma Isla did for us to be here right now.

Grandma Isla stands and uses all of her power. Every drop. Sending her healing magic in waves to cleanse the desert of death. She broke through the curse—erasing it completely–but she had to fight so hard and for so long....

The sun rises as the last of her power flares across the battlefield. A separate image appears nearby of Ella screaming at Cole to mark me at the same moment Grandma slumps to her knees, weak, and spent. She takes Grandpa's face in her hands, telling him she loves him, and then she falls to the side.

Grandma lies beside Grandpa, knitting her hand in his.

She dies there, with her mate beside her. And in the distance, her children, and her grandchildren, wake up.

I start to stumble against the rush of my powers, but Cole is behind me, steadying me with a hand on my lower back. His eyes are locked on the scene playing out–and my body freezes.

I saw this. I saw this moment months ago in a dream.

Two white wolves appear in the clearing, standing side by side. They look out over the battlefield, over a war, won.

They watch their family reunited. Parents will go home to their children because of them. The sun will set on a new Eastonia, one where goodness reigns, and evil dies before it's born.

Ella's eyes spill tears as the wolves walk through her and over the bluff, leaving footprints in the sand before their bodies disappear, carried away by the same breeze we've been healing in, embracing in, finding peace in.

I release my powers, letting them flicker out, the mist falling and bouncing around us before soaking into the ground.

No one speaks for a long, long time.

Slowly, Dad begins to gather their clothing. He folds it neatly, tucking it under his arm. Ella joins him, the siblings quiet and wearing identical expressions of grief and understanding. There will be no bodies to bury. No graves to mourn. Just… pieces to hold. A necklace. A watch. A pair of shoes…

Grief is a strange thing. It can be angry, all consuming, and desperately sad.

But I feel… hopeful as I turn to my mate and he wraps his arms around me, holding me, giving me a moment to just… feel.

Grandpa passed his torch to my Dad.

Grandma passed hers… to me.

Every time I use my powers, I'm with her. Every vision, every tear… is her gift.

THE DOOR TO MY OLD DORM SQUEAKS PAINFULLY AS I SHOVE IT OPEN. The familiar scent of Georgia's perfume and our shared vanilla laundry detergent fans the room, cutting through the lingering smell of smoke. It's untouched, surprisingly. Most of the dormitory survived the original attack and the recent war.

There's no running water, of course. It'll be cold when the sun sets again, but there's a bed, and that's all that matters to me right now.

Cole closes the door behind us and locks it. I move to the window at the far end of the snug room and look out at the campfires and groups littered across the campus square.

"Sydney and Sarah are returning to Moonrise tonight," I say into the silence. "Sydney said he's going to come back in the morning to start moving his warriors back to the border."

"Ryan and Aviva are also planning on moving out in the morning,"

Cole says behind me. I hear him pull his shirt over his head, hanging it over my old desk chair.

"What are we going to do?" I turn to face him but I'm nervous. I expect him to push me away again, tell me I'm leaving, that this… can't continue.

But he says, "We'll need to stay in Tarsian for a few weeks, at least, to oversee the transition of splitting the kingdom and the crowning of the new kings."

"Do you know who they'll be yet?"

"I gave your aunt my opinion on who should rule their territories, but the decision is hers alone."

"Then you're really giving up your title?"

"Yes." His eyes meet mine in the gloom. He runs his tongue along his lower teeth in thought. "Misty–"

"Don't you dare," I rasp, edging a step toward him. "If you're about to stay I need to return to my family, I swear to the Goddess, Cole, I'll smack you."

The corner of his mouth ticks into a smile. "I was going to say, you're a princess. I'm… about to be no one. Packless. A commoner."

"That doesn't matter to me."

"It matters to me."

"I'll always be a princess of Crescent Falls. *The* princess, actually. And you'll always be my mate. That's not going to change." But everything else will. I can see that truth on his face as I take his hands in mine. "We're going to be okay. All three of us. You, me, and the baby. We're a family, and we have a fresh start. You can finish your residency."

He leans down, pressing his forehead against mine. "You can finish your degree."

I snort a laugh. "How?"

"Well, you'll probably have to go to Wellington and major in plain old history, but then you can work there and start a protohistory program of your own, teach the next generation."

I wrap my arms around him, holding him close, breathing in his scent.

He runs a hand down my back. "Misty, I'm sorry about your grandparents."

I close my eyes, letting my grief flare for a moment. "I think she knew this was going to happen. She mentioned it to me, how Grandpa was sick and…." A tear slides down my cheek. "I'm happy they went together. I'm grateful for the way it happened. I know that sounds… crazy, but… they were together until the end. They're together now."

He cups the back of my head and kisses me long and slow.

"Promise me," I whisper against his mouth, "that we'll be the same. That we'll be together until the end."

"I promise"

I wrap my arms around his neck, deepening the kiss until we fall onto my rickety old twin bed.

I gasp in alarm when the frame gives out completely, crashing to the ground with us on top of it.

Cole groans a laugh.

"You have a real bed at your… house? Right?" I ask, then cough as dust swarms around us.

"In Crescent Falls?" he chuckles. "I was a resident doctor, Misty. I have a shitty one-bedroom apartment in the Neutral Zone."

"But is it at least a queen sized bed?"

"Yes," he laughs. "It is. It's enough for two."

4 2

WELCOME TO THE FAMILY

Cole

MISTY FALLS INTO A DEAD SLEEP IN MY ARMS ON GEORGIA'S OLD BED. I can't sleep. I try, but it's useless tonight. I'm not sure about leaving her here alone, so I bide my time, sliding out of bed and tucking her in tight before standing by the window and watching the square below as the fires turn to embers and warriors go back to wherever their comrades are bunking down for the night.

Maybe it was selfish of me to take Misty here, to sleep in an actual bed, while warriors are literally sleeping outside in the square.

The room starts to close in on me, and I make the snap decision to leave. The dorm is mostly empty. A few students mill about, their faces marred with confusion. Students who survived the attack but didn't get away from Richard and his magic. Students who were turned into voiceless, mindless warriors and remember nothing of the weeks they spent in Richard's clutches.

With our bond back in place, I can sense that she's still asleep, still safe, as I cross the square. I walk a path I carved several years ago when I was a student here. I take my usual route like it's just another sleepless night when I couldn't find the focus I needed to slouch over a book in the library.

The student commons and the new cafeteria are in pieces—a tangle of ancient rubble and the new, sleek, shattered glass that used to be a botanical garden for student use. The glass crunches under my feet as I pick my way toward the railing of the sweeping deck that overlooks the shore and the beach below.

It's high tide. Waves beat against the beach, dragging sand into its raging current. The sound is calming to my entire body, even to my wolf, which has been at full strength and dying to be unleashed since I marked Misty.

We haven't talked about that. I want to bring it up, but the only words I can say to her are that I'm sorry.

The honest truth is that I'm not. Not now that we survived, and I have some sort of a future with her. She's mine.

But I wanted that moment to be different. I wanted it to mean something other than saving her life. I have a lifetime to make that up to her, but it doesn't feel long enough.

I run my fingers through my hair and pace the beach, trying to untangle my thoughts.

Eventually, I sink onto the sand, resting my elbows on my knees.

Voices drift along the beach. Male voices—familiar. I turn my head as two men come into view, veiled in darkness, but Ryan's profile is clear as moonlight reflects off the surf.

My night couldn't get any worse.

He spots me and frowns, but his companion, Evander, the head commander of the elusive Ghost army, gives me an expressionless nod of his head. I expect them to pass behind me and carry on with their midnight stroll, but Evander sits on my left side… and Ryan on my right.

None of us speak for what feels like an eternity. Ryan picks at the sand between his legs, tossing shells back into the water as the tide slowly recedes.

Evander crosses his arms over his knees and rolls his neck, groaning under his breath like he's sore.

I suppose if they're going to kill me, this would be a graceful death. I'm not sure I have it in me to fight back. Misty would rage if anything happened to me—again—however, and I think they know that.

"I thought this war would be longer," Ryan says over the sound of the waves, rolling a shell in his hand.

Evander makes a noise in his throat in agreement, stretching out his legs. "We'll all be home by Solstice."

Ryan chuckles, rolling his eyes to the moon.

I shift my weight between them, uncomfortable with their proximity and the way they boxed me in.

Evander says, "Syd left already, right?"

"Yeah, a few hours ago. The boys have been giving my mom a hard time, I guess. Cosette's in Moonrise helping out, but they're at their wits end. Sydney's going to lay down the law, or so he says."

"Those boys have Sydney wrapped around their pinky fingers," Evander chuckles, which betrays his normally dry, emotionless voice. "He's gone soft."

"Yeah, well, so have you."

"Three kids will do that to you."

Silence falls again.

I debate standing up and walking away, but Ryan asks, "Is Misty giving you hell for trying to reject her yet?"

"We, uhm, haven't had a chance to talk about it."

Evander's mouth ticks into a faint smile. "The balls on this guy, thinking he can reject a woman from this family."

Ryan barks a laugh. "That's the first thing I thought. I know you tried and failed with Kenna."

"I didn't even try," Evander replies, smirking. "She would have killed me flat out, I'm sure."

I glance back and forth at the men, but they're still laughing. "You wanted to reject Princess Kenna?"

"Just Kenna, at least to you," Ryan says, tossing the shell into the waves. "Since you're family now. And yeah, Evander here got a little nervous when he realized Kenna was his mate, but instead of rejecting her, he pulled a disappearing act for, what, five years?"

"Something like that," Evander murmurs, his eyes on the ocean.

"Why?" I ask, genuinely curious.

"The same reason you rejected Misty. To protect her. To keep my mind clear so I could *continue* to protect her."

I glance at Ryan, noticing the faraway look in his eyes.

"Is it too soon to bring up... your first mate? Since you're throwing me under the bus?" Evander's eyes light with mischief.

Ryan scowls. "Totally different circumstances, Ev. Goddess above–"

Evander chuckles, shaking his head. "Well, I think Cole is the first guy to actually reject a mate in this family."

"It–it didn't work," I grind out, feeling utterly exposed. They're teasing each other, and me, but I barely know these guys, and up until a few days ago, I was the enemy.

Now, I have no idea where I stand.

"Yeah, because you're mated to the most stubborn person in the entire family," Ryan snorts, nudging my arm. "Congratulations are in order, honestly, but for our parents. Dad's been dying for Misty to find her mate and settle down."

I watch the waves, unsure what to say. What do I possibly say to her brother? I already told him I wasn't sorry for how things happened. I got her out. That was my only goal when I realized not only who she was but that she was my mate. I got her home.

I'd do it again–the same way.

Ryan stands, dusting sand off his pants, and says, "Aviva and I are leaving in the morning. My guys are already moving back to the border, taking their sweet time and enjoying the heat, I'm sure. I'm going to try to get some sleep."

Evander nods his goodbye, but Ryan claps me on the shoulder again. It takes all of my strength not to flinch away.

I watch him fade in the distance until he's no longer in sight.

Evander stretches out his legs beside me and says, "You get used to it."

"To what?"

"The family. The powers. The dynamics."

I shake my head. "I don't understand the–the kindness, especially from Ryan."

"Well, Sydney's the one to worry about. He chewed me out a time or two about Kenna, before we got married, at least. He's not as scary as he wants to be, though. And Ryan just… he went through it a few years ago. I'm not sure if you know or heard the rumors."

I sigh, turning back to the waves. "About the young woman from Silverhide?"

"Yeah, her name was Hadley. She was working with the Draven coven. Ryan… killed her. They were mates."

"I'd heard," I murmur. I remember the rumors swirling through Crescent Falls, especially when the news broke that the Silverhide pack was relocating to Eastonia. I'd just been starting my residency at the time. "How did Aviva react to that?"

Evander gives me a sideways smile. "She broke Ryan out of whatever haze he had been in for over two years. Ripped it right out of him. Ryan and Aviva didn't even know they were mates at first. He was so torn up about what he'd done to his first mate that he couldn't see what the Goddess put in front of him until Aviva forced him back from the brink of death. That was only a few months ago, actually. This past summer. She forgave him for trying to die on her and now has him by the balls. It's nice, actually. In a way, it was like another brother-in-law joined the family."

Now I'm laughing. It's a sound I haven't heard in a long, long time. But the laughs taper off, leaving that same sucking, all-consuming silence broken only by the waves ripping across the shore.

Evander continues, "Once we knew that Misty was with you… Ryatt and Ella fought hard to convince all of us that she was okay and safe. Even after the letter you sent saying you were going to use her as a breeder and that you'd kill her if they crossed into Tarsian. Isaac… he obviously didn't agree and fought hard to start the war days after she'd been taken, but when he saw what you'd done–how you managed to get her out–"

"I rejected his daughter in front of him."

"You got her out unscathed, in one piece. I have it on good authority that he railed on Ryatt for not taking you with them. He thought Ryatt might have known in advance she was your mate. Is that true?"

"No," I whisper, more to myself than to Evander. "It wouldn't have mattered. I wouldn't have left."

"What you did here… was incredible. The work you had to put in behind the scenes to stage a coup against Richard…." Evander tilts his head, considering. "Well, seeing as you just gave up your title, if you need a new job, let me know."

I chuckle, "I'm not cut out to be a Ghost, if that's what you're getting at."

"Maybe a contractor? Someone I call in to help design missions, then."

I hold his gaze. "I'm going back to my residency in Crescent Falls, if they'll have me. If that fails, I'll call you."

He nods, clapping me on the knee, then rises to his feet. "Kenna's probably wondering where I am. If I don't see you tomorrow, I'm sure Maddy will make us gather for Solstice, regardless of the circumstances."

I haven't even thought about Solstice. The memory of my mom and sister sprint through my head, cracking my heart into pieces. I watch Evander disappear into the shadows but take my time rising and walking back to the dorm. When I arrive, Misty's awake, sitting up in bed and picking her nails.

"Hey," I whisper, closing the door behind me.

"Couldn't sleep?"

I shake my head, sinking onto the edge of the bed. I reach for her, taking her fingers, smoothing my thumb over her skin. "I think we should talk."

Misty smiles sadly and shakes her head. "About what? There's about a hundred things I'm sure we need to discuss."

"I marked you without your consent," I say before I lose the nerve. "I had to, but I wish that hadn't been the case."

Her soft, sleepy expression splinters. "Do you... do you not want to do this? With me?"

"Misty, no. No, of course I do, I just... I wish a lot of things had been different for us, marking you included. We're mates again, but we don't have to be if this isn't what you want anymore." I can't walk away. I wouldn't be able to give her up a second time. I don't say that, but I watch her face as she drops into thought, toying with my fingers.

"So, we're going to be living in Tarsian for a while?"

"You're deflecting–"

Her eyes meet mine and hold–stern and unyielding. "I never accepted your rejection in the first place, Cole. You're stuck with me, and that's final."

I arch my brows. She throws me a cat-like glare.

"Mark me, then." I lean in, caging her in against the bed. "You spoiled, ornery little princess."

She scoffs, but the sound turns to a soft moan when my hands start their heated exploration of her curves, her breasts, especially.

It doesn't take long for our clothes to fall in a pile on the floor beside the bed. I nudge her legs apart and enter her swiftly, both of us groaning and savoring the feeling of just being together again.

But this time, it's different. It's not desperate and heartbreaking thinking we're on borrowed time because we're not. This is... forever. For a lifetime, to start.

We have the future I didn't think was possible, and I'll spend the rest of my life making that up to her.

Her moans turn to whimpers as her body gives in to mine, her pleasure roaring through our bond, falling in rhythm with my thrusts as I start coming undone at the seams.

Misty presses a kiss to my shoulder, her teeth raking over my skin in a way that has tingles of anticipation fluttering over my spine.

She bites down, hard, leaving her mark. Claiming me as her mate.

43

SOLSTICE EVE

Misty

"You need to chill," I hiss, giving Cole a nudge in the hipbone.

He adjusts my duffle bag on his shoulder and shoots daggers down at me before clearing his throat and rapping his knuckles on the front door of my grandparents' beach house in Maatua.

It's pouring down rain. Thunder snaps in the distance, sending a boom rattling over the nearby shore just beyond the house. I breathe in the familiar scent of salt and ozone and say a short, sweet prayer that the next three days aren't a total shitshow.

Normally, I'd waltz right in. I lived here for over a year, for Goddess' sake. It's practically mine.

It's been a little over a week since the war. We spent that week in Serpentia, sharing my old dorm room, while Cole dealt with his forces and the Alphas clambering for a shot at the three open Alpha King positions up for grabs. I could have gone back to Moonrise, or Crescent Falls, I suppose… but there's no way in hell I'm letting Cole out of my sight ever again.

331

Now, it's Solstice Eve, and my family is gathering like we normally would have… in Maatua. At my grandparents' mansion.

Tears sting my eyes for a second. Just a second. Grandma wouldn't have wanted anyone to cry for them. Us gathering, celebrating this holiday together like we have for decades… that was her dream and the reason she sacrificed herself. We're all together again.

The door swings open to reveal my mother wearing an apron, her cheeks dusted with flour and her hair falling out of the claw-clip fixed to the top of her head.

She beams at me, launching into my arms. "I thought you weren't getting here until tomorrow morning!"

"Kenna brought us here, but she's making a stop at the castle to see Poppy and the family." I gasp. She's squeezing the life out of me. She pulls away, dusting flour from my blue blouse. "Sorry, sweetheart. Oh!" She looks up at Cole and gives him the biggest grin I've ever seen. "Wow, you are very tall!"

"Uhm, thank you," Cole replies, clearing his throat. "I'm Cole–"

"I know." She breathes then says under her breath–as if to herself, *"Poor thing."* She turns, beckoning us into the house. "Come on, then. Get out of the rain. There's wine in the kitchen Cole, if you'd like a glass. Or… perhaps something stronger?" Her eyes are pleading, like she thinks he's going to need a stiff drink for whatever tonight has in store for him.

But Cole doesn't notice the look she's giving him. He glances around in awe at the pale wood finishes, the white carpets and walls. It's a very modern home–a sharp contrast to the dormitory we've been sleeping in for the past week. Mom apparently packed all of her Solstice decorations and brought them here because the house erupts in color and sparkling lights, and Solstice music drifts toward us from the kitchen, mingling with a few voices from within.

"You two will be staying in Misty's old room, just down there." Mom points to the left where a hallway and a row of doors stretches just before the house opens to the kitchen and dining room. "She has the best views of the beach."

"Cole can sleep in the den," Ryan says sarcastically as he walks down the stairs holding two bottles of Grandpa's best whiskey. "Seeing as they're not married yet." He winks at me.

I throw him a glare. "I'm already pregnant, you dickhead!"

Cole's face goes a bright pink, but Ryan rolls his eyes, motioning toward the kitchen with one of the bottles. "Cole? Drink? You look like you could use one."

Mom heaves a heavy sigh, giving Cole an apologetic smile. "Go ahead. I'll help Misty unpack."

I can tell the idea of joining what looks to be Ryatt, Sydney, and Ryan for a drink isn't appealing to Cole right now. I don't blame him, honestly. It's not like we've been able to sit down as a family and talk about my mate, our relationship, and everything that happened this fall and early winter.

But to my surprise, Cole hands my duffle bag to Mom and strides past us, falling in step with Ryan.

"He's very handsome, Misty," Mom says, smiling wistfully.

"I know." I smile, unable to help it. The past week has been heaven as much as it's been stressful and uncertain. With the war behind us, and Richard dead… we have a shot. We have a life to look forward to, and I'm getting to know my mate outside of the circumstances that brought us together, and that's been… wonderful. Shocking, confusing, and utterly blissful.

I follow Mom to my old room. It smells the same—like salty ocean air and lilacs. It's a simple room with just a bed, a dresser, and a desk, but I did spend a little over a year here before going to Tarsian for college. Magazines sit on the edge of the dresser. A bulletin board hangs over the desk littered with pictures of old friends and ticket stubs from concerts. It's clean but otherwise untouched.

My heart begins to quake as memories of living here with my grandparents hurtle to the forefront of my mind.

It still hasn't hit me that they're gone. I'm not sure it ever will.

I pull some old clothes from the dresser, shimmying into a pair of cotton shorts and a crewneck sweater with little evergreen trees wrapped in sparkling lights woven on its surface. It's normally warm in Maatua, but with the breeze coming off the water tonight, and the rain in the forecast… it's a bit chilly.

"I've always loved that sweater." Mom smiles, tucking her hands in the pocket of her apron.

I roll my lower lip between my teeth. "Does everyone hate Cole?"

"No, sweetheart, of course not."

"Are you *completely* sure?"

She lays her hands on my shoulders, leaning in to say, "Don't forget that all of us found our mates in… strange ways. I mean, Ryatt and Ella…" She blows out her breath. "I've told you about what happened here, in Maatua, right?"

I nod, thinking of the story of Ryatt meeting the family and being there for the birth of my brothers. He and my dad had almost dueled over Aunt Ella, but a week in paradise seems to change everyone's perspective on things.

Funny how that works.

"And," she says, reaching up to tuck my hair behind my ears, "Your dad thought my name was Jenny for nearly a month when I first came to live at the castle. I didn't know how to tell him otherwise, so I rolled with it. It could be worse, you know."

I smirk, tilting my head toward the door. "I should make sure they're not killing him right now."

"I should check on the cake," she says, wincing.

"Where's Dad?"

"He's upstairs in Grandpa's office. He's got quite a bit to sort through. Your grandfather was a bit of a hoarder in his old age—mostly books, paperwork." She sighs as we walk slowly down the hallway, side by side. "We've decided to hold off on a memorial for a few weeks, seeing as the royal army from Crescent Falls is still returning from Eastonia and… we have a large family and an even larger group of friends who will want to be there, but I've spoken with the High Priestess, and the memorial will be held at the royal temple. She's putting it together for us."

"It… it doesn't feel like they're gone."

"I know," she whispers, smoothing her hand over my hair. "One day, it will, and it will be hard but... they'll always be with us. Especially here, when we gather as a family in this house they built for us, for this reason."

"Reason being... burning cakes in the oven?" I giggle as the smoke alarm blares.

Mom curses under her breath and hurries around the corner, her shriek of alarm followed by Ryan's boisterous laugh and Ryatt saying he'll see if the bakery in town is still open.

I settle next to Cole at the kitchen table. Sarah and Kenna, who'd taken the kids to visit Poppy for the day, return, and the quiet evening turns to madness with five children under the age of five darting around, trashing the living room and the den within minutes of pulling out their toys–*our* old toys, actually.

I spent every Solstice here as a child. Brie plays with a doll I named... Steve, even though it's a girl. I watch her bounce around with the tattered thing in her arms, her eyes full of sparkling lights and the magic of the darkest night of the year.

Cole wraps his arm around my shoulders, chatting amiably with Ryatt, who tells us stories about Jaxon. Eventually, Ella joins us, dusty from working all day in her father's study, and chimes in with her own tales of Alpha King Jaxon. Cole warms to them, his eyes changing from cautiously polite to... grateful. They know a totally different side of his father than he did, and they paint that picture for him, filling in the gaps of his memory.

Aviva joins us an hour later, just as dinner's served up buffet style, all of us clambering for the best seats at the long dining room table. She's going through it during this pregnancy, that's for damn sure. She rubs her eyes and fixes a small plate of food before plopping down beside her mate with a long, exhausted sigh.

So far, I have no symptoms, but I know that'll change any day now.

"So," Sydney says between bites of prime rib, mashed potatoes with thick gravy, and an array of sides and garnishes, "When are you moving back to Crescent Falls?"

Cole answers before I can, which is great, because I honestly have no idea what's going to happen next. I'm just along for the ride, and for the first time in my life, I'm okay with that.

"I've been in contact with the hospital I used to work at. They have room for me to come back and finish my remaining years in residency, so once everything in Tarsian is patched up, I'll be free to return. But that's only if Misty wants to finish her degree at Wellington or one of the city colleges in Crescent Falls. Celestoria has a… fantastic history program, so that's also an option for us."

Suddenly, all eyes are on me, which I don't necessarily appreciate. "Uh, yeah. I should *probably* decide what I'm doing next," I grumble around the bite of food I just forked into my mouth. Honestly, I haven't given much thought to what's supposed to happen with my degree. TU is in shambles. The idea of it opening for students within the next few years—let alone *months*—is far-fetched, to say the least.

I've just been… reeling. Taking it day by day.

"I'll probably end up at Wellington," I decide, nodding to myself as my words bounce down the table. "It's a good school."

Dad replies, "Misty, it's likely you'd have enough credits to graduate *now* at Wellington, based on your course load the last two years. It wouldn't be Protohistory, but it would be history, nonetheless. Your great-uncle Ben was recently offered a tenure at Wellington. We'd be losing our royal historian if he takes the job… maybe that would be something you're interested in?"

"Being the record keeper for the kingdom?" Something bright echoes through my chest that I haven't felt in what feels like an eternity. *Excitement.* "Would you really… give me the job?"

Dad smiles at me with so much love in his eyes that it almost breaks my heart. "Of course."

I glance at Cole. He smiles down at me lovingly, resting his hand on my thigh.

"Fine, if I have to," I say, but I fail at lacing sarcasm through the words. Happiness and relief shine bright through the syllables instead.

44
UNEXPECTED GIFT

Misty

We finish dinner and eat Mom's burnt Solstice cake. The kids get tucked into bed upstairs, and for a while, the adults sit out on the covered deck, sipping wine–except for me and Aviva (we were given hot chocolate) and pouring drams of Grandpa's best and favorite whiskey. I listen to stories about my grandparents that I'd never heard before and lean my weight against Cole, his arms wrapped around me, warming me against the chill of the rain and brisk ocean air.

It's after midnight when we finally go to bed, falling into the covers, curling up nose to nose.

"Mom got you a stocking," I tell him in a whisper. "Watching us open them is her favorite part of the whole day, so act really surprised and excited about it, okay?"

He runs his fingers through my hair. "I will."

I want to ask about his mom and sister but their whereabouts, and the status of his relationship with them–whether they know what he had to do to his own father, her mate–we haven't talked about it.

I tell myself we all need time–Cole most of all.

He rolls to the side, reaching to the floor where his bag rests against the bed.

"What are you doing?"

He groans softly as he rolls back over with something in his fist. "I had a plan for this."

"For... *what?*"

"We were going to go for a walk after dinner, on the beach under the moonlight, and I was going to... do this properly. But it's raining and...." He sits up, kneeling on the bed. I balance on my elbow, absolutely perplexed by the rosy stain on his cheeks.

He fights for words for a moment, his eyes distant and glassy-fixed on his pillow. But then his eyes meet mine and... he doesn't need those words. I can see it in his eyes.

"I love you," he whispers, the words heavy, desperate, and full of feeling.

"I love you," I whisper back. "Are you... going to propose to me yet, or are you going to wait until tomorrow?"

The color on his cheeks deepens. "How did you–"

"Sydney told me, like... five minutes after we got here."

Cole closes his eyes and lets go of the breath he was holding, murmuring something under his breath that sounds a whole lot like, *"Evander was right; Sydney is the one to look out for."*

But he smiles, then chuckles, then... laughs.

I sit up all the way, beaming at him, at the sound of his happiness. It's the most beautiful sound I've ever heard.

"Gods dammit, Misty. Yes, I'm proposing to you." He unfurls his fingers, revealing the ring.

It's gorgeous. Simple and elegant. But the diamond is... familiar.

"Is this the diamond of faith?"

"Half of it," he says, holding it up. "I talked to Ella and Ryatt, and your dad, about it. It was lodged in my armor after the battle and I felt... I felt, and they felt, like it was rightfully yours."

Grandma told me the same thing. My powers sing in agreement.

"Where's the other half?"

"In a safe in the castle in Crescent Falls. Your mom helped me choose the setting. She said the whole diamond would be too heavy–"

"Is this what you've been doing all week while telling me you had meetings with Alphas about the future of Tarsian?"

His blush deepens. "Not–not totally." He chews his lip, looking suddenly boyish and nervous. "So... would you like to boss me around for the rest of our lives?"

I shoot him a cat-eyed glare.

He smirks, extending the ring. "Will you do me the honor of being not only my mate but my *wife?*"

I rise up, clasping his face between my hands, and kiss him hard. "Yes," I breathe, my eyes filling with tears–happy ones, finally. "I was planning on it!"

He smiles against my lips. I feel him slip the ring on my finger.

We don't do more than kiss–not while sharing a house with my entire freakin' family–but we're woken in the earliest hours of the morning by my bedroom door creaking open and three small beings creeping into the room and crawling onto the bed. Brie peels my eyelids open, blinking down at me.

"Missy?"

"Hmm?"

"The Yule Wolf came," she hisses.

"Brie, it's four in the morning."

"He left presents!"

I groan, rolling with the little girl in my arms, smooshing her to the bed. She squeals in delight, but now Aris and Blake are jumping on the edge of the mattress, chanting, "Get up! Get up! *Get up!*"

The sound of the coffee grinder floats through the air, followed by several muffled voices and the first smells of coffee being brewed.

Cole swings his legs out of bed, grabs the boys and tucks them under each arm, and walks into the hallway. Aris and Blake's peals of laughter echo through the house as it wakes for a very early start to the day.

It's Winter Solstice, after all.

By 4:30 A.M, all of us are tucked on the couches in the den with cups of coffee and hot chocolate, blearily watching the kids rip into presents. Laughter and joy drifts through the air, but there's an undercurrent of suppressed grief. A week ago, this wouldn't have been possible. A week ago, Blake and Liam would have lost their mother and father. Aviva and Ryan wouldn't be opening a present for their unborn child–a blanket, sown by hand by Cosette, who's spending the holiday in Crescent Falls with her family.

My dad wouldn't be kissing my mom on the temple before handing her a neatly wrapped box. Ryatt wouldn't be kneeling with his grandson, inspecting a new toy train.

I catch Kenna's gaze. She's wearing the same slightly lost expression I am. She gives me a weak smile and the smallest, saddest shrug.

Two stockings still hang on the mantle, full to the brim with treats and cards... letters... the goodbyes we didn't get a chance to say.

I wade through a sea of wrapping paper and snatch Cole's gift before Blake can get his greasy little paws on it.

"This is for you," I say, plopping down beside him and crossing my legs. I twiddle my thumbs in anticipation as Cole arches a brow and begins tearing at the poorly wrapped present.

"So, that's where all the tape went," Mom teases, a stack of new novels from my dad–likely romance, given what she believes is a *hidden* treasure trove of books in her office.

I frown playfully at her as Cole rips the paper free.

"It's silly," I say over the incessant chatter and buzzing of the toy cars whizzing around our feet.

"It's... not." His eyes meet mine. "Where did you get this?"

"Kenna helped."

Kenna smiles and waves at the mention of her name but quickly goes back to wrenching wrapping paper out of Maeve's fingers while she tries to stuff it in her mouth.

We'd taken a bit of a scenic route to Maatua. Kenna met us in Tarsian, and we jumped to Moonrise first, where Cole had a whole thirty minutes to recover before we swept him to Veiled Valley, where Kenna and I spent an evening doing some last minute shopping while Evander and Cole wrangled the kids.

Brie, Blake, and Aris appear at our knees, gazing into the finely made wooden box resting on Cole's thighs. Liam glances up from his train and darts toward us, pushing and shoving his way in front of Cole.

"Ohhh," Liam beams, wide-eyed as Cole lifts the stethoscope from the box.

He lost his medical kit in Oasia—in the fire that swept through the castle after his first battle with Richard. It's the only detail he's shared about that night so far.

"Misty," he breathes. "This is… thank you." He gives me a kiss and then realizes my entire family is watching, and pulls away, but I'm feeling incredibly smug. I'm on cloud nine.

He examines it while all three children lean in, forgetting about their new toys. He tests it on Brie, who giggles wildly as Cole smiles down at her, listening to her heart.

"Here, look." He takes it off and gently places the ear tips in Brie's tiny ears, then presses the diaphragm to her chest. "That's your heart. That *bump, bump, bump.*"

"My turn?" Liam begs, his eyes—a soft, bluish violet—going wide. "Peas?"

My heart squeezes as Cole gently guides the kids through using his new stethoscope. Everyone gets a turn.

"Trash bag?" Ryatt asks, pointing at my dad, who rises and shakes out a bag, the two Alpha King's setting to work cleaning up the wrapping paper and discarded toy boxes.

By 6:00 A.M, the kids are already starting to rub their eyes, ready for naps. Ryatt and Dad bicker over who gets to make the pancakes—a family tradition started by Grandpa Maddox. Mom and Ella get ready for their own tradition—a long walk along the beach—without the kids.

But there's one present left. Cole brings it to me, sitting back down on the couch while the kids roll around with their toys on the rug in front of us.

Maeve is slack in Aviva's arms, both of them fast asleep on the opposite couch. I smile at the image and quietly rip the paper away.

It's a book. Smaller than average and bound by fresh leather. There's no title engraved on the cover.

I look up at Cole, thinking he'd be smiling and a little pink in the cheeks in anticipation for my reaction, but he looks grave.

I open it.

It's a printed rendition of the *Book of Whispers*.

Cole purses his lips for a moment, his eyes holding heavy on mine. "Richard had the pages copied and printed, thinking that if he lost the book, he could still use the spells. He was wrong about that," he begins, gripping my knee. "This is strictly for your research. The original book held the magic, but this is just… *words*. The magic is gone."

"The book took pieces of Richard's soul every time he used it, didn't it?"

"I think so, but… you have an opportunity to figure that out for sure."

I let the book rest in my lap and wrap my arms around his neck, holding him tight. I would have never admitted that I felt a sliver of regret the moment Cole stabbed the book, the power of the diamond tearing through the book's magic and destroying it, turning its ancient pages to ash. I wanted to know what else was inside, what secrets and knowledge were housed there from people, from gods, long lost to time.

Cole must have known that about me. That I have to know *everything*. Even if it hurts.

The scent of breakfast drifts from the kitchen while we remain in a tight embrace, wordlessly letting ourselves feel everything for the first time since the battle. Our shared grief. Our shared heartbreak. Our confusion over our conflicting feelings–being both incredibly, utterly happy and unbelievably devastated at the same time.

Things will be different a year from now. Next year, there will be a baby between us, gnawing on Cole's fingers while I pass out gifts. We'll have moved on from this uncertainty. We'll have new memories that will force the memories of the past few weeks to fade.

We spend the next two days with my family before returning to Tarsian again… for the last time.

4 5

THIS IS US

Misty

One Month Later

Cole pulls our rental car into an inconspicuous apartment building parking lot under the glare of a flickering streetlight. It's bitter cold and starless–a stunning contrast to the last month we spent in Tarsian–specifically Oasia–tucked in a small house in the inner city since the palace was lost almost completely to the massive fire in the aftermath of Cole's first battle with Richard.

We haven't talked about that night very much. The night of my birthday, his rejection, and the official start of the war. It was a month of preparations, politics, and very late nights spent alone while Cole sat in meetings with the newly established Elder Council of Tarsian.

Three new kings were recently chosen by my aunt, and now... we're off the hook.

Just in time for the massive memorial service for my grandparents being held tomorrow at the royal temple.

Cole stalls by slowly killing the ignition and rifling through the backpack he's been dragging around since I first met him. He pulls out a set of keys and stares at them as if in disbelief.

He didn't think he'd ever be coming back here.

"Did your landlord just keep all your stuff for you?"

"I paid rent a year in advance," he says under his breath but refuses to meet my eye "I have a few months left of that lease." He looks flustered as he adjusts his coat then stares at his reflection in the rear view mirror before taking a deep breath and stepping out of the car into the chilly night air.

He rounds the car and opens my door as I gather my purse and the book I've been thumbing through during our drive. I smile up at him, debating making a joke about his chivalry, but the look on his face gives me pause.

"We don't have to go in. We can get a hotel," I say as he closes the door. "We could stay with my parents, actually. You could see my old room."

He smiles faintly, jiggling the keys in his hand. "I'm sorry. It's just weird being back here. It doesn't feel real."

I look past him at the pale gray siding and the four stories of square, neatly spaced windows spilling light into the parking lot.

He's right. Nothing feels real right now. I haven't been back to Crescent Falls since... well, since before TU was attacked for the first time. The war was a shift in the paradigm—an undoing of everything we knew and believed to be true. The idea that magic like Richard possessed lurks just out of reach—that it even exists—has my stomach in knots every time I think about it.

Lately, the memory of that strange woman and her fangs keeps clogging my dreams. There're worlds like ours out there—shifter worlds... with other beings so unlike us it makes my skin pebble with uncertainty.

I destroyed the Gate of the Gods.

But Arthur said it was one of many. What happens when that knowledge falls into the wrong hands?

What happens when someone comes along with the power to do

so without needing something like the *Book of Whispers* to activate one?

It's a good thing Cole kept a copy of it. I still haven't been able to find the nerve to start my research, though.

I let my thoughts tangle while following Cole up a flight of stairs, then another, until we reach the third floor. It's the middle of the night, and only a few people are up and about. A woman steps out to greet a wolf who scratches on her door just as we walk down the hallway. A young man steps out of his apartment with three of his friends, the smell of cheap beer following behind them as they brush past us.

Cole's unit is on the end, the corner, and overlooks the woods that once belonged to Ryan's pack. Seeing the wall separating the NZ from Silverhide again is jarring, to say the least. As far as I know, no one has taken over the old territory yet.

Cole unlocks the door with ease and steps inside. I follow, feeling an overwhelming sense of both excitement and worry.

I was so upset that his wing of the castle in Oasia had been so... sterile and boring. It wasn't his, at all. It was simply where he stayed.

But this place? This was his home for two entire years.

I'm about to meet my mate for the first time, honestly. *What if he's a total weirdo?*

He turns on the main light, revealing a very basic, very male living room and a small kitchen with oak cabinets. The walls are a muted grayish-blue. A stoic, comfortable looking leather sofa greets us right away. He has a TV, a few pictures hanging on the walls, and a very neglected Ficus that's so withered it flops over in its pot, brown and leathery.

Cole carries our bags down a short, narrow hallway. I follow, passing the kitchen, which is spotless and smells sharply of citrus-scented cleaning solution.

"I had a cleaning company come yesterday," he says, setting our bags down in the corner of his... bedroom.

I glance into the bathroom, desperate to open the cabinet over the sink and pick through his toiletries, but decide I'm the one being weird and follow my mate into the bedroom instead.

The first thing I notice is his scent. It's everywhere. Beautiful and instantly comforting, cutting through whatever the cleaners used to wash the bedding and mop the wood floors. This room–out of the whole apartment where he lived, alone–is his. Pictures of his family and friends I've never met sit in frames on his dresser or are pinned on a bulletin board above the desk along the far wall, which is stacked full of anatomy and biology books. His bedspread is several shades of deep green–a quilt, handmade. I run my hand over it, feeling him watching me, but saying nothing as I continue my exploration. The bed takes up the majority of the room. I sit on the edge closest to the bedside table and look through the books stacked there. More books about medicine and the body in general.

"You look disappointed," he says, tucking his hands in the pockets of his jeans. He's wearing jeans and a hoodie, which makes him look like… someone I'd see at a coffee shop and bat my eyelashes at until he noticed me. He's clean shaven and has let his hair grow out a bit. I was right about it being curly.

He shed that slightly scary, dominating shell of armor that he wore for months. That side of him is gone–and buried.

"I'm not disappointed," I tell him, giving him a weak smile. "I'm actually relieved you don't have posters of women in bikinis plastered everywhere." At that thought, I open the drawer in his bedside table. Nothing weird there, either. No… condoms or anything of the like.

I rise and move to the closet doors, sliding them open. He steps out of my way, leaning his shoulder on the wall.

Button down shirts greet me. A few white coats I'm sure he wore to work at the hospital. Scrubs. The works.

He's a normal guy.

Thank the Goddess.

"Hey," he says, trying to get my attention. "What are you looking for, exactly?"

I heave a breath and turn to him, resigned. "Honestly, I was worried I'd come up here and find the girlfriend you failed to mention waiting for you to finally get home."

He arches his brows.

I shrug, then slide his clothes to the side, giving myself room for my own clothes, which I'll have to pick up at my parents' house tomorrow, at some point, since all I have is the clothes I'd grown accustomed to wearing in Tarsian.

In fact, I'm in a pair of leggings and one of Cole's sweatshirts right now because it's all I have that's not a fantastic gown, and seeing my mate's apartment for the first time wasn't a *gown* event.

I flip my hair over my shoulder and frown at the closet.

"We won't be living here for very long," he assures me, leaning into the closet with his hands braced on the top of the doorframe. "Our next place will have a walk-in closet."

"Is it weird being back?" I ask, turning to face him.

"Yes, very." He gives me a soft smile that doesn't reach his eyes. "I'm glad you're here with me."

I wrap my arms around his waist. His hands drop from the doorframe as he embraces me back with a groan. "That was a long trip."

"I know. I'm exhausted." I close my eyes for a moment, breathing him in. I wonder if every newly mated couple feels this way–unsure. Not about each other but about the future. Things changed so fast for us. Things are still changing, still so uncertain.

I went from hating this man to loving him so deeply the idea of us being apart again is a form of torture. I went from being a wild college student to... pregnant. I went from being a year away from finishing my degree to captured, tortured, and thrown into a brutal war that claimed the lives of my grandparents and forever changed my family.

Now, I'm wondering how I'm going to fit my shoe collection into Cole's closet. It doesn't feel right. It doesn't feel real. I feel like something that minuscule could be taken from me at any minute.

He cups my face between his hands. "I know what you're feeling. It's valid. This is... a hard adjustment."

"I just want things to feel normal again."

"We have to find a new normal."

I lean into his touch, letting his warmth soak into my skin. Letting his scent and proximity untangle my thoughts and numb my senses. Eventually, I end up in the bathroom with him, vigorously brushing my teeth while he checks the water temperature of the shower.

"It takes a while to warm up," he grumbles.

"Why'd you live here for so long if you didn't have hot water when you needed it?"

"Not all of us were born in a castle."

"Okay, *Alpha King*."

He smirks, rolling his eyes as he pulls his shirt over his head. I immediately shut up, watching the way his muscles flex as he turns back to the shower. "It's close to the hospital, and I wasn't here often. I can afford more, but at the time, I didn't need it."

It dawns on me that I'm the luckiest girl who's ever lived. This man is my mate. This beautiful, kind, brave, and apparently frugal man is mine.

We made it out. Both of us.

And now, I'm stepping into the shower with him, in the apartment we now share, looking toward a future, together.

"I only have two-in-one shampoo."

"Goddess, you're such a *guy*," I tease but make a mental note to raid my mom's heavily stocked bathroom for her good shampoos and soaps tomorrow before the memorial. I pluck the single bottle off the shower shelf and gasp, holding it up to him. "Cole, this is *three*-in-one. Shampoo, conditioner, and body wash? That's worse! Who are you?"

He steals the words with a kiss that nearly knocks me off my feet. He presses me against the tiles, shielding me from the spray of the water. I fumble with the bottle of soap, deciding to just toss it over the curtain since I'm going throw it in the trash anyway, and wrap my arms around his neck.

He groans against my mouth, our bodies flush and heated, and not just from the water. I can't get enough of him. His mark on my neck burns as need thrums through my body. His hands slide down my sides, gripping my waist as he nibbles my lower lip, drawing out a sharp moan. He grips the back of my thighs and picks me up, pressing me into the tiles.

"Wrap your legs around my waist," he rasps against my mouth.

I obey. The head of his cock prods my entrance, stretching me as he grinds his hips into mine. My fingers lace through his wet hair, my mouth covering his in another heated, untamed kiss. "Please," I pant, tugging his hair. "Please, Cole–"

He groans as his cock slides home, parting my folds. I arch my neck, closing my eyes against the sensation of him thrusting into me so fully my toes curl.

He grips my thighs hard enough to leave bruises, but I'm beyond feeling anything but the way his cock is hitting places so deep I'm not sure if I'm screaming his name or just imagining it echoing through the bathroom.

He grits his teeth, burying his face in the crook of my neck.

My entire body rattles with pleasure as he grinds his hips again, slowing his pace like he's savoring this moment.

His lips brush over the mark he left on my skin before he nibbles down my neck. I moan, overstimulated and starting to tense up, my leg muscles locking and my core throbbing with desire.

"Come for me," he says, lifting his face to mine. His eyes are dreamy and hooded, dark with need.

"Make me come," I counter, gasping as he slams into me, pinning me there. I'm totally at his mercy, his whim. My body has always been his. Maybe that's why I was so willing the very first time we did this– when we were forced to do it.

It's always been great. He's always been great. But this is….

Another thrust sends me over the edge. My inner muscles tighten around him, spasming. He claps a hand on the tiles behind me and grunts with his own pleasure as he comes, filling me with warmth.

I'm boneless. My legs shake as I ride out the most intense orgasm I've ever had in my entire life. Cole kisses my temple, panting in my ear, "I love you so much."

I smile the biggest smile that's touched my face in months.

Later that night, when Cole is sound asleep beside me with his arm draped over my waist, I watch moonlight drift over sheets that smell like him—like us—like the home we get to share, in peace.

I pray. It's been a while, admittedly. But I'm not praying to the Moon Goddess tonight and thanking Her for this blessing, this gift.

"Thank you for giving him back to me," I whisper to my grandma. "Thank you for giving me this chance. I promise I won't waste it."

46

YOU CAN NEVER GO HOME

Misty

THE ROYAL TEMPLE IN CRESCENT FALLS IS THE SHINING STAR OF THE city—the center of the capital of my kingdom. My parents got married here. I attended services and funerals here. I've always been in awe of the craftsmanship that went into building this place. Every inch of the temple is detailed. Depictions of great battles, of central characters in the Goddess' narrative, sweep across the walls as I travel down a quiet corridor toward the small group of people taking refuge in an alcove.

Kenna looks solemn as she scrunches the fabric of her dress between her fingers. Evander's hand rests on her waist as he watches memorial goers leaving the temple.

Mom and Dad stand at the temple entrance nearby, shaking hands and accepting condolences.

Sydney sighs heavily, watching our parents. "Just family back at the castle for the luncheon, right?"

"That's what Mom said," Ryan replies.

It's been ages since I've seen Ryan in a suit. He looks stuffy and uncomfortable as he slides his hand over his jacket front, adjusting his tie. Aviva glows in her black midi-dress, the first hints of her pregnancy beginning to show.

I smooth my hand over my belly in reflex. Flat. It's probably–definitely too early for a bump. I'm kind of excited for it, honestly.

"I'm going to go walk around for a bit," I say to the group. I haven't been able to sit still all morning. The memorial service was lengthy but beautiful with several speakers standing at the podium, going on and on about my grandparents in a formal fashion that had my head bobbing and brain exiting my skull within the first thirty minutes... but then friends and family started to speak instead of Alphas who'd ruled alongside my grandparents.

Grandma Isla is remembered as being gracious, brave, and headstrong. Her kindness was legendary, but so was her fierceness. Grandpa Maddox is remembered for being stoic and level-headed, a firm ruler. A strong, able king. I couldn't do more than stare at the portrait Ella painted of them–over two decades ago now–which was nestled just in front of the podium and surrounded by flowers.

I turn from my family and walk back down the corridor. I have no direction in mind. I just can't stand here and feel sorry for myself anymore. The past month was busy enough to numb the grief of losing them, but now that Cole and I are back in Crescent Falls trying to piece together a new life, the grief hits hard.

Cole disappeared as the memorial drew to an end. I haven't seen him in at least twenty minutes, so I take a quick jaunt through the temple and out onto the veranda overlooking the lake, and the city beyond.

Snow blankets the rolling hills leading down to the lake. A few people walk on the bike trail, stopping to peer at the crowd leaving the temple. In the wake of the war and the news of my grandparents' death, the public began laying flowers at the base of the temple. Now wilted, frozen roses–my grandma's favorite–lift in a brisk breeze, scattered by the wind, like drops of blood against a blanket of white.

I spot Cole standing beside one of the many statues of the Moon Goddess situated around the temple. He's watching little specks skate across the frozen lake, his hands tucked in his pockets. Gray daylight dances across his profile as he turns to me, giving me a half-cocked smile, but his eyes are heavy, and dark.

I pace toward him, hugging my thick, wool trench coat around my middle. "What are you doing out here?"

He shrugs a bit guiltily. "I needed a moment. I–I didn't get to do this for my dad."

I nod, but my heart aches for him as he walks to a nearby bench and sits, leaning back and lifting his face to the single pocket of sunshine breaking through the clouds.

Getting to know Cole has been… the best month of my life. When it's just the two of us, we can talk for hours, finding out the little details we missed that didn't matter during the fight of our lives…. It helped us heal in a way.

But there was one thing he never spoke about. Not until right now.

"What happened to him?" I ask quietly.

Cole knows I'm not asking if he killed his father, because that's clear enough. I lost my grandparents, but it hadn't been by my hand, no.

"The curse was tearing him to shreds," Cole admits, shaking his head. "He was like the other's that'd been cursed early on. Silently pacing, staring into an abyss under the yoke of Richard's spells. Whenever that magic lifted, for whatever reason, he'd either have moments of lucidity or be totally, completely feral."

"Orion's mate, Lacey… she was in chains."

He heaves a breath. "Orion did that to keep her contained so he could try to save her, to treat her."

"But your dad was beyond that?"

"My dad was being used as Richard's main puppet as a means to control the kingdom. His source of the curse. Richard could make my dad do anything. He made him invite the Alpha's of Tarsian to a ball held at the castle before I came back. Most of those who attended never ended up leaving the castle… and if they did leave, they passed on the curse to their entire packs. It's how he built his army." He pauses, picking at his sleeves. "My dad wasn't the one who called me back to Tarsian. It was Richard. Punishment, I suppose, for my dad's quick thinking in getting my mom and Annabel out of Tarsian before the curse took him over completely."

Cole stretches out his legs. I'm still standing, gripping the top of the bench for support.

"My dad had a single moment of lucidity shortly after I arrived." He goes to explain those first days back in Tarsian. Orion and Lavender had their family locked away in the castle, far out of Richard's clutches. Cole stormed in and learned the order–the fraternity he once loved–had taken over his home.

"Adrian and I started planning," he says. "Orion kept shooting us down, and rightfully so. We were just wolves against a man with a magic book who was selling his soul to say his spells. Richard had nothing to lose, but we did. Adrian, especially. He had a family–a baby to think about."

So Cole decided the only way to stop Richard was to befriend the enemy, to get close.

To become the Alpha King, and stand at Richard's side while he unraveled Richard's plans from within.

"Dad was beyond help. That night everything changed–when Adrian and Elsbeth were killed… that was the same night I killed him. He begged me to do it. He was lucid, then. Begging and pleading with me to end his suffering and take over, to take back our Kingdom. He told me about the *Book of Whispers* and how Richard was devising a plot to kidnap the princess of Crescent Falls and use her powers for the book. The Gate wasn't his original plan. He wanted to raise the forges and use them to turn our world into his playground."

"The gate was his escape plan if that failed."

"Yes." He looks at me while I continue to grip the bench. "The attack on TU was already in motion, and I thought finding you, the princess, and getting you out would be easy, but… I saw you for the first time, and the bond snapped into place for me–immediately. I'd had inklings of the mate bond for about a year, but we hadn't been close enough for me to feel it fully until that moment and I… couldn't handle what he did to you. He knew, I think. About our bond."

"It's over now," I tell him softly, gently, my voice barely above a whisper.

He rises and steps toward me. I take his hand, squeezing.

"Would you be willing to go visit my mom and my sister? Possibly within the next few days?"

"Of course."

"They live on one of the islands off the northern coasts. We'll have to take a ferry."

"That's okay, Cole. We'll make a road trip out of it. You start your residency again in two weeks, anyway."

He ropes his arm around my shoulder. Instead of meeting back up with my family to finish saying goodbyes to the memorial guests, we get a head start on the short drive to the castle where everyone from our family, our friends, our royal households, are gathering to hold a different kind of memorial.

One where the stories are quiet and laced with laughter.

Because we knew them. We loved them. To us, they weren't just an Alpha King and Luna Queen.

The castle is silent when we arrive and park near the front gate. Wind whispers through the massive, decades old rose garden my grandma adored.

A strange feeling steps over me as we cross through the gate. Cole's talking about grabbing a drink with Ryan and Sydney later while my mom helps me go through my closet and pack in preparation to fill Cole's tiny apartment with my things, but I pause on the front walkway, the diamond on my finger flaring with light.

I raise my hand and let my powers flow in gentle, curling puffs of white mist.

Grandma Isla walks up the steps with a suitcase in her hands, wearing a skirt and blouse. She pauses to look over her shoulder at me, winking, her face shockingly young and nearly identical to my own.

She whirls back to the door without a hint of hesitation, without a sliver of doubt, and waits.

Once, a long time ago, she walked up those same steps not

knowing how this arrangement could possibly help her family pay their debts. She had no idea that she'd become the Alpha King's breeder, or that the man waiting within the castle would be her mate.

A single tear slides down my cheek. This vision isn't how their story went, but it's how they imagined it would have gone, had they had the ability to turn back time and try again.

A young grandpa Maddox opens the door and pulls her into his arms, spinning her in a circle before lowering her to the ground and kissing her.

They fade like specks of stars, swept away by the wind.

A feeling of utter, complete peace passes through me, erasing every pang of grief.

I look at Cole, giving him a weak smile that he returns. He extends his hand to me. "Ready?"

"For what?" I laugh, taking his hand and allowing him to lead me to the door, which opens for us, a warrior stepping aside to let us through.

"To show me your old room, seeing as you spent most of the night rifling through my apartment."

I throw him a playful frown. "Fine. I hope you like the color pink because, once my things are packed, that's going to be the main color scheme at *our* apartment."

"We won't be living there for long." He follows me upstairs, taking his time to peer at the portraits and shadowed hallways leading to various wings of the castle. "I actually wanted to talk to you about something."

"Oh?" I open my bedroom door wide, ushering him inside.

"Wow," he says, looking slightly impressed. "Bubble gum pink. I wouldn't have guessed."

I narrow my eyes as he paces toward the window overlooking the back garden.

"What did you want to talk about?"

"Sydney has an offer for us I think we should consider. He needs a new clinic in Shadowcrest, and he wants me to run it. I don't have a pack anymore and…"

"And Sydney has some really nice houses in Shadowcrest," I finish for him, regardless of if that was what he was going to say or not.

"That's not the reason," he says, sitting on the edge of the bed. "But the safety of living in Shadowcrest is appealing."

"Do you want Sydney to be your Alpha?" I ask in earnest.

"I want you to have a home and a community when the baby's born," he says.

I sit down beside him. "You'd have your own clinic."

"I would."

"And I'd be able to start working for my dad, officially."

"This could be our life, Misty. But it's up to you. Hell, I'd live in one of the tribal territories if–"

"It's going to be a while before I step foot in Eastonia again," I say under my breath, but I meet his gaze, my eyes bright with happiness. "Let's move to Shadowcrest."

47
PINK WEDDING

Cole

SNOWY SUNLIGHT DUSTS THROUGH CEILING HEIGHT WINDOWS IN ONE OF the guest rooms in King Isaac's castle. I stare at the snowflakes sticking to the frosted window as a woman with mousy brown hair and bright gray eyes adjusts my tuxedo for the eighth time, her small fingers deftly plucking invisible thread from my suit jacket.

"Mom," I say, then clear my throat. "I'm sure I look fine."

She glances up at me with glassy eyes before turning from me, walking toward the vanity. She's wearing a shimmering gray gown and a cape trimmed with white fur, possibly mink. Her braided hair is wrapped in an updo at the base of her neck, and she looks… stunning but lost in her thoughts.

She and Dad never married. Not officially. She never took vows before the Goddess, but I know they were deeply, utterly completely in love.

She lost her mate. I killed her mate, and now she's preparing me to marry my own mate.

I visited her alone shortly after the Winter Solstice. The reunion had been tense–heartbreaking, honestly. She'd spent months wondering if I was okay. It was almost impossible to get word to her about what was happening. When Lavender was rescued from Tarsian at the beginning of the war, she hadn't just been carrying a message for Misty, but one for the royal family with my mother and sister's location, and a plea to help them in the wake of my death.

She'd been thrilled to meet Misty when we moved to Crescent Falls for good, but I know her heart is still in shambles from losing my dad.

She knows I killed him. She knows I had to. I know she forgives me, but still, seeing her broken is gut wrenching.

"Are you ready?" She turns to me, smiling through her tears. "You look very handsome, Cole. You look like your father. I know he's watching over us right now."

"I know," I reply, swallowing past the lump in my throat. "I'm ready."

She shrugs her narrow shoulders and motions to the door. "The princes mentioned you'd probably need a drink before the ceremony begins. I'm sure they're waiting in the library for you."

"Is that where they said they'd be?"

"I believe so," she chuckles, unsure. "This is my first time in this castle. I'm not sure I even know how to get back downstairs."

The door opens, revealing my sister, Annabel, in her pale blue gown, her hair expertly curled and falling around her face as she hisses, "What's the hold up, Cole? The ceremony is supposed to start in ten minutes!"

"Is Misty doing all right?" I ask, checking my watch before following Mom out of the room.

"Morning sickness," Annabel shrugs. "She's a bit woozy, but she's dressed and ready to go."

The castle is a hot-bed of activity as I follow the women down an upper hallway. We pass the library, and I'm grabbed by the arm, yanked through a crack in the doorway.

Ryan kicks the door closed and shoves me toward the group of men lounging in various positions around the wide room. Three stories of bookshelves stretch to a domed ceiling while snow continues to fall in a bright, shimmering haze beyond the windows.

I glance behind me and notice my mom and sister aren't here, which is fine, I guess. They'll join the ranks of the women, while I—

"Drink up." Ryan thrusts a glass of exceedingly fine whiskey in my hand before turning to the group, which includes Sydney, Evander, Declan, Ryatt, and… Duncan.

I eye Duncan for a moment before sipping my drink then throw it back in one go. He's deep in conversation with Evander, smiling brightly. He's a handsome guy but definitely rugged—some kind of specialized mechanic.

He's my sister's mate.

I haven't had a moment to talk to him, not man-to-man. There's not much I can say to him but thank you, honestly, given that he was there for Annabel when I couldn't be.

Ryan joins their conversation, motioning me over. "We've got about six minutes before my mom tears into the room to tell us we're late, so finish that drink so we can get a second one in you."

"Why are you trying to get him drunk before his own wedding?" Ryatt tilts his own drink back, giving Ryan a playful glare.

"You've seen the decorations; he hasn't," Ryan replies smugly, rolling his eyes back to Evander. "You know what, I consider myself lucky Aviva and I got married in the Deadlands… twice. Mom's an absolute tyrant when it comes to party planning, and Sarah's no better."

"Don't bring my mate into this," Sydney laughs.

Ryan arches his brows. "I'm right, though. Your house is an explosion of pink taffeta, and you know it."

Evander sighs heavily and pours another dram of whiskey in my glass. "Anyway," he says, shooting daggers around the room.

"Anyway," Ryan drawls, looking at Duncan, "my offer stands. We could use someone like you in Silverhide if you and Annabel decide you want a change of scenery."

I don't have a single sec to process this—the idea of Annabel moving back to Eastonia–because Maddy bursts into the room with a snarl, "What the hell are you all doing up here still?"

"That's our cue," Sydney murmurs into his drink, rising and clapping me on the back.

I'm bustled out of the room and downstairs, looking around the gathered crowd for my mate, but all I see are mostly unfamiliar faces. The friends and extended family of the Alpha King of Crescent Falls and his Luna Queen crowd the ballroom, which has in fact been decorated in a… wintery type of pink, if that's a thing.

I smile despite the nerves skittering through my body as Ryan and Sydney escort me to the altar–an archway of pink and white. This whole wedding is for Maddy, honestly. Misty and I would have been fine going to the temple and having a quick ceremony without frills and fanfare, like Sydney and Sarah, but at least one of the siblings needed to have a real wedding.

The High Priestess is already waiting for me. She smiles curtly and sighs as Ryan and Sydney take their positions in the crowd.

We don't have groomsmen or bridesmaids. Misty didn't think it was necessary, but I also know she's not feeling great right now. Her pregnancy symptoms kicked in a few weeks ago and haven't let up.

I spot my mom and sister in the assembled crowd, standing beside Duncan, who leans down to whisper in Annabel's ear. She blushes brightly and swats his chest.

I feel my mouth tick into a smile at the sight.

We're fine. Everyone is fine. We made it out.

I keep telling myself every day to keep the memories of last year, of the war, at bay.

The crowd parts, and my mate comes into view. My heart stops as she's escorted by her father–dressed in his full regalia–down the aisle.

She's wearing a pearly white gown that drapes over her figure–silk, or satin–which shimmers in the chandelier light. Her veil is lace and trimmed with bubble-gum pink accents–flowers, I think, as she gets closer, and closer.

The rest of the room fades, and it's just me and her, standing before the priestess.

I barely register the vows. My eyes are locked with Misty's, and I remember the moment I saw her for the first time, in the street, just a day before all hell broke loose.

I never thought we'd make it to this point.

That shock echoes through me as I slip a new ring on her finger. A plain golden band that matches the setting of her engagement ring. I had it engraved with a date. The date of our first kiss, actually, beneath the campus in the tunnels. I'm not sure why I felt it was so important that we remember that moment given what happened shortly thereafter, but for me... it changed everything. It changed the reasons I was fighting against Richard.

I would have given up had it not been for her, and when I kissed her for the first time, I knew... she was mine.

I'm not sure the ceremony's even over when I lean down, cupping the back of her head and kissing her like I kissed her that night–fully, ravenously.

She rises on her toes and smiles around the kiss as people whoop and holler for us.

My mate. My *wife*.

* * *

"It was lovely. Just beautiful!" Lavender gushes to Maddy as Misty and I make our rounds during the reception.

We're both starving, but we haven't had a single second to ourselves since the reception started. The crowd ebbs and flows in conversation, which is broken up by multiple rounds of toasts to the happy couple, all while Misty and I are looking for an out.

Night has fallen. Misty eyes the dessert table as we pass, dropping into conversation with some of her distant relatives from a pack called Obsidian Temple, but then a woman beckons us toward the entrance of the ballroom.

It's Cosette, who works for Sydney and Sarah, running their house, and their lives, I've been told.

"Here," she whispers briskly, shoving a trio of stacked plates wrapped in tinfoil into my hands. "Take her upstairs to the Opal Room on the fourth floor. It's already set up for you both."

"Cosette," Misty laughs, "People will know we're gone!"

"No one will even notice, not after the amount of champagne that's been shelled out this evening. Go! Eat something and enjoy some peace and quiet, please."

She motions us away, and we obey, sharing feelings of relief as we jog up the grand staircase and disappear into the depths of the second, then third, and finally, the fourth floor.

The Opal Room is aptly named. Everything is a soft white. A few candles have been lit, but otherwise, the room is dim and warm as I set the plates on a small table in the back of the room and turn to my wife, who's staring at me in awe and excitement.

"We got married!"

"I know," I breathe, chuckling in disbelief. "Now what are we supposed to do?"

"I have no idea," she admits, laughing. She discarded her veil a while ago. Her hair falls loose over her shoulders, and her face is slightly flushed from the excitement of the day. "Will you help me out of my dress?"

I nod, and she gives me her back. My fingers brush over her skin as I unzip the fabric, a jolt of need coursing through my veins.

In nothing but a white shift, she walks to the far side of the room, near the ensuite bathroom, and shrugs into a satin robe before turning to face me again.

My feet move on their own accord. I grab her, pulling her against my chest, and kiss her like it's our last time, like the world is ending tomorrow.

I wonder if I'll always feel like this. Like I'll lose her if I so much as blink, but when I open my eyes again, she's still here, wearing her wedding ring on her slim finger as she unbuttons my shirt.

I've never considered myself a religious man. I like tangible things–things that make sense, that have an explanation... but I can't put into words what this woman means to me. I'd die for her. I did, actually.

I've gone to the temple almost every day to pray to the Goddess in thanks for giving me the opportunity to live a life with Misty–to have a future.

I toss Misty on the bed, thankful I had the wherewithal to lock the door behind us.

I plan to worship her body tonight. And tomorrow night... And every night after that because we have that time now. We have years... decades ahead of us.

"I love you, Cole," she whispers, wrapping her legs around my waist while I bunch the fabric of her shift up her thighs.

I steal the words with a kiss.

48
BIG BABY

Ryan

I try to flatten my back against the wall of the impossibly narrow corridor in the depths of the castle in Moonrise. It's nearly street level, and dim, with witch nurses in starched white uniforms darting from door to door tending mother's and new babies.

I've been here all morning long. Since last night, actually, when I woke up to Aviva clutching the dresser on the far side of the bedroom in our Moonrise suite, screaming in pain, and then the sound of water hitting the floor.

She's two weeks overdue. For a while, we considered just having the baby in Silverhide. During the course of her pregnancy, when her morning-sickness waned, things had been... fine. Amazing, actually. I've never seen my mate look more beautiful than she does now.... Well, maybe not *right now*.

I edge into her delivery room as silently as I can, not that it matters. Aviva screams, her face dripping with sweat. Her eyes are bright, however, and set with determination as I walk to her side, smoothing her hair away from her face.

"Am I allowed to come back in?" I whisper.

She grits her teeth, damn near arching off the bed, before hissing, "If you make another fucking joke, you're done. I'll kill you–for real."

"Okay," I breathe. It's my own damn fault. I tried and failed to break the tension when her contractions started ramping up by asking the nurses if they had a *come-along*, which is what we sometimes have to use when delivering cattle. Aviva screamed at me to get out if I wanted my balls to remain intact, so I got lost and spent the last ten minutes in the hallway listening to my wife go through wave after wave of contractions.

But I can tell she's tired. She's been at this since last night–labor came on fast. One moment, she was asleep beside me, the next, she was panting, bellowing in pain, and that pain hasn't let up.

Kenna rushes into the room followed by two assistants. "All right, Aviva." She checks her watch before donning gloves, snapping them against her wrists. "This is what we can do. I can relieve the pain pretty easily, but the potions might slow your labor, which in my professional opinion, isn't a good idea. You're already two weeks past your due date and this baby is…"

"She's giant!" Aviva hisses, baring her teeth and huffing in pain. Her eyes slide to mine full of rage. "It's your fault! You big-headed brute of a man! You did this to me!" She moans in pain, squeezing my hand so hard I feel my bones scrape together.

"I'm sorry," I say, wincing at her tone. I continue smoothing her hair back because it's the only thing she seems to want from me right now.

"We have other options, Aviva, if this fails to progress. You've been pushing for over two hours now, and I can tell you're getting tired," Kenna says.

"I just need her out. I need her out–safely. Both of us–need to get this over with!" Aviva's voice shutters as she gasps for breath and roars through a contraction. Kenna reaches between Aviva's legs in a practiced fashion, her eyes holding on the far wall. I don't like the look on her face right now. My body goes rigid with worry as Kenna withdraws her hand from my wife's body and takes off her gloves.

Kenna glances at me then tilts her head toward the door.

A nurse takes over for me, trying her best to comfort my wife. I follow Kenna into the hallway, my heartbeat booming through my ears.

"I'm not certain she's going to manage this," Kenna says in all seriousness. "I guarantee this baby is ten pounds, maybe more. I'm worried about the baby's positioning, as well. Her shoulder is tucked in a way that's making it hard for me to help her out."

"What are you saying?"

"Aviva might need a more invasive procedure–"

"You want to cut my mate open?" I ask, trying to bite back the fear in my voice.

"She's losing strength. The more potions I give her to dull her pain, the more she needs, and the more her body relaxes which… she needs to push hard, Ryan, if she's going to do this, and she's tired. Right now, the baby is doing well, but the more stress we put on the mother, the more likely it is that the baby will have complications."

I promised Aviva this would be okay. She lost her own mother in childbirth. She'd been in the room when her little sister, Lora, came into the world and stayed in that same room when her mother died before even holding the last of the four sisters.

My heart wretches. "It's up to her in the end."

"I understand, but if it comes to the point that she, or the baby, are in danger, I will ensure they're both safe, even if surgery is the answer. I just need you to be prepared for that."

I close my eyes as Kenna walks back into the room, talking in low, calming tones to Aviva. I follow her inside and take my place by Aviva's head. She grips my hand, her arm trembling. "I have to get her out!"

"We're going to try a different position, okay?" Kenna says with remarkable calm. She motions to the nurses, who start fluttering around the room, pushing carts and chairs out of the way. "Let's get you on your feet–"

"I can't–I can't stand–" Aviva screams, but it's lost the edge of determination. The fear and pain in her cry makes my body thrum with sudden power. I'm her mate. I'm supposed to be the one protecting her, caring for her.

Instead, my genetics took over this baby and turned her into a giant that's now trying to exit my petite wife's body.

Kenna looks at the other nurses, saying, "I need to try to slide the baby's shoulder free, so we're going to stand her up, have her squat–"

Aviva turns beet red and lets go of my hand. I watch her grab the back of her thighs as if in slow motion. Through our bond, I can feel the emotions spiraling through her. Fear for her life and our child's. Pain she's never experienced at this level before. A grim determination to end this before things get even worse.

I grab her shoulders. "Push. You can do it. She's almost here."

Kenna notices the change in Aviva's demeanor. Aviva has decided she's not going to stand up and be prodded. She's doing this her way.

There's a flurry of movement before Kenna's back between her legs with fresh gloves and an expression of icy decisiveness that sends a jolt of relief through my body. She is why we came here last week to deliver the baby in Moonrise instead of the Deadlands. Kenna is the best midwife around, and she's not going to let either of them die.

"Good job, Aviva," she says. "Keep pushing–pushing–okay, relax and breathe." She doesn't even look at the nurses when she says, "Get some blankets ready for the baby."

Aviva pants with pain, her face turning a deep red once again. She's soaked with sweat and trembling as she curls into herself, screaming as another contraction rips through her body. I lean down, pressing a kiss to her temple, breathing, "You're amazing. You're doing it. You're bringing our daughter into the world. I love you," over and over. She leans her head against mine as the contract ebbs away, panting, trying hard to catch her breath.

But Kenna shakes her head, muttering something under her breath as she shifts in her swivel stool and looks up at Aviva. "She has red hair."

Aviva smiles blearily, but my focus is on the way Kenna's brows pinch together with unease.

"I'm going to try to adjust her position a bit. This will hurt, but once her shoulders are out, it's done. You're a contraction away from this being all over, Aviva."

"O-Okay," Aviva breathes.

My back is on fire from bending over behind Aviva, keeping her steady while she bears down with all her strength, but feeling a pinch in my spine is nothing compared to the pain she's going through right now. I can handle it. I can take it for her. I don't have a choice.

Her body tightens with another contraction. Kenna grimaces with determination, and Aviva groans in pain when Kenna guides our daughter's shoulders into the world. "Push, now!"

I can readily admit that I'm obsessed with my mate. I love her more every day. It shouldn't be possible, honestly. *She* shouldn't be possible. Someone so strong, so perfect, so meant for me.

Watching Aviva bring our daughter into the world, both of them screaming…

It's the greatest moment of my life.

Kenna grunts under the weight of the baby slipping into her waiting arms, then holds her up for Aviva to see, smiling broadly in triumph.

Aviva shudders a gasp, leaning back as her body trembles from exertion.

I watch as our daughter is quickly dried and laid on Aviva's chest. She doesn't feel Kenna working between her knees, murmuring soft commands about her recovery. Our focus is on the baby blinking up at us—wrinkly and perfectly pink.

"Oh, my Goddess," I whisper, cupping the baby's head. I smooth my thumb through her fine, golden-red hair.

Aviva's beyond words. Tears spill down her cheeks as she presses kisses to the baby's forehead, whispering gentle blessings in the old Firestone tongue against her skin.

I'm in actual shock. My hand shakes as I stroke the baby's head. She lifts a tiny fist and catches one of my fingers, gripping it.

"Look at you, little one," I breathe in awe. "So strong already."

Aviva giggles, tears still streaming down her cheeks. I look at my beautiful, tough, brave mate and kiss her tenderly, ignoring the activity in the room around us.

Eventually, Kenna comes to take the baby to weigh her and check her vitals. I help the nurses tend to Aviva–getting her changed in a soft recovery gown, fluffing her pillows and sitting her up in the bed. Kenna returns with the baby a few minutes later, having expertly swaddled her. "Newborns are very sleepy, just so you know. You should try to let her root around on your chest for a while. She'll be hungry and already knows exactly what to do," she says to Aviva, laying the baby in her arms. "I'll have some food sent down from the castle kitchen for you and Ryan."

"Thank you," Aviva whispers. She's still in shock. I think, deep down, part of her didn't believe she'd make it through this.

But I always knew. She's the most capable woman I've ever met.

Kenna smiles at us, saying in parting, "She wins biggest baby on the floor today. *Eleven pounds.* That's significant, Aviva."

Kenna leaves, and we're alone. Aviva looks up at me, shaking her head in disbelief. "Eleven pounds? Ryan–that's insane!"

"She'll be tall, I'm sure," I murmur, wincing a bit as I look down at them. Aviva is a small woman, especially in the height department. This pregnancy took a toll on her body, and I can tell she's exhausted right now. "You should rest."

"I just want to look at her for a while," she says softly, smoothing her finger over the baby's cheek. She's asleep, nestled against Aviva's chest, making little suckling motions with her lips.

A month ago, Mercy and Jacob welcomed their son, Reuben, into the world. He was born without a hitch in Silverhide–a swift, nearly painless labor. Freya and Andrew had their son within a few days of Mercy's delivery, a golden-haired boy they named Samuel.

Aviva patiently waited for her turn.

My wife pats the bed. "Come sit with us."

"There's barely any room and you need–"

"Come here," she coaxes, sensing my hesitation. "I want you to hold her, Ryan."

I climb onto the bed and sit beside them, but my body locks up the second Aviva places our daughter in my arms for the first time.

Even for eleven pounds, which I think is probably very big for a newborn, she's... tiny. She looks up at me, surprised, before slumping into sleep again with a soft sigh.

"She looks like you," I say to Aviva, my eyes watering.

"I think she'll have your eyes," she replies, resting her head on my shoulder. "What are we going to name her?"

"I have no idea. She'll be stuck with it forever." We had a list, but over the past weeks, waiting for her arrival, we crossed out every single name. Juniper was a front runner for a while, then Thea, then Penelope. Aviva loved the name Zaila, which is a common name for women in the tribal packs, but it just didn't settle with me. I liked the name Chloe, but again, we'd come to an impasse.

"Lexa," I say.

Aviva looks up at me, smiling. "Lexa?"

"There's a little girl in Teshka named Lexa. I heard it during the festival last year. What does the name mean?"

"It's uh–It's Firestone, the old tongue. It means the dawn after a storm."

We look down at our daughter then at each other. I'm not sure why the name popped into my head, but I... like it. I think Aviva does, too.

"We can call her Lex for short. It's cute and not too frilly."

"I like it. I think that's her name."

"We'll sleep on it and decide tomorrow."

A few hours later, Aviva's moved to our private suite in the castle to rest and recover. I watch her sleep soundly against the patter of rain hitting the windows, unable to stop looking at her. I'm not sure what I did for the Goddess to give me the blessing of Aviva, but I'm grateful for it. When Lexa begins to whimper, trying to burst out of her swaddle, I decide to give my mate some peace and quiet and visit the family members desperately waiting to meet her.

49

PIECE OF CAKE

Misty

SPRING

CRESCENT FALLS HAS ERUPTED WITH SPRING BLOOMS. THE WEATHER IS soft and fair, which has been great, because this past winter royally sucked. I sigh heavily, tilting my face toward the warm sunlight dusting through the library at my parents' castle and breathing in the warmth, letting it flow over my skin.

It's been six months since the war. The war that hasn't yet been named, hasn't yet become text in some new editions of our history books. The wounded memories of my time in Tarsian are still fresh enough to send chills licking up my spine if I think about them too deeply, but lately, there's been a shift—something tangible. Something I can taste.

Grief has turned to resignation, and resignation turns to conviction while I rise from one of the tables in the library and slip the books I've been studying into my messenger bag.

I'm going to learn how to read the *Book of Whispers* because I won't allow what happened last year to ever, ever, happen again.

I pad downstairs, walking through the familiar hallways of my childhood home and feel a sense of peace when I catch my mom bustling around a corner dragging an empty suitcase behind her.

"Where are you going?" I ask, genuinely curious.

"Aviva had the baby, finally," Mom says breathlessly, her eyes watering with excitement.

"So you're heading to Silverhide?" I'm slightly jealous, but… still, the idea of returning to Eastonia soon makes my stomach tighten. I'll get there, eventually, but for now, I'm fine where my feet are planted.

"They're still in Moonrise at the moment, but yeah, I'm going to go spend two weeks or so with them while they get settled. Poor thing." She shakes her head. "The baby was eleven pounds."

"Eleven pounds?" My gasp echoes through the foyer. "H-How?"

"Ryan. That's how. Poor Aviva. It sounds like she's fine and making a full recovery, but it was a very long labor. I felt so awful when she asked me to tell her about when Sydney and Ryan were born that I skipped some very important details… like her mate being just as large as the baby she just had."

"Mom!" I tease. "You should have told her!"

"Well, I have two weeks to make it up to her, don't I?" She grins at me.

"I have gifts for them. Can you take them with you?"

She checks her watch. "Only if you have them delivered here from Shadowcrest in the next hour. Your dad and I are leaving soon."

"I'm heading home now. Don't leave without them, please?" I rush out of the foyer and through the front door as fast as my feet can carry me, but my own advancing pregnancy makes the dash to my car more like a swift waddle.

I slide into the driver seat and haul ass back to Silverhide, punching the Bluetooth on my dashboard in haste.

Cole answers his phone on the second ring. "Hey–"

"Cole? Are you at home? Ryan and Aviva had their baby, and my parents are about to leave for Eastonia. Do you remember where I put those gifts I got them?"

Cole blows out his breath, making a very male grunting sound that makes me imagine him looking around our horrible disorganized cottage while scratching his head. "No, but I can look. I have a few minutes before I need to head to the hospital."

"I'll be home in five minutes." I turn into the gates to Shadowcrest, which open for me automatically. Sydney's territory is gorgeous. It's a suburban utopia full of young families like ours. While Sydney lives in his old manor on the hillside, we moved into one of the cottages six months ago while waiting on our new house to be built. A house that will have his-and-her walk in closets and my own dedicated office space.

The house won't be ready for another month, and I'm due the next month. To say I'm stressed is the least of it.

I pass the plot of land where the new pediatric clinic is being built. One day soon, that's where Cole will be working, and he'll have a normal schedule that means he can be home there with us in the morning and come home from work before dinner, but as it stands now, he's pulling night shifts for his residency, sometimes for days at a time.

It's been insanely busy ever since we settled here together. I feel like we haven't had a single day to spend together in weeks, maybe months. Dad was right about my credits transferring from TU to Wellington, and he was also right about the fact that based on Wellington standards, I was already ready to graduate. So, degree in hand, I jumped in with both feet and started shadowing my great uncle Ben at the castle most weekdays, learning the tricks of the trade in preparation for taking over his royal position.

I pull into the wooded neighborhood of stone cottages and spot our house through the flurry of bright, spring flowers and fresh green leaves. My car is barely in park when I fly out of the car and race up the steps, ignoring the burning sensation in my lungs. "C-Cole? Did you find them?"

I edge past cardboard boxes stacked in the snug front hallway, standing on my toes to try to spot my mate over the mess. "Cole!"

"I have them right here!" he shouts from somewhere in the depths of the house. I hear boxes toppling over as he makes his way in my direction, carrying a basket full of pink toys, pink clothes, pink... everything.

I bend over as best I can around the swell of my stomach to catch my breath. "Okay–I'm going to drive back now–"

"I'll drive us."

I rise, giving him a confused look. "But your shift–"

"It got canceled," he shrugs. "Scheduling mix-up. I was supposed to be off for the next three days instead of on call."

"Three days off?" I stare at him in disbelief. I can't remember the last time in the past few months he had that kind of time off. "What are we going to do?"

"What are we going to do?" he laughs, glancing around, then down at me. "You're going to get off your feet and rest, and I'm going to sort this stuff out, once and for all."

"I can help."

"You're not supposed to be lifting anything right now, Misty." He steps past me, grabbing his keys and a light jacket. "In fact, at your last appointment, you were told you needed to spend more time off your feet."

I follow him outside to his vehicle–a sleek black SUV Ryan recommended. "Our house is a mess because of me," I argue while he holds the passenger door open and helps me in.

"Well, we both thought we'd be in the new house by now." What he isn't saying is that I went a little nuts in the online shopping department and fully furnished a house three times the size of the one we're currently living in, and everything was delivered faster than it's taking for the construction to wrap up.

I watch Cole as he rounds the car and slides into his seat, reaching behind to set the basket of gifts in the back seat.

"I'm not going to just lay there while you find a home for all the boxes."

"I already talked to Sydney about it, and he's going to drive down with his truck and store all of it at his place. It's not a big deal at all."

Shadowcrest speeds by in a blur. I stare out the window as rain clouds darken the afternoon sky. By the time we reach the castle, my parents are waiting for us, and Cole has only a minute to dart to them with the basket before Dad whisks them into the aether to meet their new grandchild.

Cole's hair is damp with rain when he gets back into the car, grinning at me.

"What's that smile for?" I ask, noticing the mischievous glint in his eyes.

"I just found out the baby's name."

"They named her? What is it!"

"I'll tell you if you have dinner with me, right now. Any restaurant you want, any pack you want to dine in."

I raise my brows. "And you won't complain when I order every dessert?"

He purses his lips. "You eat *a lot* of sugar."

"I'm pregnant," I remind him. "It's what the baby wants."

"As a doctor–"

I interrupt him with my restaurant choice, and he submits, chuckling to himself. In his defense, again, there was an entire two-month block of time when I couldn't stomach anything but chocolate cake, so I was surviving off that alone, and Cole was actually pretty worried about it.

But, Cole is my husband, not my midwife, so he can't tell me what to do.

We drive downtown to the Crescent City pack territory. We park at a familiar restaurant that has tables overlooking the lake. Cole holds my fingers as a waiter guides us through a sea of tables and finally reach one of the tables overlooking the water.

The sun is setting, and it's beautiful as it peeks through breaks in the rain clouds. Vibrant light in shades of pink and gold dance over the circular table where two people are sitting side by side, beaming at us.

"Oh my Goddess!" I shout, ignoring the other patrons in the area. "What are you doing here?!"

Georgia jumps up and throws her arms around me. Declan and Cole greet each other, and I notice Cole giving Declan a slight bob of his head... a slight bow, before pulling out a chair for me and sitting down.

It's strange, honestly. My mate gave up the title of Alpha King... passing it on to Orion, his father's old Beta, who now claims the title of Alpha King of Oasia and Serpentia–the desert territory of Tarsian.

That makes Declan the prince and heir.

Declan's cheeks glow with a furious blush at the fact that Cole just acknowledged the fact that he ranks higher than Cole now.

"Cole told us you'd choose this place," Georgia teases from across the table, resting her chin on her fist.

"They have the best dessert in the kingdom," I smile, still shocked and overwhelmed to see them here. "What–what are you doing here?"

"I wanted it to be a surprise, and Cole helped me do it." Georgia beams at Cole. "I'm here for your baby shower next week. A boy, huh?"

I look at Cole, my heart leaping out of my chest. He knows it's been a hard transition being back here, starting a new life. My old friends from childhood faded into the shadows when I returned. Georgia had been a constant in my life for three years before the war, and suddenly we were separated.

"We are having a boy," I reply. "Actually, Ryan and his mate just had their baby today."

Conversation swirls across the table for the better part of an hour. I order dessert instead of a real meal, but I have a few weeks to milk this pregnancy and the cravings that come with it and plan to do so until the bitter end.

But as the night draws to a close, I notice Declan and Georgia looking at each other, slightly... communicating.

Declan's still twenty, but Georgia's twenty-one now...

"We have something we want to tell you guys," Declan says, smiling at her before turning to us.

Cole rests his hand on my thigh, leaning back in his chair.

I meet Georgia's eyes.

"We're mates. We're getting married."

The happiness I feel for her is... so sweet. So overwhelming. A rush of relief and gratefulness to the Goddess floods my body. I think every wonderful moment like this one will make me feel that way after everything we've been through.

"It'll be a royal wedding, of course," Declan confirms after our congratulations die down to a simmer. "In Oasia. My parents are already planning for some time next fall."

"You're going to be a queen," I say to Georgia, and she blushes.

"Will you be my maid of honor?" she asks.

"I'm married and about to be a mom... can I still do that?"

"Matron of Honor, then. There's no one else I'd want by my side," she says, reaching across the table to grab my hand. "Please? I want it to be you."

Everything I had to do and endure led to this moment.

"Yes. I'll be your matron of honor."

But that means I'll have to return to Eastonia. To Oasia.

My skin prickles in warning at the thought.

5 0
NOT READY

Misty

Two weeks after Georgia asked me to be her *matron* of honor, technically, at her wedding next fall, I wake up with a start–alone–in the cottage I share with Cole.

It's the middle of the night, and Cole's at the hospital. His side of the bed is cold when I stretch my arm across it, pinching the sheets between my fingers. Echoes of pain drift in waves over my belly. My muscles are painfully tight as I roll onto my side, curling around the swell of my stomach.

It hurts enough that it's hard to catch my breath, and when I finally do, I feel... a pop, deep within me.

"Oh, Goddess," I rasp, sliding out of bed as my water breaks, soaking the sheets and falling onto the floor. My hands tremble, and my mind goes completely, utterly numb while I take the comforter off the bed and waddle to the laundry room where I do a load of laundry like... like this isn't happening. I change my clothes. I pull my hair into a bun and brace myself on the bathroom sink before turning to leave the bathroom, but another contraction begins, squeezing the life out of me. I grip the doorframe, doubling over.

I'm sure I should be prepared for this by now. I read all the books, for fuck's sake. My husband is a physician! But here I am, ripping the sheets off the bed and stuffing them in a laundry basket. I clean the mattress thoroughly, bracing myself through the increasingly steady contractions.

At exactly 2:00 A.M., my cell phone buzzes on the bedside table, the screen lighting up with Cole's name and one of our wedding pictures in the background.

He always texts me during his shifts. Little things like what book he read during one of his random breaks, whether or not he managed to get any sleep between patients, and the latest hospital drama. Tonight isn't any different.

I brace myself against the wall of our bedroom and ride out another back ripping contraction while reading his text about a man who shifted mid-surgery and ended up in the ICU.

I text him back, saying that sounds painful, and within seconds my phone is ringing.

"What're you doing up?" he asks lightly. Beeps and muffled voices sound behind him–hospital sounds. The sounds of the place I should probably be right now.

"I'm–oh–" I suck in a breath, trying to bite back a moan.

"Misty?" Cole's voice drops. "Misty, are you okay? What's wrong?"

"I'm just–just doing laundry."

Cole walks somewhere quieter. "What's the matter? Somethings– you're in labor, aren't you?"

"I can't be," I gulp, feeling my way down the darkened hallway toward the kitchen. "I'm not due for three more weeks–" My words fall from my lips in a hiss. This really fucking hurts. Why didn't I think it would hurt this much? Every class I took, and book I read, went over my head, apparently.

"I knew it," Cole rasps, sighing through the phone. "I felt a shift yesterday, in our bond. I thought it might be happening soon, but I…. Look, I'm on my way. I'm just–I'm half an hour away–"

"I'm fine," I bite out, but my body locks up as another contraction soars through me. "I'll see you in the morning, when your shift's over."

Cole goes totally silent for several seconds before asking, "How far apart are your contractions? You can barely talk through them."

"I don't know. A minute?"

"You're having a contraction every minute?" he growls. "Misty—okay, listen. Stay where you are. Your hospital bag is by the door."

"I have to finish the laundry. There's still an hour on the cycle."

The line goes dead. I waddle back into the bedroom and start making the bed like the conversation didn't happen.

But within minutes of the phone call, the front door bursts open. I'm doubled over the mattress, fighting for my life against the pain and a fitted sheet and can't find the strength to scream as heavy footsteps thunder down the hallway and a large shadow darkens my doorway.

"What the hell are you doing, Misty?" Sydney growls.

"I'm making my bed!"

"Get in the car!"

"I don't want to go. He's not ready. He has three weeks to go!" Tears sting my eyes for the first time.

"You're fine," Sydney says calmly, extending his hands in surrender. He's disheveled from sleep and wearing a plain T-shirt and sweatpants like he just rolled out of bed. "Everything's okay, but Cole just called me, and you're going to the hospital right now. I don't care if you don't want to go, you can't just stop this from happening!"

"Where's Sarah?!" I blubber, shaking from pain and uncertainty. "Why are you here instead of her? I don't want you, Sydney! Where's—where's Mom? Is she home from the Deadlands yet?"

"I will pick you up and carry you to my truck if you refuse to go," he bites out, stressed, pointing to the bedroom door. "Go."

But then I'm doubled over again, groaning and hissing in agony as a contraction spreads through my back, stealing my breath.

Sydney whispers a curse under his breath and lays a supportive hand on my back. "You're going to be okay. Liam was a bit early, too, and he was fine."

"I'm not r-ready," I admit, sniffling. "We haven't even finished setting up his crib. We-we thought we'd be in the new house by now, but we c-can't move in until next week!"

"That doesn't matter. What matters is getting you to the hospital. Mom got home last night, and she's going to meet us there–"

"I can't–"

He straightens me up and takes my face between his hands. "Please, Misty. Don't put me through delivering this baby on the floor. You're my little sister."

I grimace, shoving him away. He points to the door, and I reluctantly waddle out to his truck. He snatches my hospital bag out of my hands and helps me down the steps to the driveway, where we begin a painful fifteen minute drive that should have taken thirty minutes.

He runs every red light and ignores the speed limit completely.

I arch off the seat, groaning curses as our son tries to make his earlier arrival in the freaking truck. "Pull over–"

"I can't. We're a minute away from the hospital."

"Sydney, please! I can't–I can't sit like this!"

He revs the engine and sends us flying down a straight, mostly empty highway. The hospital lights shimmer nearby, highlighting a wide parking lot. Relief rushes over me before quickly receding, replaced by fear and guilt.

I hadn't been staying off my feet. I have a hard time sitting still as it is. Sitting still, lying around and being burdened by my own thoughts and memories gives my brain the opportunity to roil over the war, and everything that happened before, during, and after.

This is my fault, isn't it?

I'd been doing everything else correctly. I'd seen my midwife regularly. She's a witch from Eastonia who relocated here and opened her own practice performing traditional healing and midwifery. I'd wanted to deliver at the hospital, however, mostly because Cole works there but also because the majority of the women in my family have had horrific, sometimes deadly, childbirths, and I'm not dumb enough to think that couldn't happen to me.

But going early wasn't even in my mind. Aviva was *two weeks* overdue, for Goddess's sake.

Sydney says another muffled prayer while I grip the seat and scream through my teeth. He rips into the parking lot so fast my hospital bag slides across the length of the back seat.

A group waits for us at the entrance under the glow of the emergency department lights. A sleek blue sports car rests with two tires on the curb.

"How the hell did she beat us here?" Sydney gasps.

"Mom? Mom!" I shout as she comes into view, wearing her pajamas, a robe, and slippers… like she also rolled out of bed and then sped directly to the hospital in the fastest car my parents have in their arsenal.

Sydney's truck barely pulls to a stop before my door opens, and Cole appears, looking flushed, his eyes heavy with concern, then relief when he sees me in one piece. He's wearing light blue scrubs that make his gray eyes pop as he scoops me up without ceremony and carries me into the hospital.

"How far apart are her contractions?" he shouts over his shoulder to Sydney, who's running in behind us with the hospital bag slung over his shoulder and Mom gripping his other arm.

"A minute, if that." I peek over Cole's arm and watch Sydney slip his phone in his pocket.

"You were timing them?"

"I'm about to be a father of three, Misty," he says, exasperated, "This isn't my first rodeo. Is her midwife here, yet?"

"We called her but haven't gotten an answer," a man I recognize as one of Cole's colleagues, Carson, says as he rushes forward, motioning for Cole to take a sharp left. "Let's just get her to maternity. Cole, you're not the doctor right now, okay? Let me take over–"

"She's my mate," Cole snaps, and Carson gives him a thin smile.

"Exactly. You have a job to do, and it's not delivering this baby."

An absolutely epic contraction tears through me. I go rigid, biting back a scream as the pain rolls through me, splitting me apart. "Put me down!"

Cole breaks into a run. Somewhere behind us, I hear Mom breathlessly whisper, "This is so exciting!"

Cole carries me into a delivery room, following Carson, who immediately tells the nurses waiting on us that it's time... literally, right now.

Cole tries to put me on the bed, but I wriggle in his arms. "I can't–lay down. I can't! Where's my midwife?! Where–Where is she? I had–had a plan!"

Cole's reserved, emotionless doctor's expression shatters. Worry shines in his eyes, as well as guilt and fear of his own, for me. "I know, honey, I'm so sorry."

Mom rushes into the room as I allow Cole to lay me down. She kisses my cheek, and I'm instantly comforted.

But Carson, technically Dr. Drier, is now bickering with Cole at a nearby sink, telling him to tend to his wife and let him handle the delivery. "I'm the attending physician in maternity tonight."

"I'm an attending pediatrician," Cole argues.

"Then *attend* to your son when he gets here, which is any minute from now, but your mate needs you, Cole. Put those gloves on, and I'll chain you to the bed, I swear."

Cole backs away from the sink when I start whimpering through another contraction, and the nurses begin adjusting my position. I'm wearing a nightgown, but they're trying to coax me to change into a hospital gown.

I feel a shift. The contraction ebbs into another contraction immediately. I sit up, grabbing my knees. Cole turns to me in shock, pushing past the nurses with Carson by his side.

Mom grabs my hand, her eyes going wide.

Cole catches our son as I bring him into the world in a single push.

I slump against the pillows in shock and relief, watching through hooded eyes as Cole stares down at our baby.

His eyes slowly meet mine before the rush of activity in the room reaches a pitch. His eyes water with unshed tears, and his smile is… heaven.

"I love you, Misty," he says over the chaos.

"Is he okay?"

Before I can even take a breath, the baby is placed on my chest and roughly dried. He's small, and hasn't cried yet, but makes grunting sounds like he's pissed about being thrust from his warm bed and into the cool, dry air of the hospital.

"Why isn't he crying?" I gasp.

As if on cue, our son chokes on a cry before erupting with noise that betrays his size. It's the most beautiful sound I've ever heard.

"Is she okay?" Cole asks Carson. "My mate–"

"She's totally fine," Carson says from somewhere between my legs.

Cole is still at my side in somewhat of a haze. I glance through the few inches of space between him and my mom, who's fawning over me and the baby, and notice Sydney pale white and wide-eyed in the doorway, still holding my hospital bag.

"This is a family record for sure," Mom laughs, her eyes full of happy tears. "Oh, sweetheart, you did such a good job."

The next ten minutes are a chaotic blur of activity. I'm changed into a hospital gown and settled in the bed with snacks and the biggest bottle of water with crunchy ice. The baby's cleaned off, examined, swaddled, and tucked in my arms. Mom gives me huge, wet kisses on my cheeks but refuses to hold the baby, telling me this is my time, but I watch Cole walk her to the door, and Mom tells him in just above a whisper, "My baby just had a baby."

"She did great," Cole smiles. "We'll call you later this morning. You should come back and see them."

"I will. I know Isaac's waiting for my call." She looks at me with happy tears in her eyes. "He's so worried. He'll be so happy to hear this went so well. Oh, what's his name? Have you decided?"

The nurses leave the room, skirting around them, leaving us alone.

"Adrian," I tell her. "His name is Adrian."

Mom smiles at us, murmuring something about getting a few things monogrammed, and hurries out the door, taking a still shell-shocked Sydney with her.

Cole walks to me, sitting on the edge of the hospital bed. He's slightly disheveled as I place Adrian in his arms.

"Look at what we made," I whisper, meeting my mate's eyes.

"Thank you," he whispers, his voice cracking with emotion as he holds my gaze. "*I love you.*"

"I love *you.*"

51
A NEW STORY BEGINS

Aviva

Three month old Lexa's dark blue eyes are wide and round as she grips Mercy's arm. Her eyes go glassy as her lower lip begins to tremble, her little face twisting with pitiful sorrow.

"I'll be back tomorrow morning," I try to assure her, but my voice wobbles with sudden heartbreak. I look at my sister, desperate and unsure. "It's too early, isn't it? Leaving her like this?"

Mercy rolls her eyes. "You're going to be gone for like... ten hours, Aviva. She's fine. She has plenty of milk–"

I take a single step away, and Lexa wails.

We're attached, that's clear. I've been wearing her on my chest since the day she was born. We're rarely apart, and if we are, Lexa firmly believes she'll never see me again.

She wants nothing to do with Ryan recently. It's not that she doesn't like him, or can't find comfort in his arms but... I'm her mother. I smell familiar, feel familiar....

"I'll be back very soon, love," I croak, trying not to burst into tears myself.

Lexa gives me the most heartbroken face as I whirl, running out of

Mercy and Jacob's house and across the village, where I close myself in our quiet, empty house and let my own tears flow free.

Over the past couple of months, we've added a second story to the house... not that Lexa needed her own room because she sleeps with us every night, cuddled tight against my chest, nursing whenever she wants.

I blink back tears, drying my face on the back of my hands as Ryan comes out of our bedroom carrying my weapons belt and halter. He notices the look of utter dismay crossing my features and sighs, setting the items in his hands on the kitchen table. "That bad?"

"It's far too early to spend a night away from her, isn't it? She was devastated, Ryan!"

"She's not going to remember this," he assures me. "You need this, Aviva."

"I know," I grind out. "But that doesn't make it any easier."

"It's just a night. We'll be back before dawn tomorrow, I promise."

I nod but feel guilty about how excited I am to get out of the village for the night, to shift and run free in my wolf form for the first time since her birth. I'm excited to go hunting with the men and feel the cool, summer night air whispering through my fur.

I'm excited to be myself again, just for a few hours, before going back to being Lexa's mom.

I didn't get to go on the spring hunt in Endova this year. Lexa was less than a week old, and Ryan stayed behind to tend to both of us while most of the men in our pack left for four or five days. This hunt he planned... it's just for me.

He wraps me in his strong arms and holds me close. "If you don't want to go, we don't have to."

"I need this," I echo, laying my cheek against his chest.

"You've needed this," he smiles. "So let's go."

I make quick work of preparing for our night in the forest around Silverhide. If I linger long, I'm going to lose my nerve. I know Lexa's in great hands with Mercy, who dotes on her endlessly already, but still. I wasn't expecting motherhood to feel like this–all-consuming and fragile, like if I blink, I'll miss this time with her when she's so young and dependent on me, while also dying to recognize myself in the mirror again.

The sun sets on Silverhide as we head out, shifting and racing over the mountain top together and dropping into the endless forest beyond our sheltered valley.

There's a stillness to the forest I realize I remember from my youth. Once, years ago, the Deadlands were a calm place. A place teeming with ancient magic that settled in the ground and thrummed deep beneath us... but a few years ago, when I was still becoming the warrior, and hunter, I am today... that changed. The forest—our old hunting grounds—changed. Evil coasted over the forest floor. Rogues moved in, traveling in droves. Hellhounds separated from their witches long ago woke from their endless slumbers to stalk through the forest.

It was Richard and his magic all along.

But now, the Deadlands are free.

I sprint through the woods, weaving and leaping, reveling in how easily I shifted and how good it feels to be in my wolf form again. My crippling brain-fog brought on by long, sleepless nights lifts completely, and I feel... amazing. Amazingly myself again.

I'm not sure where Ryan's taking me tonight. He didn't mention any specific plans or hunting grounds, but after an hour, we reach the western edge of the forest where it bleeds into plains again, and stretches another hundred miles to another row of towering mountains where Moonrise is nestled somewhere in the valleys.

But the mountains to the south are draped in moonlight and beckoning to me, so I turn in that direction. The last time I hunted in these mountains, I got a mountain goat in an... unprecedented way. By nearly falling to my death, actually. Ryan had been there to witness it, of course, and it's a story he loves to tell anyone willing to listen.

Ryan follows me through the plains under a cloak of moonlight. I feel light as air, darting over rocks and leaping over dry creek beds, sailing through the night.

We reach a small valley with a patch of woods—a new place, a place I don't think I've ever been–but I notice smoke rising from the thicket below and skid to a stop.

'Other hunters?' Ryan asks through the mind-link.

'Possibly,' I reply, hesitating as I step from paw to paw. Adrenaline races through my veins. It's later summer now–prime hunting season. The last chance to gather meat and furs before the animals return to their winter grazing lands far from the reaches of the tribal packs that inhabit this area.

'I want to check it out,' Ryan says, his voice calm but stern. He's been on edge lately. I've chalked it up to being a new father, but two new packs have settled in the Deadlands this summer, one of which he's not fond of.

The Alpha of Narrow Valley, a pack now only twenty miles east of Silverhide, is Ryan's age. He's mateless and hungry for power. His pack isn't any different. Mostly young, eager men looking for adventure and… women.

They've already gotten into some trouble with my father in Endova, hunting in Endovian territory, harassing the women they come across. Ryan's had to put his foot down several times, and the Alpha of Narrow Valley isn't too keen on bending the knee to an Alpha King.

Not yet, at least.

The last thing I want right now is to come across a band of Narrow Valley hunters, but I follow Ryan toward the woods, toward the smoke, nonetheless. Ten minutes later, we shift into our human forms, hugged by our Endovian leathers, and walk into a camp of… Teshkan hunters.

"Long way from Teshka," Ryan says, clapping the shoulder of the leader of the group, a warrior named Saul.

Saul rolls his dark brown eyes, motioning to the full moon over our heads. He's a young man, and a kind one. His uncle is the patriarch, and his father is an elder, so he's of high rank. "We weren't going to waste the new moon."

"Any luck?" I ask the men as I sit next to the fire, settling beside Ryan.

"We've seen a few elk, but that's it," answers one of the hunters with a shrug. "We're not here to hunt, though."

"Why are you here then?" Ryan is genuinely curious.

I am, too. These guys are dozens of miles away from their village right now, and they're all dressed for a long journey, based on the supplies scattered around the camp.

"We were actually on our way to you, Alpha," Saul says wearily, giving Ryan a knowing look. "There's been an incident in Teshka, on the shore."

Ryan furrows his brows. "What happened?"

Saul looks to his friend, Ezra, who continues, "A man washed up on the beach, about ten miles from Teshka. We thought he was dead, but we brought him to the village, and he eventually woke up in a panic."

Saul says, "We thought he might've been in the war last year, in Tarsian. We share the sea, you know. I thought he might've been swept away and ended up here, but where he was in the meantime is a mystery."

"What does the guy say about it?" Ryan asks, his voice low and gravelly. "Where was he, all these months?"

"That's the thing." Saul sighs, glancing at Ezra, who shares an equally concerned expression on his chiseled face. "He only speaks the old tongue. That's not totally uncommon, but it's mostly the oldest of the elders who still converse in Firestone…. He's young. Only a teenager… maybe fourteen or fifteen at the most."

"You said he was a man," I argue, but the men ignore me.

"He said he was in a wreck on the water. His boat sank. He can't find his parents. He has no idea where he is."

"Where is he from, then? Somewhere in Tarisan?"

"No," Saul grinds out, looking worried and skeptical. "I don't believe so. I think he came from… across the water."

Ryan glances at me. "So… where?"

It's common knowledge, at least in Eastonia, that those who travel into the Southern Sea don't return. There are small islands, of course, but eventually they fade to nothing but raging, angry, open water and waves as tall as mountains… or so, the legends go.

We argue back and forth with the Teshkan group, trying to piece together the boy's history. He's not from the islands. He's not from Serpentia, or the other cities along Tarsian's shore. He's young, hurt, and terrified, and Saul was coming to Silverhide to ask us for help.

"He says he's from a place called Emberfyll," Saul says in conclusion, shaking his head. "We have no idea where that is, and the poor kid insists it's in the sea, far away. He said he'd been traveling for months when their boat sank in a storm."

I roll the word Emberfyll over my tongue. It doesn't sound that familiar. I dig through the legends and tall-tales I know from my childhood and come up with nothing regarding the Southern Sea, other than the storms and the monsters that guard it, for some reason, stopping people from venturing too far.

"Why was he traveling?" Ryan asks into the gloom of night. "What was his destination?"

Saul heaves a breath, his eyes holding Ryan's gaze. "He told us his parents were on the run. An Alpha and Luna, apparently. They left Emberfyll, wherever that is, to try to take him somewhere safe."

"Why?"

It's Ezra's turn to speak, but he glances at Saul before saying, "He won't say. He gets really upset when we ask him. We thought maybe he'd answer to you, instead."

Ryan looks around the fire before his eyes meet mine. Inside my head, he asks, 'Is Emberfyll familiar to you at all?'

'No, it's not. But if he's really from somewhere in the sea… If there're people that far south, people that might come looking for him…'

"Where is the boy now?" Ryan asks the group.

"In Teshka, recovering. He's badly malnourished, but he'll be fit for travel soon."

"Bring him to Silverhide as soon as you can." Ryan rises, nodding at Saul. "We can house him there until we can find a way to return him to his people—or whatever."

Ryan walks away from the camp. I rise, and follow.

We walk through the woods side-by-side in silence for a while before he finally speaks, saying, "I have an odd feeling about this."

"So do I," I admit, a chill snaking through my body. "What do you think it means?"

"I think it means we involve my aunt and uncle," he says quietly. "And… Sarah, who can look into his mind… and Misty, who can paint us a picture of what happened to the boy."

"Sarah and Misty haven't wanted to come back to Eastonia since the war."

"I don't think we have a choice," Ryan says to me.

I take a deep breath, knowing he's right and wondering what the hell we're getting ourselves into now.

We're about to find out….

ALSO BY BELLA MOONDRAGON

The Alpha King's Breeder series:

Bought by the Alpha: The Alpha King's Breeder Book 1

Loved by the Alpha: The Alpha King's Breeder Book 2

Lost by the Alpha: The Alpha King's Breeder Book 3

Luna of the Alpha: The Alpha King's Breeder Book 4

Legacy of the Alpha: The Alpha Kings's Breeder Book 5

Daughter of the Alpha: The Alpha King's Breeder Book 6

Descendants of the Alpha: The Alpha King's Breeder Book 7

Shadow of the Alpha: The Alpha King's Breeder Book 8

Son of the Alpha: The Alpha King's Breeder Book 9

Spare of the Alpha: The Alpha King's Breeder Book 10

Claimed by the Alpha: The Alpha King's Breeder Book 11

Atonement for the Alpha King: The Alpha King's Breeder Book 12

Rejected by the Alpha: The Alpha King's Breeder Book 13

The Luna's Vampire Prince series:

The Culling

The Kingdom

The Conquered

Pregnant With Four Alphas' Babies

Chosen As the Breeder

Mated to Four Alphas

Threats Against the Breeder

At War for the Breeder

The Stolen Breeder

Four Alphas, Four Babies

Becoming the Luna Queen

Descendants of the Breeder

Desired by the Devil series

Whispers of the Devil

Banter of the Devil

Murmurs of the Devil

The Mafia Kings series

Indebted to the Mafia King

<u>Loved by the Mafia King</u>

Claimed by the Mafia King

Secrets of the Mafia King

Burned by the Mafia King

Kidnapped by the Mafia King (coming soon!)

Dark Stalker Romance series

Tempted by Sin

Fated by Sin

Secret Billionaires series

Finding the Secret Billionaire by Olivia Bhelle Kildare

Falling for My Secret Billionaire by Bella Moondragon

Driven by the Secret Billionaire by ID Johnson

Wolf Shifter Alpha Kings series

Ravens and Ruins

Sundrops and Shadows

Snowflakes and Sabotage (Preorder now!)

The Vampire King's Feeder series

Claiming the Alpha's Daughter

Loving the Alpha's Daughter

Finding the Alpha's Daughter

Writing as B. Moon

The Boy Who Died

Sign up for Bella's newsletter here.

Or get a free novella from The Alpha King's Breeder series when you sign up here:
The Beta and the Maid

Follow Bella on Facebook here.

Follow Bella on Bookbub here.

9 781964 125718